J. Ryan Fenzel

Inherit All Things

A Novel

Ironcroft Publishing

Inherit All Things

Copyright © 2009 by J. Ryan Fenzel

Cover Artist: Julie L. Hamilton

Interior Design: Thomas Gideon

Printed in the United States of America

First Printing: April 2009

Library of Congress Information:

Fenzel, J. Ryan.

    LCCN: 2008941756
    Inherit All Things / J. Ryan Fenzel
    1st ed.
        Hartland, MI : Ironcroft Pub., 2009.
        p. cm.

ISBN-10: 0-9771688-1-6
ISBN-13: 978-0-9771688-1-1
1. Fiction – Action & Adventure
2. Fiction – Mystery and Detective, General

For Melynda,
Marisa, and Keira

Michigan

(Contemporary Map)

Lake Superior

Granite Island

Marquette

Mackinac Island

Leland

Sleeping Bear Dunes

Frankfort

Traverse City

Lake Michigan

Lake Huron

Marion

Grand Haven

Mt. Pleasant

Carson City

Port Huron

Grand Rapids

Saugatuck

Allegan

Linden

South Haven

Milford

Battle Creek

Detroit

Lake Erie

PROLOGUE

Kalamazoo River Light
Allegan County, Michigan
November 17th, 1842

Harlan Coates listened to wind thrash against the rubble stone tower from his bed in the lighthouse guestroom. A ceiling truss creaked under the weight of snow, and he wondered if it would give way. That would be a rude welcome to this wilderness territory. He'd come to a village named Singapore at the bend in the Kalamazoo River to find work. Back home jobs had become scarce, and a wife and two small boys were depending on him. A Singapore saw mill supposedly needed help, and Coates had made the trek from Detroit to investigate the claim. He did not appreciate winter's eager march across Lake Michigan to greet him.

Despite the snowstorm he counted himself fortunate to have met Lightkeeper Nichols upon his arrival in town the previous day. If not for Nichols, Coates would be sleeping in a crowded boarding house with his wallet a little lighter and his stomach a little tighter.

Sleep nearly closed his eyes when a desperate pounding suddenly cut against the grainy clamor of the gale. A frantic rhythm played out on the front door, too urgent to be characterized as knocking. Something was wrong.

Coates threw off the heavy blanket he'd been huddling under and set his feet on the cold wood floor. He scooped up his clothes from the foot of the bed and dressed in haste. A silver crucifix chained around his neck dangled in sight as he stooped to pull on his leather boots. He tied each lace into a haphazard knot and left the guestroom.

Lightkeeper Nichols had heard the racket too, and raced across the parlor room wearing nothing but his long underwear. He pulled open the front door.

Coates followed but stopped dead when he got a look at the visitors across the threshold.

There were five of them, maybe six. Men, or what was left of them, huddled together against the cold. They stood with shoulders slumped, caked in ice and dirty white paste that didn't quite fit the look of melting snow. One of them pleaded for entry into the warmth of the lighthouse. Nichols obliged and assisted him inside. "Sarah," he called to his wife. "Blankets, quickly!"

The frozen man stumbled and Nichols struggled to keep him on his feet. Coates came forward and helped the next man through the door. This one had a beard of ice and frosted eyebrows. Coates led him to a chair in front of the fireplace. "What happened?"

The man tried to form a word but failed through chattering teeth and trembling blue lips.

Coates grabbed a log from the stack near the hearth and tossed it onto the fire.

"She's lost."

The voice came from behind. Coates turned.

The last of the ice-laden men stared blankly into the room from the doorway. A mixture of slush and sand dripped from his oil-stained overalls. White blotches of powdery paste matted his hair and covered him head to toe. "She's lost," he said again.

Sarah Nichols appeared from the back room with an armful of woolen blankets and quilts. Her husband grabbed half her burden and went about distributing them amongst the snowmen gravitating toward the fireplace. Coates took a quilt to the man who had spoken. "Get near the fire before the cold takes you."

The man shuffled forward. "It's Whitmore's fault," he said.

"Who's Whitmore?" Coates asked.

"Captain Whitmore...*Milwaukee*'s skipper."

Milwaukee, the three-master laid up in port all the previous day. Coates recalled her being loaded when he arrived in town. She took on hundreds of barrels throughout the afternoon; barrels of flour. That pasty powder covering those men wasn't snow or ice. It was the ship's cargo. "What happened to the *Milwaukee?*"

"Whitmore happened." The talker slid onto the floor and leaned against a chair occupied by one of his shipmates. He stared into the flames. "None of us wanted to make sail after loading in St. Joseph. Whitmore ordered us out just the same. One more stop." He raised his hand to feel the warmth of the fire. "A gale was coming. We smelled it in the air. Hell, even the rats knew it. They left the ship in droves at St. Joseph."

Nichols suggested Sarah put on kettles of coffee.

"You were still in port at dusk," Coates said. "When did you ship out?"

The man pulled a melting chunk of ice from his hair. "After dark. Long after dark. The wind had shifted northeast. The cold was on us by then. We didn't make it far. The gale grew strong, took command. It blew us hard into the outer bar." He paused, recounting the moment in memory. "Whitmore laid into us, said we weren't workin' like we should to save the ship. The horse's ass didn't understand that heaving barrels all day saps a man's strength."

"You ran aground on the bar. How did you get ashore?"

The man nodded to one of his shipmates near the fire. "Mead got a line to shore. He dressed in oilcloth overalls to keep the water off him and swam in, tied off on a tree. Told us to dress likewise. He saved our hides out there."

Coates counted six shipwrecked sailors. "How many are in your crew?"

"Fifteen. Whitmore and the rest of them were still on deck when I came across on the line. If they didn't try to make shore by now they're in a bad way."

Coates considered the survivors and thought about the ones still stranded aboard *Milwaukee*. He picked Nichols out of the crowd in the parlor room. "More men are out there," he said to the lightkeeper. "Some may have gotten to shore. I'm going to look for them." He grabbed his black frock off the peg rack near the door and ran into the storm.

A frigid gust of wind nearly blew him back inside the lighthouse. He buttoned his coat from bottom to top and lifted the collar. Ice rain stung his cheeks and hands. Above his head the beam of light from the lighthouse lantern struggled to punch through swirling snow and pre-dawn darkness. He surged forward, maneuvering toward the beach. Dead ahead Lake Michigan boiled like an arctic cauldron.

Two miles north of the river along the lakeshore, Coates found the site of the disaster. The first tease of daylight had turned the ink-black sky to heavy grey and revealed *Milwaukee* in her death throws. Indeed she was driven hard into the outer bar, leaning fore and starboard at an unnatural pitch. Two of her three masts had snapped and lay tip-down in the crystallizing water collecting at her load line. Ribbons of sail whipped horizontal in the wind on the last mast standing. Heavy seas beat against her hull without mercy. The blows had begun to break her apart.

Coates ran toward the water but then slowed his steps. What could he do? He searched for the rope that the sailor named Mead had towed to shore and found it caked in ice and snow lying on the ground. The shifting ship had snapped it in two, leaving the end tied to the tree to snake into the lake in a worthless coil. Coates scanned the white beach. A human shape lay in a heap near the water.

He hurried over and knelt beside the body, rolling the hapless soul onto his back.

The man shivered uncontrollably. His face was blue, his lips purple, and his eyes dark and dilated. He grabbed hold of Coates' arm. "Ti—Tipton. You made it."

Coates didn't bother to correct him. "I'll get you to shelter."

"Where...are...the others?"

"Mead and his group are at the lighthouse."

The man shook his head. "Not Mead...not them. Where are the rest...of us?"

Coates regarded the severed rope, the turbulent water, the *Milwaukee* buckling on the outer bar. Wind howled through the coastal tree line. Ice and snow swept across the beach in great squalls. The desolate scene made him shudder. No one else was going to make it off that ship.

"Don't try to speak. There's a cabin just up the beach. I'll take you there."

The sailor's arms shook like the ribbons of sail on *Milwaukee's* mast, and he made a clumsy attempt to take hold of Coates' hand. Coates obliged. Icy fingers clamped on. "Find the barrel," the man rasped. "Don't let it be lost."

Coates felt something press into his palm.

The sailor stared at the gray clouds overhead. "They don't need it like we do."

Coates lifted his head. "Hang on."

The man's rigid arms loosened and fell limp, and he rolled his gaze to Coates. "I marked it...with pitch. A black...X. Don't let it be lost."

Coates watched the life wither from the sailor's eyes. The man had to know he was dying. Why did the ship's cargo mean so much to him in these final moments?

"What's in the barrel?"

The man's frozen stare fixed on the sky.

No reply. No breath. No more survivors from the *Milwaukee*.

A dreadful cold seeped into Coates' bones. He gently closed the sailor's eyes and stood. Out on the lake the ship moaned as sheets of ice closed in around her. The lower decks looked to be a deathtrap, and there were no signs of life topside. Nine men were gone. Nine men who just yesterday had been alive, healthy, and strong were all gone.

Coates' shoulders sank and he turned away. *They don't need it like we do.* What was that supposed to mean? He opened his hand to inspect what the dead man had given him. Shining in his palm against the murky light and swirling snow was a gold coin. He studied it closer. It was a five-dollar denomination with a North Carolina inscription. His mouth fell open and his fingers curled tight around the coin.

The *Milwaukee* floundered on the bar with hundreds of barrels of flour stacked in her disintegrating cargo hold. One of those barrels was marked with black pitch and contained something else.

Harlan Coates didn't feel cold anymore.

Part I

P I E C E S

The best place to hide something is in the past...

- ONE -

Present Day
Mt. Pleasant, MI

Jack Sheridan sat in his Jeep Cherokee and considered the gold band on his hand. He'd been wearing it a long time. Every now and then he had to marvel at the fact that he still had it in his possession. He'd almost lost it on a number of occasions. During a salvage dive in Lake Huron, it had slipped from his finger into lakebed silt. It was a miracle he managed to scoop it up before running out of air. He once removed it to work on an overhead gantry aboard the *Aeneas* and had to sift through a thousand brass fittings strewn across the deck to get it back. And then there was the Rafferty salvage, the project doomed from day one, the dark voyage from which he almost didn't return.

Jack closed his hand into a fist as if holding the ring tight to keep it from slipping away. There were so many ways to lose it. Time apart from his wife Lauren and mixed priorities nearly swiped it from his hand for good a few years back. That memory gave him pause, and he reached deep for the reason he'd come here tonight.

He pushed open the door and stepped down to the street. Mud from the running board streaked the back of his pant leg, and he reached down and brushed it off. The absence of the shoulder holster felt strange. Ever since the Rafferty incident a year ago he'd been carrying an old Colt semi-automatic, just in case. Now his first day without it felt a bit like stepping onto a tightrope without a net.

The scent of a storm carried into town on a wind gust. He pulled his windbreaker closed and locked the Jeep with the remote. Before crossing he checked down Main Street for traffic. A single pair of headlights pierced the late June dusk. He considered crossing ahead of the approaching car but decided to wait. No need to hurry. This meeting was years in the making. A few more seconds wouldn't hurt.

The car drove by with tires thumping over an expansion joint in the road.

Jack hesitated. Warm light spilled from the storefronts on the other side of Main. A string of white lights ringed the front window of the Daily Grind Café. Beyond the pane of glass a crowd populated the tables and milled about a coffee bar. He couldn't tell if she was there. The distance, the dim lighting, concealed the faces of the customers.

Raindrops began to pop and ping on parked cars. He grumbled and started across the road. Cold rain fell hard around him. He ducked his head and hustled to the sidewalk.

Beneath the café's clapboard overhang, he shook off a covering of droplets and peered through the front door glass. He could make out the faces now. She wasn't there. Relief washed over him. Maybe she'd bluffed, jerked his chain just to see if he'd come. Well, if she bluffed, he just called. Game over. He turned to leave and collided with someone rushing in.

Wet and curly brunette hair. Dark green eyes searching his face. It only took an instant for them to recognize each other. "Bobbie." It's all he could get out. Part of him wanted to run.

Bobbie read his body language. "Are you coming or going?"

Her gaze set him on edge. "I wasn't sure if you were really going to show up," he said. "Thought you might be, you know, pushing my buttons." He flashed a wise little smile.

She sidestepped a stream of water falling from the overhang. "I could say the same about you." She swept back a wave of hair. "Not showing up is your game."

Jack snapped his fingers. "That didn't take long. Five short seconds and we're back twenty-four years."

"Sounds like you're still sensitive." She crossed her arms. "That's called guilt."

"Hey, we could have done this on the phone. It would've been a lot easier just to hang up on each other." He walked into the rain but stopped at the curb. "You know, you almost had me. I actually thought you might be serious about needing help. My mistake."

Bobbie raised her hands. "Jack, I'm sorry."

He didn't reply.

She watched him soak in the downpour. "I'm going to get a coffee," she said. "You do what you want. I half expected you to say no anyway."

He stood firm on the curb. "You're not very good at this."

"Okay. I need help, and despite everything you're still the one I called. Better?"

"A little."

She stared him down. "I'm not begging you. I didn't back then and I won't do it now." She pushed through the café door.

Rainwater swirled into a sewer drain near Jack's feet. He glanced across the street at his Jeep. Dirt melted down the sides in brown smears. An oversized raindrop splashed into his eye. He wiped it away and checked inside the café. Bobbie took a seat at a table in the corner, her back to him. She was setting the hook.

"Jackass, Jack," he said. "What did you expect?" He kicked a newspaper box on the sidewalk. "Forget it." He stormed into the street and pulled the Jeep's keys from his pocket. He unlocked the doors, and the headlights and taillights flashed. A passing car swerved around him. He barely noticed. At the double yellow line he turned about-face.

It was warm inside the café. A dozen quiet conversations droned just below the jazz flowing from hidden speakers. Fresh coffee and cinnamon replaced the cold, wet scent of early summer outside. Jack approached Bobbie's table. She sipped black hazelnut from a white ceramic mug and gave no indication she knew he was behind her. A second mug sat on the table across from her.

"Expecting someone?" he said.

She didn't react to his voice beyond setting her coffee down. "You're predictable." She glanced back. "That's not a bad thing."

"Right." He took the opposite chair and began fixing his brew with cream and sugar from an antique-looking pewter tray.

"One cream, two sugar," she said.

He raised an eyebrow. "Good memory."

She smiled and silence settled between them.

He lowered a spoon into his coffee. "What is it you need my help with—"

"How's Lauren doing?" She locked her gaze on him and waited for an answer.

Jack paused to shuffle his thoughts. "Lauren's well. We've had our struggles, but I think we've worked through the worst of it."

"At Steven's wake I heard you two had reconciled. I'm happy for you."

Jack noted how well she held her voice while mentioning her husband's passing. He studied the pewter tray. "I'm sorry about the funeral. You needed a friend. I did a poor job of it."

She shook her head. "If you feel you let me down in some way, it's only because I expected too much from you. That wasn't fair. You were trying to rebuild your marriage. You didn't need me dredging up the past. A friend of mine told me she thinks I was displacing grief with anger."

"Leave it to a person in therapy to come up with that one."

She gave him a look like she might kick him under the table.

"There's the Bobbie I know." He toyed with the handle of his mug. "How is Alyson coping?"

"She's strong. It's in her blood. She delayed her senior year at MSU to help me out on the island. Last fall she went back to finish her degree."

"And what about the renovation? Restoring a hundred and forty-year-old lighthouse has got to be a monstrous challenge."

"You wouldn't believe. Buying the island and light was a huge dream of Steven's. We started to realize we were in over our heads a short time before the accident. Now with Steven gone, there's just my income to work with. What with college tuition, the mortgage, renovation costs, and day-to-day survival, money is spread pretty thin."

Jack settled into his chair. "Is that why you asked me to come here?"

Embarrassment flushed her cheeks red. "No! It's not like you're thinking."

"What am I thinking?"

"That I'm going to hit you up for a loan."

He didn't reply.

"It's something else."

"Something else?"

"Something you're uniquely qualified for."

"Bobbie, the things I'm uniquely qualified for make for a very short list."

"Steven thought you could help. Looking back I think he was right."

"I have a hard time believing Steven would consider my help for anything."

"Don't be like that. You two were friends in college. We were all friends; you, me, Steven, even Wallace. The things that happened between us, Steven didn't let them get in the way. He wanted to call you."

Jack sat forward and set his elbows on the table. "Call me for what?"

She matched him. "You're good at finding things."

He ruffled his brow.

"You spent twenty years with that undersea salvage company, Poseidon something."

"Neptune's Reach," he corrected. "Go on."

"In all those years, did you ever hunt for sunken treasure?"

"No. We were contracted to salvage contemporary wrecks and

cargo, sometimes to map sections of sea floor." He paused. "You've got a treasure hunt for me?"

She nodded.

"Did Steven have a line on some Great Lakes shipwreck loaded with gold?"

"Not quite, but you've got the general idea."

"I think I've heard this one before."

"No. Not this one."

"Bobbie, there are thousands of wrecks in the lakes; hundreds of legends about lost treasure, precious cargos. Most of these stories are just that, stories. What makes yours different?"

"When you learn the details you'll understand."

He shrugged. "All right, let's talk details. What type of treasure is it?"

"Coins."

"Potential value?"

She grinned. "Steven believed it would be enough to set up retirement plans through to our grandchildren, provided Alyson gives me grandchildren one day." She glanced at the crown molding above their heads. "Except, I'm not so sure this treasure is sunken. It might be buried."

"Sunken, buried, whatever it takes. Treasure is treasure, right?"

She folded her arms with an irritated huff.

"It doesn't sound like you've got your story straight."

More irritation.

"Bobbie, are you serious about this?"

"Would we be sitting here if I wasn't?"

Their eyes connected. She didn't flinch. "Okay," he said. "Tell me everything."

"I'm not going to *tell* you anything. You need to decide for yourself if this…opportunity…is real." She reached into the black purse sitting in her lap and pulled out a small leather-bound book zipped closed around the edges. She slid it across the table, jostling Jack's coffee mug. "This is Steven's. He kept his notes and research material in there. Study what he collected. Do your own research. Come back to me when you decide if it's plausible or not."

Jack picked up the book and studied it. "Is there a map with an X on it in here?"

She smiled. "If it was that easy I wouldn't need your help."

He returned the smile. "Why now? Why did you wait a year to contact me?"

"Honestly? I had my doubts. This was Steven's discovery. When he died the possibility that it was real seemed to die with him, but recently I've had second thoughts."

"What changed?"

She looked away. "I think I've gotten desperate. Things are falling apart, getting out of control. Bills, creditors, other complications. If this treasure is real it would solve a lot of problems."

He noticed her eyes dodging. "Is there something you're not telling me?"

She brought her gaze around. "There are a lot of things I'm not telling you."

He squirmed in his chair.

"It's all in Steven's notes," she added. "I don't want to distort or misrepresent the information by trying to explain what's in there. I want your first impression to be untainted."

Jack nodded but a tremor of unease rippled through him.

Bobbie took a sip of coffee and stood. "Thank you for meeting me, Jack. I know it sounds kind of crazy, but look through the notes and draw your own conclusion."

He stood too, and realized he hadn't had any of his coffee. They walked to the counter to pay the tab. "I'll look into this," he said, gesturing with the book, "but don't get your hopes too high. Even if there is a pile of gold out there, it might be impossible to find, or someone else may have already found it."

"I know, I know, but I have to try." She rummaged through her purse to pay the cashier.

Jack already had his wallet in hand. "Let me get this."

He paid and they walked out of the café. The rain had stopped, and the street and sidewalk glistened in the street lights. Bobbie faced him. "Tell Lauren how much I appreciate her letting you meet with me tonight."

He kept quiet and scratched the back of his head.

"You didn't tell her you were coming to see me, did you?"

"Like I said, I wasn't even sure you were going to show, or what this was all about. Lauren and I have a good shot at a second chance. There's no need to complicate things at home any more than they already are."

Bobbie lifted her car keys from her coat pocket. "I understand, but if we move forward with this little adventure, you're going to have to tell her something. You better start thinking about that." She gave him a quick hug and started down the sidewalk toward her car.

He watched her go and then considered the worn book in his hand, wondering where all this was heading. She drove away and he climbed into the Jeep. He started the engine and checked for traffic in the rearview mirror. All he could see was the back seat. The mirror was cocked. It hadn't been like that earlier. Then he noticed water droplets beading on the passenger seat. A spot check of the windows showed them all closed tight.

He suddenly remembered unlocking the doors before going into the café.

Jack jumped from the driver's seat and out the door. He stepped away from the Jeep and peered through the rear windows, searching for...someone. It was the first day in eleven months that he wasn't carrying the old Colt .45, and the first instance in all that time that he really wished he had it.

He threw open the rear door. Nobody there. He stepped back and checked underneath the Jeep. Nothing. Nothing seemed to have been stolen, either. The only thing out of place was a scrap of paper sticking out from the glove box. He flicked open the front panel and saw that the compartment had been rifled.

He plopped behind the wheel and locked the doors. Maybe Rafferty had finally decided to make an appearance. It'd been a year since their last contact, long enough for Jack to consider the issue closed, which is why he had left the Colt at home. But if this was Rafferty paying a visit, why did he choose this particular night? And why here? It didn't make sense.

After a moment of indulgent paranoia Jack chastised himself. Probably just kids looking for cash or something to sell on the street. Fortunately he had neither on board. He shook his head. Don't overreact.

And then he recalled Bobbie's words.

There are a lot of things I'm not telling you.

TWO

Benjamin Higgs knew how to seize an opportunity. Barreling down 31 in his black 300C he was about to prove this fact again. In the passenger seat Nate Kisko slept fully reclined. They'd been driving for over an hour and had about twenty minutes left to go before pulling into the driveway of the next rung on the ladder.

A newspaper lay folded in Kisko's lap. Higgs grinned at the headline. *Battle Creek Diver Discovers Pieces of the Past.* He didn't usually read the *Grand Haven Tribune,* but that headline in yesterday's edition had caught his eye. Seconds after reading the article he set a plan in motion. You had to be quick in life. Hesitation leads to failure, and Benjamin Higgs refused to fail. On the contrary, he knew the value of pressing circumstance quickly, of driving events to where you wanted them to be. Control the ball, control the game.

He veered off the expressway at Exit 100 and headed south on Beedle Lake. Roadside trees shielded the car from the setting sun. He removed his sunglasses and checked the GPS unit. He really hated backtracking. The next turn-off was just a few miles ahead, after Beedle Lake turned into 8 Mile. He drove the distance and jerked the wheel to slide the car onto a gravel side street.

Kisko rolled in his seat and stirred awake. "How far?" he said without opening his eyes.

"A few more miles," Higgs answered.

Kisko raised his seat. "Who is this guy again?"

Higgs glanced at the GPS unit; two more miles. "He's a local diver. About a month ago he found some things at the bottom of Lake Michigan that might be of interest to us."

"Not likely."

Higgs turned an agitated eye toward him. "Did you bother to read the article?"

Kisko lifted the newspaper. "Yeah, the first few paragraphs. Says he's given the junk to a museum. I'll bet he doesn't even have it at his house anymore."

"If you'd read the whole damn thing, you'd know he's keeping everything until July, when the museum takes possession for the exhibit."

Kisko sneered. "Twenty bucks says it's all garbage."

Higgs steered the car down a long gravel drive through a wooded piece of property. The area was too rural for his liking. Houses were spread so far apart he couldn't see two that were close enough to call neighbors. The small ranch home with faded blue siding at the end of the drive was no exception. It was the only residence for a mile in either direction; nice if you liked that kind of isolation, but Higgs had lived among apartments and suburbs all his life and had become accustomed to the crush of civilization. A rural setting was a nice place to do business, but he wouldn't want to live there.

He stopped the car in front of a garage door made of faded white aluminum panels. Kisko clicked open his door. Higgs grabbed his arm. "Leave your nine, take the camera."

Kisko cursed under his breath but removed the 9mm Glock from his belt and set it at his feet. He reached back into the rear seat and grabbed a digital camera.

Higgs exited the car, shook off the stiffness of the drive, and straightened the sleeves of his black sports jacket. He walked across a crumbling concrete sidewalk to the front door and squared himself with the doorframe. Kisko stood next to him with the camera in hand. Higgs knocked and they waited.

The door opened. A man in his late twenties with wavy blond hair greeted them. A few inches shorter than Higgs, the man looked up to his visitor. "Good afternoon. You must be Howse."

Higgs flashed a courteous smile. "Yes, and you are Rob Hamilton. Correct?"

"That's me. Come in and I'll show you the find." Hamilton stepped aside.

Higgs walked in and gestured to Kisko. "This is my photographer, Greg Brady."

Hamilton chuckled. "Like that old TV show?"

"Yeah," Higgs said, "something like that."

Kisko sneered and followed him through the door.

The house felt small inside and suffered from bachelor's house-keeping. There seemed to be more things than places to put them, and nothing appeared to be in the place it had. The living room furnishings consisted of a twenty-year-old black sectional couch and a dark-paneled television cabinet. A wetsuit hung from a curtain rod above the sliding glass door on the back wall. An aroma of stale laundry and last night's pizza hung in the air.

"I like your writing," Hamilton said. "I read all your articles in the *Detroit News*."

"You might be confusing me with the other Howse. See, there're two of us, and he's the one who gets all the front-page space."

"Oh, sorry."

"Don't sweat it. Happens all the time. Now tell me about this find of yours."

Hamilton became animated, like he'd just been asked to tell how he scored the winning touchdown in the big game. "I've been diving the Manitou Passage for a long time. A bunch of ships have gone down near South Manitou Island, and I'm always trying to discover new wrecks. Well, a few weeks ago I figured I'd give it another go."

Higgs pulled a notepad from his jacket pocket and scribbled something on the front page. "You do that a lot? Just dive in and hope to find something?"

"Every chance I get. There are a slew of wrecks out there. If you think about it, the odds of finding one are pretty good—if you know the shipping routes the old mariners used."

"Apparently so."

Kisko stepped back and snapped a picture of the wetsuit.

"This time was a little different though," Hamilton said. "Someone put a bug in my ear about a wreck that matched the description of what I found in the place I found it."

Higgs raised an eyebrow. "How do you mean?"

"Over a year ago I met this guy, Steve somebody, and he asked me about the Manitou Passage. He wanted to know if I ever dove on a wreck named *William Barclay*, or any schooner that may have gone down in 1868. He never told me why it interested him, he just asked me to call him if I ever found a ship from that era in the Passage."

"Did you?"

"I might have. A few miles southeast of the island, I came across a wreck that looked like it could be from the mid-to-late-nineteenth century. No signs of a boiler or mechanized propulsion, so she's most likely a schooner, probably a scow. There wasn't much left, just a faint outline of the keel and some skeletal cross members with a few broken sections of hull around the perimeter." Hamilton paused. "I guess I should give him a call."

"Maybe you should."

"Anyway," Hamilton continued, "an odd rock was sticking out from between a pile of split planks. It looked too regular shaped, too rectangular to be a natural rock. I checked it out and found it was a sea chest, you know, like people used to lug around when they traveled."

"Your lucky day."

"You bet. The chest was deteriorated pretty badly, but I found some interesting stuff inside."

"What sort of stuff?"

Hamilton gestured to the couch cluttered with newspapers. "Have a seat and I'll show you." He disappeared around a corner across the room. Higgs and Kisko did not sit down. They made eye contact. "Garbage," Kisko said.

Higgs didn't reply. He knew better. He'd read the whole damn article.

Hamilton returned carrying a blue plastic tote about the size of a laundry basket.

"I didn't know they were so handy with injection molding back then," Kisko said.

Hamilton smiled and set the container down on the couch. He peeled off the lid and reached inside. The item he pulled out set Higgs at full attention. It was a small copper plate that had been wiped clean. Engraved letters darkened by imbedded sediment spelled out the name H. W. COATES across the face.

"This was on the trunk," Hamilton said. "I did some research on this name. There was a guy, a Lieutenant Harlan W. Coates, who worked for the Lighthouse Board in the mid-1800s. This stuff could be his."

"Could be," Higgs said. "What else have you got?"

Hamilton dipped again into the tub and produced something wrapped in plain black cloth. He folded the corners back to reveal a white ceramic plate whose surface pattern had been worn and stained by a century and a half immersion in lakebed silt.

Kisko looked sideways at Higgs. *Garbage.*

"And this." Hamilton rolled a discolored piece of metal shaped like a five-point star in his fingers. He angled it in the light coming through the living room window. "The ornamentation right here looks like an anchor. I did some checking on this, too. The navy gives out a Medal of Honor that resembles this shape. I think this is one of those." He continued his presentation with the unveiling of a glass decanter stained brown and a tarnished pewter fork.

Higgs calmly listened to Hamilton's account of how he'd recovered each item and waited for the other shoe to drop.

"Here's my favorite piece." Hamilton lifted the last item from the tote and carefully removed black cloth wrapping to reveal a dulled silver crucifix. The corners were rounded and tiny nicks marred the surface. A ringlet at the top point indicated it had at one time hung on a chain.

Higgs eyed the cross. "May I take a closer look?"

Hamilton handed it over. Higgs inspected every facet, ran his thumb over the faded engraved text. It matched the description he'd been given. Exhilaration ran through to his fingertips.

Kisko suddenly became interested.

Hamilton rocked on his heels. "What do you think?"

"Very nice artifacts," Higgs said. "I can see why the museum wants to exhibit them." He handed the cross back to Hamilton. "Have you uncovered any information about this crucifix? Any interesting tales associated with it?"

Hamilton shook his head and wrapped the cloth around his prized find again. "Nothing yet." He turned and placed it back in the tub. "Why do you ask?"

He never saw it coming.

Higgs swung hard. His fist slammed Hamilton's jaw and made the diver stagger, dropping him to one knee. Higgs followed through with a knee to the face and put Hamilton down.

Kisko swiped up the tub and pressed the lid back on. "You didn't tell me you were going to do that."

Higgs massaged the ache in his knuckles. "I didn't know I was going to do that." He surveyed the disheveled room. "Wipe anything you've touched."

"I didn't touch anything."

"Did you hear what he said? Weller put him on to the wreck. Sneaky prick was holding out on us." Higgs searched and found a kitchen adjacent to the living room. He pondered the old appliances and furnishings. "Nate, bring Hamilton in here, now." He grabbed a towel off the countertop and used it to open cabinet doors until he found pots and pans. Still using the towel, he lifted a fry pan off the shelf and set it on a stove burner, and then took a carton of eggs from the refrigerator and set it open on the counter.

Kisko dragged Hamilton into the kitchen.

"Lay him near the table and knock a chair over," Higgs said. "Get it?"

"Got it."

Higgs ignited the burner under the pan and stuck the edge of the towel in the blue flame. It caught, and he laid the smoldering towel in an open drawer full of other towels. The fire spread. He stepped back and considered all the items in the kitchen that would eventually combust. This wouldn't take long.

Kisko overturned a chair next to Hamilton's body on the floor.

Higgs gave him a nod and they headed out, snatching the tote from the couch on their way out the front door. Kisko shouldered it closed. They were barreling down the gravel drive in fifteen seconds.

Higgs flipped open his cell phone and hit speed dial one.

The voice that answered didn't bother to say hello. "Did he have it?"

"Yes, sir," Higgs said.

"Is there writing on the face?"

"There is."

"Does he still have it?"

"No, sir."

"Should we expect trouble from him concerning your visit today?"

"No, sir. The issue is closed."

Silence.

"I'll have it in your hands in the morning," Higgs said to fill the void.

"Good. We need to get moving on this. We've lost a lot of time, and there are too many people taking interest again."

Higgs paused. "This may not have been a coincidence."

"How so?"

"Weller told this guy to be on the lookout for the Coates wreck. Seems our partner wasn't being very honest with us."

Another stretch of silence, this one more uncomfortable than the last. "It doesn't matter now. It's played into our hands. This was very fortunate for you, Mr. Higgs."

"Agreed."

"In the morning then, at the normal time and place."

"Yes, sir."

The line disconnected and Higgs closed the phone. "Sounds like things are heating up." He glanced over at Kisko. "Ehrlich and Barnett must have found out that Bobbie Weller is getting involved."

Kisko shrugged. "She's been warned."

Higgs pulled out of the driveway and accelerated down the dirt road toward 8 Mile. Above the trees behind the car, a column of black smoke rose into the sky. Higgs watched it in the rearview mirror for a moment and then set his gaze back on the road. "No more warnings—for anyone."

- THREE -

"One of the most time consuming things is to have an enemy."
— E. B. White

Jack Sheridan lay propped on his elbow in bed watching Lauren sleep. The sun had been up nearly an hour and its first rays were breaching the treetops beside the house, streaming into the bedroom through an open window. Robins chirped back and forth in the branches of the old oak out front. The serenity struck Jack. He had imagined moments like this while stuck on salvage vessels half a world away. He'd reflected on them during the darkest hours of the Rafferty incident, relied on them to stay focused, to give him that one strong reason to keep fighting for survival. The thought of getting back to Lauren had kept him sane and alive. Now having found his way home, he savored these moments like each might be the last. He took nothing for granted anymore, and yet...

Lauren stirred on her pillow as if sensing his thoughts. She opened her eyes and brushed back tousled auburn hair from her cheek. "Why are you looking at me?"

He smiled at her. "There's a big drool puddle on your pillow."

She lifted her head and wiped her mouth, and then checked the dry pillow case. She slapped him on the shoulder. "Liar." She rolled on her back and stretched under the covers. "You got in late last night. How did your business meeting go?"

"It went fine." He wasn't good at bold-faced lies. "We threw some good ideas back and forth." Sometimes he could muster little white ones.

"You think he'll invest in the charter boat idea?"

Jack sat up and leaned against the headboard. "It's hard to say at this point."

"Your heart isn't in this charter thing, is it?"

"How can you tell?"

"Twenty-four years married."

"Oh, that."

She reached over and took his hand. "You're not convincing me that you want to do this. You were different with Neptune's Reach. You got excited talking about the things you did there, the Russian Trawler salvage, how you raised that ironclad off the Virginia coast. You have to admit, despite the negatives you loved the work."

He squeezed her hand. "The payoff wasn't worth the cost."

"I know, but it did give you something that you're missing now." She added, "Even when you talk about the Rafferty project you get—animated."

He touched her hand with a kiss. "That's not funny." He dropped his legs over the edge of the bed. "Calm seas. That's what I'm looking for now."

She studied him a long while. "Is that really what you want?"

He managed to subdue a shoulder shrug. "It's hard to say at this point."

"It might be hard to say but it's easy to see. Deep down you don't really want to ferry clients out to fish for big mouth bass."

"Large mouth bass," he corrected. "And sometimes you're right."

"Then why pretend it's what you want to do?"

He glanced at her. "I'm not pretending. Besides, I don't have many alternatives."

She sat cross-legged and smoothed the material of her silky green night gown in her lap, and then tilted her head in thought. "Tell me then, in those moments of doubt, what is it you desire to do with the rest of your early retirement?"

"Desire?" He raised an eyebrow.

"Stay on task, dear."

"I like that night gown on you."

She leaned forward and gave him a sexy pout. "Focus."

"I'm only forty-six. I've got plenty of tread left on me." He thought a bit. "I could be a tour boat captain and ferry tourists through Michigan waterways at two knots while reading a corny script. I'd only have to do it seven or eight times a day."

"I think you'd enjoy charter captain-hood better."

He turned and faced her. "You know what—"

A sharp bark split their conversation. Prancing paws and a jangling name tag preceded a sixty-pound German Shepard's leap onto the bed. Dark-haired and playfully alert, the dog stood between Jack and Lauren and woofed. Lauren scratched the Shepard's chest.

"Ike, off the bed!" Jack reached for the dog's collar, and the Shepard playfully gnawed on his forearm. Jack stood and snapped his fingers. "Now."

Ike's ears went back. He hopped to the floor with a thud and spun around, then fixed Jack with wide eyes and barked.

"Right, time for the morning hunt." Jack walked from the bedroom, gesturing the dog to follow. He welcomed the interruption. He wasn't ready for this conversation yet.

He stepped onto the front porch, appraised his rural property, and wondered what it would be like to drive a boat around in circles all day long. Ike slipped by him, bolting over the steps and down the hill that the house was built upon. Jack walked the gravel drive to the mail box and retrieved the morning paper. Maybe being a charter boat captain was the best solution for him. A lot of men dreamed of such a job. There were certainly worse occupations to have, a lot worse.

He returned to the house and climbed the steps to the wraparound porch. Ike trotted along the wall of weeds surrounding the manicured lawn searching for groundhogs. Jack went inside to start a pot of coffee. He dropped the newspaper on the hutch near the front door. Stepping into the kitchen, he heard the spray of water coming from the shower in the master bath.

He set up the coffee maker and took a seat on one of the stools around the island in the kitchen to wait for his brew. Atop the hutch, beneath the newspaper he'd brought in, Steven's leather notebook that Bobbie had given him commanded his attention. It felt as if the thing had eyes and was staring at him. Jack stared back.

He hadn't opened it yet. To do so would be crossing a line. Those pages were going to put him on a road leading into the unknown. It'd been a while since he'd put himself out on a limb. Bobbie's involvement just complicated matters.

Ike, the great hunter, cut loose with a barrage of barks outside. Jack rolled his eyes. He went to a window in the great room and spotted the Shepard stalking the tree line at the base of the hill out back. The Jeep break-in came to mind and he tried to see through the trees, looking for anything or anybody that shouldn't be there. Nothing materialized under the shadowy foliage, but ominous thoughts had surfaced. He turned back into the room and considered the oak china cabinet in the kitchen. He wasn't thinking about formal place settings. He opened the top drawer and lifted the Colt pistol he'd put there the day before. The magazine was missing from the butt of the pistol grip just as he had left it. He cycled the action and verified the chamber was clear.

It'd been over a year since he had fired the weapon outside of a range, and on that occasion he had killed a man in order to save his son Connor from being gunned down. The memory held him there gazing at the weapon. Jack had been eluding Rafferty's men aboard the *Aeneas*. One of the gunmen searching for him stormed into a cabin and found Connor instead. Jack had two seconds to act, to decide whether to take a man's life or not. It only took him half a second to make the decision. He shot the man three times. The thundering reports pounded in his head.

A full magazine lay in the china cabinet drawer. Jack picked it up and slid it into the Colt.

"He's not coming back."

Jack looked over his shoulder toward the sound of Lauren's voice.

She stood in the bedroom doorway draped in a white bath robe with a towel wrapped around her wet hair. "Donovan Rafferty is not coming back for you."

Jack didn't reply.

"He's as far from here as he can be," she continued. "Probably not even in the country."

"You may be right." Jack set the Colt on the island. "But being cautious doesn't hurt."

"There's a fine line between cautious and paranoid."

"You know what they say."

"Yeah, when people are out to get you, being paranoid is just good thinking." She wiped a water droplet from her cheek. "Rafferty's not out to get you. He called you on the phone a year ago to shake you up, that's all."

"He called from a car parked on the road in front of the house."

"Scare tactic."

"It worked." Jack considered the pistol. "When's the last time you were at the range with your .32?"

"You going to cook eggs to go with that coffee?"

"Of course. Scrambled. I'm also making an appointment for both of us to do some target practice."

She walked into the great room. "How about some bacon, too?"

He opened the refrigerator and retrieved a carton of eggs and a package of bacon. "You still carry your pepper spray in your purse?"

"No, but there's a shaker in the spice rack right there."

He fixed her with an agitated stare. "Rafferty is a dangerous man, he's still on the loose, and I really pissed him off. Will you at least indulge me in this?"

She took a seat on a stool and balanced the wrapped towel on her head. "I think we can pull back to Threat Level Orange. There hasn't been a single incident, not a phone call, a sighting, nothing, since that first and only encounter. Don't you think he's a little busy staying ahead of the CIA or the FBI or whoever chases people like that? Besides, if he does pop his head up the police will notify us."

Jack grabbed a pan from a drawer beside the stove. "Sure, the authorities will notify us if they happen to see him when he pops his head up."

"You know, sweetheart, I'm starting to think you feed off this in some way."

He set the pan firmly on a burner and cracked an egg into it. "That's ridiculous."

"I thought we were having scrambled eggs."

"Changed my mind. I got a taste for over easy."

"Okay, so it's not Rafferty stressing you out. Maybe it's retirement. Maybe it's Neptune's Reach. You miss it and want to go back. Possible?"

"We've already had this discussion and agreed that going back is not on the table. I don't want it and you don't want it."

"Sometimes I think I don't want it more than you don't want it."

He ignited the burner. "Are we still talking about Neptune's Reach?"

She laughed. "Now you're the one dodging."

"I'm not…"

Ike broke into another barking tirade on the porch. A glint of sunlight reflected in through the front window and drew Jack's attention. A Cadillac CTS was rolling up the driveway. He recognized the car. "Damn."

"What is it?" She stood to get a look at the car. "What's he doing here?"

"How should I know? I haven't talked to him in months. And I certainly didn't invite him over." Jack put the Colt back in the drawer.

She pulled the towel from her head and straightened her hair. "Interesting timing, don't you think?"

Jack flushed red. "Now wait a minute. Our conversation and Lloyd Faulkner showing up is just a coincidence."

Ike stopped barking. Lauren saw through the window that Lloyd was petting the Shepard on the porch. "Your dog doesn't know who to keep away from the house." She went to the door and met their visitor.

Lloyd made a big plastic smile. His suit and tie looked out of place against the oak trees and gravel drive, and his strong cologne polluted the air. "Lauren, you look great! What's it been, six, seven months now?" He extended a hand.

She didn't offer hers. "However long it's been it hasn't been long enough."

He retracted his hand and put it in his pocket. "It's still good to see you. Is Jack around?"

"You can't have him."

Lloyd's mouth fell open, apparently shocked at the comment. "I'm here on a social call, as a friend. I haven't spoken with Jack in a long time, and I wanted to see how he was doing."

She tilted her head. "A friend? How can you call yourself that? You put a paycheck ahead of my husband's safety, ahead of the whole crew."

"I had no way of knowing what Rafferty was up to. Nobody did. Don't you believe me?"

She turned her back and walked to the corner of the porch. "You had my husband on a leash for eighteen years. You're not getting him back."

Lloyd waved his hands in surrender. "I just want to talk to him. Is he home?"

Jack stepped into the doorway. "Of course I'm home. It's seven in the morning and my Jeep's in the drive."

Lloyd smiled. "Hey, how've you been? You look great. Tanned, rested, and ready to go."

Lauren flashed him an angry glare.

Jack rolled his eyes. "What do you want, Lloyd?"

"Just to talk and let you know how your buddies at Neptune are doing."

Lauren turned her back again. Jack gave her a sideways glance. "Wipe off that Hi-Karate, Lloyd, you're making my eyes water." He gestured inside with a nod.

They walked into the kitchen, and Jack poured coffee. Lloyd sat on a stool. "How've you been keeping yourself busy these days?"

Jack loaded his coffee. "This and that. You have a point in asking?"

"Just curious. You know, the maritime world is a small community. Everyone knows everyone else and word gets around. You hear interesting things sometimes."

"Things like what?"

Lloyd shrugged. "Are you really opening a charter business?"

"Who'd you hear that from? Was it Berry?"

"Like I said, word gets around. Is it true?"

Jack sat down. "What's it to you? Neptune's Reach doesn't hold title to me anymore."

Lloyd shook his head. "It's none of my business, I know. I'm just concerned. I'd hate to see a friend of twenty years make a bad decision, that's all."

"Why, you trying to corner the market on bad decisions?"

"Jack, I didn't know Rafferty was—"

"Was what, an arms dealer trying to steal a Defense Department prototype aircraft using Neptune's Reach manpower and equipment?"

"Don't put it all at my feet. You had your suspicions but went along for the ride anyway. I didn't force you to ship out."

Jack stared hard at him.

Lloyd braced himself on the island and exhaled. "You're baiting me, and I'm dumb enough to bite. Look, I didn't come here to argue, or admit I made a mistake, or blame you for anything."

"Then why did you come?"

Lloyd took a breath and exhaled slow. "The truth is the company is going through a tough time. Neptune's Reach new business dropped fifty percent over the past eight months. The economy is tightening up. Organizations and industries aren't so quick to spend the dollars it takes to mount a first-class maritime salvage operation or an ocean research project. And the potential clients who do walk through the door are looking for the guy from the *Newsweek* cover. When I tell them you don't work for us anymore, they lose interest in the company."

"Then they weren't viable clients in the first place."

"Jack, you have cachet. You can bring million-dollar contracts back to Neptune."

"You lied to my wife out there."

"We need you to come back, just to get us on our feet again. We've got a little thing going on in Lake Michigan right now that's perfect to ease you into the swing of things. It will be different this time. You'll call the shots on the projects. You'll choose your clients."

"It wasn't just the Rafferty project. It was eighteen years being away on some ship across the globe. I missed my son growing up, and it nearly cost me my marriage."

"We'll double your salary."

"Never again."

"Being a charter boat captain isn't a big enough challenge for you. We both know it."

"What do you mean we; you got a mouse in your suit pocket?"

"You thrive on the hunt for a wreck. You're consumed by devising just the right strategy to bring it to the surface or salvage its cargo. The only reason you hung with Neptune for eighteen years is because you loved it."

"Loved it, past tense. I loved it until I realized my priorities were completely screwed up. That's one thing Rafferty showed me. You get one life, one shot at making it right, and if you waste your time chasing the wrong things, you might not get a chance to correct your course. I'm on track now, Lloyd, and Neptune's Reach is off the chart."

"Okay, that's your decision—for now." Lloyd stood and straightened his tie. "Just remember this conversation when you're untangling fishing lines for weekend warriors and the biggest thrill of your day is locating a school of lake trout on your echo sounder." He turned to leave. "Call me when you change your mind."

Jack took a sip of coffee.

Lloyd stepped outside and spied Lauren sitting in a deck chair at the far corner of the porch. She was putting Ike through his paces with a game of fetch. "Take care of yourself, Lauren," he said. "And take care of that stubborn husband of yours."

She ignored him and picked up the stick that Ike had just dropped at her feet.

Lloyd got in his car and backed down the driveway, giving a short beep as he drove off.

In the kitchen Jack toyed with his coffee mug. That notebook was staring at him again. He averted his eyes. Outside, Ike requested another stick toss with a bark. Lauren obliged. She seemed intent on staying out there until she had calmed down. Breakfast was apparently on hold. Jack returned his gaze to the notebook. Before he realized it he had the book in his hands and was sitting down in his little study.

You need to decide for yourself if this...opportunity...is real.

- FOUR -

"It doesn't mean what you think it does, pinhead."

Connor Sheridan zipped the front of his neoprene wetsuit and laughed. He stood in the stern of a thirty-foot Boston Whaler Conquest anchored a mile from the Sarnia, Michigan shore. A Lake Huron swell rolled beneath the boat and upset his balance. He compensated with a step forward and reached for his diving hood. "When will you listen to me?"

Markus Sweetwood sat on the starboard bench and inspected the octopus arrangement of hoses on his buoyancy compensator (BC). "Since when are you bilingual, Sheridan?"

Connor cinched a weight belt around his waist. "For some reason my one semester of high school Spanish stuck with me. *Pomposo* doesn't mean dangerous. *Peligroso* is the word you wanted."

Two hundred yards north of their position another boat had dropped its anchor. Markus observed it pitching in the waves. "So what are you telling me?"

Connor grinned. "You named your boat *The Pompous One* instead of *The Dangerous One*— El Pomposo."

"Whatever." Markus shrugged. "I thought about naming her *Man of Steel* too, but I didn't know the Spanish word for steel."

"Acero."

"What'd you call me?"

"*Acero* means steel in Spanish."

"Connor means *wise ass* in English." Markus nodded toward the other boat. "Looks like that twenty-foot Trophy we saw back at the marina. Isn't that the boat those yahoos boarded?"

"You mean the guys you squared off with in the parking lot because someone opened their car door into the side of your Explorer? Yeah, I think so."

Markus spit into the water.

"I guess the Great Lakes aren't big enough for the four of us," Connor said.

Markus frowned. "If those cork stackers go under first they'll stir up the silt around the wreck and ruin visibility for the rest of the day."

"Then let's get wet before they do."

"We better. These rubber pants are melting my shorts."

They continued to suit up. Markus pulled his fins on. "Is your dad starting up a charter company or what?"

Connor twisted the air valve on his tank to the full open position and then backed it off a quarter turn. "I doubt it. He's talkin' the talk but not walkin' the walk."

"Well, talk him or walk him into it. I could handle being a deck hand on a fishing charter. Working at CCG is getting under my skin."

"Right. Slapping together equipment for Crittenden Controls Group to sell to the automotive industry is not what I call fulfilling and meaningful employ, unless you like aggravation, pressure, and a kick in the teeth every once in a while."

Markus lifted his air tank and threaded his arms through the BC vest. "Going back to work after the Rafferty thing sort of sucked too."

"I know what you mean." Connor thought on it a moment. "It's hard to explain. We were nearly killed out there. Coming back to normal after that was tough. I wanted to dump engineering and go off and do—something else, something more satisfying, more important."

"This is all borrowed time," Markus said. "I want to live like there aren't twenty-five years and a 401(k) ahead of me." He pulled the neoprene hood over his head. "SCUBA, skydive, beer, women—not necessarily in that order."

Connor put his hood on too. "I hate this thing. When I put it on I feel hearing impaired and look like a dork."

Markus cocked his head. "What?"

"Wise ass."

"By the way, you always look like a dork."

Connor checked on the Trophy. "Your friends are splashing in. Come on."

They put their dive masks on, adjusted snorkels, set their regulators in their mouths, and checked air flow. Connor rolled off the side of the Boston Whaler first, splashing a few yards from the Diver Down buoy. Markus followed suit. After a quick equipment check they gave one another the okay sign, drained their BC vests of air, and sank below the surface.

Water distorted sounds in a weird way. It always took Connor a few minutes to adjust to the new environment. The motor of a nearby boat sounded like a high-pitched buzz. He hated that. And his breathing through the regulator boomed in his ears like a Darth Vader soundtrack. Visibility was good near the surface, however, and that helped balance him out. Glancing left, he found Markus floating beside him. Another okay sign and they started their descent.

According to the marker buoy on the surface the wreck was a hundred yards or so northeast, eighty feet down. Connor checked his wrist compass, corrected his bearing. The depth needle indicated he was at twenty feet. They could have followed the mooring line down from the marker buoy to the wreck, but what fun would that be? Talk about taking the sport out of sport diving.

They sank deeper into Lake Huron, gliding through a thermo-cline that registered to Connor as a fifteen-degree drop. The bottom materialized beneath them. The wreck wasn't in sight. Connor tapped the fill button on the octopus of his BC vest and fussed with the air volume until finding neutral buoyancy. He swam above the silt and seaweed on a bearing that would lead him to the wreck. Markus stayed at his side.

A large dark shape appeared ahead in the green-tinted light from above. Overturned and encrusted in zebra mussels, the steel hull of a 250-foot long ship lie on the lakebed. She was the freighter *Regina*. Eight decades ago she traversed the Great Lakes in support of turn-of-the-century maritime commerce. A 1913 storm brought her to an untimely grave.

Connor kicked his legs and propelled himself toward the ship. He rounded the bow. The *Regina* was nearly inverted. A large portion of her topside deck was concealed by sand, silt, and seaweed. An immense smokestack lay next to the wreck. It had come off so clean it appeared as if it had been unbolted and carefully set aside.

The somber majesty of the scene captivated Connor; that is, until another pair of divers appeared. One in a red wetsuit and the other in black, the guys from the Trophy swam up from *Regina's* stern. They kept close to the overturned deck. A silt cloud billowed in their wake. Connor cursed into his regulator. He glanced left and caught Markus' attention. Markus nodded and made a limp gesture with his wrist, apparently trying to communicate some derogatory comment on the new arrivals.

The four SCUBA divers crossed paths amidships. The guy in the red wetsuit flipped the Italian salute in passing. Markus began to turn back after him. Connor grabbed hold of Markus' arm and kept him moving forward. They continued swimming down the length of the wreck, drifting up to peer into the numerous portholes along the hull.

They circumvented the entire ship and came back around the bow. Connor marveled at how well the cold, fresh water had preserved her.

He wanted to stay down longer, but his oxygen gauge read that he had only a quarter tank of air left. He connected with Markus, and they gave each other the thumbs up sign—time to surface.

Connor tapped some air into his BC. Above his head and a bit north one of the other divers, the guy in the black wetsuit, was making his ascent. The diver in the red suit wasn't with him. Not good practice. The buddy system only works when you stick with your buddy. It's not a social thing, it's a safety thing. Before kicking toward the surface, Connor scanned through the dispersing silt cloud around the wreck and debris field.

A steady stream of bubbles flowed from the base of the giant smokestack. It seemed like a free-flow discharge, not at all in accord with the breathing pattern of a calm diver. Connor reached out to tap Markus on the shoulder, but his partner had already seen the red flag. A sense of urgency took hold and they swam toward the bubbles. Connor noticed his breathing accelerate in his ears.

Inside the giant steel smokestack, the diver in the red wetsuit fought a frantic struggle. Exposed and twisted steel had entangled his BC octopus and had severed his primary regulator hose. Compressed air rushed from his tank. He flailed and kicked to break free of the steel tendrils with eyes wild and lips pressed tight together.

Connor swam into the mouth of the smokestack to try and help. The entrapped diver was in full panic mode, completely focused on his battle to get free. Connor waved his arms to get the guy's attention. Through their dive masks their eyes connected. The guy was scared. Connor reached over to untangle the hoses from the steel, but as he did the bubbles pouring from the severed hose dwindled and then stopped flowing altogether. The tank had emptied itself.

The guy shifted gears from scared to frantic. The last of his air supply drifted up and out of the smokestack. The jerk in the red wetsuit, the one who had nearly come to blows with Markus in the marina parking lot, the dip-shit who stirred a cloud of silt around the *Regina,* that poor bastard was seconds away from drowning.

Connor didn't even think about it. He pulled the regulator from his mouth and held it up so the trapped diver would see it. The guy reached out and scooped it into his mouth, sucking in an enormous breath. Connor checked his oxygen gauge. Just an eighth of a tank remained.

Markus hovered above with eyes nearly as wide as the guy in the red wetsuit. He worked at separating the hose from the steel. Lips pressed closed, Connor pulled off his glove to gain some dexterity and worked a fold of sheet metal out of the trapped diver's weight belt. He fought the impulse to take a breath. Without the regulator in his mouth it would be suicide. He thought about grabbing the secondary regulator on his octopus but stopped short. With the way the trapped guy was breathing, both of them sucking from the tank would draw it down to nothing in no time flat.

Markus seemed to be reading his thoughts and offered him his backup regulator for a few replenishing breaths. Connor accepted, took three controlled draws, and handed it back. He signed him—okay.

Markus untangled the last hose from the steel. The diver in the red wetsuit was free. He'd gotten himself somewhat under control but was still in crisis mode. Connor and Markus led him out of the smokestack, one of them on either side.

Once out in open water, Connor took another hit off Markus' backup regulator and considered the situation. Three men were breathing from two nearly empty air tanks with eighty feet of water above them and a decompression stop in between. This was going to be tricky.

Connor and Markus coordinated their movements and began the ascent. The guy in the red wetsuit started kicking like he wanted to get to the surface right now. Connor and Markus fought to hold him back. If the guy shot to the surface, his lungs would likely burst from rapid air expansion in his chest. If he made it to the surface with organs intact, the bends would probably strike him down. Any way you cut it, they had to go up slow, and they had to make their air last, somehow.

They inched up to twenty-five feet and hovered. Diving by the tables, they had to make this decompression stop to ensure their bodies and blood would adjust properly to the decreasing pressure. Connor kept an eye on his oxygen gauge. The needle barely registered any air in the tank. The guy in the red wetsuit seemed to be gaining more clarity and slowed his breathing to a minimum. Markus' air tank was faring just as poorly. With Connor and Markus both drawing from it, despite how shallow they tried to breathe, it wasn't going to last much longer.

Seven minutes into a ten-minute stop they had to move. Red wetsuit stayed tethered to Connor through the regulator hose. Connor was tied to Markus in the same fashion. They floated upward, cloistered together like fish on a string. The shallower they got the quicker they rose. Connor fought to draw his next breath. Nothing entered his lungs. The tank was dead. Sparkling light and wave ripples materialized overhead. Connor's lungs reflexively tried to suck in air that just wasn't there. The surface seemed so close. Why the hell wasn't he there yet?

The guy in the red wetsuit drifted away, apparently abandoning the second empty tank.

Connor reached skyward, trying to break the surface, trying to get out of the water. A cool breeze blew over his hand. Water receded from his face. He gulped in the biggest breath he'd ever taken in his life. Kicking his legs and treading water, he filled his lungs over and over again. His thoughts began to clear. And then...

Markus! Where was he?

Connor whirled about. Ten yards to his left the guy in the red wetsuit floated on his back, panting.

"Come on, Sheridan."

Connor spun another sixty degrees toward Markus' voice and found him paddling toward the old Boston Whaler, which happened to be just thirty yards away. Connor turned to the guy in the red wetsuit. "Are you all right?"

The guy came off his back and treaded water. "Yeah, thanks. You saved my bacon down there. Thank God. You saved my bacon."

"Our boat's over here," Connor said. "Think you can make it?"

"Yeah, yeah."

Connor swam toward the stern of the boat. The blue script writing on the back made him smile. *El Pomposo.*

Markus reached over the side and seized Connor's hand and pulled him aboard. After struggling to his feet with the empty tank on his back, Connor unbuckled the BC vest and lowered the assembly to the deck. It felt like five hundred pounds had just come off his back.

The guy in the red wetsuit came alongside the boat, and Connor and Markus pulled him out of the water. He plopped on the deck in the stern and leaned back, gasping and squinting at the sky. "You guys saved my ass. Thanks."

Markus sat on the starboard bench seat and pulled off his gloves off. "You got a name?"

The guy lowered his eyes to his saviors. "Dave. Dave Wright." He extended his hand.

Connor leaned over and shook it. "Connor Sheridan. This guy is Markus Sweetwood."

Markus settled back on the bench seat. "Don't get the wrong idea, Dave. I didn't pull you out of there just to save your life. See, I wasn't about to let you get out of paying my car insurance deductible to repair that dent in my door."

Wright burst out laughing. "Just tell me who to write the check to."

Connor set his weight belt on the deck. "Markus, what do you think my dad will say about this little adventure?"

Markus unzipped his wetsuit. "He'll say 'Those guys are just the kind of men I want working for me.'"

Connor chuckled. "More like, 'I thought I told you to stay away from dangerous situations.'"

"Yeah," Markus said, "like your dad's one to talk about playing it safe."

- FIVE -

Jack Sheridan held the worn leather notebook in one hand and knocked on the front door of the old house with the other. He'd read completely through the material Steven had assembled and, to his surprise, found the pieced-together story of lost coins undeniably compelling. But the raw information lacked factual support. Jack needed more. He needed someone who could put flesh on the bones of the tale, and had spent half the night searching the Internet for just the right person to help him do that. Now, after a two-hour drive to reach Portage, Michigan, he stood on the front porch of a pre-World War II home with faded red brick hoping he'd come to the right place.

Mature maples lined the street in front of the house and shielded the sidewalk from the blistering sun. It was a hot day with humidity so thick Jack's shirt stuck to his skin. The heat seemed to oppress the sleepy neighborhood. No one ventured outside, no lawn mowers were running, and the only sound competing with the birdsong was the buzz of air conditioners.

A little impatient, Jack tried to peer into the house through a pane of glass above a window-mounted air conditioner to the right of the door, but the combination of outside heat and inside cool had fogged over the glass. It was the same on the left side of the porch. He raised his hand to knock on the lacquered front door again, but it opened under his fist.

A thin, elderly man with Ben Franklin glasses and a narrow face greeted him. A scrap of gray hair lay frizzled on the man's head, and he wore a long black scarf wrapped once around his neck.

Jack gave him a polite smile. "Eugene Elliot?"

The man adjusted his glasses with bony fingers that poked through fingerless black knit gloves. "You must be Sheridan," he said. They shook hands, and Eugene Elliot waved his visitor inside. "Quickly, before I lose my cool." He smiled at his quip.

Jack entered the house and shivered. The temperature difference between outside and inside was so stark that goose bumps rose on his skin. Elliot closed the door. "Hope you don't mind the climate. Cold air is good for the lungs, and the books."

Jack surveyed the house. Every wall was covered by a bookshelf, and every shelf was packed with books. They were all tucked neatly in place with their bindings flush. The place smelled of pulp and print. A hardwood dining table sat in the middle of the large room but it didn't seem to have been used for dining in quite some time. A few note pads covered in ink scrawls were lying open on its surface along with a short stack of books. An odd little cylinder sat in the corner of the table, and an old desktop computer and monitor occupied the far side. An antique wooden office chair sat behind the table. On the back wall two more air conditioners hummed in windows between bookshelves, kicking additional chill into the space.

"Thanks for seeing me on such short notice," Jack said.

Elliot gave him a thin smile. "I'm a retired history professor who has taken up studying the nooks and crannies of West Michigan history in his retirement. Judging by the sales volume of my last two books on the subject, I'd say I have a rather select audience." He paused and assessed the contents of his study. "Demands on my time are somewhat meager." He took measured steps across the room and lowered himself into the office chair. "You mentioned a name on the phone and bits of local history that you're interested in, so I've collected some reference material to look at." He patted the stack of books on the table. "Now tell me, what is it you are after, Mr. Sheridan?"

"Call me Jack; and I'm looking to flesh out the life of Harlan Coates."

Elliot settled back and the chair squeaked. "The Coates family has been in the area since the turn of the eighteenth century. They helped build Allegan County out of wilderness territory."

Jack came forward and opened the leather notebook. "I'm only interested in Harlan. He supposedly lived in Allegan County from 1842 to perhaps 1870. Is this something you can confirm?"

Elliot rooted around in his shirt pocket. "We can check census records, tax bills, land deeds, things of public record that would place him here or there." He pulled out a pack of Marlboros and extracted a cigarette. "Is this Coates fellow family?" He lit the cigarette with a butane lighter and pulled the cylinder toward him. He flicked a little switch on the side of the cylinder and the thing began to whir.

"Not family; he's a little more interesting than that."

Elliot puffed on the cigarette. "You smoke, Jack?"

"No, I quit a couple of years back."

"So did I." Elliot chuckled. "You know, quitting is easy. I've done it a dozen times."

Jack smiled. "Cold air might be good for the lungs, but smoking is definitely bad."

Elliot set the cigarette in the open end of the cylinder. The smoke was sucked in and disappeared. "I calculate the one offsets the other." He took a book with a black cover off the stack. "Harlan Coates did live in Allegan County. Late in 1842 he was added to the payroll of a saw mill built by pioneer Oshea Wilder in a little village named Singapore near the shore of Lake Michigan, north of what we call Saugatuck today." Elliot flipped through some pages to a scrap of paper serving as a bookmark. The book seemed to be an atlas compendium of some type.

"Coates purchased a piece of land at the corner of River Street and Cherry Street here." Elliot pointed to a plot on an old hand-drawn village plat showing the street grid of Singapore as it appeared in the late 1800s. "At the bottom here you see two saw mills near the Kalamazoo River. Coates worked at the west mill, the original mill that Wilder built."

Jack referred to Steven's notebook. "There's a similar sketch of a village layout in here. Okay, Coates lived in this Singapore place. Did he also work with the U.S. Board of Lights about twenty years later?"

Elliot took a puff off his cigarette and pulled another book from the stack. He didn't open this one but tapped a finger on the cover. "Coates joined the Union Navy at the outbreak of the Civil War, reaching the rank of lieutenant before being discharged in the wake of Appomattox. After the war he served the Board of Lights as a lighthouse inspector in the Great Lakes." Elliot considered Jack a moment. "Do you want to know this man's life story for purely inquisitive reasons, or is there a more specific point that you're tap dancing around?"

Jack smiled. "You're more than a historian, Eugene."

"The study of history is really the study of human nature, and for fifty years I've researched the motives that have made the world go around. After a while you get a sense for certain things. Right now I have a sense that Harlan Coates once possessed something you very much want today."

"He might have," Jack said, "but I'm afraid the answer I'm looking for won't be packaged neatly between the covers of one of your books."

"Not one book perhaps, but the pieces we need might be scattered throughout several volumes. That's the beauty of history. The answers are all there. All of man's conflicts, the clash of cultures, ambition, freedom, tyranny, progress; these elements flow through time like threads, entwining and intersecting to stitch together an elegant tapestry. Looking into the weaves and wefts that make up the past can answer any question we face today, reveal any secret ever kept."

"Any secret?"

Elliot laughed and the overhead light reflected in his glasses. "The best place to hide something is in the past." He snuffed out his cigarette in the cylinder opening. "What else do you have in that notebook of yours?"

"Rumors," Jack said. "Harlan Coates supposedly came into possession of a fortune in gold and silver coins. He hid them away with the intent of revealing their location to his sons as an inheritance. Unfortunately for his sons, Coates died unexpectedly in a shipwreck on Lake Michigan without revealing the coins' location. They're still out there somewhere."

Elliot meshed his fingers together. "Where did this information come from?"

"A friend of mine was active in the lighthouse restoration community and stumbled across anecdotes concerning an inspector named Harlan Coates. Most of what's in these pages is hearsay, scattered sentences from letters Coates sent to his wife, and some creative thinking on the part of my friend." Jack considered the notebook. "I need to know if there is concrete evidence to support the story in here."

Elliot adjusted his glasses. "Sounds like you have little to go on." He tucked the cigarette pack back into his shirt pocket. "Nonetheless, let's pick a place to start." A touch of excitement slipped into his demeanor. "How did Coates obtain these coins?"

Jack rubbed his forearm to ward off the chill. He mulled over just how much information he should divulge. Certainly not everything, just what the historian needed to know.

"Jack, you still with me?"

"Milwaukee."

"Coates got the coins in Milwaukee? From who? From where?"

"It's a little fuzzy. My friend Steven referred to the coins from Milwaukee a few times in his notes. He didn't get any more involved in their origin than that. I figure Coates had to have obtained them in some shady deal if he felt it necessary to hide them instead of putting them in a bank vault."

"Why don't you ask your friend for clarity on the the issue?"

"I'd like to but Steven died a year ago."

"My condolences." Elliot sat quiet a moment. "Are you taking up this pursuit at his request?"

"In a way I am." That's all the historian needed to know.

Elliot slowly swiveled his chair toward the desk. "Did your friend have any idea at all where Coates may have deposited the coins? Is there any reference in the notes that we can…"

Jack shook his head. "That's the problem—"

"Deposited," Elliot said. "Deposited. That could be it." He swiveled back around. "Do those notes say the coins came from Milwaukee or from the *Milwaukee?*"

"Steven wrote in sort of a shorthand so it's not clear…" Jack caught on. "The *Milwaukee.* Like a ship. The *Milwaukee.*"

Elliot rose from the chair with an energy and alertness in his eyes that made him seem ten years younger. He walked to the bookshelf behind him and scanned for a title. "What do you know about banking?"

"Not nearly enough I imagine." Curiosity moved Jack closer.

"In the late 1830s Michigan had a deeply flawed banking law on the books that allowed just about any group of investors with fifty thousand dollars between them to open their own banking business."

"What does this have to do with a ship named *Milwaukee?*"

Elliot waved him to silence. "These institutions were permitted to print and issue their own paper money, but only had to underwrite thirty percent of those notes with hard specie, or coinage." Elliot found the book he was after and pulled it down. "They called these institutions wildcat banks, and one of them opened in Singapore."

"You think Coates robbed the Singapore Bank?"

Elliot chuckled. "It didn't take long for the worthless notes from these banks to flood the state. The Michigan legislature quickly realized their mistake and suspended the flawed law but the damage had been done. Here's where it gets interesting. The Bank of Singapore issued a large number of notes that ended up being redeemed for customers by the Bank of Michigan. When the law was suspended, the Bank of Michigan demanded that the Singapore Bank reimburse them for the payout on the worthless notes. Singapore refused. The Bank of Michigan filed suit to get their money back. The Bank of Singapore lost the court battle and was ordered to surrender a large percentage of their remaining hard specie to cover the damages."

Elliot leafed through the book. "The coins to settle the lawsuit were loaded onto a ship for transport to the Bank of Michigan's main branch office."

"That ship," Jack said, "was the *Milwaukee*."

Elliot laid open the book. It was a comprehensive compilation of Great Lakes shipwrecks and he had opened it to a page with the heading MILWAUKEE. "The *Milwaukee* was a three-masted schooner that made port in Singapore on November 17th, 1842. She was loaded with flour, in addition to the coins from the Singapore Bank, which were not entered on the ship's ledger for security reasons, and shipped out that night as the Great Blizzard of '42 hit. By dawn the next day the ship was a complete loss."

Jack flipped back and forth through pages in Steven's notebook. "Coates spent his first night in Singapore at the lighthouse at the mouth of the Kalamazoo River. In a letter to his wife he told a story about survivors from a shipwreck coming to the lighthouse for help. That letter was dated November eighteenth, 1842."

"The *Milwaukee* was relatively close to shore and in shallow water when she went down." Elliot adjusted his glasses. "But the coins were never recovered."

"Because Coates got his hands on them first." Jack stopped and thought about the difficult logistics of what he had just said. "How did he get them off the ship? Maybe one of the survivors got them to shore somehow."

"The blizzard raged for forty days and forty nights." Elliot chuckled. "It was a truly biblical event. The entire area was snowed in for months. Roads were impassable and no supplies could get through to the surrounding villages. The *Milwaukee*'s misfortune, however, saved many lives. The barrels of flour that made up the bulk of her cargo were salvaged by a pioneer named William Butler. During the darkest days of the storm, he distributed flour to the people in the area."

Jack pondered that a long while. "Maybe the coins were in one of those barrels."

Elliot smiled. "History is fun, isn't it?"

"It just might be a barrel of fun." Jack mulled it all over, contemplating the possibility that this tale of lost treasure might actually be true. "How much coinage did the Bank of Singapore load onto the *Milwaukee*?"

"Court records indicate the Bank of Michigan was awarded twenty thousand dollars from Singapore's capital. It doesn't sound like much by today's standards, does it?" Elliot returned to the bookshelf and scanned the titles again. "Remember, this was over a hundred and seventy years ago, and the dominant currency of the day was gold and silver." He peeled another tome from the shelf. "One of the Singapore

Bank investors, a gentleman named Hill, came from a wealthy mining family in North Carolina."

He plopped back in the chair with the book in his lap. "An interesting thing about North Carolina back then is the large number of gold mines that were in operation around Charlotte. Prospectors were pulling chunks of yellow rock from the ground but they lacked a convenient means to process it into currency. One enterprising man named Christopher Bechtler sought to meet the need of these miners by opening a private minting operation. He produced gold coins of such quality that the US Mint authorities allowed him to continue his practice after inspecting his work."

"You're losing me again, Eugene."

"Weaves and wefts, Jack, follow the thread. The Bechtler Mint stayed in business a number of years and then closed. Today coins from this mint are extremely rare and extremely valuable. If Hill came north from North Carolina with a sack full of Bechtler coins, it's likely he used them as his capital to buy into the Bank of Singapore scheme." Elliot cracked open the book in his lap, which was a numismatic reference guide, and found a page with a blown-up photograph of a gold coin. "This is a Bechtler five-dollar piece consisting of eighty-three percent pure gold. Today this coin is worth five thousand dollars, or more."

Jack studied the photograph. "How many of these coins could be mixed in with the hard specie from Singapore?"

"No way to know for sure, but let's make an educated guess. Hill was among the top three investors in regards to investment proportions. Let's assume Bechtler coins make up five thousand dollars of the total amount awarded to the Bank of Michigan. If the coins are five-dollar pieces that would mean there are one thousand coins."

Jack calculated. "One thousand coins at five thousand dollars each total five million dollars."

"And that's not counting the value of the other coins in the cache. That era of U.S. minted silver dollars is rare as well, some going for seven hundred dollars a piece at auction today. Depending on the mix this trove could be worth ten to twenty million dollars."

That assumption sounded appealing to Jack. "Coates intended to give the coins to his sons upon his death. If that's the case he must have made mention or left a clue to their location in his will."

"County clerk's office," Elliot said. "If Coates had a will it should be of public record there. But if he included the coins in his will, why didn't his boys get them?"

"Maybe he just left a clue to the coins, and that clue was an article or item that Coates carried on his person, something he could leave to his sons that would show them where the coins were hidden. When he went down on that ship the clue went with him."

Eugene huffed. "Why wouldn't he just tell them plainly where to find the coins?"

"Think about it," Jack said. "A barrel of coins falls into Coates' lap. He discovers they've come from the Bank of Singapore. He's not entitled to this money and fears that if the bank investors find out about his windfall they might put two and two together and take the money back. He decides to keep it real low profile, so low that the coins won't surface until his death."

Elliot thought about it a few seconds. "It's possible, but if the clue you suppose in your theory went down with Coates, I'm afraid your quest is going to end here in my study."

Jack didn't reply.

"If nothing else," Elliot said, "you've helped me fill in some holes in my research."

Jack regarded him. "Why do you know so much about the Bank of Singapore?"

"It's one of the more interesting pieces of West Michigan history I've studied." Elliot turned to the back cover of the numismatic book. A clear plastic bag containing a gold coin was taped to the hard back. The coin was a Bechtler five-dollar piece. "This came from the Singapore vault and was saved as a memento when the bank was dissolved. I've been wondering where the rest of these things have disappeared to for a long time now."

"If I find out I'll let you know." Jack rubbed his hands for warmth. "Better yet, I'll buy you a new central air unit."

Elliot's laughter crackled in the crisp air. "I'll hold you to that, Jack."

"It's the least I can do."

They spoke another hour, cross checking tax records, deeds, and census reports to triangulate on Harlan Coates. Before too long Jack grew anxious to get to the county clerk's office. He bid farewell to Eugene and left his icebox of a home. The humidity outside wrapped around him like a wet blanket. He climbed into the dusty Jeep and drove off. He hit Lauren's speed dial number on his phone. She answered on the second ring.

"It's me," Jack said. "I'm going to be a little longer out here than I thought."

"The meeting went that well?"

"You could say that. I just need to follow up on a few issues."

"Okay, I won't wait on you for dinner. Oh, Connor called. He was excited about something and wanted to talk to you. He said he'd call back in the morning."

"All right. I'll see you tonight." He added, "Love you."

"Love you too." Disconnect.

At the next stop light he dug into his pocket and unfolded the paper he had written Bobbie's phone number on. He keyed in the digits and held his thumb over the "send" button. Making this call would set everything in motion. He hesitated. The traffic light turned green. The guy in the car behind him honked his horn.

Jack took his foot off the brake and pressed the button on the phone. The cell connected and rang once. She answered.

"Bobbie, this is Jack."

"I didn't expect to hear from you so soon."

"I've done some investigating into Steven's theory."

"And?"

He lowered his foot on the gas pedal and accelerated down open road.

"And?" she said again.

He switched ears with the phone. "It's plausible."

"How plausible?"

"Enough to really stoke my interest."

"Meaning what?"

Jack ran through everything in his mind one more time: Coates, the coins, Steven, Bobbie, Rafferty, Lauren, guilt, trust, redemption—twenty-million dollars. He wet his lips and toyed with the cell. "I'm in."

SIX

Bobbie realized she was clenching the phone. "Thank you, Jack."

She'd taken the call in the lighthouse kitchen, and as Jack talked she looked out through the south window. The blades of a wind generator out back spooled up to a frantic spin in an easterly gust. It always seemed to be windy on Granite Island. The little stone lighthouse perched atop an island of rock five miles into Lake Superior was in prime location to bear the brunt of the northern lake's desolate climate.

Lately the gray desolation of Granite Island complemented Bobbie's sense of isolation. Since Steven's passing she'd taken on a lot of responsibility. Finishing the lighthouse restoration alone, getting her daughter through college, and keeping the bank at bay was crushing her. Dark days had arrived, and the luster of Steven's fanciful treasure hunt seemed the only means she had to light the path out of the hole.

"Don't thank me yet," Jack said. "I haven't done anything to deserve it."

"You will. Once you commit to something you don't give up on it." She added, "Getting that commitment is the trick."

He didn't reply.

"I didn't mean anything by that."

"You meant something, or you wouldn't have said it."

"I really appreciate this, Jack. You could have easily said no."

"What are friends for?"

"If we find the coins it's fifty/fifty."

He didn't say anything for a long while. "That's not the only reason I'm doing this."

Bobbie's voice caught in her throat. "So…what's the next step?"

"I've got a theory of my own I'm going to look into. For now I'll keep you in the loop with reports by phone. Fair enough?"

"Just let me know when I need to grab a shovel."

He laughed. "Let's not get ahead of ourselves."

"Thank you."

"Take care."

She lowered the cell from her ear. For the first time in months she didn't feel like she was all alone on a big piece of granite in a cold great lake. Jack's acceptance to help find the coins sparked in her a glimmer of hope, a way out.

She walked out to the deck across the rear of the lighthouse and scanned the water. Her daughter Alyson would be arriving from Marquette this afternoon with the supply run for the week. Thad, one of the contractors who had worked on the restoration, had offered to ferry her to the island on his thirty-foot Zodiac. Bobbie had not seen her daughter in months, and when the boat came into view her spirits jumped.

The sun was bright and the temperature warmer than usual for June on Lake Superior. Down in the choppy water the Zodiac with the enclosed cabin looped around the two-acre island and maneuvered toward its southern tip. Bobbie hurried down a set of wooden steps that ran from the deck to the lower part of the island, and then down an aluminum ladder to the suspended dock at the south landing. Thad guided the Zodiac between walls of granite and touched the boat's durable soft side against the dock pylons. Bobbie helped him tie off the mooring lines and thanked him for making the trip. Alyson emerged from the cabin with a wide smile and a travel bag over her shoulder. She'd grown her blonde hair out again and had it pulled into a ponytail. Her tall, slender frame put her half a head over Thad's height.

"Hi, Mom."

Bobbie helped her up to the dock and they embraced. "How does it feel to be a graduated Spartan?"

"Relief," Alyson said. "Now the hard part: getting a job in the field of marine biology."

"Never time to relax, always taking on the next challenge." Bobbie appraised her daughter with a flush of pride. "Just like your father."

Thad hefted a pair of boxes from the boat to the dock.

Alyson nodded toward them. "Speaking of Dad's challenges, what's on this week's agenda?"

Bobbie signed the shipper for the painting supplies. "The utility room off the kitchen. We're painting, trimming, and touching up the plaster. It's the last room to finish."

Thad wasted no time in preparing to head back to Marquette.

Bobbie helped him throw off the mooring lines and bid him farewell. She regarded Alyson. "Let's get you settled in. We'll come back for the boxes."

They climbed the ladder up and off the dock. Bobbie scurried up the rungs without effort. "Looks like you're keeping yourself in good shape," Alyson said.

"Easy to do around here." A wind gust blew Bobbie's hair into her face. She pulled it back into a ponytail and snapped a yellow band in place. Mother and daughter now matched. "Keep climbing steps."

They settled in the lighthouse kitchen at a small table for two, each with bottled water in hand. Alyson noted the fresh plaster and paint on the walls and the varnished wood trim. "You did a great job in here. I remember the rotted studs and debris when we first bought the place." She peered out through the door behind her mother. "Dining room's awesome, too. I love the wide base molding. And it looks like you're ready to host a dinner party with the place settings on the table."

"There's a Web cam in there," Bobbie said. "I keep it set up like that for display. Steven wanted cameras mounted around the island so that everyone could enjoy the views of the lake and the lighthouse by way of the Internet."

Alyson smirked. "What other rooms have Web cams?"

Bobbie laughed. "That's the only one. The other cameras are outside watching the horizon and the south landing and the house exterior."

Alyson sipped water from her bottle. "How many trips have you made this season?"

"This is the third."

"Are you doing okay being alone?"

Bobbie gave her an appreciative smile. "It's been over a year. This is my life now, and I'm all right with it."

Alyson nodded. "Is the bank working with you on the mortgage?"

"They're becoming less and less understanding."

"When I get a job I'm going to help you out, and don't say no."

"No."

"I owe you for school. It's the least I can do." She added, "You need the money. Dad's insurance policy stunk. It didn't cover half of what it was supposed to cover."

"Don't take on my problems. They're mine to deal with. I'll get by."

"How?"

Bobbie thought a long while before speaking. "Remember before the accident how Steven was researching that story about the lighthouse inspector?"

"Yes."

"Remember how excited he got trying to find those old coins?"

"Mom, First National isn't going to accept Dad's treasure notebook as collateral."

"No, but they'll take the money from the sale of the coins."

"*Please* tell me you're joking."

"No joke. I'm going to find those coins, and I've asked Jack to help me out."

Alyson stared quietly at her. "Are you serious?"

"Why do people keep asking me that?"

"Are you?"

No reply, but the answer was there in the silence.

"You don't even know if that story is true."

"Steven's notes were enough to convince Jack to give it a shot. If Jack thinks the story is credible, that's good enough for me."

Alyson twisted the cap on to her bottle. "Sounds a little desperate."

"I am desperate."

"I'm not just talking about the money situation."

Bobbie crinkled her water bottle. "What do you mean?"

"Didn't you and Jack have a thing together back in college?"

"Where did you hear that?"

Alyson rolled her eyes. "I lived in the same house with you and Dad for twenty years; I heard things."

Bobbie exhaled. "Whatever happened between Jack and me ended a long time ago."

"How close were you?"

"Very close, but I don't think it would have worked out if we had tried to stay together. We were still kids back then. We didn't know where we were going or what we wanted out of life."

"You must have been about my age. I don't consider myself a kid."

"From my vantage point you are. Perspectives change through the years. You'll see."

Alyson set her elbows on the table. "Whose fault was it?"

"Fault?"

"The end. Who broke off the relationship?"

Bobbie studied the refinished floor. "It was a mutual decision."

"It's never a mutual decision."

Silence. "Jack saw his future taking him to the East Coast for a career in maritime research or industry," Bobbie finally said. "I saw my future here in Michigan with the university. We agreed those paths weren't parallel."

Alyson thought about it a bit. "Do you still have feelings for him?"

"Yes, as a close and trusted friend."

"Nothing more?"

Bobbie set her water bottle down. "Our romance ended long before you were born."

"But do you ever find yourself thinking about what it would have been like if you two had gotten married?"

Bobbie paused half a second longer than she thought appropriate before answering. "I've reconsidered every important decision I've made in life at one point or another, just like you will. I haven't regretted a single one yet."

Alyson settled into her chair looking unconvinced.

"I didn't tell you about the coins to explain my history with Jack."

"I'm just interested in my mother's social well-being."

"There's not much to be interested in."

"Okay," Alyson said, slapping her legs. "Anything else you want to get off your chest?"

"I didn't raise the issue."

"Yeah, you did. You brought up the coins and how you asked Jack—"

"Aly."

"How about the break-in, did the police ever contact you with any new information on that?"

Bobbie felt anxiety creep into her chest. On her second trip to the island, she discovered someone had broke into the lighthouse through a living room window. The police suspected it was the work of vandals but nothing had been vandalized. She thought it looked more like someone had searched through the place, looking for something in particular.

"No news yet," Bobbie said. "The police told me that type of breaking and entering is commonplace for seasonal homes around here. They also told me the perpetrators are usually not caught."

A box of Steven's paperwork concerning the coins and other research items had been dumped out and sifted through. Something may have been taken. She wasn't sure.

"I think it was a couple of teens," Alyson said, "looking for a little rendezvous, if you know what I mean."

"We're eleven miles from Marquette across an unpredictable lake with a tricky granite alcove as a boat landing. They must have been really motivated."

Alyson glanced into the dining room. "You have the cameras up now. If they do it again you just might capture some pictures of them."

Bobbie shrugged. "Maybe, but I only retain the last eight hours of images from the Web cams. I'd just about have to catch them in the act real-time."

"Kinky."

"I'd rather it be vandals."

Alyson laughed. "At least you have a chance to catch them now."

Bobbie nodded, but she really didn't want to catch them. She had no desire to face those people...not again.

- SEVEN -

Jack sat in front of a flat-screen monitor at a document viewing station in the Allegan County Clerk's office. The county had recently undertaken the task of digitizing their records and had succeeded clear through to the end of the nineteenth century. Good news for Jack, as he needed to find the last will and testament of Harlan Walter Coates, who happened to have died in 1868.

Rolls of microfiche and old documents were packed in boxes and piled on tables surrounding the viewing station. The digitization project was a work in process. Rose, the clerk's assistant who escorted him to the viewing station, informed him that copies of documents cost ten dollars each. That seemed a fair price considering the outcome of this search might net twenty million.

Jack maneuvered the mouse and drilled through the archiving system's file structure. Top level comprised a timeline interface dating all the way back to 1790. He selected the appropriate decade and then the year 1868. A subdirectory menu opened. He selected Probate, followed by Wills. A folder arrangement cascaded across the screen, each one labeled with a letter of the alphabet. He clicked the 'C' folder. Names scrolled top to bottom on the screen. Carole, Carter, Cedric, Chavez...Coates. There it was in digital black and white, Harlan Walter Coates.

Jack double-clicked the name. A scan of the will blinked onto the screen. The original document paper had taken on an aged sepia hue, but the handwritten black ink text was neat and legible. After reading through a bunch of legal preamble he got to the meat of the document.

In the name of God, Amen. I, Harlan Coates, considering the uncertainty of this mortal life and being of sound mind and memory, hereby set forth my last will and testament.

Item First: I will that my debts be paid from the contents of my estate.

Item Second: I leave and bequest to my beloved wife Elisabeth the balance of monies from said estate on account and in material possessions found in my home on the plot in Singapore, Michigan. I further leave and bequest to Elisabeth all my Real property, including the plot of land in Singapore and the tract of land north of town, whose bounds are duly recorded in the county clerk's office.

Item Third: I leave and bequest to my sons Daniel and David the symbol of my salvation. As their inheritance I give my quarreling sons the cross I bear over my heart so that it might lead them to their salvation as well, and with this bequest the hope that their discord will dissolve, their eyes will see what is to be seen, and they will discover life to the full.

Jack read it three more times. It seemed the answer to the question of where to pick up the search for the coins lie embedded in Item Third. He had supposed the key might be an article that Coates had carried on his person, and that it had been lost in the shipwreck. In the will, "the cross I bear over my heart" lent itself to literal interpretation as a crucifix, perhaps the type strung on a chain around one's neck. And the bit about dissolving discord and seeing what is to be seen; Coates was telling his sons there was more to their inheritance than met the eye but he wanted them to put aside their differences and figure it out for themselves. It made sense in the context of the secret inheritance. Sure, the wording might have been intended to carry the obvious spiritual meaning, but in light of the circumstances that interpretation seemed unlikely.

Jack had caught the scent of a trail.

He noted the file name and location of the Coates will and left the viewing station. He went to the front counter and found Rose waiting. She lifted a pair of dark-framed glasses and put them on. "Did you find what you were after?"

"I think I did." He handed her the slip of paper he had written the file information on. "I'd like a copy of that document."

Rose took the paper and walked to a computer monitor on the counter a few steps away. She started typing with stubby fingers. Her keystrokes slowed. "Ever get the feeling of deja-vu?"

Jack looked at her funny. "Do you have the feeling I've been here before talking with you?"

"No, it's not you. It's this document."

"What about it?"

She adjusted her glasses and caressed her chin. "I've made a copy of this will before. I'm sure of it. Last time it was on microfiche."

"When?"

"About a year ago. Yeah, I remember it was sometime in late spring. The man who asked for it mentioned something about getting back to his restoration project up north for the summer."

"Do you remember his name?"

Rose crinkled her eyebrows. "Something Keller?"

"Weller?"

"Yeah, that's it. He said he was fixing up an old lighthouse. That's why I remember. I thought it was an interesting project. Do you know him?"

"Yes. He passed away several months ago. We were old friends."

"Oh, I'm sorry." A printer below the counter clicked and whirred. She retrieved the copy of the will and handed it to him. "You two must have had similar interests."

He took the paper from her. "We did." He appraised the print out. "Ten dollars?"

"Uh-huh."

He paid her with a bill from his wallet. This just might be the deal of the century. "Thanks for your help."

"If you need any more assistance, come on back." She handed him a receipt and smiled.

Jack reciprocated and left the building. He sat behind the wheel of the Jeep and assessed his visit. It surprised him that Steven had followed this trail too. The notebook Bobbie had given him didn't contain any information about the cross, yet it was supposed to have included everything Steven knew about the coins. There was a hole there somewhere. Did that mean anything? Maybe not. Maybe Steven died before he had a chance to incorporate his latest discoveries into his notes. That would be a damned big omission. It got Jack to thinking of what else might have been left out.

He started the engine and backed out of the parking space. The Jeep's muddy rear bumper came close to a silver Camry across the aisle. The Camry's taillights flashed. Jack shifted into drive. "Don't worry," he said under his breath. "I won't hit you."

He pulled out of the parking lot and onto Chestnut Street. It was about four o'clock, and traffic had just begun to thicken. He flipped open his cell phone and called Lauren.

"Hey, honey, it's me. I'm finished out here and I'm leaving Allegan."

"Did it go well?"

"I think I made some headway."

"Oh good, should I call you Captain Jack now?"

"I'd hold off on that one. I'll give you the details later."

"How long a drive back is it?"

"Over two and a half hours, but don't wait up. I'm making one more stop on the way home."

Lauren let out an exasperated breath. "Where?"

"Since I'm so close to Grand Haven, I thought I'd pop in and see

Wallace at the marina, maybe get some legal advice on my business decision." Jack stopped the Jeep at a traffic light.

"All right," Lauren said, "but don't spend all night reminiscing about the old college days."

He smiled. "Wallace Garity doesn't recall those days as fondly as I do. He's all business now. Come to think of it, he was all business back then." Jack glanced in the rearview mirror. A silver Camry was behind him at the light. "Don't forget to play fetch-the-brick with Ike. He's restless all night if he doesn't burn that energy."

"I know. Tell Wallace I said hello. Be careful on the drive home. Love you."

"You too."

They ended the call as the traffic light turned green. Jack accelerated into the intersection. He checked the rearview mirror again. The Camry followed a car-length behind. Was it the same one from the clerk's parking lot? Odds argued against it. There were a million cars of that make, model, and color on the road.

At the next light, for no good reason, he made a left turn. The Camry followed. He told himself that it didn't mean anything, but instincts stood the hairs of his neck on end. Ever since the Rafferty incident he'd grown increasingly paranoid. Any face in the crowd that appeared remotely out of place deserved a second look. Any bump in the night had him checking over his shoulder. All this paranoia had apparently developed into a problem. He'd gotten so used to the feeling of being followed that he couldn't seem to tell if someone was actually doing it now.

At the next light he steered the Jeep through a left turn. The Camry stayed with him.

Why would someone be following? Even Rafferty hadn't been so brazen.

The Colt was in the glove box. Jack resisted pulling it out. That would be an overreaction.

The intersection of Cedar and Trowbridge was coming up, and traffic was moving pretty good. He decided to pull a tight right. If that Camry stayed on his bumper, he'd have the pistol in his lap with the action cocked and a round in the chamber in two seconds flat.

Up ahead the traffic light blinked from red to green. Jack found a pocket and switched lanes. The Jeep's tires squealed over the blacktop around the corner. A few people on the sidewalk shot him an annoyed glare. He popped open the glove box and checked the rearview mirror.

No Camry. He waited a few seconds, checked again. Still no

Camry.

Jack Sheridan suddenly felt stupid.

To top it off, he'd made so many random turns that he'd gotten himself completely turned around. A restaurant parking lot came up on the right, and he pulled into it to collect himself and get his bearings. He grabbed the MapQuest map from the passenger seat and traced a path to Route 89. It wasn't that far off. He merged back onto the road and met up with the expressway junction a few blocks west of the restaurant.

The glove box was still open, and the Colt sat inside atop a pile of receipts and fast-food napkins. Jack reached over to close the compartment but stopped before flipping the panel shut. He considered the pistol a moment or two before putting his hand back on the steering wheel.

He accelerated toward Grand Haven, checking the rearview mirror one more time to see if a silver Camry had slipped in behind him.

- EIGHT -

Benjamin Higgs reclined in his chair and crossed his burly arms. A toothpick dangled between his lips. Overhead a tarnished copper light fixture cast a yellow glow down on the barroom table and made three o'clock feel like midnight. Higgs alternated his gaze back and forth between a Blackberry phone and a sheet of paper lying in the middle of the table. Three names and addresses were written on the paper. He read each name for the tenth time. No new insight came to him. He checked the Blackberry for the twentieth time to see if the e-mail had somehow come in without his noticing. It hadn't. He split the toothpick between his teeth.

Higgs hated to wait. He hated it almost as much as backtracking. Languishing in limbo derailed his momentum like slamming into a brick wall. It frustrated him. He'd crafted an entire philosophy based on taking decisive action with the express intent of constantly advancing the ball forward. Move the ball, score the points. Score enough points, win the game. Waiting meant he wasn't moving forward, it meant he wasn't getting any closer to scoring points. It meant he wasn't winning, and above all else Benjamin Higgs loved to win.

Annoyed with the Blackberry, he directed his attention across the table to Nate Kisko, who seemed equally as thrilled with the wait. Kisko was calculating the optimum spot on the tabletop to bounce a quarter so that it would jump into his mug of beer. Higgs noted the proximity of the sheet of paper to the mug. Before he could get out a word of warning Kisko tossed the quarter, which bounced tails-down off the table and into the mug. A few drops of amber ale splashed the paper.

Higgs yanked the sheet off the table. "Damn it, Nate."

Kisko feigned innocence. "What?"

"You'll smear the addresses."

"What's it matter? More names, more addresses, more roads to nowhere."

"These names are different. We've jumped to the next level."

"I've been hearing that for a year and a half."

Higgs dabbed the beer drops with a napkin. "You want out?"

"I didn't say that."

"Weller wanted out."

Kisko didn't reply.

Higgs appraised the names and addresses. "We're closer than we've ever been. I feel it."

"You sound kind of new age." Kisko drank a slug of beer. "I never knew."

"Don't be such a simpleton. If you'd pay attention once in a while, you'd understand that each step we've taken has gotten us closer to the prize. We're damn near there."

Kisko swirled a mouthful of beer, skeptical.

"Don't forget where all this is going to land us. In less than a year—"

The Blackberry buzzed on the tabletop. Higgs snatched it up and checked the screen. He frowned. "Ehrlich." He lifted the phone to his ear and answered. "What is it, Mr. Ehrlich?"

"We've got competition," the voice said, drowning in wind and road noise.

Higgs cocked his head. "Explain."

"There's a guy looking for the same coins we are, and he's coming up to speed real fast."

"How'd you find out about him?"

"I got put on assignment to watch him for a few days, see what he's up to. I don't ask questions. Know what I mean? Anyway, it looks like he is up to something, and that something is our business."

Higgs thought on it a moment. "He won't get very far. We've got the cross and an eighteen-month head start."

"Yeah, but he seems to know what he's doing."

Higgs leaned forward. "Who is *he*?"

"I don't know. Weller's wife got him involved. I think his name is Sheridan. Yeah, that's right, Jack Sheridan."

Gears began spinning in Higgs' head. "You sure about that?"

"Pretty sure. Why, you know him?"

Higgs smiled. "Maybe. What are you supposed to do about him?"

"Just stay in his shadow for now, report back what he does."

"Hey, Ehrlich, do me a favor. Keep me in the loop, okay?"

"Sure, as long as it doesn't get my ass in a wringer."

"It won't. I just don't want to get caught flat footed by this guy if he does something unexpected. Capice?"

"Right. I gotta get moving. Thought you'd find him interesting."

"I do."

Ehrlich disconnected. Higgs smirked at Kisko across the table.

"Why are you smiling?"

Higgs set the Blackberry down. "Jack Sheridan has gotten into the game."

"Jack who?"

"Oh that's right, you don't read, so you wouldn't have seen the *Newsweek* article last year. Sheridan made the cover."

Kisko didn't follow. "Made the cover for what?"

Higgs settled into his 'I'm going to teach you a lesson' posture. "According to this *Newsweek* article, Sheridan was working with an undersea salvage company on some project in the Atlantic that turned out to be a big espionage plot orchestrated by an international arms dealer. The operation went sour when Sheridan found out what was going on. The arms dealer took the crew of the salvage ship hostage with a band of mercenaries he'd smuggled aboard. Apparently Sheridan is a real bad ass when he wants to be. He routed the mercs and freed the crew. In the process he prevented a sensitive piece of military technology from being auctioned off on the black market. He's a regular national hero."

Kisko downed the rest of his beer. "Great. Now Captain America is after the coins."

"Do you always turn this yellow when someone challenges you?"

Kisko slammed his mug down. "Damned if I'm worried about this guy. If he gets in our way I'll put a bullet between his eyes myself. Mercenaries my ass."

Higgs smiled. "That's more like it. You just needed someone to light a fire under you." He glanced around at the sparse crowd in the dim bar. "Just keep it down. No need to attract attention."

Kisko sneered. "I didn't waste a year and a half on this treasure hunt to let some Boy Scout on steroids walk home with the coins."

"Nor did I."

"Don't know what I'm so worked up about. We have the cross. End of story, right?"

Higgs glanced at the Blackberry. "End of story."

Kisko seemed to take solace in the confirmation.

Higgs didn't. He too had dedicated eighteen months of his life to recovering the cache of gold and silver coins worth millions. He'd taken extreme measures to make sure no one else could lay a finger on it. He'd stained his hands with blood that would not wash off. No, he'd gone to the edge and beyond to claim the prize, leading right up to the diver's house in Battle Creek. Now he had the cross, the key that opened the door to the next level. No one else would be allowed to unlock its cryptic message, especially not Jack Sheridan.

But Sheridan's arrival on the scene did not stir up anxiety. If anything Higgs believed the opposition would charge his efforts. He'd be more alert. He'd be more perceptive. He'd make damn sure he didn't let his guard down. Thanks to Jack Sheridan he'd just stepped up his game.

"Now what are you smiling at?" Kisko said, watching him with a quizzical eye.

Higgs broadened his smile. "I'm envisioning our success. You should try it sometime."

"I'll celebrate with you." Kisko snapped his fingers to call a waitress over. "Another round."

The Blackberry buzzed again, this time with the expected e-mail. The message was short and sweet. *Old men keep old things.* In an instant Higgs knew what it meant.

"Forget the beer," he said, "we're on the move."

Kisko cursed but followed the lead of his partner up and out of the bar.

It was all coming together. Higgs knew which of the three names held the most relevance, and what address they were going to visit. A worthy adversary had stepped up to oppose him. Momentum built in his chest. A few more points were about to go on the scoreboard. He climbed into the car with a slight kick of adrenalin.

Benjamin Higgs loved to win.

- NINE -

Grand Isle Marina
Grand Haven, MI

"Can the Turks build a boat, or what?"

Wallace Garity stood in the bow solarium of his seventy-five-foot sailboat and spread his arms to display his possession. Afternoon sun gleamed off his white polo shirt. The dark tint of his sunglasses protected his eyes from the glare. "There's more mahogany in my cabin than in the whole state capitol building."

Jack Sheridan smiled and gave the polished stainless steel bollards, handrail, and fittings along the sailboat's wooden deck a quick once-over. "When did you pick up this beauty?"

"Last summer." Garity tilted his head to admire the ship's aluminum fore and mizzen masts against the blue sky. "I bought her off an Exxon executive I met at the economic forum on Mackinac Island. He was looking to upgrade to the next class of sail. I got her for a steal." A Lake Michigan breeze upset Garity's precision-cut white hair. He set it back in place with a sweep of his hand. "Guess I shouldn't say that too loud."

"Better not, your honor, that's the way rumors start." Jack took a minute to study the lines of the boat. "She's a Transom Gulet. Who built her?"

"Bodrum. She's pure Turkish origin. Keel laid in '97."

"Twin diesels, I'll bet."

"That's right, Caterpillar 210s, and she has seven guest cabins. You and Lauren should come out with me for a week. You're not with Neptune's Reach anymore; you must miss the water."

Jack took a deep breath of lake air. "That's real tempting, Wallace, but—"

"That's not why you're here."

"That's not why I'm here."

Garity nodded toward an open hatch leading into the deckhouse. "Let's get something cool to drink." He started down the steep steps. "Hope you're not in trouble."

Jack waited for Garity to clear the hatch. *I hope I'm not in trouble too.*

Wall-to-wall lacquered mahogany adorned the ship's air-conditioned galley. Bench seats, chairs, and a table configuration portside looked capable of entertaining about ten people. Sunlight spilled in through a series of starboard windows. Garity stepped behind a wet bar just left of the stairs leading down from main deck. A thirty-two-inch plasma television hung on the far wall and displayed C-SPAN coverage of a debate taking place on the floor of the U.S. Senate. The sound was muted. Jack didn't notice any difference in the content of the politicians' speech.

A dozen crystal glasses hung suspended above the wet bar from an overhead rack. Garity took a pair down and set them on the black marble countertop. "Dewars?"

Jack grinned. "I'm not big on Scotch whiskey. How about Michelob?"

"You haven't changed since college."

"Neither have you, which is creepy. I mean, your hair went white real early, didn't it?"

Garity peeled off his sunglasses. "Can't we act like adults? We're certainly old enough."

"I think you were an adult while you were still in diapers. You missed all the fun of growing up and being young and stupid."

"And for you the fun never seems to have stopped. Hasn't that been your problem, gallivanting around the globe on one adventure after another while leaving your family behind? It almost cost you your marriage."

"It's a good thing we're friends. I would have taken offense at that if another man had said it, but I know your social graces are somewhat lacking."

"I call it as I see it. I do it from the bench, and I do it in private." Garity pulled a beer bottle from a refrigerator below the bar. "Red Stripe is as close to Michelob as you're getting here."

Jack stepped up and took the bottle. "Figures." He popped off the cap with the opener mounted on the side of the bar.

"Now, what brings you to Grand Haven?"

"A business decision I need legal advice on."

"Business?" Garity smiled for the first time. "You're the one always accusing me of being absorbed by my work, and yet here you are on a beautiful sailboat in Lake Michigan with nothing but business on your mind. You can't let it go any more than I can."

"I'm retired. I let it go just fine. I'm just looking into a little part-time project."

"You don't do anything part time. It won't be long before you're so involved in whatever endeavor you're undertaking that Lauren will get roiled at you for neglecting her, again. You and I are more alike than you care to admit."

"Don't get nasty. I don't have the blood of a politician in my veins."

Garity poured a Dewars over ice. "The sins of the father don't always fall on the son."

"Sometimes they do."

Garity swirled his glass to stir the contents. "Tell me your business dilemma. I'm in terrible suspense."

"Does Michigan have a finders-keepers law?"

"Depends on what you find that you want to keep."

"What if I find some coins that have been lost for a hundred and fifty years?"

"Depends. Who legally possessed them at the time they were lost?"

Jack downed some Red Stripe and thought over the question. "For the record let's say the Bank of Michigan possessed them. Don't say 'depends' again."

"Were the coins lost by means of a bank robbery?"

"No, by means of a shipwreck."

"Did the bank attempt to recover them from the wreck?"

"Good question. I'll need to get back to you on that."

Garity regarded Jack a long while. "Do you have these coins?"

"Not yet. I'm just trying to determine what kind of legal challenge I might face when I do find them. I read that the French government caused a lot of problems for the salvager who found the wreck of the *Griffin* in the Great Lakes, and I'd like to avoid that kind of headache if I can."

"You seem certain you're going to succeed."

"I am. Inflated confidence goes with the territory of not growing up."

"A sense of immortality does too. Do you have that?"

"I used to, but my little adventure last year kind of ruined it for me."

Garity smiled for the second time. "We're at that age, aren't we? We've started thinking about what kind of legacy we're going leave behind, about the paths we've followed and if they're leading us to where we want to end up. Is that a factor in this treasure hunt? Are you looking for something to leave behind?" Garity finished his drink. "Or are you just bored?"

"Which one are you?"

"Neither. I'm proud of what I've accomplished in life, and if I died today I'd have one hell of an epitaph. Son of a distinguished United States senator, doctorate in law, brilliant legal career, ascended to a judgeship on the Michigan Supreme Court. You have to admit it's not too shabby."

Jack flashed his best wise guy smile. "But are you happy?"

Garity deflected. "What's this quest going to do for you?"

"It's not about me. Actually, Bobbie asked for help searching for the coins."

Garity crinkled his brow. "Bobbie? Bobbie Weller?" He laughed. "This is worse than I thought. It's a full-blown midlife crisis, isn't it?"

Jack walked up to the bar. "I'm helping out a friend who really needs it. Friends do that, but then you always had a tough time grasping the concept of friendship."

"You derailed the woman's life, Jack. You two were practically walking down the aisle when you abandoned her, and you talk about my social graces. Now she's found the internal fortitude to ask you, of all people, for help. Pretty gutsy. Sounds like she's trying to even up the ledger."

"We settled that issue years ago. I'm helping her out because she's in some trouble."

"And you owe her."

"You're an irritating man, Wallace."

"What's Lauren's take on this whole thing?"

"I haven't told her about it yet."

"When you lose control you completely let go of the wheel, don't you?"

"At least I admit to my mistakes. I even learn from them, which is more than you can say. What is it now, three failed marriages and working on number four?"

"It's good to see you, Jack. Why don't we do this more often?"

"Because you're an adult, I never grew up, and we both can't resist the urge to point out each other's mistakes in life. Now what kind of legal minefield am I walking into when I find these coins, Judge Judy?"

Garity poured another drink. "You shouldn't have much to be concerned about. First, a foreign government is not involved in the equation. Second, the amount of time that has passed since the coins have been lost and the lack of action by the Bank of Michigan to recover them should shield you from a credible legal challenge. That being said, banks don't like to give up their money, no matter how long it's been lost." He swirled his glass, apparently taking a mental sidebar. "At Steven's funeral Bobbie mentioned something interesting. She said Steven had been obsessed on a research project concerning some old coins. Are the coins we're talking about the same ones?"

"They could be. I don't know what she told you at the funeral."

Garity tilted his glass from side to side. "How's life with Lauren post reconciliation?"

"We're doing well."

"So this interaction with Bobbie is a purely platonic, friend-helping-friend situation."

"Of course it is. Don't be such a buffoon."

"Are you certain old embers haven't rekindled the flame?"

"This might be hard for you to understand, but not every man's actions are influenced by his second brain."

Garity scoffed. "I've been wading through the bilge of criminal justice for thirty years. You'd be surprised how many crimes are fueled by carnal desire."

"Crime? You're equating my coin search with a crime?"

"You miss my point." Garity sat on a bar stool. "Desire motivates a man. Sometimes it drives him to formulate a miracle drug. Sometimes it drives him to put a bullet in another man's head. It all depends on the man being motivated. You, my friend, if I can use that expression without a lecture on its definition, you're what they call a romantic, and what could be more romantic than coming full circle in life to sweep your one true love off her feet for a happily ever after worthy of the final reel." Garity smiled again. He was really on a roll.

Jack set his beer on the bar. "I have no doubt that I married the right woman. That's more than one of us can say."

"Well, this is obviously a tender subject and one I should broach carefully."

"Don't broach anything. I had a legal question, you gave me your opinion, and that's all I was after. Let's keep this simple."

Garity gazed into his glass. "All right. Simple it is, but for your own sake make sure you're not fooling yourself."

"I appreciate your concern." Jack fought the urge to roll his eyes.

Garity checked his watch. "I'm expecting my deck hands back within the hour. Why don't you stick around? We're cruising the lake this evening. You'd love it, and you might even get a chance to meet future wife number four."

"Thanks for the invite, but I'm still working on wife number one."

"Look who won't take time to play now."

"Yeah, things aren't as they should be. Wallace Garity is having fun, and Jack Sheridan is passing on a sailing opportunity. I might have to rethink my opinion of you."

Garity shook his head. "Stand on your convictions."

"Right."

"But do talk with Lauren about a sail vacation. Better yet, I'm planning a Fourth of July cruise from Grand Haven to Mackinac and you two have to join us. I've got crates full of fireworks we'll be shooting off in a private offshore show. It's going to be fantastic."

"I'm sure you've got all the permits and licenses you need to pull that off."

"It's all covered."

"I'll talk to Lauren." Jack noticed the sun nearing the horizon through the starboard windows. "I need to hit the road. Any other legal entanglements I need to look out for with my treasure hunt?"

"Obtain written permission before digging on privately owned land, don't even tell me if you break ground on state-owned land, and if you pull the coins from a shipwreck be prepared to defend against a counter claim from the bank. It's not likely but be prepared. I'll let you know if anything else comes to mind."

"Thanks." Jack tipped his beer one more time. "I'm under the limit so don't call your buddies in blue." He started for the steps leading out of the deckhouse.

"Jack."

He turned.

Garity walked over to him. "Let me know if you need any other help."

Jack regarded him. "You got a new shovel you're dying to use?"

Garity ignored the comment. "You're retired from Neptune's Reach and don't have their resources at your fingertips anymore. I might be able to offer some logistical assistance."

"I should be good, but thanks for the offer."

Back on main deck Jack appraised the sailboat again. He really did admire the vessel. It's the kind of ship he hoped to own one day. With any luck this quest just might make that happen. "So what did you name her?"

A touch of pride lit up Garity's suntanned face. "The *Distinguished Gentleman*, after my father."

Jack smiled. "I have to admit, I envied the relationship you had with your dad."

"My father made a difference during his time in the senate. I respected the man." Garity scanned the reddening horizon. "His tenure ended too soon. It's a shame how fickle constituents are, shifting with every political wind that blows through their district. I can only hope to accomplish half the things he did."

"Well, I'm working on making up lost time with Connor. Don't want to repeat the mistakes of Sheridan family history."

"You do that." Garity offered his hand. "Good hunting."

They shook, which struck Jack odd. Such bonding wasn't par for the course with the judge. They must have made some breakthrough in their relationship. Jack couldn't let it go at that. "If you want to keep number four around longer, throw some Grecian Formula on that mop."

"If you exercise that kind of social etiquette with Lauren, it's a miracle you're still on wife number one."

"I'm sure she'd agree with you." That's more like it.

Jack left Wallace Garity to prepare the *Distinguished Gentleman* for her dusk sail on Lake Michigan. He drove off the marina parking lot and set course for home. An hour into the journey the sun disappeared from the sky behind him. The Jeep's headlights clicked on. Rolling through the gathering darkness on Interstate 96, Jack found himself mulling over Garity's comments concerning Bobbie. The judge had it all wrong. Jack wasn't helping her to re-fire the flame. There was no romantic subtext underlying his efforts to find the coins. The whole—affair—so to speak, was innocuous as to his marriage. The only bit he couldn't rationalize was why he hadn't told Lauren about it yet. She would understand, once she heard the whole story. Yes, he had to get it all out on the table. Soon.

A pair of headlights appeared in the rearview mirror. Was it the Camry? He couldn't tell in the darkness. He watched it for five minutes. It stayed half a mile back, no closer, no farther. He switched lanes. It switched lanes. A week ago he would have thought it was just a guy drafting in the wake of his radar detector, but a lot of things have happened since last week. Besides, the detector wasn't on tonight.

His cell phone rang and startled him. Caller ID displayed an unknown number. He hated those. "Hello."

"Jack, this is Lloyd. How've you been?"

"Lloyd? Didn't we already speak to each other once this year?"

Lloyd chuckled. "Hey, I didn't want to let our last conversation set a sour tone."

"Too late."

"I hope not. Have you given any more thought to my offer?"

"None."

"Come on, Jack, I just want what's best for you, and Neptune's Reach. It's a win-win."

"Yeah, you win and the company wins. I don't see myself coming out on top in that scenario."

"It's going to be different this time. You'll call the shots. As much as it pains me to say it, I don't have the leverage over you that I once did. Neptune's CEO is personally driving this recruitment effort."

"Sound's like his faith in his Operations VP is flagging. If I were you I'd be concerned about that."

"We're all feeling our throats over here. This is the first time Neptune's backlog has been this thin. We need something to inoculate us against this economic downturn. The CEO thinks that something is you."

"He's grasping at straws, Lloyd, just like you are. Times are tough; you have to tighten your belt. Downsize. Mothball some of the fleet. Quote new work aggressively. Why am I the one who has to tell you this?"

"We're making changes, but you're the lynchpin to get us through the crunch. I'm being told that if you come back, Neptune will secure twenty million in new contracts."

"Sounds like I won't have all that much say in what projects we take on. That's a little different than you've been telling me."

Lloyd stammered a second or two. "Damn it, Jack, you're getting a sweetheart deal no matter how you look at it."

"I'm not looking at it."

"Three times your salary."

"Unplug your ears."

"Don't turn your back on us. We took care of you for eighteen years."

Anger fueled Jack's grip on the steering wheel. "I think you've got that backwards."

"Turning me down is a mistake." Lloyd's tone lowered. "A mistake you'll regret."

Contacts started clicking in Jack's thoughts. The headlights in the rearview mirror suddenly appeared more ominous. "Mess with me, Lloyd, and I swear you'll be the one with regrets."

"Stubborn jackass, I'm trying to help you."

"Thanks for the concern, but I'm doing all right."

"If you strike out alone, you're going to crash and burn."

"Is that a prediction or a threat?"

"Take it however you want, just make the right decision."

"I already have." Jack disconnected and threw the phone on the passenger seat. He checked the headlights again. Were they getting closer? Had Lloyd sunk to strong-arm tactics? He wasn't about to wait around to find out.

Just beyond mile marker 56, the east and westbound sections of divided highway split to curve around a dense patch of forested terrain. Nice. He dropped his foot on the accelerator and crowned the outside lane. The trailing headlights disappeared behind the arc of the road. Jack shot out of the curve and searched for cover. The wide median between east and westbound 96 dipped below the road height and was awash in tall grass. He cut across the passing lane and started braking. The embankment sloped down from the soft shoulder in a gradual pitch. He steered the Jeep toward it. The tires left the pavement and the suspension rattled. Weeds beat against the grill. He switched off the headlights and lifted his foot from the brake. Darkness enveloped the Jeep as it rolled to a stop in the median.

The car that was following emerged from the curve and raced down the expressway. Jack watched it pass in a blur from the bottom of the shadowy embankment. He couldn't make out the model or color, but at this point it didn't matter. He shifted into drive and climbed the embankment. When the tires hit pavement he switched the headlights on and gunned the accelerator. Two miles down the road, a car sat on the right-side soft shoulder with its trunk open and hazard lights flashing. Jack picked up his cell phone and dialed 911. "I'd like to report an accident on 96 East near mile marker 58."

He slowed the Jeep, cautiously rolling up behind the car on the shoulder. It was a silver Camry. A guy standing in front of the car watched him approach. Jack threw open the glove box to put the Colt in reach. He glided up beside the car and scrolled the passenger window down. "You need some help?"

The guy looked at him a little perplexed. "No, we've got a call in to AAA. Thanks."

Jack showed his cell. "Didn't know what was going on so I reported an accident. Police should be here in a few minutes to help out. Take care now."

He accelerated away, a little smile creasing his face.

TEN

Harbor Springs, MI

Higgs and Kisko sat at a cast aluminum table behind an Alpine-themed condominium unit. Early morning sun warmed the air, and a light breeze carried fresh-cut grass aroma to them from a lawn mower buzzing in the distance. A tiny black Chihuahua sat on its haunches near the condo's sliding glass door and growled at their feet. An elderly man came through the door and set two cups of coffee down in front them.

Sparse threads of silver hair splayed on the man's head, and a chevron of crow's feet wrinkles textured his sun-darkened skin. He lowered himself into a patio chair and regarded Higgs. "Tell me, Mr. Nugent, why has the university become interested in my family?"

"Please," Higgs said, "call me Ted." He took a sip of coffee and arranged his delivery. "Are you aware, Mr. Coates, that some artifacts belonging to your great-grandfather were discovered in a shipwreck on Lake Michigan a few months ago?"

"Yes, people from the museum down near Sleeping Bear Point called me about it. They asked for permission from the family to display the items in an exhibit."

"You agreed." Higgs smiled.

"Yes, of course. Those things they found weren't doing Great-Grandpa Coates any good anymore, and they weren't doing me any good, either."

The Chihuahua inched closer to Higgs' foot and bared its teeth.

Higgs ignored it. "A few history professors at Western Michigan heard about the proposed display, and it got them to think that a class focused on Great Lakes maritime history in the 1800s would be a good addition to the university's curriculum."

The elderly Coates rested his arms on the table. "You want my permission for that, too?"

Higgs shook his head with an affable smirk. "Not exactly. See, the professors believe that if the course material is presented from the perspective of a local family, it will be more interesting for the students. They want to build on what was found in the wreck."

Coates seemed a bit nervous. "They don't want me to speak to the class, do they?"

Higgs chuckled. "No, but they would like to supplement the course material with actual historical documents or articles from the family, and have sent me here to ask if you have anything you're willing to share with the class."

"Documents or articles?" Coates straightened a few strands of hair on his head. "Like what?"

The dog started barking. Higgs glanced at it from the corner of his eye but carried on. "Letters, journals, birth or death records, heirlooms…a family Bible. Items that would help convey a sense of the time."

"Oscar!" Coates said to the dog. "Quiet." The Chihuahua slinked back toward the sliding glass door with a quiet growl in its throat. Coates thought a moment. "I don't think I have anything of historical significance."

"It doesn't have to be significant, and I don't have to take it with me when I leave." Higgs gestured to Kisko. "Forgive me for failing to make an introduction. This is my associate Clarence Clemens. Back in the car he has digital scanning and photographic equipment we can use to capture images of documents or items of interest."

Coates searched his memory. "You mentioned a Bible. I used to have one that my father gave me. I'm not certain but I think it came into the family with Great-Grandpa Harlan."

"Used to have?" Higgs sat forward. "What happened to it?"

Coates shrugged. "It got to be that time and I passed it on. My father gave it to me, and his father gave it to him. It was my turn."

Kisko stared at Higgs, irritated. *Road to nowhere.*

Higgs ignored him. "Who did you give it to?"

"To my son, Lewis."

Oscar started barking again, yapping from beside the sliding glass door.

Higgs shifted his weight in the chair and straightened his jacket. That dog might not make it through the morning. "A family Bible could be just the thing. A book that has survived several generations and embodies the Coates saga is exactly the kind of thing the professors are after. I think it would be perfect."

Coates opened his hands to show them empty. "I don't have it anymore."

"Do you think your son would be willing to let us take a look at it?"

"I don't see why not. You want me to call him?"

"Yes, if it's not too much trouble." Even if it was trouble that call had to be made.

Coates pulled himself to his feet and ambled into the condo through the sliding glass door. Oscar followed him in but turned around on the other side of the screen door and stood guard, growling.

Kisko picked up a pebble from the patio and tossed it at the screen. Oscar jumped back. Kisko laughed. "Piss-ant dog." He faced Higgs. "Nice three-hour drive last night. It led us right into another detour."

"Quit complaining." Higgs surveyed the wooded common area behind the condo. "This is another step closer to the end game."

Kisko scooted his chair forward "Wonder what your buddy Jack Sheridan is up to today."

"Chasing his tail most likely, but we can't afford to ignore him. The guy's sharp."

"Sharp enough to take the cross from our back pocket?"

"Ehrlich called with an update last night. Sheridan knows he's being shadowed."

Kisko grumbled. "If he's going to be a problem we should just take him out."

"That kind of thing needs to be approved at the top, like with Hamilton. Didn't you learn a damn thing after Weller?"

Kisko reclined in his chair and chose not to reply.

Higgs prepared to continue his rebuke but noticed Coates returning.

"I've got some gentlemen here right now who are asking about it." Coates slipped out through the sliding screen door with a cordless phone pressed to his ear. He kept the barking Chihuahua back with his leg. "I can't hear you. Oscar's making a fuss."

Higgs hand twitched. He wanted to pull his 9mm and put that dog out of his misery.

"Okay, I know you have to go, but hold on one minute." Coates addressed Higgs. "Can you go to the Grand Rapids area tomorrow afternoon?"

"Yes, but I'd prefer to—"

The buzz of a gasoline-powered line trimmer drowned out Higgs' voice. A guy from the lawn crew swept the machine across the edge of the patio. Higgs glared at him.

"Lewis," Coates said into the phone, "can you show them the Bible tomorrow?"

Higgs waved to get the old man's attention. "Mr. Coates, may I speak with him?"

Coates was concentrating on the call too much to notice, blocking the buzz of the line trimmer with a hand over his ear. "Five o'clock."

Oscar wedged his nose into a crack between the screen door and door frame and came through, latching onto Kisko's pant leg with sharp little teeth. "Hey!" Kisko shot to his feet.

"Oscar, no!" Coates pushed the dog back into the house with his foot. "All right. I'll tell them."

Kisko was ready to go after that short-haired Mexican rat.

Higgs stood and stopped his partner with a steely glare.

"Thank you, Lewis." Coates lowered the phone from his ear and contained Oscar behind the sliding glass door. The buzz of the line trimmer faded around the corner of the condo. "I'm sorry about that," Coates said. "Oscar's not usually like that with visitors."

"It's okay," Higgs said. "Dogs don't like Clarence. What did your son say?"

"He was in the middle of something important at work. He's a biotech engineer and is always busy. He's so wrapped up in scientific things I doubt he's even opened the Bible."

"You mentioned a meeting," Higgs said to keep him on track.

"Yes. Lewis works in Grand Rapids and said he'd try to get home a little early tomorrow. He said to come to his house at five p.m."

Higgs considered the hasty plan. Not perfect but workable. "That should be fine. I'll need his address of course, and his phone number so I can call him tomorrow to confirm our meeting."

"Sure, you have some paper and a pencil?"

Higgs searched his jacket pockets and found the notepad and pencil he used at the diver's house. "Ready." Coates recited Lewis' phone number and address. "Thank you for your help, Mr. Coates. I'm sure the professors will be pleased."

"That's his cell number," Coates said. "When he's involved at work like he is today he might not answer. He only picked up my call because he knew it was me."

"We'll hook up just fine." Higgs slipped the notepad into his pocket.

"Hope the Bible is something you can use."

"Me too."

Higgs and Kisko walked to the front of the condo unit where they'd parked the car. "We could have saved ourselves a little trouble by picking the second name on our list to visit first," Kisko said.

"We're not paid to make those types of decisions. We're paid to follow orders."

Kisko looked back at the condo unit and sniffed the air. "Do I smell a gas leak?"

Higgs stopped. "What would be the point of putting a match to this place, besides getting rid of Oscar?"

"Coates saw us, he talked to us. Loose thread."

"And if anyone questions him about us, he'll tell them he met with Ted Nugent and Clarence Clemens. You think that conversation is going to go any further?"

Higgs shook his head. Kisko's flippant willingness to torch the old man and his house irritated him. It wasn't necessary, and it hadn't been signed off. Not that he was squeamish about such things. If it made sense he'd do it in a heartbeat. But a hammer wasn't always the right tool. Circumstance dictated method. Sometimes a situation required friendly banter, and sometimes it required busting teeth. This morning it was the banter. Tomorrow—who knows?

He climbed into the driver's seat of the 300C. "Get in the car, Nate. We're done here."

ELEVEN

New Hudson, MI

Jack Sheridan raised the Colt, drew a bead, and squeezed off two quick shots. The thunder from the pistol pounded through his ear plugs. Spent shells ejected from the firing chamber and tinged on the concrete beside him. Twenty-five yards down range two .45 caliber slugs ripped through the black epicenter of a paper target. Jack grinned.

Three pops from a .32 caliber pistol rang out from the stall to his right. He glanced over. Lauren stood crooked to the target, left elbow dipped, right arm not extended. Sloppy stance. She fired the Kel-Tec semi-auto in her hands. A tiny dust cloud burst on the dirt pile above and behind the target. She shrugged.

"Sweetheart," Jack said. "Did you pay any attention to my little lesson?"

She faced him and lowered her safety glasses. "There're about a dozen places I'd rather be right now than a shooting range."

Someone fired a Glock .40 a few stalls down and she jumped.

Jack smiled. He set his stance and gestured to his posture. "Stand with your left side in line with the target, feet spread shoulder width apart. Don't lock your knees."

She smiled. "Right."

"Raise the pistol in your right hand and aim down range, extending your arm across your chest with a slight bend in your elbow. Keep your finger alongside the trigger guard."

"How am I supposed to shoot with it there?"

"Patience, woman. Cup your right hand with your left and stabilize your aim. Observe." Jack brought the Colt up and settled into a firing posture. His nose twitched as he lined up the barrel. "Finger inside the trigger guard, line up your target with the sight, squeeze the trigger on an exhale." He fired his last two rounds. The shells ejected and the slide locked open. Another pair of holes tore through the target. He ejected the empty magazine and set it beside the pistol on the table top in front of him. "You're on, babe."

Lauren imitated his stance, even his nose twitch.

"The twitch isn't necessary."

She smirked and fired the Kel-Tec twice.

He picked up a pair of binoculars and checked her target. Two holes perforated the outer ring. "Congratulations, you actually broke paper."

"Good, can we go now?"

The range officer in the observation booth switched on the PA system and instructed all shooters to fully discharge their weapons for the scheduled cease fire. Up and down the row of stalls the shooters responded by firing the ammunition remaining in their magazines. Lauren quickly popped off her last three rounds. One of them hit the target.

"You're improving," Jack said.

Cease fire arrived. The range officer prompted the shooters to table their weapons and leave the shooting area. Jack helped Lauren ready her pistol for inspection by ejecting the magazine and laying the Kel-Tec on the table pointing down range. They grabbed some fresh targets and exited their stall, taking up positions behind the yellow line designating the clear zone to allow a range official to come through and verify the weapons were made safe.

Jack pulled out his ear plugs. "We need to discuss something."

Lauren removed her safety glasses and ear plugs as well. "Your charter business?"

"Yeah, that." He rolled a spent shell under his shoe. "There've been some developments over the past couple of days that have rearranged my plans."

"What, do we need to take out a huge bank loan for start up?"

"No." He scratched an imaginary itch on the back of his head. "I've gotten another job offer that I've decided to accept. It's going to require me to do some traveling within the state, probably on an unpredictable schedule."

Lauren spun around and squared off with him. "An offer from Lloyd?"

Jack noticed her foot had crossed the yellow line. "Honey, you're in the restricted area."

She stepped forward, forcing him back. "Is this job with Neptune's Reach?"

"Of course not, I know better than to do something that stupid." She looked at him like she didn't believe him.

"Look, it has nothing to do with Lloyd or Neptune's Reach."

"All right." She softened her tone. "Then what is this job offer?"

He took a breath. "I've been asked to head up a salvage project."

"A salvage project?"

"Yeah, and I'll be doing it on sort of a freelance basis."

She didn't say anything for a long while. "What are you going after?"

"Uh, it's cargo from a shipwreck. Pretty valuable cargo."

"How valuable?"

"Ten, maybe twenty million dollars."

"Wow, what is it?"

"It's a load of coins."

"Coins?"

"Yeah, coins."

The range officer announced over the PA that the kill zone was safe.

"Hey, we got the all clear. Let's go change out our targets." Jack headed for the trail leading down range, merging in with the other shooters. Lauren followed.

"What are these coins," she said, "Spanish Doubloons?"

"They're not quite that old."

She hurried to catch up to him. "How old are they?"

"About a hundred and seventy years."

"This doesn't sound like a salvage project. It sounds more like a treasure hunt."

Jack kept walking.

"Didn't you once tell me a treasure hunt is just a wild goose chase for the desperate?"

"Most of them are." He walked along the wooden fence stretching across the dirt embankment to where their targets were hung and tore Lauren's down. "You want it framed?"

"What makes this one different?"

He held the target up so sunlight came through the holes. "You actually got three hits."

"Not the target, the treasure hunt. What makes this treasure hunt different?"

He handed her the perforated paper. "The story behind the coins has a good foundation. Peripheral facts are cross referencing nicely. I think with a little research, some deductive reasoning, and basic search and recovery skills I'll be successful." He stapled a new target on the rail for her.

She took his target down. He had a cluster of hits in the black center and three or four in the outer rings. "How do you do this?"

"It's called practice, which is something you are supposed to be doing once in a while."

"We're not talking about me. We're talking about you and your wild goose chase." She thought a moment. "Who asked you to do it?"

He lifted his new target into position and drove staples into the corners. "Time's almost up. Let's beat the rush out of the kill zone." He headed for the trail.

"Who hired you to do this, Jack?" She rushed to catch up with him. "It's Lloyd, isn't it?"

"I told you this doesn't involve Lloyd."

"Then who does it involve?"

He walked a few more paces. "An old friend."

She circled around and got in front of him. "Abner Wilson asked you to do this in conjunction with some sort of historical project for the navy. Right?" She walked backwards to stay ahead of him.

"Strike two."

She started counting off names on her fingers. "Rezner, Garcia, Harper, Oz, who is it?"

He couldn't put it off anymore. "Bobbie."

Lauren stopped walking backwards. Her expression fell blank. "Bobbie who?"

He knew she'd catch on before too long. In her suspended moment of confusion he skirted around her and staked a position across the yellow line behind the shooting stalls. *Come on people, get back up range.* Lauren turned slowly about. Her confusion seemed to be dissipating. Realization settled in its place. Yeah, a face had been associated with the name.

"Bobbie Weller?"

Jack thought it best to just nod his head.

She marched over to him. "Is that who you've been meeting with this week?"

"Just once, three days ago. Since then I've been doing preliminary research—"

"Why didn't you tell me?"

"I didn't know if I was going to go after the coins or not. Bobbie came to me with a story of lost treasure in the Great Lakes, for Pete's sake. I sure as hell wasn't going to just hop on board without looking into it first. And since there was a good chance nothing would come of it, I opted not to tell you right away. I didn't want to have this conversation if it wasn't necessary."

"So you decided it wasn't necessary to tell your wife you had a secret meeting with your ex-lover?"

The other shooters were returning from down range. Jack lowered his voice. "Look, Bobbie's had a rough year since Steven died. She's in financial trouble and thinks these coins arc her only way out. She asked me to help search for them because of my salvage experience with Neptune's Reach."

"I'm sure that's all there was to it."

"Don't read anything into it. I agreed to help her because she's a friend, nothing more."

"You hid it from me, Jack. It makes it look like you've done something wrong." She searched his eyes. "Don't you understand where I coming from?"

"I'll admit my approach to handling the situation seemed like a better idea three days ago than it does now, but I explained why I didn't rush home and spill my guts about Bobbie and her treasure. Now I'm telling you."

"A little late."

"Better late than never."

The PA system crackled and the range officer announced the cease fire was over. Jack left Lauren stewing behind the yellow line and returned to his stall. He opened a box of ammunition. Guilt pecked at him. He thought about trying to explain himself again, but she had turned her back to him. He began reloading the Colt. Eventually she came up alongside him.

He glanced over. "You need help with your reload?"

She took the Kel-Tec's clip into her hand and began feeding in .32 caliber shells.

He pressed another round into his magazine. "Guess you were paying attention."

They continued reloading in silence. Jack started thinking that putting a loaded gun in his wife's hand right then might not be a good idea. "There's no reason to be upset about this."

She jammed the clip into the pistol. "Don't tell me what to be upset about."

"I'm sorry I didn't tell you."

"I can see that." She drew back the slide on the pistol and let it snap forward to load a shell into the chamber. "We've been married too long, been through too much together to start keeping secrets from each other."

"I know." He slid the magazine into the Colt. "Did I mention the fact that I'm sorry?"

She put her safety glasses on and ear plugs in. "You did. I just like hearing you say it. You do it so infrequently." She lifted the pistol and set her stance.

Jack donned his safety gear. Lauren's first shot missed the target. "Relax," he said. "Exhale, and then fire."

She said something under her breath and squeezed the trigger twice. One shot hit the black.

"Better." He chambered a round in the Colt.

"So," she said, "have you and your client discussed terms of your agreement?"

The .45 thundered and a hole blew into Jack's target. "Terms?"

"Is Bobbie giving you a cut, or are you helping her out of the goodness of your heart?"

"We haven't really talked about it."

Lauren let out an exasperated breath and sent three more shots down range.

Jack responded with a single blast. "Unofficially it's an even split."

She paused. "Half of ten million dollars is a lot of money."

"You think?"

"What's the next step in your wild goose chase?"

"I need to find a shipwreck in the Manitou Passage."

"You got your resources lined up, equipment, charts?"

"I'm working on it." He lowered his pistol. "I had to put everything on hold to consult with my wife."

She smirked. "Sounds like you need help with negotiations and logistics."

"I'm sole proprietor of Jack's Treasure Expeditions, Inc. There is no one else."

"You're wrong about that."

He faced her. "How so?"

"I'm Mrs. Jack Sheridan, half of this business concern is mine, and from here on in we're working together."

- TWELVE -

Sheridan Home
Linden, MI

It was a long ride home. Lauren squeezed Jack for every bit of information he had on the coins. He told her everything; the Singapore bank, the *Milwaukee*, Harlan Coates, the will, Steven's notebook, Eugene Elliot's North Carolina coin theory, and the cross that just might hold the key to unraveling it all. He told her everything except the part about being followed by a suspicious silver Camry. He needed to come to grips with that himself before presenting it to her.

He still hadn't determined where the Camry fit in. Was it tied to the coins, or did it have something to do with Rafferty? And what about Lloyd? His peculiar behavior really added an odd ingredient to the mix. There were too many angles to consider. Back when the only phobia on his plate was the ubiquitous Rafferty threat he had managed to find a livable balance between paranoia and normalcy. Now this balance had been upset.

He found one positive aspect to Lauren's joining the hunt. At least he could keep an eye on her this way, protect her from Rafferty or anyone else who might happen along.

Jack steered the Jeep into his gravel driveway. Ike came bounding through the yard. That wasn't right. "Didn't we put him inside when we left for the range?"

Lauren glanced at the dog. "I thought we did."

Ike ran after the Jeep, barking as it came around the bend in the driveway.

Jack saw an old S-10 pickup parked in front of the house and knew why the dog was out. "We've got company."

Connor and Markus sat on the porch waiting for them to arrive. Apparently they'd raided the kitchen because they had a big bowl of chips between them and cans of cola in their hands. Jack and Lauren climbed the porch steps. "Hey, guys, what's the occasion?" Jack said.

Connor raised his cola in a toast. "You're looking at a couple of heroes."

"Oh, good," Lauren said, "and your father is a treasure hunter.

What an extraordinary family I have."

Markus cocked his head at Jack. "You're a what?"

"Never mind," Jack said. "What happened with you two?"

"We were diving the *Regina* in Lake Huron yesterday and saved a guy's life."

"Even when he didn't deserve it," Markus added.

Jack slid a patio chair over to them. "Give me the details."

Connor and Markus told him the SCUBA rescue story from splashing in to surfacing with dry tanks. Jack felt a good portion of pride in his son's actions; nonetheless he said, "I thought I told you to stay away from dangerous situations."

Connor slapped Markus' arm. "See, he's so predictable."

Markus made like he was going to respond with a punch in the nose and then shifted his attention to Jack. "Hey, what did Mrs. Sheridan mean by 'treasure hunter'?"

Lauren took that as her cue to exit. "I've heard this before. Boys, if you get hungry for lunch, come in and I'll find something for you."

"Thank you, Mrs. Sheridan," Markus said. "We appreciate it."

Jack kicked his foot. "Why do you turn into Eddie Haskell when my wife's around?"

Markus grinned. "You're avoiding the question. What's this about a treasure hunter?"

Jack debated what to say. His knee-jerk reaction was to not tell them anything, but Lauren had shown the cat the open end of the bag and it had started to crawl out. He decided it best to try and wrap a leash around its neck. "I've got a summer project going. Some might call it a treasure hunt."

Connor's eyes widened. "Say no more. I want in."

"Yeah," Markus added, "We want in."

"Easy guys, I haven't told you anything yet."

Connor leaned forward. "Give me the details."

Jack took a breath, hoped he wouldn't regret this decision, and then recited everything he had told Lauren in the Jeep on the way home. The guys sat there slack-jawed. Ike came onto the porch and sat in front of the bowl of chips. Jack scratched behind the dog's ears. "What do you think, guys?"

"Dad, this is cool. I want in."

"Yeah," Markus added, "We want in."

"Connor, your mother has expressed interest in lending me a hand. If you've got some time off work, you can tag along here and there." Jack figured that since he had Lauren under his wing, he might as well get Connor there too.

"I've got five days left," Connor said. "Let's start burning them."

Markus grabbed a chip from the bowl. "Mr. Sheridan, I can't help but notice that you're sitting on your porch at home instead of chasing down these coins. What's the hold-up?"

Jack squared his chair with his new recruits. "The hold-up is a ship named *William Barclay* that sank in Lake Michigan back in 1868. Steven's notebook says that Harlan Coates commissioned that ship to haul some lumber for one of the lighthouse construction projects he was supervising. Coates' last letter to his wife said he was returning home to Allegan County onboard that ship. *William Barclay* never made it."

"What happened?" Connor asked.

"That's the twenty million-dollar question. Steven believed the *William Barclay* had set sail from somewhere in northern Lake Michigan. In those days ships traveling between the Straits of Mackinac and southern Lake Michigan would have made the trek through the Manitou Passage. It was a tricky stretch of water to navigate. Storm, fog, and collision claimed dozens of vessels. Steven believed the ship went down there. I agree with him."

Markus burped some cola. "What are you going to find on the *William Barclay?*"

"The resting place of Harlan W. Coates, and hopefully his personal effects."

"The cross," Connor said.

"Bingo." Jack tossed a potato chip to Ike.

Markus narrowed his eyes. "Forgive me for asking, but how did Coates manage to carve a treasure map on the face of a silver crucifix?"

"I doubt it's a map," Jack said. "I figure it's a destination, perhaps the name of a town or building, or maybe it's a message."

Markus stood. "Let's get my boat to the Manitou Passage. Come on."

"Sit down, Markus," Jack said. "You can't just randomly pick a coordinate inside the hundreds of square miles of water in the passage and hope to get lucky. You have to uncover information about the ship and her route, and make an educated guess on where she went down."

"Boatnerd.com," Connor said. "The guy who runs that site has got detailed information on every wreck in the Great Lakes."

"I've already exhausted the Internet for information on the ship. The *William Barclay* is one of the true mystery shipwrecks out there. All that was ever reported about her is that she was lost in Lake Michigan in 1868. I contacted the Great Lakes Historical Society and the Coast Guard to try and find the ship's registration and enrollment documents, or any other information that might shed some light on where she disappeared. I came up empty."

Markus bounced on his heels. "How about other known shipwrecks in the area? Plot out where they are in the passage and find the greatest concentration. That would identify the most dangerous part of the passage. Wouldn't that be a good place to start looking?"

Connor gave him a double take. "Jeez, Markus, that actually sounded intelligent."

"Good line of thinking," Jack said. "I was heading that direction myself."

"It hurt too. I think I'm getting a headache."

Connor seemed to be contemplating. "Okay, Dad, this might seem like a dumb idea, but did you Google Harlan Coates as well as the *William Barclay*?"

"Google?" Markus laughed. "Sheridan, you kill me."

Jack smiled. "Connor, the man died over a hundred and forty years ago. I don't think he has a lot of postings on the Internet."

Connor took offense. "Hey, the Web's an infinite resource. There's probably stuff posted about this guy in places you haven't even thought of looking."

"Yes, it's possible," Jack said. "But the information you find won't tell us where the ship went down. I've already farmed that territory."

"What if Coates was never aboard the *William Barclay*?" Connor paused for effect. "Searching the Manitou Passage would be a bad idea then, wouldn't it? All it would take is for us to find one record of him being alive after 1868. Think about all the crap posted on the net. Diaries, genealogies, college term papers, old newspaper articles; if we find him in just one reference, it would prove he wasn't on the ship and we wouldn't have to waste a lot of time and effort searching for the shipwreck." He stood. "Where's your computer, Dad? I'm looking up Coates now."

Jack slid his chair back. "You actually have something there. I haven't looked it from that perspective before. PC's in my study." He led the guys into the house and took a seat in his office chair in the study. He booted the computer and fired up the Web browser. Touchtone sounds of a phone dialing came through the speakers.

Connor glanced sideways at his father. "You've got to be kidding me."

"Nearest cable is about half a mile away. I'm not paying eight thousand dollars to pull a line to my house."

Markus plopped in a leather recliner sitting in the corner. "Wake me when we're online."

The computer screeched to make its connection.

Connor crouched beside the desk. "There's a sound you don't hear in America anymore." He stared at the blank screen.

Eventually Jack's home page popped up and they jumped over to Google. Connor typed Harlan Coates into the search field. Every conceivable combination of Harlan and Coates that appeared in any document anywhere had been flagged.

"Great," Connor said. "One hundred and seventeen thousand hits."

Markus extended the leg rest on the recliner. "Rookie, put quotes around the name."

"Get off me." Connor re-entered the name with quotes. "Down to six." He read through the reference hits. "A listing for a lawyer in Tennessee, a university student in Wisconsin, the same student's physics lab report, a hybrid of two other names listed next to each other in the same document, a couple of repeats. Looks like I'm striking out."

"Search his full name," Jack said. "Harlan W. Coates."

Connor did. One hit came back. "Hey, there's something in a *Grand Haven Tribune* online article." He clicked the link. The newspaper's Web page slowly assembled on screen. "Dad, you won't believe this but the article is dated last week. Headline reads, *Battle Creek Diver Discovers Pieces of the Past*." He skimmed through the text. "Holy shit, this guy found an unidentified wreck in the Manitou Passage and brought a trunk belonging to Harlan W. Coates to the surface."

Jack came out of the chair. "Print that article!" He threw open a cabinet door beside the computer and switched on the power for the printer stored inside. "Go."

Within a minute he and Markus had copies of the article in their hands. They all read through the story in dead silence. "I guess this proves that Coates was aboard the ship," Markus said.

Jack highlighted some sections of the article with a yellow marker. "This Hamilton guy did us a huge favor."

"It doesn't say he found a cross," Connor said. "The article mentions the trunk and some mundane stuff like a ceramic plate and a bottle, but it doesn't list a cross."

Markus set his copy of the article on his lap. "It also says he donated the stuff to the Sleeping Bear Point Museum and they'll be displaying it in an exhibit this month."

"Let's get the story right from the horse's mouth," Jack said. "Connor, look up Hamilton's phone number."

Connor took the office chair in front of the computer. After a minute of searching online directories he found a phone number listing for a Robert Hamilton in Battle Creek. Jack dialed the number on his cell phone. A recorded message told him the number was no longer in service. He dialed it again just to be sure he got it right. Same result. "Plan B: Find the phone number for the Sleeping Bear Museum."

Connor located it in a Western Michigan directory. Jack dialed.

"Hello, Sleeping Bear Point Maritime Museum, Roger speaking."

Jack took the chair back from Connor. "Hello, may I speak with the director of exhibits, please?"

Roger chuckled. "You're talking to him."

"This must be my lucky day."

"We're a small operation, so museum members wear a lot of hats. Today in addition to curator and president of the board, I'm the receptionist."

"Good, I've got some questions about the Coates exhibit you're opening this month."

"Oh." Roger's voice dipped. "I'll help how I can, but that exhibit ran into some trouble."

Jack spun the office chair away from the computer screen. "What sort of trouble?"

"The pieces for the exhibit were destroyed in a fire two days ago."

"Are you kidding me?"

"No, the man who was donating the pieces was killed in the fire too. It's a real tragedy"

Jack absorbed the news.

"Are you still there, sir?" Roger asked

"Yes, I'm sorry, just a little taken back."

"It shocked me too. Mr. Hamilton seemed like a good man. Obviously the exhibit will not be opening. Perhaps I can still help you. What questions did you have?"

Those little hairs on the back of Jack's neck were standing up. It was coincidence enough that someone had recently discovered the Coates wreck. Now the recovered articles from that wreck had been destroyed days before going on display, and literally hours after Bobbie had solicited his help to find the coins. Something reeked about the whole thing.

"Sir?"

"I'm collecting some genealogical information on the Coates family," Jack said. "The pieces you were going to display might have helped me with my research. Do you have a complete listing of the items that Mr. Hamilton found on the wreck?"

"Yes, we thoroughly catalogue exhibit pieces."

"Do you recall if one of the items was a silver crucifix?"

"I believe there was one."

Jack felt his heart kick a little harder. "Do you have a photographic record of it?"

No reply.

"Roger?" Jack heard a clatter on the line. "Roger, you okay?"

Someone fumbled with the phone on the other end. "I'm back," Roger said. "I went to grab the file. Now, you asked for a photographic record." Papers shuffled. "I've got a couple of different shots of the cross."

"I sure would like to see those pictures."

"Do you have access to a fax machine?"

"Uh, yes, I can receive a fax in my office—"

Connor waved to nix the suggestion. "Don't fax a photograph. The image quality stinks. Ask if he can scan it and e-mail it over."

"Roger, do you have a scanner you can digitize the photograph with and e-mail that?"

Roger grumbled. "One minute." He called for someone offline. A short muffled conversation took place. He came back. "This *is* your lucky day. My daughter's here this afternoon. She understands all this digital super-highway mumbo-jumbo. Give me your e-mail address and I'll have her send it over."

Jack gave him his home e-mail address twice, had him read it back. "Thank you for the help. I'll wait for your message." He ended the call and spun the office chair back toward the computer screen. Connor and Markus looked over his shoulder. Jack accessed his e-mail account and displayed the inbox. No new message yet.

Markus scanned through some SPAM. "You going to take advantage of that Viagra offer, Mr. Sheridan?"

"Quiet, Markus."

Ten minutes elapsed. Connor sat on the desk. "We could have driven there by now."

A chime announced the arrival of the e-mail from the museum. The subject line read: Coates Artifact – Catalogue Number 135: Silver Cross. Jack found two JPEG files attached. He clicked the first. The slow connection stalled the resolution of the image. "Come on."

After thirty seconds the full picture had assembled. A tarnished silver crucifix set against a black cloth background filled the screen. The surface of the cross was smooth with nicks and mars scoring the edges. No engraving appeared.

Connor leaned closer. "No lettering. There's no writing on it."

"No map carved on it either," Markus said.

"It's the front face," Jack said. "I'll bet the other JPEG shows the reverse side and the engraving will be there." He closed the first image and opened the second, initiating the lethargic picture resolving process. *There better be something written on the back.*

The next picture appeared to be identical to the first, with one significant exception.

"There," Connor said, "engraving along the vertical!"

Markus crept closer. "We're not blind, Sherlock, we can see it."

"Let's get a closer look." Jack magnified the view and rotated it ninety degrees. Darkened script lettering stretched from one end of the screen to the other. He read it several times. It wasn't what he had expected.

To my sons, seek your legacy in the Word - Rev. 21:7

Connor glanced at Jack. "Looks like Coates took the cheap way out and left his boys some spiritual advice instead of money. Are you sure about the coins?"

"Of course I'm sure." Jack stood and searched through a small bookcase above the computer. "He's directing his sons to read that Bible verse for a reason."

"Then let's look it up," Markus said.

Jack pulled down an old NIV translation Bible. "Way ahead of you." He cracked open the Bible and flipped through the pages, feeling pretty certain that Revelations was the last book of the New Testament. Thank goodness for Sunday school. He found chapter twenty-one, verse seven and read it aloud. "He who overcomes will inherit all this, and I will be his God and he will be my son."

Markus shook his head. "That's not helping me picture the hiding place of a cache of gold coins."

"Me neither," Connor said.

Jack wanted to agree with them but held his tongue. "He who overcomes—Coates was definitely challenging his sons."

"Why make it so difficult for them?" Connor asked.

"The Coates boys apparently had some sort of feud going on between them. I think Harlan was trying to get them to bury the hatchet posthumously. In his will he said he hoped his sons would resolve their differences to see what is to be seen and have life to the full." Jack considered the Bible. "This verse may have meant something in particular to them."

"If that's the case we're never going to figure it out." Markus said. Connor sat in the office chair. "Nice positive attitude."

"Maybe the meaning Coates was trying to communicate through the verse is lost in translation." Jack said. "They didn't have an NIV Bible in 1868."

Connor scanned the bookshelf. "What version would they have had back then?"

"My guess is King James, but you won't find it up there. This is the only Bible we have in the house."

"No it's not."

Lauren's voice came from behind them. Jack and the guys turned around. She stood in the doorway to the study with her arms crossed. "I heard you quoting Bible verses and thought I'd better get in here to witness the revival."

"It's not a revival," Jack said. "It's a treasure hunt. Remember? What did you mean there are more Bibles in this house?"

"I have a parallel Bible on CD. It includes a bunch of translations. It's great for studying context and to get the full meaning of a passage, especially when your husband does something infuriating and you need divine guidance to figure out how to deal with him."

"The part about your husband notwithstanding, tell me where you keep the CD."

Lauren walked to the computer and put a hand on Connor's shoulder. "I need the chair, kiddo." Connor vacated and she sat down. She opened a drawer in the desk, sifted through some jewel cases, and loaded a disc into the CD drive. "What verse and translation are you looking for?" Jack told her and she opened a series of windows on the software. "Okay, Revelations 21:7. The left column here is the King James Version, the next column over is the NIV, third is the Noah Webster version. I included that one because it's from the timeframe you're interested in. I didn't think the Greek or Latin Vulgate versions would do you much good."

"Thank you for your speedy and thorough assistance." Jack read the King James translation. "He that overcometh shall inherit all things; and I will be his God, and he shall be my son."

Connor mulled it over. "That didn't sound very different from the NIV."

"It's not supposed to be different," Markus said, "just nuanced."

Jack stared into the screen. "The nuance doesn't set it apart either. And the Webster version is identical to the King James Version." He caressed his chin. A disappointing thought occurred to him. "The clue is not in the verse."

Markus sat in the recliner. "If the clue is not in the verse, then we don't have the clue."

"You never have a clue," Connor said. "But if the clue is not in the verse, then why put the verse on the cross?"

"It's a marker," Jack replied, "a flag to let his sons know where to look for the clue."

"Yeah, he told them to look in a Bible." Markus rocked the recliner. "We did that and struck out."

Connor's face lit up. "No, not just any Bible; he expected them to open a particular one."

Jack nodded. "Right, he expected them to open the family Bible, and that's where he divulges the location of the coins."

"Your logic is making me dizzy," Lauren said. "How did you arrive at that?"

"It makes sense." Jack faced her. "No verse could reveal exactly where Harlan hid the coins in 1868, so he needed to put that detailed information in the one Bible his sons would turn to after seeing the engraving on the cross." He glanced at the screen with the translations again. "Now we've got to find the Coates family Bible. That might be more difficult than finding a shipwreck. At least a shipwreck stays put once it hits the bottom. A Bible changes hands every generation. It might not even stay with the family."

Connor settled back on the desk. "Where do you look for something like that?"

"The family," Lauren said.

"Exactly." Jack grabbed his cell phone and dialed a number. "And I know just the guy to get us going in the right direction."

THIRTEEN

Jack waited for the cell to connect. The number rang three times. "Hello?"

"Hello, this is Jack Sheridan. Am I speaking with Eugene Elliot?"

"Yes, Jack, how are you?"

"Good. Are you keeping warm over there?"

"Warmer than I'd like. To what do I owe the pleasure?"

"I'm working on that new air conditioner for you, and I have a little favor to ask."

"York has a nice high efficiency model. They're on discount at Home Depot this week. What is it you need?"

"The Coates family tree."

Eugene laughed. "The past bleeds into the present, eh?"

"Sure does. I need to contact some direct descendents of Harlan Coates. A phone book won't do. It has to be a clear lineage back to Harlan. I figure you can trace this genealogy a lot quicker than I can."

"I probably can. When do you need it?"

Jack hesitated. "I need it just as soon as you can possibly pull it together. My quest may have become time critical."

"This world just keeps going faster and faster. You know, there was a time when historians never had to rush to do anything." Eugene exhaled. "I'll sketch something out as soon as possible, but don't expect a miracle."

"Thanks, Eugene, I really appreciate—"

Call disconnected.

Jack checked his phone's signal strength. Four bars. "I think Eugene hung up on me. I hope I didn't tick him off." He scanned the study. Only Lauren was still there. "Where are the guys?"

"They went to get something to eat," she said.

"I think they've got the right idea. It's way past lunch."

"Hold on a minute." She motioned him to sit.

He lowered into the recliner. "This feels like one of *those* conversations coming."

"I just realized something while you were talking to Eugene Elliot."

"I'll bet I don't like what you say next."

"If you contact a Coates relative and locate the family Bible, are you going to tell this person what you're doing?"

"Hmmm, let me think…No."

"Jack, we're going after an inheritance that Harlan Coates intended to leave to his sons. Aren't his living descendants more entitled to these coins than we are?"

"Not at all."

"Why?"

"Harlan Coates acquired this 'inheritance' in a somewhat underhanded way. He took coins that didn't belong to him. He didn't offer them back to the Bank of Singapore, and he didn't offer them to the Bank of Michigan. Just because he intended to give them to his sons as an inheritance doesn't change the fact that they weren't rightfully his to begin with."

"Won't you feel a little underhanded yourself when you use a Coates relative to siphon information on your way to the treasure?"

"Do you really need to ask me that?"

"They're not ours to take. That's what's bothering me."

"Then let's just go through all this trouble and give them back to the Bank of Michigan. The coins were technically theirs to begin with. Would that make you feel better?"

"No."

"Honey, I consulted with Garity on this. The Bank of Michigan owned the coins at the time they were lost, not Harlan Coates. The bank failed to make any noteworthy effort to recover them from the shipwreck. A century and a half has ticked away. The bank can't make a credible claim on them now. Possession is nine-tenths of the law. Finders keepers, losers weepers."

"That would have been a more convincing argument without the 'finders keepers' part."

"Sorry, I lost my head."

"Still, Harlan didn't really steal the coins, so I think his relatives deserve something."

Jack regarded her a long while. "Can I take that under advisement?"

"Fine."

"Okay, I'm getting food."

They joined the boys in the kitchen for leftover fried chicken and potato salad. Jack felt relaxed having his family together in one place where he could keep an eye on them. They weren't out of his reach today. They weren't easy prey if Rafferty decided to return. Today, he had his family, including Markus, home where he could protect them.

* * *

Eugene had warned not to expect a miracle. In light of this Jack didn't think he'd hear anything back for at least a day. When the historian called after only three hours, it was a welcome surprise. Eugene explained that the Coates family wasn't very large and that he only needed to trace five generations. He faxed a handwritten diagram to Jack's study showing the Coates tree. Jack took the diagram to the porch to inspect it. Lauren and the boys followed.

"If there are any hot, young Coates women around today just tell me where they are," Markus said. "I'll get whatever we need from them personally."

Connor positioned a chair adjacent to his father. "What's the tree look like?"

Jack studied the diagram on the sheet of paper. "David and Daniel were Harlan's only children. David was the eldest. His line carries through to today, even after tuberculosis, war, and influenza swept through his descendants. Daniel had a son and daughter. The son died young without children so the direct Coates bloodline stopped there. The daughter married and had two sons. That branch continues under the name of Cabbin."

"What branch should we follow, David or Daniel?" Connor asked.

"Let's see." Jack scanned the diagram. "Harlan seemed to be a religious man, and religious men tend to pay heed to biblical tradition. Keeping that in mind, first-born sons were favored in the Bible. Their birthright entitled them to special blessings, a larger portion of the inheritance, and the promise of stepping into their father's social position. Given that, and the fact that his line spans the years unbroken, I'd have go with David. Harlan most likely gave him the family Bible, if one exists, and it would have been up to David to pass it to the next generation."

"What's my birthright?" Connor said.

"Hanging around with Markus," Jack replied.

"That's it?"

"Do you really want my social position?"

"Pass."

Lauren listened from the railing. "What if a family Bible doesn't exist? If it does, what if Harlan died before he had a chance to plant the coins' hiding place in it?"

"Then we're having a very interesting conversation for nothing."

"So who are they?" Markus said. "Who are these modern Coates folks, and where do they live?" He checked the time on his cell phone. "We're burning daylight."

"Settle down, Markus. Fools rush in." Jack referenced some of Eugene's notes. "According to my historian, two direct descendants from David's line are in Michigan. A seventy-five-year-old man named Samuel Coates lives in Harbor Springs. His son, a forty-two-year-old man named Lewis Coates, lives in Grand Rapids." He read another bit. "A Cabbin relative lives in Allendale, too."

"Okay," Connor said. "Since we're starting with David's line our focus is Samuel and Lewis. Of these two who's most likely to have the Bible, the old guy or the not-so-old guy?"

Markus shrugged. "Depends if the old guy thinks the not-so-old guy would appreciate a family heirloom like that."

"Let's assume Lewis is established in life," Lauren said. "My guess is Samuel would recognize this and start preparing his son to take over as head of the Coates family."

"And Samuel knows his time is limited," Jack added. "If he up and died unexpectedly, he wouldn't want to leave it to chance for the treasured family Bible to get into Lewis' hands. I think he's already given it to his son."

"That's what I think," Lauren said.

Connor felt his father's eyes on him. "I know. I'm on it. Lewis Coates' phone number." He got up and headed inside to search the online phone directories. It took him fifteen minutes to come up with a Grand Rapids residence listing for Lewis.

Jack dialed the number. It amazed him how much progress they'd made in one afternoon. He went from planning a full-fledged shipwreck search of the Manitou Passage to calling a descendant of Harlan Coates to discover, he hoped, the final resting place of the coins. It seemed this treasure hunt was going to be a lot easier than he had imagined.

"Hello?"

"Hello, my name is Jack Sheridan, and I'm participating in a genealogical research project that involves Western Michigan families. Do you have a few minutes to talk?"

"I just walked in from work…is this a survey or something?"

"No, sir, the Coates family is part of our research efforts. I only have a few questions to ask you. It shouldn't take long."

The voice on the other end of the line paused. "Are you with the university?"

Jack balked. Would being with the university add credibility to his story? He decided it would. "Yes. Western Michigan launched this project to get a grassroots perspective on Michigan history."

"Then can we talk tomorrow at five o'clock? I'd really like to get some dinner now."

"Tomorrow at five? Certainly. I would like to ask one question now, however. It helps our research to study a family Bible that has been handed down through several generations. My notes here indicate the Coates family may have such a Bible. Is this true?"

"Yes, and I'll have it out tomorrow when we talk. Did you get my address?"

Address? Why would I need his address? "No, sir, all I have here is your phone number."

"Dad's slipping."

Jack didn't understand the comment. "Sorry, Mr. Coates, could you repeat that?"

"Nothing...Do you have a pencil handy?"

Jack fumbled around his shirt pocket. The guy wanted a face-to-face meeting to discuss the Bible. This was turning out better than he had planned. "I'm sorry, sir, give me one second." He cupped his hand over the phone. "Connor, get me a pencil, quick."

Connor ran inside to find something to write with.

Lauren stared at Jack. He figured she was trying to generate a bit of guilt in him based on their earlier conversation. He turned his chair around to avoid her eyes and grabbed the pencil from Connor upon his return. "Mr. Coates, I'm ready." Lewis dictated the address. "Okay, I've got it. Thank you for your assistance. I'm looking forward to our meeting tomorrow."

"No problem, Mr. Sheridan, see you then." Click.

Excitement brought Jack to his feet. "I'm going to Grand Rapids tomorrow."

Lauren smiled. "So am I."

Markus wagged his thumb between he and Connor. "Don't think we're staying home."

"Come on," Jack said. "This is a quick trip to GR and back. I don't need a posse."

"What if you find out where the coins are located?" Markus asked. "You won't want to come home. You'll want to hit the ground running."

Connor added, "Yeah, having the team in the field will make us agile. We'll be more flexible to respond to whatever turn the hunt takes."

"I'm just coming along," Lauren said. "Partner, remember?"

Jack figured arguing the issue would be a lost cause. The guys sort of had a point, and Lauren wasn't budging. Besides, if everyone were with him he could keep his arms around the situation. "You all want to come? Fine with me. But remember, I call the shots. Anyone have a problem with that?"

The guys shook their head. Lauren nodded.

"Markus, you actually made some sense. Just in case we get good information from Lewis, let's plan for about a week on the road. Pack for it. We may come home tomorrow night but we may not. I don't want to be sidetracked by day-to-day needs."

"What time do you want to head out?" Connor asked.

"Meeting's at five. No need to rush. Let's plan on hitting the road at noon."

"What about Ike?" Lauren said.

"See if the Krebs can keep an eye on him."

Lauren started into the house. "I'll give them a ring and then get packing."

Jack thought about the silver Camry. "Guys, give me a call around eleven o'clock. There're a few last minute details I want to address."

Connor and Markus acknowledged and headed out in Connor's little S-10. Jack lifted his cell and dialed Bobbie's number. Her voice mail greeting answered. "Bobbie, this is Jack. I've made some progress today. I'm following a lead to Grand Rapids tomorrow, and if all goes well I might have good news for you." He paused. Missing information regarding the cross and the fact that he was being shadowed topped his thoughts. He needed to know if she was hiding anything from him. A voice mail wasn't the way to ask. "I'll call with an update tomorrow. Keep your phone close—we need to talk."

FOURTEEN -

Travel bags filled the Cherokee's cargo area. Jack tossed in the last soft case and closed the filthy rear hatch. He brushed dried mud from his hands, marveling at how much dirt had accumulated since the rain storm on the night he met with Bobbie. A light brown layer of grime coated the rear of the vehicle, window, license plate and all. Jack wiped the taillights clean. No need to invite a rear end collision.

Lauren came out of the house. Small leather handbag over her shoulder, she made sure the front door was locked and then descended the porch steps. Jack watched her approach. She had on jeans and a sky-blue sleeveless shirt with buttons up the front and a collar. She'd done a good job of staying in shape. He and Lauren were both forty-six and had thus far been blessed with good health. On most days they didn't feel any older than thirty. In Lauren's case she didn't look much older than that either. Not a single strand of gray had imbued her auburn hair, vigor brightened her blue eyes, and the lines of her face remained soft, youthful. She retained a natural grace in her movements, and her effortless charm still held irresistible sway over him.

Jack reflected on their past. They'd started their life together at twenty-one years old, pretty young but legal nonetheless, and had Connor early in the relationship. Their son was now twenty-three. It didn't seem possible. An awful lot of challenges had tested their marriage in the intervening years, the ultimate challenge culminating in a separation that coincided with the Rafferty incident. Jack surmised that if they could pull it together after that mess, they should be able to weather any storm.

Jack walked around the Jeep to the driver's door and Lauren stepped up to the passenger side. "I'm only planning for a week on the road," he said to her. "Looks like you cleaned out the closets and packed it all."

"No, dear," Lauren said. "If I packed it all we'd need three Jeeps."

"Right."

They climbed in and drove off the rural piece of property. They hooked up with 23 South and headed for the 96 interchange. Jack checked the rearview mirror three times within six miles. Lauren noticed.

"Worried about getting a ticket?" she said.

"Oh, you know me, always cautious."

She studied him a few seconds. "Yes, I do know you." She read the speedometer. "You're not speeding, what's the worry?"

Their exit to 96 came up. He didn't take it. "I want to get a sandwich at Lee Road. You want anything?"

"No, I grabbed something at the house before we left." She sat quiet a minute or two. "Why didn't the boys car pool with us?"

He drifted onto the Lee Road exit ramp and slowed the Jeep. "I wanted two vehicles to work with. You never know how our schedules will splinter." The familiar front end of the Camry appeared in the rearview mirror. Jack casually noted its arrival.

Up ahead a pair of side-by-side roundabouts funneled cars in a circular stream to cross streets, service drives, and expressway exits. Jack merged in with the counter-clockwise flow of traffic and followed the lane around to the 96 overpass. Once across the overpass another roundabout spun the Jeep off to the Green Oak Mall entry drive. A Panera restaurant stood at the corner of a retail plaza to the right. Jack pulled into the parking lot.

Waiting in line to place an order, he glanced out through the store windows. The Camry drove by the entrance at a slow speed. Jack ordered his sandwich and a pop to go. He paid the cashier and then checked the time on his cell phone.

Lauren crossed her arms. "What are you doing?"

He shrugged. "I want to clock how long it takes us to drive to Grand Rapids."

"We're not on the road yet."

A cook set a bag containing Jack's order on the counter. Jack picked it up. "Let's go."

They climbed into the Jeep and drove onto the mall drive. After completing the obligatory Michigan Left he headed into the single roundabout.

"No, no," Lauren said, "stay right. The ramp to 23 North is the outside lane."

Jack continued through and shot onto the 96 overpass, missing the on ramp. "Oops. These things always mess me up. I'll turn around at the dual circles up here." He glanced into the rearview mirror. The Camry was with him again. He drove the Jeep down the backside of the overpass and merged into the traffic orbiting the side-by-side roundabouts. As he came around the far circle, the Camry entered the traffic flow at the other end. They passed each other going opposite directions at the center of the figure eight. Jack picked up speed, changed lanes, and exited to the overpass again, this time heading back toward the mall.

Lauren sat with a hand over her eyes. "Take me around that thing again and I'll be sick."

"Sorry, honey." He checked behind the Jeep and smiled.

Connor's S-10 suddenly entered the dual roundabout from Old 23 just ahead of the Camry and slid to a stop crosswise, straddling the lanes. Cars screeched to a halt to avoid colliding with it. Horns started screaming. The Camry was locked in. Jack turned on the radio. "Gotta have my talk shows to keep me awake for the drive."

"Someone's laying on a horn out there," Lauren said.

Jack pretended to listen. "I don't hear it. Hey, we're coming up on this next roundabout. What lane should I be in again?"

"Outside lane." She pointed across the circle. "The ramp is about eleven o'clock from where we are now."

He nodded. "Oh, right." Back in the mirror he saw what looked like Markus standing on the hood of the S-10, waving his arms at the people honking as if to tell them to shut up. Cars were already backed up onto the overpass. Jack coughed into his hand to conceal a laugh and put his eyes back on the road ahead. "Next stop, Grand Rapids."

He accelerated to the 96 interchange and hopped into the westbound lanes. After fifteen minutes his cell rang. It was Connor. "You guys on your way yet?" Jack asked.

"Yeah. Brighton Police helped me get my truck started. It magically turned over right after they arrived. I had to stop Markus from getting into three fights with some of the people we were blocking."

"Did you get to see your friends off before leaving?"

"No problem there. After we cleared the road, those guys in the Camry drove across the overpass but didn't know which way to go and just sat there for ten minutes. They were really pissed." Connor laughed. "Markus and I watched them from the McDonalds near the intersection. They eventually went south on 23. We're grabbing a quick lunch and then we'll hit the road."

Jack smiled over at Lauren. "Your son is leaving for GR now." He spoke into the phone again. "Okay, drive safe and we'll meet at the hotel."

"See you there."

Jack clipped the phone to his belt.

Lauren stared at him. "Why do I get the feeling I just missed something?"

"Beats me. Will you get my sandwich out?"

She opened the Panera bag. "Normally you get mad when I direct you through the roundabouts. You didn't mind today." She handed him a turkey sandwich.

"I'm trying to not let the little things rile me. It must be working." He took the sandwich. "Thanks for making the hotel reservations for tonight."

She took a sip of his soda. "You're almost giddy. Are you always this upbeat at work?"

He bit into the turkey and thought while he chewed. "You know, I think I must be. How else could I have lasted at Neptune so long?"

"It's like I said." She reclined her seat back. "The deeper you get into a project, the more intense it becomes, the happier you are. You feed off it."

He thought about that. It sort of made sense. He had to admit, after getting out of dangerous situations he would always feel a visceral sense of victory. He'd always thought it was just a normal adrenalin rush. He wouldn't begin to characterize himself as an adrenalin freak, but somewhere deep inside he reveled in facing danger. Maybe a part of him did feel immortal as Garity had surmised. That could be trouble, especially with the family along for the ride.

The drive to Grand Rapids was uneventful. Lauren slept half the way. They rolled into the Comfort Inn parking lot just after two-thirty and were able to check in a little early. They carried their overnight bags into the room. Jack pulled out Lewis Coates' address and the map he had marked up last night. He double checked the route from the hotel to Lewis' house. It would take about fifteen minutes to get there. He retrieved his camera case from the Jeep. The case contained a digital camera, an extra battery pack, a USB cable, two memory cards, a battery charger, and a long-range lens attachment. He took out the camera and powered it up to make sure the battery had a full charge. He aimed it at Lauren, who was watching the Weather Channel from one of the two beds in the room. "Smile," he said.

She did, and he snapped a shot. The image popped up on the display. Lauren was a natural. The woman couldn't take a bad picture.

"What do you think you'll find in the Bible?" she said.

He turned off the camera power. "Not sure. I just hope it's still there. If the clue was written on a sheet of paper or if it's in the form of a photograph, it may have been lost after all these years."

"Maybe notes are written right on the pages."

"Could be anything." He tucked the camera into the case. "Whatever it is I'll get plenty of shots of it. I'm guessing Lewis won't want to hand the Bible over to me for study. It would be nice, but I've got to plan otherwise."

Pounding erupted from the hotel room door. It startled Jack. He immediately thought about the Colt in the glove compartment of the Jeep. "Open up, it's us," a voice called. Jack peered through the peep hole in the door. Connor's distorted face stared back through the fishbowl lens. Jack unchained the door and let him in.

"Hey, boys," Lauren said.

"Any problems on the drive?" Jack asked his son.

"Nope, flat-out eighty most of the way here."

"Any traffic?" Jack gave more weight to the question by making eye contact.

"Light," Connor said.

"No one behind us or in front of us," Markus added.

Lauren eyed the three of them.

"All right." Jack clapped his hands to break the moment. "In about an hour I'm off to see Lewis. After my meeting we'll know which direction we're headed. Guys, stay here with Lauren."

"Mr. Sheridan," Markus said. "Shouldn't you take your muscle with you?"

"I'm taking my muscle, but you two are staying here."

"Then why did we even come?" Connor said.

"I tried to make that point yesterday." Jack went to the bed and folded the map.

Connor followed him over. "I think we should go with you. Know what I mean?"

Jack faced him. "I think you should stay with your mother. Know what *I* mean?"

"I don't know what either of you mean," Lauren said. "What's the big deal, Jack? Let them go with you."

"Honey, Lewis is only expecting me. I don't want him to get nervous." Jack gestured to Markus. "Imagine a tall, dark, goofy guy like this showing up unexpectedly at our house."

"Hey," Markus said. "I resemble that remark."

Connor looked at Lauren like he wanted to tell her something.

Jack warned him to keep quiet with a stern eye. "You two coming to Grand Rapids didn't necessarily have anything to do with my meeting. It was more about keeping the team flexible. Remember?"

Markus nodded. "Yeah, Connor, you mentioned something about

agility, too."

"Whose side are you on?" Connor said.

"Hey," Markus stepped back. "This is a Sheridan family issue. I've got no dog in this fight." He back peddled. "No offense, Mrs. Sheridan."

She ignored him. "Jack, I don't need chaperones, especially when one of them is my son."

"Let me handle this meeting the way it was arranged. When I get back we'll come together and plan our next move." Jack's tone suggested the debate had ended.

Lauren huffed. "Fine."

"Whatever," Connor said.

Markus shrugged. "I still want to go."

Jack plopped onto one of the beds. "No." He grabbed the TV remote and clicked through fifty channels of nothing good. The next hour played out in relative silence but the "issue" simmered close to the surface. At four-thirty he stood, grabbed the camera case and the Jeep keys, made sure he had his wallet in pocket, and headed for the door. "I'll call when I'm done with Lewis Coates." He left them frowning in the room.

- FIFTEEN -

It took Jack twelve minutes to drive to the Lewis Coates address.

The house was in a historic Grand Rapids neighborhood named Ottawa Hills. To Jack 'historic' translated into 'old.' The mature trees that lined the streets and populated the yards confirmed that fact. Many of the streets had Native American names like Iroquois and Seminole. Most of the houses had been there decades; but unlike more recently built subdivisions, a wide range of architectural styles had been employed throughout the years. The mix of brick, stone, cedar, and vinyl siding on colonial, ranch, contemporary, and farmhouse models gave the neighborhood a rich American heritage feel.

Coates lived on Alexander Street in a modern-looking home. A complex roof line with a steep pitch capped a story-and-a-half house with a fieldstone exterior. It seemed like the stonework had been redone recently. Jack parked beside the curb in the street instead of pulling into the concrete drive. It was 4:45. Nobody appeared to be home. He waited in the Jeep.

Within five minutes a gray Ford Taurus turned into the driveway. Jack waved to the driver and then climbed out of the Jeep. He shouldered the camera case and walked up to the house. A tall man with dark hair and a slight build got out of the Taurus and emerged from the garage to greet him. "Jack Sheridan?"

Jack extended his hand. "Yes, and you must be Lewis Coates."

They shook. Coates smiled and the lines around his blue eyes crinkled. "So Western Michigan University thinks my family has some historical relevance?"

"Yes, the Coates family has been in the area since the formation of Allegan County. Your ancestors can give us an intimate perspective on Michigan history, and like I mentioned on the phone, a family Bible is a great resource to reveal that perspective." Jack patted the top of the camera case. "I'd like to get some pictures of the Bible and any historical notations therein."

"That'll be fine," Coates said. "Let's take a look." He motioned Jack to follow. "I don't believe I've actually read the thing myself."

They entered the house. Coates led Jack to a study with deep burgundy walls, a floor-to-ceiling bookshelf, and crown molding trim. A divided light window faced the street. Jack could barely see his Jeep behind a maple tree in the front yard. A second window on the adjacent wall provided a view of the garage where Coates had parked and a six-foot hedgerow defining the neighbor's property line.

Lewis walked to a cherry wood office desk in the corner. "Are you one of the guys who visited my dad yesterday?"

Jack turned from the front window. "Your dad?"

"Yes, he called me to set up this meeting when some gentlemen from the university came by and asked him about the Bible." Coates opened a desk drawer and lifted out a book. "I assume you're all members of the same research team."

Jack nodded. A flare of anxiety radiated through his chest.

"You must have a lot of people collecting information for this project."

"There's a few of us out in the field." Apparently a few more than he thought.

Coates handed him the Bible.

Jack took it. The tome was smaller than he'd imagined, about five inches wide by seven inches tall, but the leather binding was just as worn and faded as one might expect a nearly two-century-old book to be. His excitement at holding the Bible was tempered by apprehension. Someone had prompted Samuel Coates to set up a five o'clock meeting for them with his son Lewis. That explained the ease in which his conversation with Lewis drifted toward a face-to-face get together. The groundwork had already been laid. Jack checked the time on his cell phone. It was 4:54. Other visitors were due to show up at any moment. He didn't care to meet them.

"Mr. Coates, I just realized that I have another appointment across town in a half hour. Can I take the Bible with me for a couple of days?"

Lewis thought it over. "Um, you mentioned photographing it earlier."

"Yes, but I didn't realize I had a time constraint then." Jack began thumbing through the pages of the Bible, working toward the Revelations chapter. "I'd hate to rush through my inspection and miss something important."

Movement in the street drew Lewis' attention to the front window. A black 300C pulled into the driveway. "Are you expecting anyone to drop by and give you a hand, Mr. Sheridan?"

Jack found Revelations. He stopped flipping with his thumb and began turning individual pages. "Can't say that I am." He peered through the window. "Might be an insurance salesman or a Jehovah Witness."

"I've never seen a Jehovah Witness drive a 300C." Coates turned from the window. "I'll go see who it is. Be right back." He left the room.

Jack kept turning pages. Chapter twelve, thirteen, the thin paper crinkled under his fingers. Chapter sixteen, seventeen, almost...there. Revelations 21:7. He that overcometh shall inherit all things. Handwriting ran up the sides and across the top margins.

Jack glanced out the window. A big, imposing guy wearing a black sports jacket stepped out of the 300C. He had gelled black hair, a neck like a linebacker, and a jaw like a slab of granite. A second man exited the passenger side. This one was a bit shorter and leaner than his partner, had a crop of wavy brown hair on his head, and sneered like he wasn't happy to be making this visit. Jack really didn't want to meet these guys.

He read the writing up the left side margin. *A hundred yards south of the Beach, To the north and touching the River.* This had to be it.

The guys from the 300C were walking up to the house. Time was running out.

The camera! He forgot about the camera. Jack laid the Bible open on the desk and removed the case from his shoulder. The two men walked past the front window. Damn! The zipper on the camera case jammed. He yanked it free and pulled the camera out. Switching the power on, he stepped back and lined up the Bible in the lens. He clicked the button. Nothing. A message flashed on the screen. *Card Full.*

The doorbell rang. Coates was there to answer it right away. Jack didn't have time to swap the memory card and take another picture. He had to get out of there. He dumped the extra battery pack, charger, and lens attachment onto the desk and tucked the Bible inside the case. The camera barely fit along side of it. He zipped the cover closed and shouldered the case.

Lewis' voice carried down the hallway. "One of your research partners is looking at the Bible right now in the study."

"Really," another voice said. "What's his name?"

"Jack Sheridan," Coates answered.

Not good! Jack spun to the closest window and tried to open it. Locked. He unlatched the lever and lifted the lower pane. A scuffle broke out in the hallway. The dull thud of dead weight falling on a hardwood floor rolled into the study. Jack crouched and squeezed through the small window frame.

A voice thundered from the hallway again. "Nate, go around front!"

Jack tumbled through the window and free-fell to the driveway. He cradled the case like a football and hit hard on his left side. His palm scraped against rough concrete as he scrambled to his feet. The Jeep waited at the curb. He tucked the case under his arm and broke into a run. He'd cleared the corner of the house when a blur came at him fast from the right. Something hit him solid against his midsection and knocked him off his feet. The guy with the wavy brown hair had tackled him. They crashed down in front of the 300C. Pain shot through Jack's hip. The guy rose to one knee and closed his hand into a fist. Jack struck first. He clapped the guy's ear with an open hand and slammed his head into the car's front end, cracking the grill.

Jack kicked his assailant over with a boot heel and struggled to his feet. He had one second to catch his breath. The big guy in the black sports coat had followed him through the window and was on him. The guy threw a fist like a cinder block. Jack pulled back. A massive set of knuckles nicked his chin. The linebacker threw another punch. Jack ducked under the swing and landed a sharp right into the guy's abdomen. He was pretty solid but groaned on impact and hunched over a bit. Jack stood straight, snapping his head into the man's granite jaw. The guy fell back a step and caressed the throb in his chin.

Jack clutched the camera case and looked toward the Jeep. The guy with wavy hair got up and blocked his escape route.

The linebacker let loose a chuckle. "I'll hand it to you, Sheridan, you're not a disappointment."

Jack checked behind him for another way out but found the hedgerow. He backed up to a section where the branches appeared thin. "Glad I'm meeting your expectations. Who the hell are you and what do you want?"

"Call me Ben." Higgs shook off the head butt and extended a hand. "Gimme the case."

"Get your own."

"I saw the crap on the desk. I know you stuffed the Bible in the case. Hand it over."

Jack sidestepped closer to the thin branches. "Don't suppose we can cut a deal."

Higgs snapped his fingers at his partner. "Nate, stay there in case he makes a break." He focused on Jack again. "Here's the deal. You give me the case and we only break your legs."

"What if I don't give you the case?"

Higgs stepped forward. "That's not an option."

Jack sucked the case in close to his body, rolled left, and dove into the hedgerow. The branches resisted him, tried to throw him back. A cut split open on his cheek. His jeans ripped across the thigh. Fingers were trying to grasp the back of his shirt. He shouted and powered ahead with a massive heave, breaking through, stumbling forward. An Adirondack chair in the yard he'd just entered cracked him across the shin. Gravity pulled him down. Inertia tumbled him forward. He tucked his head and rolled on his shoulder. In three strides he was back on his feet. And then he heard the barking.

A black mastiff came at him from the edge of the lot thirty yards away. The dog had to be a hundred and eighty pounds. Jack picked up his pace and made for the six-foot cedar fence straight ahead. A quick glance behind. The two thugs were tearing through the hedgerow. The dog must not have seen them yet, or it didn't care about them yet. Jack heard its massive paws scraping through the turf, a low growl, a deep bark. He leapt into the air and grabbed hold of a pair of spires atop the fence. He lifted himself with his arms and kicked his legs up. The dog went airborne and slammed against the fence, shaking the boards and loosening Jack's grip. He managed to hold on, and then noticed the thugs had gotten through the hedgerow. The dog suddenly noticed too. Jack dropped down the other side of the fence. The mastiff went ballistic toward the new intruders.

Jack found himself in another yard, this one with a large in-ground pool, a thick cluster of old maple trees, and a twenty-foot shed with doors wide open along the far edge of the property. Behind the cedar fence the two thugs were shouting at each other, and the dog. Jack had bought himself some time. He ran across the yard, around the pool, and into the open shed.

He figured he only had a few minutes before his pursuers would evade the dog and close in on him. He couldn't keep running through Ottawa Hills. They'd catch up to him sooner or later. Even if he got away today, they'd keep breathing down his neck to get the Bible. He had to give them what they wanted.

He pulled the case off his shoulder. A worktable cluttered with tools and small engine parts ran along the wall. He swiped a section clear with his forearm and set the case down. The zipper stuck again but he just wrenched hard and ripped the lid at the seam. He pulled out the camera and worked the memory card cover open. The damn card was so small he could barely work his fingers to pull it out. Extra cards were lying on the bottom of the case. He inserted one into the camera and set the Bible open on the worktable.

The buzz of a line trimmer surged along the back side of the shed. Someone was coming around. Jack centered the Bible in the viewfinder and clicked a picture. He took two more shots and then stuffed the camera and the Bible back into the case.

"Hey, what the hell are you doing in there?" A gray-haired guy with a sweaty face stood in the doorway. Cut blades of grass speckled his jeans and T-shirt, and he held an idling two-cycle line trimmer in his hand.

Jack put the case back on his shoulder. "I'm not a thief. I just needed some shelter."

The homeowner cocked his head like he didn't get it. "Get out or I'm calling the cops."

Jack saw Big Ben striding up the driveway over the guy's shoulder. "Mister, you've got more trouble than me coming this way."

The homeowner turned around. "Now who are you?"

Higgs ignored him and focused on Jack.

Cornered. The shed walls seemed to close in. Jack's breathing quickened. Which way out?

Higgs was spitting distance away.

Jack leapt forward and seized the idling line trimmer from the homeowner.

"Hey!" the man snarled.

Jack pushed him aside and wielded the machine like a broadsword.

Higgs laughed. "Desperation is an embarrassing thing, isn't it, Sheridan?"

Jack hit the throttle trigger and thrust the machine forward. The spinning trim line cut through the air with a wicked hiss. Higgs stopped laughing when the nylon buzz saw nearly severed his nose from his face. He instinctively raised his arm in defense. The trimmer shredded the sleeve of his sports coat. "Son of a bitch!"

A dark blur clouded Jack's peripheral vision. He stayed on the trigger and swung the trimmer in an arc. Nate Kisko was advancing, but the hissing line tickled the fibers of his shirt straight across his chest and stopped him cold. He stumbled back with arms spread and tripped over a deck chair behind him.

Higgs attempted a rush. Jack pivoted about and held him at bay with the two-cycle weapon. The homeowner freaked and ran into his house. Jack withdrew, stepping back toward the pool. Kisko got to his feet.

Higgs shook his head. "Fun's over." He reached under his jacket and drew a 9mm pistol. "Hand over the Bible."

Kisko laughed. "Hey, Captain America, not so smart bringing a weed whacker to a gunfight."

Jack retreated another step, getting closer to the edge of the pool. "All right, close your eyes and count to ten, and I'll leave the Bible at your feet."

Higgs advanced. "No damned deals. You're lucky I don't shoot you dead and take it off your body. Now hand it over, or you'll walk with a limp the rest of your life."

Jack was somewhat surprised that Ben hadn't pulled the trigger yet. Perhaps he wasn't the murdering type. That didn't seem like the right answer, but Jack wasn't about to ask. He took the line trimmer in one hand and slid the Bible out of the case with the other. "You want this?"

Higgs read his thoughts. "Don't do it, Sheridan."

Jack struggled to wield the trimmer single handed. "Here you go." He tossed the Bible into the pool.

Higgs cursed. "Nate, get it! Quick!"

Kisko hesitated. "Sheridan, you bastard." He jumped into the pool after the sinking tome.

Higgs raised the 9mm. He didn't seem too concerned with taking a non-lethal shot anymore. Jack hurled the line trimmer at him, directing the engine's hot muffler to hit his face. Higgs shouted and deflected it with his free hand.

Jack spun around and leapt over a black iron fence that surrounded the pool. He darted into the cluster of old maples across the rear edge of the property line. The crack of pistol fire echoed in the leafy canopy. A chunk of bark splintered off a tree trunk near his face. The camera case slapped against his body as he dashed into the back yard of the adjacent house. He poured on the speed. His hip ached, his shin ached, blood trickled down his cheek. He crossed into the front yard and ended up in a street. He spun around to get his bearings. It was Alexander Street. His dirty Jeep sat parked at the curb a hundred yards west. He made a break for it.

Forty yards into his sprint, a car turned onto the road in front of him from a perpendicular side street named Cadillac Drive. Jack stopped dead and nearly lost his balance. It was the silver Camry. The car parked in the middle of the road and the doors opened. Two guys climbed out. One of them held a pistol. Jack recognized him from that night on 96.

They came around the front of the car and advanced toward their mark. "Remember," the unarmed guy said, "kneecaps only." The other one smirked.

Jack walked backward, keeping an eye on them. He searched for an escape route.

And then he spotted the truck.

Connor's S-10 pickup came rolling up Alexander Street from the west, behind the Camry. It slowed when it neared Jack's Jeep, snaked left and right in indecision, then barreled full on ahead. The little pickup devoured forty yards of road in a heartbeat and didn't look to be slowing. Its revving engine turned the guys from the Camry around. They scattered in panic. The S-10 blasted into the Camry's open passenger door, ripping it off its hinges. The deep crash of heavy things hitting each other pulsed down the street. Connor's front quarter panel grazed the armed guy and spun him around. He lost his grip on the pistol and fell backward onto the road.

The car door came skidding across the blacktop, spinning like a top. Jack jumped to the curb to dodge it. Connor locked up the truck's brakes and slid sideways to a stop ten feet from his father. He leaned out the window. "Get in the back!"

Jack leapt into the bed of the S-10, and Connor fishtailed back down the road toward the Jeep. The Camry guys picked themselves up off the ground. One seemed to be looking for something. Probably the gun. Markus slid open the rear window of the cab. "Did you see that, Mr. Sheridan? We smashed that door to flinders!" He giggled like a kid.

"Markus," Connor said, "You need help." He stopped the S-10 beside the Jeep.

Jack jumped out of the truck bed and pointed at Connor through the passenger window. "I told you to stay at the hotel."

"You're welcome," Connor replied.

"Hey, those guys are coming this way," Markus said.

Jack climbed in the Jeep and started the engine. "Get back to the hotel and make sure your mother is safe."

Connor nodded and gunned the accelerator. The S-10 squealed away amid burnt rubber smell and blue smoke. Jack backed the Jeep into the road and scrolled the passenger window down. The Camry guys had scurried back inside their battered sedan and had turned the car around. They were rolling now, bearing down on the Jeep's broadside. Jack threw open the glove compartment and pulled out the Colt. He chambered a round and aimed at the Camry's windshield just right of center. An arm holding a pistol extended from the car's doorless passenger side. Jack fired. The Colt thundered and ejected a shell into the Jeep's rear seat. A hole burst in the Camry's windshield. Cobweb cracks spread across the glass. The shot hit just shy of the driver's head, right where Jack had aimed. The driver flinched and the car veered left. Jack aimed again, this time at the exposed front tire. He sent two slugs into the rim and rubber. The Camry rode up on the curb behind the Jeep and clipped the trunk of an oak tree.

Jack slapped the gear shift into drive, spun the steering wheel, and gunned the engine. He raced down Alexander Street as the Camry rolled to a stop on the easement. He turned onto the main drag and kept the camera case close at his side. A drop of blood trickled down his cheek. He took a deep breath.

Bobbie's treasure hunt had just taken a deadly turn.

Part II

BLACKENED BONES

Jack made a beeline for the hotel. That first mile he watched the road behind him more than the road ahead. He'd roiled some people back there and figured they weren't quite ready to let it go. It was a good bet the Camry wouldn't show up in the rearview mirror. More likely the black 300C would slide out of Alexander Street and give chase. Jack drove with white knuckles until he melted into the city side streets. No one followed him out of Ottawa Hills. Apparently Ben thought it more important to retrieve the Bible and salvage the clue than to race after that troublesome Sheridan guy. That suited Jack just fine.

When he'd gotten his breathing under control, he swiped the cell phone off his belt and speed-dialed Lauren's number. After one ring he got anxious. Two rings and he cursed at the dashboard. Three—

"Hello, dear."

"Lauren?"

"Yes, why do you sound surprised? You dialed my number, didn't you?"

"Yeah, but—"

"How did it go with Lewis?"

Jack rolled through a stop sign. "Uh, kind of intense. I'll tell you about it when I get back. Should be about ten minutes."

"Ten minutes? That was quick."

"Well, you know I don't like to waste time."

"Okay…" She seemed distracted. "I'll see you back in the room. Love you." She disconnected.

Jack stared at the phone a second. Something in her voice sounded odd. Maybe it was nothing. Maybe the confrontation with Ben and his boys had kicked his instincts into overdrive and he was looking for trouble around every corner. *Get a grip, Jack, she's fine.*

He considered the turn of events. It was a good bet that home-owner or one of his Ottawa Hills neighbors had called the police. Right now the authorities might be on the lookout for a filthy Jeep Cherokee. Fortunately, the dust from Jack's dirt road had covered the license plate. The best the police could have is a general description of the vehicle.

He was near 28th Street. A car wash came up in the next block. After a good cleaning the Jeep would look completely different. He turned sharp into the entry. Only two cars were ahead of him. He paid the attendant for a full wash and waited his turn. Once the water jets hit the windshield, he removed the camera from the case and checked out his shots of the clue inside the Bible. The first image was too bleary to read. The second was better. The third was the charm. It was crisp and captured all of the handwriting. He read it completely through for the first time, but his mind was racing too fast to focus clearly. He leaned back, and closed his eyes.

A knock on the window startled him. The kid at the end of the wash motioned him to drive forward. Jack put the Jeep in drive and rolled out of the building. Two teens wiped water from the side windows as he drove off the premises. Back on 28th Street he spotted the Comfort Inn. Connor's S-10 was parked in the lot. Jack pulled up alongside it and his cell rang. It was Connor.

"Dad, she's not here. Mom's not in the room."

"What? I just talked to her on the phone." Jack grabbed the case and jumped from the Jeep. He ran into the hotel. The door to the room was open. The guys were inside. He checked the room's four corners and inside the bathroom for his wife. She wasn't there.

"I don't get it," Markus said. "She didn't have a car. Where could she have gone?"

Connor paced to the window. "Dad, you think those guys knew you checked in here?"

"No one knew." Jack called Lauren's cell again. Her ring tone sounded in the hotel hallway. He set the case on a bed and ran out of the room. The boys followed. Lauren was there, walking toward them with a brown bag in her hand. They all stared at her.

"Why are you looking at me like that?"

"What did you do, go shopping?" Jack asked.

She walked by him and into the room. "No, I was on the job."

"On the job?" Jack followed her into the room. "Explain, please."

Connor closed the door and hooked up the chain. Markus pulled the curtains shut.

Lauren noticed they were a little wired. "Come on, guys, crime in Grand Rapids isn't that bad." She sat on a bed, picked up the TV remote, and turned on the television.

Jack stood at the foot of the bed, staring at her. "On the job?"

She clicked through some channels. "Hey, on the phone you said your meeting with Coates was intense." She noticed the cut on his cheek and the rip in his pants. "Why don't you explain that one first?"

Jack stood silent, trying to decide the best way to tell her about the incident.

Lauren settled on a local news channel displaying a *Breaking News* banner.

"I met with Lewis," Jack said. "He showed me the Bible. I found what I believe is the clue written in the margins of Revelations, chapter twenty-one. And then these other guys showed up looking for the same thing."

A helicopter shot of a residential street appeared on the television. The crawl across the bottom of the screen read, *Suburban violence in Ottawa Hills.* Lauren fixated on the picture. The image of a wrecked silver Camry replaced the view from the helicopter. "Jack, tell me this isn't your mess."

"It isn't mine," he protested. "It's theirs!"

"Theirs? Who are they? Tell me what happened."

"These two guys were about to work over Mr. Sheridan in the street," Markus said. "Connor and I flew over there in the pickup—"

Jack threw up a hand to stop him from talking.

Lauren stood. "You got Connor and Markus involved in this?"

Jack poked an indignant finger into his chest. "Hey, I'm the one who wanted the guys to stay here. Remember? They shouldn't have even been out there."

"Lucky for you we were," Connor said.

Lauren absorbed his comment and looked Jack in the eye. "Were two guys really going to work you over?"

"No, they were going to shoot me in the kneecaps."

"Why?"

"I don't know. I'd already given them the Bible by then."

"You gave up the Bible?" Markus said.

"I was staring down a 9mm, of course I gave up the Bible."

"Then we've lost the clue," Connor said. "Game over."

Jack picked up the case from the foot of the bed. "We have the clue. I snapped a picture of the page it was on."

Lauren gestured to the television. "If you snapped a picture of the clue and gave them the Bible, how did the rest of this happen?"

"I didn't give them the Bible right away. I thought I could make off with it before the trouble started. I was apparently wrong about that."

"But you had the camera," she said. "Why did you think you had to take the Bible too?"

"Honey, it all happened kind of fast. Don't be a Monday morning quarterback."

"Let's see the clue," Connor said. "If they have it too, we need to get moving."

"Yeah," Markus added, "power up the camera."

Jack and Lauren made eye contact. He knew what she was thinking. The treasure hunt had crossed a line. It wasn't just a benign search for a sack of gold anymore. It had gotten serious. If they kept going, odds were excellent that they'd cross paths with those men from Ottawa Hills again, and next time someone might get hurt, maybe even killed. Jack didn't fear so much for his own hide. His concern was for Lauren and Connor. If events kept escalating, his ability to protect them would suffer. "Guys, we need to think about this," he said. "This has gotten more dangerous than I ever thought it would." He glanced at Lauren. "I think it might be a good idea to call it a day."

Connor and Markus stared at him dumbfounded. Jack saw resistance welling up inside them.

"Are you crazy?" Connor said. "We're talking about twenty million dollars. One little bump in the road, and you want to throw in the towel?"

"This wasn't a bump. These guys had guns, and they weren't afraid to use them."

"Forewarned is forearmed," Connor countered.

Markus slapped his shoulder. "Hey, that sounded kind of gutsy for you."

"Too gutsy," Lauren said.

"Mom, we know these guys are out there now. We can work around them."

"Or roll over them," Markus said. "Damn near did that today."

Jack considered them. "Do you guys really know what you're saying? This isn't a game anymore." He waited for Lauren to jump in and tell everyone to pack up and go home. She didn't.

"Dad, Markus and I were both out there when Rafferty went psycho. If we made it though that, then we'll skate through this."

Jack snapped to attention. "I almost lost you because of Rafferty. I'm not going through something like that again."

"I'm not a kid anymore," Connor said. "I've been legal to buy alcohol or carry a rifle in the army for a long time now. Don't take this the wrong way, but your license to run my life expired five years ago."

"I will always try to protect my son, and if protecting you means stopping this hunt, then that's what's going to happen."

Connor grumbled. "You may stop hunting for these coins, but I'm not going to."

"Me neither," Markus said.

"And if we're still looking," Connor continued, "you might as well stick with us. It'll be a little easier to protect us that way, don't you think?"

Markus threw up his hands. "Why are we even talking about this? Quitters never win."

Jack turned to Lauren. "What do you think?"

She frowned. "I hate to admit it but Connor's right. He is an adult."

"Then do we continue on, together?"

She paused for what seemed a minute. "When you and Connor were out there with Rafferty I was afraid I was going to lose you both, but I always felt a glimmer of hope. I've come to realize that hope was my faith in you, that you would know what to do to get home safe, and you did it. Now with this treasure hunt I feel the same way. If anyone can lead us to the coins and back again it's you. In these kinds of situations you seem to know what you're doing, I can't argue that. So whatever you think we should do I'm with you."

If Jack was the crying type he'd have a tear in his eye. Instead he smiled and gave his wife a kiss. "Let's make this official," he said to the group. "We're going to vote on it. All in favor of continuing the treasure hunt show your hand."

The decision was unanimous. Even Lauren raised her hand, after a bit of hesitation.

Markus howled and clapped. "Now get that camera out, Mr. Sheridan."

"Wait a minute," Jack said. "Lauren, you never explained where you were or what you have in that bag."

"Oh." She turned around and lifted the brown paper bag. "I got to thinking, Harlan Coates had two sons and he wanted them to work together to find their inheritance, right?"

"Yes."

"Well, if he gave just one son all the clues, they wouldn't have to work together. So I thought, what if there were two Bibles, one each for David and Daniel? We found the one David had. I looked into the possibility of a second Bible from Daniel's line."

Jack listened very closely. "How did you do that?"

"I looked up your historian friend Eugene Elliot's phone number and gave him a call. He got me the address for the Cabban lady in Allendale. Her number was listed and I called. She's such a nice woman. She invited me over to have a look at the Bible her father gave her. I took a cab to her house. Guess what?"

"Her Bible had a clue written in the margins of Revelations chapter twenty-one," Jack said.

She feigned disappointment. "How did you know?"

Jack switched on the lamp between the beds. "Let's have a look."

SEVENTEEN

Lauren removed the second Coates Bible from the paper bag. The general appearance was identical to the one Jack had seen at Lewis' house. Worn and faded leather binding. Paper yellowed by time. She handed it to him. He opened it to Revelations.

A television reporter droned in standard newsroom cadence in the background. Jack paid no mind as he flipped through the pages. He raised his head when the guy on TV said something about Lewis Coates. Markus and Connor took note as well.

"One of the intruders apparently struck Lewis Coates on the head," the reporter said, "rendering him unconscious. Coates was taken to Grand Rapids General, where his condition is listed as serious but stable. He remains unconscious and has been unable to speak to police about the incidents surrounding the break-in."

Lauren eyed Jack.

"Them again," he said.

"How bad is Coates hurt?" she asked.

"I don't know. He was walking those guys back to the room I was in when they jumped him. That's when I hopped through a window."

"Won't the police think you assaulted Lewis?"

"Right now they don't even know I was there. I don't like saying this, but Lewis being incapacitated has bought me some time. He can't tell the police about my visit. Mud was covering the Jeep's license plate, so any witnesses to the events in the street couldn't get my number. I wasn't officially there."

"They'll eventually find out you were. Shouldn't you make a statement to the police explaining what happened?"

"In a perfect world, yes, but I doubt the police have any idea who committed the assault. If I go in and tell them I was there, I become the prime suspect and they'll hold me until Coates can clear me. Even then, they might think I was working with those other guys. I'm not voluntarily walking into a cell."

"Are you sure we should go forward with this treasure hunt?"

Jack took her hand. "This will all shake out okay. If I have to I'll get Garity to throw his weight around on my behalf. He's an SOB but we do have history together."

"What about those men you ran into? How certain are you that we can avoid another confrontation with them?"

"Look, if we do this right we'll find the coins before they even get close. We should be cashing in while they're still digging holes in the ground somewhere."

She nodded.

"Okay." Jack found Revelations 21:7. "There's handwriting in the margins just like the Bible Lewis had." He read up the side and across the top of the pages. "The words aren't the same. Honey, I think you're right. Harlan Coates gave each son a different clue."

Connor grabbed the camera from the case. "I'll get my laptop so we can look at the picture of David's Bible on a larger screen." He ran out of the room.

Jack and Lauren sat on one of the beds with the Bible between them. He smoothed the hairs of his mustache. "Daniel's clue reads: Revelation awaits, Above the ground, For in the wildcat's bones, The answer is found, Engraved and sealed, Read north to south, Selah."

Markus cocked his head. "Selah?"

"It's a Hebrew word used in the Bible at the end of some Psalms," Lauren said. "Its meaning isn't clear. Some think it means to stop and listen. Some think it's interchangeable with amen." She turned to Jack. "When I read the clue at Cabban's house, it conjured up some pretty bizarre images. What's your take?"

He thought a second. "Did you tell Ms. Cabban why you were interested in her Bible?"

Lauren angled the Book so she could read it. "Engraving on an animal's bones up in a tree somewhere. That's what came to me. Not very helpful."

"You didn't tell her about the coins, did you?" Jack smirked. "Whatever happened to sharing the loot with the family of Harlan Coates?"

She frowned. "No point in getting her all excited about treasure until we find it."

Markus flopped on the opposite bed. "Share the coins with the Coates family? Whose stupid idea is that?"

Lauren gave him a cross look.

He shrunk back. "It would be sort of an honorable thing to do."

"Engraving," Jack said. "It's the one clear thing I see. Engraving arranged in some particular orientation reveals the location of the coins. I was hoping the Bible clue would put an X on the map, but it's starting to look like just another link in the chain."

"Above the ground," Markus said. "At least we won't have to dig."

Lauren lifted her gaze from the Bible. "What species of cat are wildcats?"

"The wild kind," Markus said.

"No, you bonehead." Jack kicked the bed Markus was lying on. "Wildcat is a vernacular term for certain types of cat like a lynx or an ocelot or something."

"An oce-what?"

"Why would Coates engrave the location of the coins on the bones of some dead cat?" Lauren made a face. "Disgusting."

Connor stormed back into the room. "What's disgusting?" He had his laptop booting up already. As the computer came to life he plugged the camera's USB cable into an open port on the laptop's back side. He set both the camera and computer on the pressed wood table near the television cabinet.

Markus came over. "Come on, pull it up. Pick up the pace, Sheridan."

Connor drilled through to the camera and found the pictures of the Bible on the memory card. Jack told him to open the third image. He did and read aloud.

"A hundred yards south of the Beach, To the north and touching the River, That which you seek, In Singapore lie, Cherry and Cedar flank the great find."

"Singapore?" Jack walked to the computer.

Connor narrowed his eyes at the screen. "This could be a problem. I don't do Southeast Asia."

"Go ahead and back out," Markus said. "I'll take your cut."

Connor hung his head. "Seventeen-hour plane ride, vaccination shots, customs officials, bird flu, caning—"

"Not that Singapore," Jack said. "Didn't you guys listen when I told you about the coins?" He read the clue from David's Bible to himself. Bursts of recognition flashed like heat lightening in his mind. "I've seen a lot of these words grouped together before. I think I know what Coates is saying."

He tore into his overnight bag. Steven's notebook sat on top of the clothes packed inside. He opened it up and flipped through the pages until finding the sketch of the village layout that matched the street map Eugene Elliot had shown him. Connor, Markus, and Lauren gathered around.

"Remember the little milling town named Singapore from the

story of the coins?" Jack said. "Coates lived there. This sketch is a map of that town." He ran his finger along the street names. "See right there? Cedar Street. It runs north and south. And Cherry Street parallel here."

"Look," Connor said, "the Kalamazoo River south of town. All right, no passport required."

Markus shrugged. "How can you be a hundred yards south of the beach but touching the river to the north?"

"Wait." Lauren tapped the notebook page. "There's also a River Street that intersects Cedar and Cherry. Coates may have meant the street and not the actual river."

"Check out the northern-most street." Jack traced a road across the top of the map with his finger. "Beach Street. If we measure off a hundred yards south...we have..." He slid his hand to the lower half of the page. "This block of lots right here. Cherry and Cedar flank the sides, River Street touches the lower boundary, and a hundred yards south of Beach appears to define the upper boundary of the block. Coates may have buried the coins in his own back yard."

"What about the second clue," Lauren said. "Revelation above ground."

"I haven't figured that one out yet." Jack studied the map a moment longer. "I'm certain the first clue is directing us to this block in Singapore. The second clue will pinpoint a particular location within the block, but the first clue gives us our heading."

"To Singapore?" Lauren said. "Does it even exist anymore?"

Jack opened his cell phone. "Let's find out." He dialed Eugene Elliot's number.

"Hello, Jack, what can I do for you this time?"

"I apologize, Eugene, but I need one more thing today."

"Between you and your wife's requests I'm getting exhausted."

"This one's worth it. We're getting close."

"I hope so. I lost a window unit on the porch today; burned out because of all the heat and humidity lately. I'm down one air conditioner, and I already feel inside ambient rising."

"Help's on the way but I need some information on Singapore."

"What is it you need?"

"It's exact location."

The historian broke out laughing.

"I didn't mean that to be funny, Eugene."

"I know, but it is."

"Why?"

"Singapore, or what's left of it, is located one and a quarter miles upriver from present day Saugatuck, on the north bank of the Kalamazoo River."

Jack thought about the description. "I'm not seeing the joke."

"You will when you go there."

"Is the land in use as a cemetery or something?"

"No, but you're close." Eugene chuckled. "By the late 1800s the mill owners and lumberjacks had managed to clear cut the land surrounding Singapore. Without the protection of the trees, the westerly winds off Lake Michigan began to blow the coastal sand dunes inland. At the same time, the loss of milling jobs led to an exodus of residents. Singapore became little more than a ghost town. Not long after the turn of the century, the remains of the village were buried beneath the shifting dunes." Eugene paused. "Singapore didn't die, it committed suicide."

Jack exhaled and sat on the desk. "This could be a problem."

"Do you think the coins are hidden in Singapore?"

"Possibly. Thanks for the help, Eugene. I should be able to give you a break for a while."

"Your calls for help really aren't a problem. Keep keeping me informed. I'm on pins and needles over here."

"Will do. Take care now." Jack disconnected. "There may be some digging involved after all."

"How much?" Markus asked.

"A lot." Jack glanced about the room. They were all staring at him. "I think we should leave tonight, get out of Grand Rapids and into Saugatuck. The remains of Singapore are near there. We'll formulate a plan on how to reach the city block once we're at the site."

"What about the second clue?" Lauren said. "We haven't deciphered it yet."

"We can hash it out on the way. I want to put some miles between us and Ottawa Hills."

Lauren agreed and went about repacking their things and buttoning up their bags.

Jack put a hand on Connor's shoulder. "We'll need a place to stay in Saugatuck. Get on line and find a B and B that we can fill up. I don't want any neighbors while we're there."

Connor nodded.

Jack continued. "Markus, when you guys are on the road watch for a tail. We don't know if Lewis' neighbors reported the S-10 to the police, or if those yahoos you ran off the road took special note of the car that ripped their door off."

Markus snickered. "Flinders, baby."

"I don't care if it's a police car or a 300C, if you suspect you're being followed, call me right away. Got it?"

"Got it."

Jack lifted the overnight bags. "I'm throwing these in the Jeep." He strode into the hotel hall. In the lobby he flicked open his cell and called Bobbie's number.

She answered this time. "Hey, do you have some good news for me?"

He walked through the lobby doors and stood beneath the main entry overhang. The sun was still well above the horizon at six-thirty on the eve of July. "I have a mixed report, but before I get into it you need to come clean with me right now."

"You sound angry. What happened?"

"I damn near got shot today."

"Shot!"

"Other people are looking for the coins, and they don't like competition. Did you know about them?"

She hesitated. "I—I knew someone else was interested in the coins but I didn't know they were out there looking."

"Why didn't you tell me?"

"I didn't think it mattered."

"Damn it, Bobbie, you can't hold anything back. These people are serious trouble."

"All I know is that they're interested in Steven's research. They…visited me on one occasion to ask for some of his notes. I don't know how they heard about what he was doing, but they definitely wanted me to help them with their research."

"Did one of them look like an Italian linebacker for the Detroit Lions?"

"I'm not sure. It was a short meeting, the lighting was bad. One of them could have matched that description."

Jack closed his eyes and craned his neck back. "Did you give them anything?"

"No. As a matter of fact it was their interest in Steven's notes that convinced me the coins might actually be real. That's when I decided to call you."

"Anything else?"

"Well, this may not be related, but someone broke into the lighthouse last winter. They rifled through some of Steven's papers. I don't know everything he had in his files, so I'm not certain if anything was taken."

Jack thought a moment. "I uncovered some key information that was missing from the notebook. Maybe the people who broke in took it from Steven's papers. That would explain how they got so far ahead in the search."

"I'm sorry I didn't tell you these things up front. I didn't connect the dots. Or maybe I was afraid to connect the dots."

Jack walked to the Jeep in the parking lot. "This information might have affected my decision to join your treasure hunt."

She stayed silent a long while. "I know. I needed someone's help. I needed you."

He didn't reply.

"It sounds like this has gotten too dangerous. Please stop looking. I don't want you to get hurt."

He threw the bags down behind the Jeep. "It's not me who's going to get hurt. I'm in it, damn it, and I'm going to win it."

"Jack, you don't know how much I appreciate that. I want to help you. I don't want to just get field reports."

He opened the Jeep's rear hatch and threw the bags in. "Stay put. I'm making good progress. No need for both of us to get tangled up out here."

"I can't just sit home anymore. I got you into this, and I want to help you out of it."

"Don't think you need to make amends. Guilt is my game, remember?"

She exhaled. "There's plenty of guilt to go around, then and now."

He didn't reply.

"Hello, hello, are you there?"

"Sometimes I'm not sure what angle you're coming at me from."

"I'm not trying to be cute and hit you with a cheap shot."

"I know." He closed the hatch. "I'll be in Saugatuck tomorrow to follow up the latest lead. There's a place called Singapore near there that might be the end of the road. I'll give you another update in twenty-four hours. Okay?"

Silence on the line. "Okay, but I don't like sitting and doing nothing. That has to change."

"We'll discuss it tomorrow."

"Yes, we will. Be careful, Jack."

"Be patient, Bobbie. Talk to you soon."

- EIGHTEEN -

Higgs accelerated the 300C down the Blue Star Highway. His chin throbbed where Sheridan's skull had popped him, and black threads dangled from his shredded jacket sleeve. Kisko frowned in the passenger seat with a bruise on his cheek shaped like the pattern in the car's front grill. Ehrlich and Barnett silently fumed in the rear seat. Higgs shook his head. "You sorry sons of bitches."

Kisko sneered. "What?"

"In case you ladies haven't noticed we won back there. We have the Bible and the last clue to the coins, not him."

"In case you haven't noticed," Ehrlich said, "we got our asses handed to us by a guy who got into the game less than a week ago."

Higgs laughed. "Speak for yourself. I've still got my car."

Ehrlich slapped the seat back. "Blow me."

"How did Sheridan get to the Bible before we did?" Kisko said. "We had the cross."

"I told you he was sharp." Higgs punched the accelerator and passed an ambling minivan in front of him. "I also told you to take him seriously. By the way, how's that cheek feel?"

"About as good as your chin."

Higgs swerved into the lane ahead of the minivan. "Sheridan may have gotten there first, but we took the prize from him."

"He had help," Barnett said.

Ehrlich nodded. "Yeah, I want to meet those guys in the pickup again. They just about ran me down. I want to repay the favor."

"You'll get your chance," Higgs said.

Kisko stared hard at him. "You just said we won. We have the Bible. How the—"

"We had the cross too," Higgs interrupted. "Get it through your head, Nate, Sheridan isn't going away quietly."

Kisko flipped open the glove compartment and wrenched out the wet Bible wrapped in a dry towel. "He isn't going anywhere without this."

Higgs tensed. "Easy! That thing's two hundred years old and soaked in chlorine water. If you rip, tear, smear, or smash those pages

I'm going to snap your neck!"

Kisko placed the tome back in the glove compartment.

Higgs set a stern gaze on the road ahead. "Back at Coates' house I saw some camera equipment spilled out on a desk. That bag Sheridan was carrying the Bible in was probably a camera case, and I'd bet your life he got a few nice shots of the clue."

"We're still racing with Sheridan?" Kisko cursed. "I say we take the gloves off with this prick. We see him, we take him down."

"I'm working on it," Higgs said.

"We've got to get the Bible clue deciphered before he does," Ehrlich added.

"I'm on it. Once I drop you guys off at the dig, I'm hand delivering the Bible to the front office. My bet is I'll be back in the morning with the solution."

"Good," Ehrlich said. "I heard the academics are at a standstill out there. They need some direction."

"They'll have it." Higgs veered onto Holland Street leading into Saugatuck. "If you guys cross paths with Sheridan before I get back, do not go lethal on him. We need clearance first. Capice?"

Kisko crossed his arms. "He might leave us no choice."

Higgs thought on it a bit and then lifted his cell phone and hit speed dial one.

"Are you on your way?" the voice answered.

"Fifteen minutes and I will be," Higgs said.

"I saw some news reports from Grand Rapids. It looked like obtaining the Bible was a little more difficult than you said it was earlier."

Higgs clenched his teeth and his face flushed red. "You know how the news media is, sir, blowing everything out of proportion, making everything a crisis."

"You do have the Bible, don't you?"

"Absolutely. Sheridan may be a pain in my ass but I'm not going to let him beat me."

"You best not, Mr. Higgs. I've been chasing this rainbow too long, invested too many resources to lose the pot of gold now."

"Agreed."

"You can't afford to let your guard down with Sheridan around."

Higgs nodded. "We were just discussing this issue and agreed that if Sheridan gets in our way again we need to eliminate him from the mix. Do we have the authority to do that?"

Silence. "Sheridan is high profile. If something happens to him, it will make the news and there will be an investigation surrounded by a great deal of buzz. Answers tend to shake out quickly in investigations under that type of scrutiny. I don't think I need to explain why this would be a bad thing."

"Understood, but what if Sheridan jeopardizes our recovery of the coins?"

"If it comes down to him getting the coins or us, then you have the authority. Do it discretely, and do not leave a trail leading back to us. If we're implicated in such an event you will be the first to suffer, Mr. Higgs."

"Understood as well. I'll be at our usual meet with the Bible in two hours."

"Looking forward to it." Disconnect.

Higgs snapped the phone closed. "We officially have the go-ahead to pop Sheridan if he gets in our way."

Kisko smiled. "First good news I've heard in weeks."

"That doesn't mean if you see him on the street you can shoot him," Higgs said. "It was made very clear. We take him down only if he's stopping us from getting the coins."

"Why risk it?" Ehrlich said. "Eliminate him and we eliminate the chance of losing."

Higgs frowned. "Use your head. Sheridan's had some national press. If he's killed, a spotlight is going to shine on his case. We don't need the police and the media investigating the activities leading up to his death. All that attention might put us on their radar."

Kisko grumbled. "If you ask me—"

"I didn't."

"As long as Sheridan is breathing he lowers our chances of getting the coins. I think if he pops his head up again we cut it off."

"Yeah," Barnett said. "If I see him in town I just might have to whack him in self-defense."

Higgs thumped his palm against the steering wheel. "You dumb shits aren't going to do anything stupid while I'm gone. If I come back to yellow crime scene tape, there will be hell to pay. Capice?"

Barnett fished around in his shirt pocket. "So what do we do while you're off getting the clue decoded?"

"Stay out of trouble." Higgs glanced into the rearview mirror and saw that Barnett had a cigarette in his hand. "Hey, don't smoke in the car."

"Who are you, the Surgeon General?" Barnett dangled the cigarette between his lips.

Higgs rolled the car to a stop at the Lucy and Butler Street intersection just outside of town. Without a word he reached back and yanked the unlit cigarette from Barnett's mouth.

"Hey!"

Higgs closed his hand into a fist. Tobacco leaf and paper squashed between his fingers. "Keep this shit outside or you'll be sucking food through a straw for weeks."

Barnett sat still but his eyes darted around to the others in the car.

Kisko twisted around. "He means it. If you want to keep your teeth where they are, don't smoke in the car."

Higgs kept the heat on. Barnett swallowed hard. A red Impala pulled up behind the 300C and its horn beeped. Higgs paid it no mind. "Do we have an understanding, Mr. Barnett?"

Barnett squirmed. "Are you seriously jacked about me lighting up?"

Higgs didn't answer.

Kisko and Ehrlich sat quiet.

Barnett stammered. "Yeah, Ben, sure. What the hell? No smoking in the car."

The Impala's horn beeped again.

"I appreciate the cooperation." Higgs slammed the gear shift into park and settled back into the leather seat. It really wasn't about the stink or hazard of secondhand smoke. It was more about control. He needed these men to know who had it and who didn't.

"Hey, asshole, get moving!" The guy in the Impala laid on the horn again.

Higgs adjusted his head rest.

The Impala backed up half a car length and then jerked forward. It swerved around the tail of the 300C. Higgs kicked open his car door. The Impala screeched to a halt. Higgs stepped out of the car and stood in the street.

The Impala's driver leaned out his window. "What the hell are you doing?"

Higgs walked toward him. "Giving you a lesson in patience."

The guy jumped from his car. He looked college age, athletic build, full of piss and vinegar. "Let's go."

Higgs squared off with him. "You get one shot."

The guy smirked. "Your mistake." He swung hard.

Higgs caught his fist with a hand the size of a bear claw and threw a jackhammer right jab. The guy's nose cracked and he staggered. Higgs slammed the Impala's door into his body and folded him into the driver's seat.

Higgs jabbed a finger at him. "Lay off the horn and never, ever screw with me."

The guy lay crumpled in the front seat trying to stop the blood flow from his nose.

Higgs got back into the 300C and shifted into drive. Nobody said a word to him. Nobody looked at him. Nobody was going to go after Jack Sheridan that night.

Higgs drew a satisfied breath.

It's all about control.

- NINETEEN -

The great lake's beautiful sapphire breast
Kissed by the crimson rose of the west,
'Neath that sandy plain is Singapore,
The buried town by the great lake's shore.

— Stella D. E. Calkins, "The Road to Singapore"

Jack reached through the blackness of the room to the nightstand and flipped open his cell phone to check the time. The brightness of the display made him squint. It was six o'clock in the morning. He gently rolled out of bed and pulled his pants on as quietly as he could. Lauren stirred on the other side of the bed. She always was a light sleeper.

He fumbled through the dark and unfamiliar room to find a shirt he'd thrown over a chair.

"You're up early," Lauren whispered.

"Couldn't sleep. Mind's working on overdrive." He found the denim shirt and pulled it over his shoulders. "Trying to figure out how to move a mountain of sand."

"I couldn't sleep either. I dreamt about those clues."

"We'll figure it out." He threaded his arm through the Colt's shoulder holster and adjusted the pistol to a comfortable position.

"There's something there," she said. "I sense it but I can't pull it forward."

He put on a blue Nautica windbreaker to conceal the holster. "I'm going to get a coffee in town. You want one?"

"Sure. Don't wake the boys when you leave. And be careful."

He leaned over and gave her a kiss. "I'm always careful, but you call it paranoia."

"Hey, when people are out to get you…"

"Don't worry. Think about Daniel's clue instead. I'll be back."

Jack left the bedroom. Early daylight lit the kitchen and adjacent living room of the Beechwood Manor Inn. It was an ideal lodging arrangement. Connor had found the inn online and discovered that a last-minute cancellation made the detached cottage available for a few days. With three bedrooms and a thousand square feet of space, the whole group could stay under one roof yet not be pestered by other guests.

Jack headed into downtown Saugatuck on foot, thinking about an excursion to the Singapore site along the way. Clear sky and spreading sunlight foretold a beautiful day ahead. The fresh scent of Lake Michigan washed over him in a westerly breeze. The rumble of lake surf rose from the horizon. It was an intoxicating mix. He felt the itch for open water.

He picked up coffee at the Saugatuck Coffee Company in the paver stone alley off Butler Street and started back, but that scent of lake air drew him like a magnet. Lake Kalamazoo and Sergeant Marina were close. A little detour wouldn't hurt. He walked to the water and strolled amongst the boats laid up in the docks. There were vessels of every type and size, from thirty-foot cruisers to sixty-foot sail boats, from nineteen-foot Chris Crafts to eighty-foot luxury yachts, all moored in slips just a short jaunt north and around the river bend from Lake Michigan. One day he'd have one of those sail boats, maybe a transom like Garity's, and each summer he and Lauren would spend weeks at a time sailing the Great Lakes. One day.

He walked the stretch of docks near the Butler Restaurant and recalled Eugene Elliot's story about pioneer William Butler distributing flour salvaged from the wrecked *Milwaukee* to local residents during the Great Blizzard of '42. Jack had read somewhere that the Butler building started life as a mill, spent half a century as a hotel, and evolved into the restaurant it is today. The massive wooden deck that sprawls the length of the back side was added when the building became an eatery, apparently to give patrons a view of the sloping greens of Cook Park and the water of Lake Kalamazoo.

The picturesque scene distracted Jack from noticing the boat at first. He nearly spit out a mouthful of coffee when he saw it. A twenty-foot Bayliner with the blue Neptune's Reach trident logo emblazoned on the bow was moored in the slip ahead. He recognized the boat as the runabout attached to the *Achilles*, a large research and salvage vessel stationed in the Great Lakes. Jack knew the ship well. He'd spent months on board throughout his career with the company. The fact that she was cruising Lake Michigan didn't surprise him. The fact that her runabout turned up at Sergeant Marina the same time he did stretched credulity.

The maritime world is a small community, Lloyd Faulkner had said. *You hear interesting things sometimes.* Did Lloyd catch wind of the hunt for the coins and dispatch the *Achilles?* It didn't seem possible. He had no way of finding out; at least no way that Jack could imagine. But that might explain Lloyd's recent contact with him.

There didn't seem to be anybody aboard the Bayliner. Jack left the docks and headed across Cook Park. He made it to the cottage at Beechwood Manor without incident. Lauren had gotten up and was sitting at the kitchen table with Daniel's Bible open in front of her.

Jack handed her one of the coffee cups. "Guess what I just saw."

"Two men holding hands?"

"No, a Neptune's Reach boat down at the docks."

She leaned back from the Bible. "Coincidence?"

"Never when Lloyd's involved." He sat across the table from her.

"Is he still trying to get you to come back to work for them?"

"I don't know." Jack took a sip from his cup. "It might be something bigger."

"What do you mean?"

He glanced at the Bible.

"How could Lloyd know about the treasure?"

"I have no idea, but then I don't know how those guys at Lewis' house heard about it either. I'm starting to feel like I was the last one invited to the party."

"Do you think Neptune's Reach wants you back to help find the coins for them?"

Jack balanced his chair on the rear legs. "Perhaps, but that's not what Lloyd told me."

She thought a moment. "Maybe they're trying to keep you out of it by putting you on the payroll and sending you off to unrelated projects. That way you'll be out of their hair."

"Hey, that's a good one. With duplicitous thinking like that you'd be a good candidate for Lloyd's job."

"It is possible that boat is here by coincidence."

"Possible but not likely." He brought the chair back down on all four legs.

"What are the odds Lloyd and those guys from Lewis's house are on the same team?"

Jack exhaled. "Lloyd's a weasel but I like to think he wouldn't get into bed with people like that. I could be wrong."

Lauren feigned astonishment. "Wrong?"

"Don't let that get around. Let's table this issue for the moment. I'll deal with Neptune if it becomes necessary." He nodded to the Bible. "Any luck with Daniel's clue?"

She set her gaze on the pages. "Revelation awaits, Above the ground, For in the wildcat's bones, The answer is found, Engraved and sealed, Read north to south, Selah—Wouldn't an animal's bones be buried? I can't get past the above ground reference. I tried to compare the two clues to determine if there are common threads but I couldn't find any. Even the styles don't match. The meter of David's clue is different from Daniel's."

"I'm concerned about the engraving part," Jack said. "It's been a hundred and fifty years. Depending on where this engraving is located it may not be legible any longer."

"I think I need to get a little off the wall with this—"

Jack's cell rang. He checked caller ID. It was Bobbie. "Our client is calling," he said. Lauren's expression narrowed ever so slightly. He held the phone and waited for her ceremonial permission to answer. She waved her hand. So let it be done.

"Good morning, Bobbie. You're up early today."

"I'm up early every day. You are too, if memory serves."

"Everything okay? I thought I was to report in this evening."

"Remember we discussed changing the reporting arrangement?"

"Yes." Jack glanced at Lauren.

"Well," Bobbie said. "I'm in Saugatuck."

"You are?"

"Yes, Alyson and I drove in last night. Probably got here before you did."

"How did you do that? When we talked yesterday, you were at Granite Island."

"No, when we spoke I was actually on the road heading to Grand Rapids. I changed course to Saugatuck after you told me it was your next destination. Like it or not, I'm going to help you."

He ran a hand through his hair. "Bobbie, I said you didn't need to come out here. I've got things under control."

"Are you sure?"

"I haven't been shot at yet. I'd say the day's off to a good start."

"I searched around town last night," she said. "There's something I need to show you."

Jack didn't like the sound of that. "What is it?"

"Meet me in town in an hour. You have to see it."

He leaned forward and searched for a pen or pencil. "Where do you want to meet?" Lauren rolled the pen she had been using across the table to him. He picked it up.

"There's a boat that takes tourists on a cruise up the Kalamazoo,"

Bobbie said. "It's called the *Star of Saugatuck*. Do you know it?"

"Yeah, off Water Street. I saw it when we came through town. You want to meet there?"

"Yes. I'll see you in an hour." She hung up.

Jack closed his phone. "Bobbie's in town," he said. "She needs to show me something."

"I'm sure she does," Lauren said deadpan. "What is it?"

He shrugged. "She didn't say, but it sounded like it could be a problem."

"Of course."

"This wasn't part of the plan. Bobbie and I never discussed her joining me on the road."

"I didn't ask you about that."

"No, but you were thinking about it."

Lauren stood and walked to the kitchen counter. "Revelation awaits. Let's not keep it waiting too long. We need to figure out the meaning behind the clues and find the coins. If Bobbie's presence will help us do that, then I'm glad she's here."

Connor came walking from his bedroom with a tired step. "Wow, I haven't heard a Bobbie discussion in fifteen years."

Lauren faced him. "This isn't a Bobbie discussion."

Connor eyed his dad. "Sounds like one."

Jack just shook his head.

Markus burst from the opposite bedroom door. "What's a Bobbie discussion?" He looked around the kitchen. "Is that coffee?"

"I didn't think you guys would be awake this early," Jack said, "so I didn't get you one."

Markus took Lauren's vacated chair at the table. "Who could sleep with all this talking?"

Connor went to the kitchen and opened the cupboard they'd stocked with protein bars and bagels. "Did I hear you say Bobbie is in Saugatuck?" He grabbed a chocolate protein bar.

"Connor, toss me a peanut butter," Markus said raising his hand.

Connor swiped another bar from the cupboard and lobbed it over his shoulder without looking. Markus snatched it from the air.

"Bobbie and Alyson are both here," Jack said. "They drove down last night."

Markus peeled back the foil wrapper from the bar. "Bobbie Alyson." He chuckled. "That's funny. Is the family into stock car racing or what?"

"She doesn't look like a race car driver," Connor said.

"One of the pit crew?"

"Hardly. I saw her at her dad's funeral last year. It was the first time in a decade that I'd seen her. Wow, she's smokin' hot now."

"Hmm." Markus took a bite of the protein bar. "Is this Bobbie person a blood relative?"

"No," Lauren said. "She's an old friend of Jack's—and mine."

Markus smiled. "Well, that's good. I was afraid Connor was getting a little taboo on us."

"Markus!" Lauren opened the refrigerator and grabbed a grapefruit.

Connor sat on the kitchen counter. "Keep talking like an idiot, Sweethead."

Lauren swung the fridge door closed. "Boys, keep the trash talk between yourselves."

Jack concealed a smirk. "Okay guys, listen. We're hiking to the Singapore site today to find out just how much sand we might have to dig up. Dress for it. I'm heading off to a business meeting shortly, but when I get back be ready to go."

"A business meeting?" Connor tore open his bar.

"With Bobbie," Lauren said.

Connor nodded and took a bite. "Right, this wasn't a Bobbie discussion."

Jack grabbed a bagel and apple to go with his coffee. He and the guys kept the conversation light but inside he wondered what Bobbie intended to show him. Maybe she had a newspaper article announcing someone had recovered a trove of gold coins once owned by a man named Harlan Coates. Maybe some investor with an interest in the Bank of Michigan found out about the treasure and has filed a cease and desist order against all hunters. He would soon find out.

Fifteen minutes before the meet he left the cottage and headed for Water Street. People were starting to populate the streets of Saugatuck. Café and shop owners opened their doors. Vendors set up their sidewalk displays with American flags and streamers in preparation for the coming Fourth of July weekend. Kids climbed on the play structure in the park at the intersection of Main and Butler. Two women played tennis on the court across the street. The day seemed off to a bustling start for the harbor town. Jack had a feeling he wouldn't get much relaxation out of it.

With two minutes to spare he walked up to the ticket office and souvenir shop for the *Star of Saugatuck* on the Kalamazoo River. Bobbie stood near the front door, waiting to ruin his day.

TWENTY

Bobbie smiled when she saw him. Jack smiled too and gave her a hug. She stood on her toes and held him tight. "Thanks again for doing this."

"No thanks required."

His shoulder holster pressed uncomfortably between them. She let go and peered beneath his open windbreaker. "Jeez, is that a gun under your jacket, or are you just happy to see me?"

"I've attracted some new friends on this expedition. I needed a little life insurance."

"Is that legal?"

"Got my CCW permit two years ago." He smoothed the windbreaker over the Colt. "Michigan is a great state." He stepped back and looked around. "First cruise is at eleven-thirty. If you're taking me on the boat we're a little early."

"No problem." She eyed a pair of elderly women walking toward the ticket office. "A seniors group chartered a morning cruise and I finagled a couple of tickets for us. Just be nice to them and we'll be okay."

He chuckled. "So what is it you need to show me on the *Star of Saugatuck*? You got me a bit concerned on the phone."

"It's not on the boat," she said.

The ticket office doors opened and Alyson walked out. "Jack!" Her green eyes brightened and her broad smile beamed. She threw her arms around him. She didn't need to stand on her toes. "It's great to see you again."

"You taking the cruise with us?" he asked.

"No, Mom says it's all business. I'm going to check out some of the shops in town."

Jack recalled his run-in with Big Ben and his boys. He turned to Bobbie. "You think that's a good idea, considering…"

She gave him a thoughtful glance. "I did until you said that."

"Come on," Alyson said. "It's Saugatuck. We're not talking Detroit here."

"Wait a minute." Jack grabbed his cell and called Connor. "Son, take a quick shower and put on some clean clothes. I want you and Markus to hang with Alyson for a few hours."

Alyson smiled. "Connor is here?" She looked across Spear Street. "Have him meet me at the corner in front of River Market."

Jack relayed the instructions and hung up. "Alyson, let me apologize in advance for Connor's friend Markus. He's a sexist pig and drools around pretty girls, but he's a good guy, mostly."

"Don't worry," Alyson said. "I've dealt with guys like that at State for five years. I can handle him."

They chatted up the small things until Connor and Markus arrived. Alyson headed off with them, and Jack and Bobbie boarded the *Star of Saugatuck*. The boat was a two-tier paddlewheel vessel. They climbed to the upper level and took a chair at a table in the stern portion of the deck that was open to the air. The last of the seniors group ambled aboard. Dock hands threw off the mooring lines, and the captain announced their departure.

Jack watched the captain pilot the boat from the wheelhouse on the upper level, listened to him recite his spiel of historical facts and bad jokes over the PA. Any thoughts remaining about the tour boat captain career option vanished at that moment. Jack just wasn't ready for that yet.

The *Star of Saugatuck* glided down the Kalamazoo River, her stern paddlewheel splashing through the water to propel the ship forward. She drifted past boats in dock and period homes on the water with manicured lawns and renovated exteriors. A dozen members from the seniors group climbed to the upper level and watched the scenery pass by at a sedate pace. Jack filled Bobbie in on the Bible clues leading to Singapore. The *Star of Saugatuck* left the dense cluster of civilization behind and neared the bend in the river nestled between tree-covered hills. "Are you going to show me this thing or not?" Jack said.

She leaned closer to him so he could hear clearly over the wind, water, and surrounding conversations. "On the phone yesterday you said Singapore might be the end of the road. I think someone else agrees with you on that."

The captain steered the boat through the bend and started into a bit about a buried ghost town that used to be a thriving milling village.

"He's talking about Singapore," Jack said. He tried to get his bearings in respect to the river. "The village was on the north shore just ahead. Good idea taking this cruise. It'll be useful reconnaissance."

"That's what I thought last night," Bobbie said. "I took the tour and saw it."

Jack gave her a puzzled look. "Saw what?"

The captain continued through his script. "After the milling operation exhausted the surrounding tree supply the jobs disappeared. Singapore became a ghost town, and shifting sands from the western shore covered the deserted village. But the story doesn't end there."

Jack kept an eye on Bobbie and an ear listening to the captain.

"An archeological team from Michigan State University arrived at the location of buried Singapore this past spring to learn more about the culture and tools of the time. They began excavating the site in April, and after nearly three months of work they've reached the remains of Singapore. If you look to starboard you'll see the dig in process."

Jack came to his feet and stood at the handrail. The *Star of Saugatuck* glided by a bank of trees and cleared a line of sight to an open plain. Center stage and thirty yards back from the water, a small cluster of rotted building remains stood half-buried in a dune. Roof peaks jutted from the ground, their rafters laid bare, their ruined shells filled with sand. Collapsed walls left lonely facades to mark the vestiges of the settlement like tombstones. A grid of rope suspended on wooden stakes criss-crossed the site and segmented Singapore into cells, and each cell was labeled with a coordinate marker. Small white flags punctuated the ground at various points. Members of the archeological team moved about the grid, crouching in cavities, delicately brushing sand from embedded items, cataloging cells, and removing earth from around larger structures.

Jack fixed on the scene.

Bobbie came up beside him. "What do you think?"

"This dig isn't purely cultural."

"Do you think the university knows about the coins too?"

"I doubt it. It's more likely that the university is a tool. They're doing the hard labor for someone else." He chuckled despite the feeling of having just been sucker punched. "I wish I'd thought of this."

"The Bible clue pointing to Singapore turned up just yesterday," she said. "This dig has been going on for three months. The events don't coincide."

He glanced at her. "That just means someone is way ahead of the curve." He put his eyes back on the dig. "Whoever it is suspected Singapore as the resting place for the coins a long time ago. He probably didn't know precisely where to dig; just that he had to unearth the village. My guess is the guys I ran into yesterday are involved with this, and now they have the clue from David's Bible. If they're able to decipher it, they're going to get real close to the coins."

Bobbie watched resurrected Singapore grow smaller on shore in the wake of the boat. "Does this mean we've lost?"

"Lost?" He faced her. "I can't even spell that word. It's never lost."

His confident tone made her smile. "How can you say that? Someone is a couple of shovelfuls away from finding the coins."

"I've got an ace up my sleeve."

"What do you mean?"

"There are two Bibles with clues, remember? David and Daniel's. My competition and I both have David's clue. That one narrows the search parameter to a particular city block in Singapore. But I'm the only one with Daniel's clue, and I'm certain it's Daniel's clue that's going to put an X on the map."

"It doesn't sound like you've deciphered Daniel's clue yet."

"We're close."

"So you're guessing that the exact location will pop out of Daniel's Bible."

"The important thing here is we have the second clue and they don't."

"Let's say you determine a more specific location with the second clue. How do we slip onto the dig site and make off with the coins undetected? The 'bad' guys are probably monitoring things pretty close in Singapore."

"There are always ways to get over a wall or under the radar."

"You're pretty good at that," she said, "the way you make things sound easier than they are."

Jack leaned on the handrail. "You sound like my wife."

"I almost was."

The words twisted his gut with a shot of guilt. He'd been wondering when the issue would come up; he just wasn't sure if he should address it head-on right then. He watched water swell around the hull of the boat. It was as good a time as ever. "Believe it or not, Bobbie, ending our relationship was the hardest decision I've ever made."

She fell silent with the shift in conversation.

Keep going, Jack. "In a weird way I think I was protecting you. I had tunnel vision on getting my career in high gear. I was prepared to throw myself headlong into the maritime industry and knew there wouldn't be enough of me left for you." He turned from the view of the lake. "I never meant to hurt you."

"It's amazing how well we do things we never intend to do."

He made eye contact with her. "You deserved someone who could commit to you one hundred percent. I couldn't walk into a marriage knowing that wouldn't be the case. I wouldn't lie to you like that."

"And a year later you committed to Lauren."

"That was a different situation. She took a big risk with me. The first five years of our marriage, I was away more than I was home."

"I don't remember you giving me the chance to take that risk."

"Before I left for Virginia, you made it clear that kind of arrangement wouldn't work."

She stopped and took a breath. "I did, but our dialogue ended as soon as you left the state. We might have been able to work something out if we'd kept talking."

"You don't know how many times I wanted to call you that first six months, but I thought if I did it would only make it worse."

"Clean cuts heal quick. Isn't that what they say?"

"Then you and Steven got together and you were expecting with Alyson. It seemed you had moved on just fine."

"It all played out in your favor, didn't it?"

"Bobbie, I'm trying to tell you I'm sorry. For everything. It all falls on me. I know that."

She saw his frustration and placed a hand on his arm. "We've spent a couple of decades perfecting this tit-for-tat conversation and it never gets us anywhere. Let's stop." She took his hand. "What happened between us back then wasn't your entire fault. I'm sorry if I made you feel that way. We both suffered symptoms of being young. You weren't ready to settle the way I expected, and I was naïve to think I could change your mind. I realized that years ago. I couldn't say it to you until now."

The *Star of Saugatuck* had sailed through the mouth of the Kalamazoo River and was circling around in Lake Michigan. The sandy beach of the western shore shimmered in the sun, and the lush green of the trees capping the sand dunes stood bold against a clear blue sky. The perfect summer scene seemed to be melting the ice of a twenty-five year winter. Jack gave Bobbie's hand a squeeze and released it. He stood near the handrail watching the captain pilot the boat back through the mouth of the Kalamazoo. "You asked a good question," he said after a long while.

She regarded him. "Which one?"

"How do we get the coins from under the nose of the other people looking for them?"

"Oh, that one. I agree. That is a good question."

"That's an MSU archeological team at the dig site, right?"

"Yes."

"You have twenty years in at MSU as an English professor, right?"

"Yes, but I rarely crossed paths with anyone in the Department of Anthropology."

"But you have contacts inside the university."

"Yes."

"I want you to make some calls, see if your friends on campus can get a few answers for us. Ask if they can find out who is supervising the dig; perhaps arrange an official meet with them on site. Maybe even find out who initiated the dig or if any outside benefactor pushed for it. I'd like to know who's sitting across the table from me."

Bobbie nodded. "I'll find out what I can."

They drifted past Singapore again on the way upriver. Jack watched students work among the ruins. The problem of moving a mountain of sand had been solved. The problem of operating invisibly under the competition's nose had replaced it. He thought about the choices and decided he'd rather have a shovel in his hands.

TWENTY-ONE

Connor walked on Alyson's left and Markus stayed to her right. They wedged through the crowded sidewalk on the west side of Butler Street, hitting all the craft shops and art galleries that struck Alyson's fancy. She was as attractive as Connor had remembered, so he didn't mind the chaperone duty. Markus enjoyed the task as well and dispensed his irritating charm at every opportunity. Sometimes the guy could be annoying.

Connor's cell rang and he checked caller ID. "Yeah, Dad."

"We're on our way back," Jack said. "I want everyone to meet at the cottage in forty-five minutes."

"No problem. We'll start back now. See you soon." Connor disconnected. "Alyson, our parents are finished with their meeting. We're going to meet up at our cottage."

"Okay," she said. "Let's finish this street." A Caribbean-themed gift store caught her eye and she headed in. Connor and Markus exchanged an anguished glance but followed her inside. A shelf loaded with wooden crafts defined the aisle to the right. Alyson picked up a little treasure chest and opened the lid. "Connor, how did you get mixed up with Mom's treasure hunt?"

"My dad," Connor said. "After Bobbie, or rather, your mom recruited him, Markus and I heard about what was happening and volunteered."

She smiled and snapped the lid closed on the chest. "It's great that Jack and Mom are still good friends after all these years and all the stuff that went on between them."

Markus stood at the end of the aisle with a wooden pirate sword in one hand and a cap gun shaped like a flintlock pistol in the other. "Jack?" He chuckled. "Have you no respect for your elders, young lady?"

"Hey," Connor said. "It's Johnny Depp without the looks, talent, or money."

Markus pointed the sword at him. "What did she mean 'all the stuff that went on between them'?"

"Somewhere back in Sheridan lore, Dad and Bobbie dated."

Connor pushed the tip of the sword away. "Put that thing down before you hurt yourself."

Markus withdrew the wooden saber and raised the plastic flintlock to Connor's head. "How serious were they?"

Alyson giggled. "Serious enough that they still walk on egg shells around each other."

"Yeah," Connor added, "and serious enough that my parents have Bobbie discussions to this very day."

"Oh, so that's a Bobbie discussion." Markus set the pistol back on the shelf. A smile spread across his face. "Wait a minute. Jack and Bobbie. Jack and Bobbie, get it?"

Alyson and Connor didn't respond.

"Come on. John Kennedy and Robert Kennedy. Jack and Bobby."

Connor just shook his head.

"Why am I the only one picking up on these things?"

"Things like the Bobbie Allison congruence?"

Markus put the sword down. "The race car driver analogy was close to the money. Alyson is definitely in the same league as Danica Patrick."

Alyson smiled and rounded the corner to the next aisle.

Connor slapped Markus on the shoulder. "Nice. I think she's being taken in by these suave one-liners."

"Sometimes it's hard to see the cracks on the surface," Markus said. "But they're there."

Connor circled around the end cap. Alyson stood near a display shelf staring at a small ceramic lighthouse in her hand. She wasn't smiling anymore. He walked up to her. "Is that like the lighthouse on Granite Island you and your mom are renovating?"

She set the sculpture down. "No, my dad kept a lighthouse just like this one on his desk at home. He loved the Great Lakes lights. It's a shame he didn't see Granite Island finished."

Connor noticed her eyes had become glassy. "Well, I definitely want to see the island. Think you can arrange that?"

"I know the owners," she said wiping the corner of her eye. "I'll see what I can do."

"It has to be a guided tour."

"I'll make sure Mom's there." She nudged him with her elbow. "Let's go."

She headed out of the shop. Markus walked up beside Connor. "Cheater. You played the sympathy card. Even I won't go that low."

"I didn't play any card," Connor protested. "And nothing is

beneath you."

"Come on now. It may be hard to tell, but I do have a moral compass."

"Yeah? There must be a magnet stuck to it somewhere."

They left the Caribbean shop and caught up with Alyson on the sidewalk. They crossed Hoffman Street. A couple of art studios were too much for her to resist. She led the guys into each one. They hurried her through the exhibits as best they could. A few storefronts down Alyson paused at the Art & Angels shop. The guys held their breath until she decided to keep walking. They bumped knuckles behind her back. Connor eyed a wine tasting room ahead. He nudged Markus.

"I see it," Markus said.

"Hey, Aly." Connor gestured to the wine room. "You thirsty?"

Across Butler Street a place with an old movie marquee above it called Phil's Bar & Grill grabbed Markus' attention. He stared like he'd rather visit that establishment.

Connor realized the wine tasting room wasn't open and became dejected. He noticed Markus gazing at the bar. "I doubt they're open yet either," Connor said.

"That's a drag but that's not what I'm looking at."

Connor scanned the storefronts through the thin crowd on the opposite sidewalk. He didn't see anything particularly intriguing. Markus stayed focused and seemed to be coiling up like a spring. Connor had seen him like this a few times before, usually right before a fight broke out. "We're in an arts and crafts harbor town. How can you possibly be gearing up for action?"

Alyson walked up between them. "What's the matter?"

Markus smirked. "Connor, let's play I Spy."

"What?"

"I spy with my little eye, a couple of guys you nearly ran over with your truck yesterday."

"Where?" Connor scanned the sidewalk again.

"Loitering in front of the bar and grill." Markus nodded. "I didn't get a real good look at them yesterday, but I think they're the same guys."

Connor found them amongst the crowd, a short, stocky guy with a brush cut and a cigarette hanging from his mouth, and a tall blond-haired guy with a thin face and a week's worth of beard. The tall one really stirred the memory. He was the one who bounced off the S-10's front quarter panel. "You're right."

Alyson peered over Connor's shoulder. "Who do you see?"

"A couple of assholes." Markus kept his eye on them. "Let's go say hello."

"Are you insane?" Connor kept his voice down. "They haven't seen us yet. We need to evaporate into the crowd."

"Connor, these guys were going to blow a hole in your dad's knee-caps."

"You had to bring that up." Connor stared hard at them. A part of him wanted to march over there and thrash the thugs for what they tried to do to his father. Reason held him back. "We can't get Alyson mixed up in this."

"Too late," Markus said. "That tall guy spotted us. I don't think he recognizes who we are yet, but he's suspicious." Markus stepped into the street. "I'm going to jog his memory."

"Get back here!" Connor tried to grab his shirt but failed.

"Where's he going?" Alyson said.

"Into the breach." Connor stepped off the curb. Alyson started to follow but he warded her back. "Stay here. I need to reel him back in." He jogged ahead and caught up with Markus. "Slow down. We need to keep a low profile."

"Right." Markus kept walking. "Hey, they're coming to greet us."

The tall blond and the short guy with the brush cut moved to the edge of the sidewalk. They were seeing but they weren't recognizing. They knew enough to be on alert though. Connor clenched his fist. "It's not too late. About face and let's get Alyson out of here."

They got within five feet of the men. Markus grinned at them. "Hey man, what's up? Got your car in for service?"

That did it. The blond guy's jaw dropped, and the veins in the short guy's temples pulsed. They knew who they were facing. A wave of panic rushed through Connor. There was no turning back now.

The tall blond huffed. "You stupid bastards actually showed up in town. Bad move."

Connor bristled. "What are you going to do about it, shoot us in the kneecaps?"

The guy with the brush cut flicked his cigarette at Connor's feet. "These piss-ants on the no-hit list?"

"Don't think they are."

Markus laughed. "It's funny when pussies talk tough."

The knife came out of nowhere. The short guy snapped a blade open in his palm and thrust it forward. Markus sidestepped and grabbed the guy's forearm. The tip of the knife stopped an inch short of Alyson's chest.

What's she doing here? Connor wheeled around. "Get back!" He pushed her away from the blade and sent her stumbling backward. Markus and the short guy struggled for control of the knife. Connor pivoted back to the fray. A bony set of knuckles cracked him in the eye. A burst of light and a shot of pain rattled his head. The tall guy laughed.

Connor lunged at him on a surge of fury. They collided near the curb and grappled in the street, each trying to wrench the other to the ground. People scattered from the melee. Connor lost his footing and slammed into a parked car. He regained his balance and charged, forcing the tall guy back three steps. From the corner of his eye, Connor saw Markus head butt the ass with the brush cut. The clang of metal on concrete rang out. The knife had fallen.

The tall guy tried to drive his knee into Connor's groin but missed and bludgeoned his thigh instead. Connor found his right hand free. He jabbed the guy in the jaw. Blondie loosened his grip. Connor jabbed him a second time, a little harder than the first. Blondie let go and fell back a step. Connor cocked his right again. Third time's the charm. He threw the punch but the guy blocked with his left and struck with his right. The blow rocked Connor's head back. Pinpricks of light spotted his vision. His knees buckled. He tried to stay focused.

It didn't make sense at first. A shapeless black mass flew in front of his eyes. It glistened in the sun, changed shape. It flowed like a wave and covered the tall guy's face, and he shouted and cursed and wiped steaming liquid from his eyes. It smelled like coffee.

Alyson stepped up and hurled a half-empty cardboard cup. It bounced off the tall blond's forehead. He keyed in on her and advanced.

The precious seconds of delay cleared Connor's head. Strength returned to his legs. Alyson was in trouble. He sprang, intercepting the tall guy, slamming a forearm into his chest and seizing a handful of shirt.

They drew back their fists to pulverize each other in perfect synchronicity.

And then a voice thundered from the periphery of people watching the fight from the sidewalk. "Ehrlich, Barnett, back off!"

The tall guy held fast and glanced sideways into the crowd. A large man with short black hair and a muscular neck stared so intently on the scene that the weight of his will held everyone still. He roared again. "Back off, now!"

TWENTY-TWO

The *Star of Saugatuck* gently bumped against the pilings, and dock hands tied her off. Senior citizens began their exodus from the lower deck. Jack stopped by the wheelhouse to give the captain his regards and shake his hand for a flawless cruise. He and Bobbie descended the stairs and filed out with the other passengers to the lot in front of the ticket office.

"Start making calls," he said to her. "I want to get on that dig site."

Bobbie lifted her Palm Pilot from her purse. "Let me run through my contacts."

A black 300C crossed the intersection of Spear and Butler a block east of where they stood. Jack recalled Ben driving the same make and color car the previous day in Ottawa Hills. He tapped Bobbie on the shoulder. "Follow me."

He led her up Spear Street to the intersection. The 300C had headed south down Butler. Jack rounded the corner, looking for it amongst the sparse number of cars on the road. Pedestrian crossings and stop lights kept traffic moving slowly, and the 300C was just crossing the next intersection. Jack weaved around the people on the sidewalk to catch up to it.

Bobbie followed him close. "Who are we chasing?"

"Don't know yet." He tracked the car beyond the tennis court and playground he'd seen earlier and got within fifty feet of it when it crossed Hoffman Street. Farther down Butler some commotion had gathered a knot of people in the road. Traffic was backing up. The 300C slid into an open parallel parking spot. Jack pulled Bobbie inside an art studio and watched the car through the front window. Benjamin Higgs emerged. There was nobody in the passenger seat.

Jack narrowed his eyes on him. "Is that the guy who wanted Steven's research from you?"

Bobbie nodded. "That's him."

"He's also the guy who shot at me yesterday. This is good. We're connecting dots."

Higgs headed for the commotion in the street, a bit of urgency in his step. Jack moved for the door. "Stay here. I want to see where he's going."

"No, I'm going with you."

"What is it with women not listening to me?"

"How long have you been married?"

Jack shook his head and they left the studio. They shadowed Higgs to the ring of people standing in the street. Something had the crowd's rapt attention. Jack stood on his toes to peer over their heads. At the center of all the excitement, Connor and Markus were fighting the men from the silver Camry. In a blink Jack switched modes from spy to soldier. He put a hand on Bobbie's shoulder. "Stay here. No argument this time."

"What's happening?"

"Just stay here!" He walked into the street and marched toward Higgs. Big Ben had wedged through to the front row of spectators. Jack slid a hand under his windbreaker and freed the Colt from the holster. He kept it concealed and worked his way behind Higgs. Connor and Markus flailed away in the chaos of an all-out street fight. Seeing them engaged in a violent struggle turned Jack's stomach. He closed within inches of Higgs and jammed the pistol into his back. "Morning, Ben."

Higgs didn't flinch. He exhaled and lowered his head a fraction of an inch. "Sheridan."

"In case you're wondering, this is a gun in your kidney. Yank the leash on your dogs now."

"What does it matter to you?"

"Let's just say I'm a Good Samaritan."

Higgs thought in silence a moment. "Or are my guys kicking the shit out of your guys? Is that what's happening here?"

"What's happening here is you're a hair trigger from a dialysis machine."

"This is a tactical error, Jack. Now I know you've deciphered the clue. That's what brought you to Saugatuck, isn't it? It would have been smarter to stay low, try to sneak around town without me noticing."

Connor took a hard hit and staggered.

"Ehrlich scored some points with that one," Higgs said.

Jack pressed the Colt deeper into his back. "If one of my guys fall I shoot."

Higgs scoffed. "I don't think you've got it in you."

Markus traded blows with the short guy. Connor looked like he was in trouble. Alyson appeared from the crowd and threw coffee into

Ehrlich's face. Jack grabbed hold of Higg's shirt collar and leaned closer. "My son is out there, you son of a bitch. I won't have any problem dropping you right here if anything happens to him."

Higgs tensed up.

Ehrlich rushed toward Alyson. Connor intercepted him. They drew back to strike each other.

"Your life is in their hands, Ben."

Higgs shouted, "Ehrlich, Barnett, back off!"

Higgs' men froze in place. Connor and Markus did likewise. Time seemed suspended. Higgs bellowed again. "Back off, now!"

Ehrlich shook himself free from Connor's grip. Barnett stepped away from Markus. The guys were confused. Alyson searched the crowd of bystanders to find the man who shouted the order.

Jack released Higgs' collar. "Smart decision."

Higgs kept his eyes forward. "You're going to regret you didn't pull that trigger."

Someone announced the police were coming. A siren pulsed behind them. Jack glanced back. A police cruiser was rolling up the street, parting the crowd. Jack nudged the Colt into Higgs' back one last time. "You go your way, I'll go mine, and let's hope we never meet again."

Higgs chuckled. "That's not very likely now, is it?"

Jack stepped away from him and discretely slid the Colt back into its holster. The ring of onlookers broke up. Jack melded into their ranks. Ehrlich and Barnett had already vanished. Connor, Markus, and Alyson stood in the street trying to figure out what was happening. Jack worked his way over to them. He took Alyson's arm and made eye contact with his son. "You and Markus scatter. The police are here. Get back to the cottage."

Connor nodded and slapped Markus on the shoulder. They ran south down Butler before the cruiser arrived, weaving around the people and cutting across Mason Street. The police car stopped where the fight had taken place. Officers got out and started asking questions. There was no shortage of people willing to give their account of events.

Jack led Alyson to the sidewalk. "Are you okay?"

"Yes. Who were those men?"

"Other people interested in your father's treasure hunt."

Bobbie pushed through the crowd to reach them. "What happened?"

"I don't know," Alyson said. "Markus recognized those guys

across the street. He and Connor went to talk with them, and the next thing I knew they were all fighting."

Jack checked behind them. One of the witnesses talking to a police officer was looking around, like he was trying to point someone out of the crowd. Jack walked faster. "Keep moving, ladies. We don't need to get tangled up with the police."

"Where are we going?" Bobbie said.

"The cottage at Beechwood Manor."

They hurried across Mason Street and kept their stride brisk. The crowd on the sidewalk thinned out. No one seemed interested in their nonchalant flight.

At the corner of Butler and Culver they stopped for traffic. Saugatuck City Hall stood on their right. The white colonial two-story with columns flanking the front door provided a peaceful counterpoint to the conflict they'd just escaped. A historic marker stood in front of the building. The words SINGAPORE, MICHIGAN in large letters across the top of the plaque commanded Jack's attention. He started reading through the text on the marker.

"Come on, Jack, the traffic cleared," Bobbie said.

He held up a finger. "Hold on."

The marker recounted the story of Singapore, Michigan, in a brief narrative. The information wasn't new. Jack had heard it all from Eugene and the captain of the *Star of Saugatuck*. He almost stopped reading. And then he saw it. He slapped his forehead and whispered to himself. "Of course, how did I miss it?"

Bobbie and Alyson came alongside him. "What is it?" Bobbie asked.

He read from the marker. "Singapore was in fact, until the 1870s, a busy lumbering town. With three mills, two hotels, several general stores, and a renowned "wild-cat" bank, it outshone its neighbor to the south…"

Alyson shrugged. "What's the significance of that?"

Jack read it again in silence. The clue in Daniel's Bible suddenly had a very clear context. He couldn't believe he hadn't made the connection before. "For in the wildcat's bones the answer is found."

Bobbie shook her head. "What are you talking about?"

Jack stood straight. "Let's go." He started across the street.

Bobbie raced after him. "Damn it, Jack, what did you just discover?"

He was almost jogging down the sidewalk now. Bobbie and Alyson hustled to keep up. "That ace up my sleeve," he said, "the clue in the second Bible, I think I just figured it out. The wildcat is the bank. Harlan Coates went full circle to the origin of his treasure."

"Went back and did what?" Bobbie said.

Jack smiled. "He engraved where he hid the coins somewhere inside the Bank of Singapore."

- TWENTY THREE -

Jack made sure Higgs and his boys were nowhere in sight before walking up to the cottage. He pushed through the front door with Bobbie and Alyson on his heels. Lauren was cleaning a cut over Connor's eye at the kitchen table. Markus sat on the kitchen counter top sucking down a lime-flavored sports drink. He had his left hand wrapped in a towel packed with ice.

Lauren noticed Bobbie standing there and gave her a tepid hello.

Jack scrutinized the guys. "How the hell did that fight start?"

Connor stopped Lauren from dressing his cut and sat forward. "We were minding our own business shopping in town when we ran into those idiots. You know, the ones who wanted to blast your kneecaps. They didn't like what we did to their car yesterday. One thing led to another. It was crazy."

Jack stared at the floor. "That's your story?"

Markus took a swig from his bottle. "Yeah, that's about it." He looked casually about the room. Connor crossed his arms and stayed quiet. Markus gestured with the sports drink bottle as if remembering something. "Oh yeah, I called them a couple of pussies too." He cringed. "Sorry for the language, ladies."

Jack pulled a chair from the table and clapped it down on the floor. "So you two instigated the fight, is that right?"

"Instigated is kind of a strong word," Markus said.

"I'd say those boneheads instigated the fight yesterday in Grand Rapids," Connor added.

"Did either one of you geniuses consider the advantage of not letting them know we're here?"

Connor sheepishly raised his hand.

"And you let this happen anyway?"

Neither of them answered.

"If you two weren't serious about this, you should have told me up front." Jack sat in the chair. "If you can't get serious about it now, then pack up your things and get your asses home. What's it going to be?"

The guys slunk their shoulders and avoided looking at him, suppressed by shame only a father could dish out. Connor lifted his chin. "Sorry, Dad, no more mistakes." He fixed Markus with a glare. "I'll make sure of it."

Jack shook his head. "What a stellar morning. First I find out about the dig and now this."

Connor cocked his head. "The dig?"

"Bobbie and I took a boat ride upriver past buried Singapore. There's an MSU archeological team working the site. They've been there three months and have dug their way down to the ruins. Somebody has been on this treasure hunt a long time."

Markus pulled his hand from the ice pack. "Hey, how are we going to dig anything up if the other guys are already there?"

Jack leaned forward and set his hands on his knees. "I can't get anything past you, Markus."

Bobbie and Alyson had not ventured into the cottage much beyond the front door. Lauren waved them in. "You don't have to stand there, girls, come in and take a seat."

Bobbie walked up and gave her a short hug. "Thanks for helping out."

Lauren exchanged a quick glance with Jack over Bobbie's shoulder. Her eyes seemed to be saying, *You owe me for this, mister.*

Alyson gave her a more affectionate embrace. "Good to see you again."

Connor stood and surrendered his seat.

"This MSU dig is a mixed bag for us," Jack said. "Most of the sand covering Singapore is gone, but as Markus so aptly pointed out, the other team is on the field."

"At least we have the clue from the second Bible," Lauren said.

Jack perked up. "That's right, sweetheart, and I figured it out!"

"You did?"

"Yeah, the wildcat is not an ocelot."

Markus toyed with an ice cube. "An oce-what?"

Jack ignored him. "The wildcat is the bank."

Lauren went to the kitchen table and collected sheets of paper she'd been scribbling her thoughts on. "Excuse me, Bobbie." She sifted through the pages. "Which bank?"

"Singapore," Jack said. "Eugene told me the Bank of Singapore opened and operated under a flawed banking law. It printed its own paper money but didn't have enough hard coin to back it up. They called these types of institutions wildcat banks. The bones of the wildcat. Get it?"

"That fits." Lauren skimmed through her notes.

"Of course it fits. That's why I said I figured it out."

"No, it fits with what I found in the clues while you were gone." She handed him one of the pieces of paper and traced a portion of her notes with her finger. He studied it a moment and his eyebrows arched. "This is really good. How did you piece it together?"

"I like word puzzles. My mind latches on to them for some reason. Sudoku, crosswords, word searches, the patterns just jump out at me. This one took me some time though."

"Well, let's see it," Connor said.

Jack slid his chair over and laid the paper on the table so everyone could see.

Lauren had rewritten the clues and had arranged them in a more traditional poetic structure. They appeared as two stanzas of a poem now, David's clue above Daniel's. Lauren stepped up and put a hand on Jack's back. "In each Bible the clue is written out in the margins as one long sentence. The sentence is broken by commas at rhythmic points." She motioned her hand like it was a knife cutting a rope. "It dawned on me that after each comma Coates capitalized the first letter of the next word. The way it strung out on the page gave me the impulse to rewrite the clue and start a new line with each comma. I did and it turned out like you see here."

> A hundred yards south of the Beach
> To the north and touching the River
> That which you seek
> In Singapore lie
> Cherry and Cedar flank the great find
>
> Revelation awaits
> Above the ground
> For in the wildcat's bones
> The answer is found,
> Engraved and sealed
> Read north to south
> Selah

Lauren bounced on her heels. "Does anybody see it?"

Nobody spoke. Jack kept his lips sealed to give them a chance to pick it out.

"Come on." Lauren frowned. "Haven't any of you ever seen an acrostic poem before?"

Connor scratched his head. "What's an apocryphic poem?"

"Not apocryphic," Alyson said with a laugh. "An acrostic poem."

Bobbie leaned closer to the clues. "I see it, Lauren. Good eye."

"Care to enlighten the rest of us?" Markus said.

Lauren crossed her arms. "An acrostic poem is simply a poem in which the first or last letter of each line is part of a hidden word or phrase. When the letters are read in sequence the word is revealed."

Connor seemed unconvinced. "Yeah?"

"Guys," Jack said, "look at the first letter of each line and read down."

Connor did. "A-T-T-I-C R-A-F-T-E-R-S. Very cool, Mom, I get it."

Jack stood. "Honey, you just salvaged the day." He gave Lauren a kiss and hurried off to his travel bag in the bedroom. He returned with Steven's notebook and opened it to the street map of Singapore. "Time to get up to speed. Everybody listen up." He glanced at Bobbie. "Especially new arrivals." He laid the notebook on the table. "David's clue told us to look in Singapore and focused on this city block right here. At that point it seemed like Coates had buried the coins in the foundation of one of the old buildings in the block."

"Isn't that still the assumption?" Markus asked.

"Not necessarily. Now we've deciphered Daniel's clue and the acrostic element. It tells us we'll find engraving on the attic rafters inside the Bank of Singapore, not the actual coins. This engraving will tell us where the coins are, and I'm guessing they won't be in Singapore proper."

"Why not Singapore?" Bobbie said.

"Let's think about it." Jack reclaimed his chair. "Harlan Coates takes coins that aren't rightfully his. He learns that the coins came from a group of investors who ran the defunct Bank of Singapore. He doesn't know the reason they loaded the coins on the ship. All he knows is those investors still live in the area and he doesn't want them finding out that he has their capital. If they find out they'll take the coins, put him in jail, and his sons won't have an inheritance. Now if I'm Harlan Coates, I want to get the coins as far from those investors as possible. In the overall scheme of things it makes sense that he wouldn't dig a hole in Singapore."

Bobbie tapped the tabletop with her finger. "But if Coates was afraid the investors would find out, why would he hide the location of the coins inside the bank?"

"Because when he did it the building wasn't a bank anymore. The

Singapore Bank was dissolved three years before Coates found the coins. The building itself was probably a boarding house or a hotel or something. I'm sure Coates appreciated the irony of putting the final clue there."

"So Singapore isn't our last stop," Lauren said.

Markus finished off his lime drink. "Good, no digging with the bad guys."

"We still have to play ball with them," Jack said. "We need to get inside Singapore and find the engraving, and to do that we need to know where the bank is located." He swiped his hand over the notebook. "This map isn't detailed enough to show us where it was, but I'd bet my 401(k) it's somewhere inside this city block."

"How are we going to pinpoint it?" Connor said.

"Eugene Elliot." Jack opened his cell and called the historian's number. "If anyone can tell us the coordinates of the bank it's him." The line rang several times. Eventually Eugene's voice mail greeting answered. Jack left him a brief message explaining the dilemma. He closed the phone and addressed Bobbie. "You're up, sweet—" His brain caught up with his mouth and he stammered. "Uh, Bobbie, call your MSU friends. We need to set up a meet with the dig supervisor."

She switched on her PDA. "I'll see what I can do."

Jack felt some heat radiating nearby and realized it was Lauren's glare.

"Dad." Connor stepped between them. "I just had a thought. Those idiots got a real good look at my truck yesterday, and we're parked out front. It'd be pretty easy for them to find out where we're staying. I think we should try to get a townie to let us park it in his garage."

"Good thought." Jack pulled a twenty dollar bill from his wallet. "Offer a homeowner this and tell him you're throwing a surprise birthday party for your girlfriend at Beechwood Manor and you don't want her to see your truck when she arrives."

"Wow, that's good. You're pretty sneaky."

A witty comment correlating sneakiness and marriage came to mind, but Jack decided it wasn't a good time to throw it out there. "Take Markus with you. Stay out of trouble."

Connor nodded. "Markus, quit whining about your finger. Let's go." They dashed out of the cottage.

Bobbie dialed the first number on her contacts list.

Lauren and Jack moved off into the living room. "Those men know we're in town," she said, "and they know we need to get into

Singapore. How are we going to find the engraving without them knowing?"

"I haven't figured that out yet." He watched through the front window as Connor pulled his truck out of its parking spot. "First things first. We have to find the site of that bank." He flashed a sarcastic smile. "It'd be a real shame if those rafters have disintegrated under that sand after all these years."

Connor's truck disappeared down the road.

Lauren turned from the window. "A part of me wouldn't mind that at all."

Jack regarded her a moment. "Why? You have something against being a millionaire?"

"No, I'm just concerned over what it might cost to get there."

He took her hand. "I won't let anything happen to you or the boys. You've got my word on that. If it ever comes down to a decision between recovering the coins or ensuring my family's safety, then to hell with the millions."

She mustered a weak smile. "You were there for Connor today. Tomorrow might be a different story. You can't be there for everyone all the time. It just isn't possible."

Jack's warm expression receded and a resolute cast replaced it. "Watch me."

TWENTY-FOUR

Bobbie's efforts to reach the MSU dig supervisor carried into the afternoon. After several calls, messages, return calls, and collected favors, she managed to get the cell number of Professor Collin Dodd, Director of Field Projects, Department of Anthropology. A friend of a friend of a colleague came up with the final links in the chain to make contact. Bobbie reached the professor, dropped a few university staff names, and arranged a four o'clock meeting on the deck behind the Butler Restaurant.

Lauren did not appreciate her exclusion from the invite list to the meeting, but Jack had other plans. He and Bobbie would attend the meeting alone. No need to come at the guy with a committee. Keep it simple. Downplay the entire affair. Just try to get Professor Dodd to escort them on site after hours with no one else around. That was the goal.

Jack posted Lauren and the guys in and around the restaurant to keep watch during the meet to make sure Ben didn't happen by and cause a problem. That's the last thing he needed. Eugene Elliot hadn't called back, and this meeting with Collin Dodd was Jack's best hope to find the location of the Bank of Singapore and get a look at its ruins.

At five before the hour, he and Bobbie took a seat beneath an umbrella on the Butler's immense outdoor deck overlooking Lake Kalamazoo. An early dinner crowd had already gathered. Lauren and Alyson were seated among them at a table near the entrance to the deck. Connor and Markus kept an eye on the front door and the docks from Cook Park.

Jack wanted a beer real bad but thought it better to stay sharp and ordered an iced tea instead. Bobbie took ice water. The waitress brought them their drinks. A moment after she set them on the table, a suntanned man with pattern baldness and a scraggly salt-and-pepper beard walked onto the deck. He scanned through the people seated at the tables through a pair of dark sunglasses with rectangular frames. He wore khaki Bermuda shorts and a white button shirt smudged here and there with dried dirt. Jack considered him a few moments. "That's got to be our man."

"I think you're right," Bobbie said. She stood and waved to him. "Professor Dodd?"

The man homed in on her voice, waved, and walked over. "Ms. Weller, good to meet you."

She shook his hand. "Thanks for making time for me."

Jack stood. "Professor." They shook as well.

"This is Jack, my research assistant," Bobbie said.

Assistant?

They all sat down at the table. Professor Dodd brushed at one of the dirt smudges on his shirt. "Forgive me," he said. "I came right over from the dig." The waitress returned and asked him for a drink order. He chose iced tea.

"How is it going out there?" Bobbie said. "We took the paddle-boat upriver this morning and saw the ruins. It looks like you're making good progress."

"It's getting very exciting now. Everyday we're opening the window into Singapore's past a little wider." Dodd leaned to the side to get under the shade of the umbrella. "So tell me what piqued your interest in our little village buried in sand, Ms. Weller."

Bobbie settled back and crossed her legs. "I'm writing a book on Michigan's transformation from a territory to a state. Some notable pioneers in Allegan County lore lived in Singapore during the boom times. I heard about your project here and thought it a wonderful opportunity to actually see the place these men built out of the wilderness."

Jack decided her legs still looked pretty good.

"We're concentrating on a section of town where the buildings are clustered close together," Dodd said. "It's dramatic to stand in the street of a village rising from the dust. If you'd like to see it I can take you there this afternoon."

Bobbie smiled. "That would be fantastic."

Jack raised a hand. "We don't want to be a distraction to your team."

The waitress delivered Dodd's iced tea. He thanked her and took a sip. "Your presence won't be a problem at all."

Jack fidgeted in his seat. "The other thing is that we'd love to get some photographs of the ruins, alone in the sand if possible. I want to invoke the desolate feel of a ghost town dead and buried being exhumed for an autopsy, so to speak. If we can visit after the dig team has left for the day it would be great."

Dodd thought about that for a little bit. "That won't be a problem." He checked the time on his wristwatch. "We take advantage of the long summer days and work pretty late into the evening. We pack up about nine o'clock. We're usually clear of the site in a half hour. Is that too late?"

"No, that's perfect," Bobbie said.

"Why work so late?" Jack said. "You in a hurry?"

"We're on a timetable of sorts." Dodd smiled. "It must sound funny, an archeological dig in a time crunch. The fact is our sponsor wants to display some of our finds at an exhibit in July, and I don't want to disappoint." He set his glass down on the table. "I've got a feeling some really good pieces are down closer to the foundation of the buildings."

The sun made Bobbie squint. "Are you looking for something in particular?"

Dodd shook his head. "No, it's just that people tend to lose things near the buildings in which they live and work. Mundane things misplaced two hundred years ago are extremely interesting to us today, like tools, jewelry, buttons, boots, tin cans, coins—"

"Coins?" Jack sat up straight. "Have you found any?"

"No, we haven't reached the depth those types of things are most likely imbedded."

"I'll bet a coin from that era would be pretty valuable today."

Dodd nodded. "Most likely."

"Who is the sponsor for this dig?" Bobbie said.

"The Blue Water Project. It's a foundation for the historical preservation of Great Lakes culture."

"Do representatives from the foundation direct site activities, or do you get full rein?"

"I direct activities." Dodd looked at her funny. "That's an odd question, Ms. Weller."

"I'm just curious if you have to deal with sponsors wanting too much control over your dig sites. It's something I've dealt with on research projects in the past."

Jack glanced at Bobbie and gave her a slight nod for the nice recovery.

"It's my dig," Dodd said. "I wouldn't have accepted the position if it were any other way."

"Well, we appreciate the invitation to your site," Jack said.

Bobbie added, "It'll be an invaluable experience for my book."

Dodd reminded them to dress for walking through sand and dirt. For the next hour they ate dinner while discussing the Singapore dig and how the MSU team whisked away a towering sand dune to reveal the village remnants beneath. Dodd seemed very proud of his work there. Jack had to admit it was a massive undertaking. Once again he found himself giving credit to whoever had thought up the scheme.

Jack felt certain the Blue Water Foundation was a front, just a paper organization to mask the real intent of the excavation. As to Dodd and the students on the dig site, he leaned toward the belief that they were oblivious to the importance of unearthing Singapore. He believed this of the students for sure. He chose for the moment to reserve judgment on Professor Collin Dodd. It would make sense for the man directing dig activities to know about the coins. Then again, keeping that same man in the dark could be argued made just as much sense. Jack wasn't sure which way to go with it, so he fell back on the axiom that had served him so well in the past: In the absence of certainty, abstain from trust.

In any event, Jack Sheridan knew he had an ace up his sleeve, and he had to be very careful of when and how he played it. At nine thirty that night he would read the cards at the Singapore site. If the hand before him looked favorable, he'd find out how far that ace would get him.

Professor Dodd left the Butler Restaurant after a Chicken Caesar salad dinner.

Bobbie watched him disappear from the crowded deck. "You think they've uncovered the bank?" she asked Jack.

"Depends how much information the Blue Water Foundation had at the start of the dig." Jack played with a French fry on his plate. "I'm banking on them having unearthed our clue without realizing what they've done." He smiled. "No pun intended."

Lauren and Alyson came over to the table from their surveillance post.

"How did it go?" Lauren asked.

"Good," Jack said. "We were invited to go up to the site tonight."

"'We' meaning all of us?"

"'We' meaning Bobbie and I."

Lauren paused just long enough to let him know she was nonplussed at this second lack of an invitation. "Did Professor Dodd know about the coins?"

"He didn't let on that he knew, but then again he didn't say he that he didn't know. I guess that's a double negative. Those are hard to prove one way or the other."

Lauren started to look annoyed. "How did you get him to invite you up there?"

"I told him seeing Singapore would really help research a book I was writing," Bobbie said.

"What if Ben and those men Connor and Markus fought with are waiting for you at the dig site when you get there?"

"I won't be alone," Jack said. "I'll have my team backing me up."

"Well then, you better tell your team the plan."

"Let's get Connor and Markus over here to hash it out." Jack summoned the boys with a cell call. Everyone gathered around the table. "We need to find the bank in Singapore and get a look at the rafters," Jack said. "This morning from the river, it seemed the dig team had cleared enough sand to allow that. If I handle it right, Professor Dodd will lead us to the clue without realizing it."

"Why deal with Dodd at all?" Markus said. "Can't we just sneak onto the dig site at night and find the engraving on our own?"

"We don't know the location of the bank or in what state of deterioration it's in. I don't think fumbling through the ruins in darkness will be very effective. Dodd's been working the site for three months. He knows every inch of the excavation and likely has more detailed maps and charts than we do. If the bank structure is uncovered and intact, it should be a simple matter for him to point it out."

"Why didn't you ask him about the bank at this meeting?" Connor said.

"I didn't want to tip him off to what we're doing, at least not yet. Once we're on site I'll get more in-depth with him. He won't have as much time to think about it then."

Markus caressed his fist. "What if those retards we keep running into show up in Singapore while you're there?"

"I'll judge the situation and make a threat assessment. Who knows? If they're there they might want to talk. They might want to negotiate. Remember, you guys were the ones who kicked the hornets nest this morning." Jack let the boys gnaw on that a bit. Of course, he didn't really believe Ben and his cronies were interested in civil discourse, either.

"Okay," Connor said. "For the sake of argument, let's say they want to kick your ass."

"Bobbie and I aren't going to hang around and let them do it. We'll have an exit strategy."

Alyson looked at her mother. "What will that be?"

"Back door," Jack said. "We're walking into Singapore through the front but if we need to get out quick we're exiting through the back."

He slapped Markus on the bicep. "And you're going to be there waiting for us."

Markus smirked. "I don't know, Mr. Sheridan, I'm not comfortable being someone's back door man."

"Don't worry, you'll like it." Jack glanced at Alyson. "You up for keeping him in line?"

"What is it we're doing?" she said.

Jack assured her with a smile. "The river is the back door. The Kalamazoo runs just south of Singapore. Dugout Road is the only road leading to the dig site. Bobbie and I will drive in on the road, but if something happens and we need to get out quick, we'll make a break for the water. You and Markus will be there with transportation. Details to follow."

"What are Connor and I going to be doing?" Lauren said.

"Surveillance and cavalry call. You two will watch Dugout Road and make sure no one follows us in. If you see anyone, you call me immediately." Jack gestured with his phone. "Our communication will be failsafe, too. Every five minutes I'll dial your cell and let it ring once. That's my heartbeat. If I don't call on time, you dial 911 immediately. Tell them there's a fire raging at the Singapore dig site and there are people hurt. They'll dispatch the entire fire department."

"Why not just call the police?" Connor said.

"We'll get a bigger response from the fire department. Police will come with the package. We'll even get EMTs." He chuckled. "That might be very helpful."

Lauren frowned. "That's not funny."

"Plan for the worst, hope for the best," Jack said. "Chances are we'll be in and out with the clue in fifteen minutes."

"If you get in trouble and we call 911, I'm heading into Singapore," Connor said.

Jack shook his head. "Negative. If you show up there'll be a target painted on your chest."

"That's not what happened in Ottawa Hills."

"They didn't know about you then. Now they do, and I'm sure they'll be more than willing to take you out of the equation if given the chance, especially after this morning."

Connor didn't reply.

Jack surveyed the pensive faces of his team. "This is going to go smooth, we're going to find the coins, and we're all going to retire early. Got it?"

"There you go again," Bobbie said.

"Making it all seem so easy," Lauren added.

Jack regarded them. "Stereo." He picked up the tab for the meals and calculated the tip. "We need to get ourselves prepared." He pulled the cash to cover the bill out of his wallet and set it on the table.

They left the restaurant and went about arranging logistics for the Singapore visit that night. Jack set up Markus and Alyson for their river duty. Markus was pleased. The group scouted Dugout Road, getting a lay of the land leading up to the dig site and picking out a surveillance location for Connor and Lauren to stand post. After shopping for some last minute necessities they returned to the cottage to wait for the meeting time.

Jack tried to call Eugene Elliot a few more times but never got beyond voice mail. At eight thirty he left with Bobbie to get her car from the hotel she and Alyson were staying at. The group reconnected in the parking lot at the corner of Mason and Griffith in town. They ran through the plan one last time and then broke. Markus and Alyson headed toward Hoffman Street and the launching point for their role. Lauren took the wheel of Jack's Cherokee and rolled toward the parking lot's east exit to circle around Saugatuck and take up her post at the appointed time. Jack signaled her to stop and walked up to the driver's window.

"Keep your phone in your hand," he said. "We're heading in fifteen minutes early to keep Dodd off balance, so my first call will come in at quarter after nine."

Lauren nodded. "Okay."

"Got your Kel-Tek with you?"

She patted the purse sitting on the center console. "Right here. And it's loaded."

"Mom's packing heat," Connor said. "That's cool. Can I take a look?"

She snatched the purse into her lap. "No playing with guns. I don't care how old you are."

Jack smiled. "You won't need it but it's a good comforter."

She returned his smile. "If Ben is there, turn around and get out."

"We need the clue."

"You won't get it if you walk into a trap."

"They're still digging out Singapore thinking the coins are there. Ben doesn't know he's wasting his time. He doesn't know I have something he needs. If he's there when I show up, the worst he'll do is try to kick me off the site."

"Why won't he shoot you?"

"He's in defense mode. He thinks he's close to the treasure and doesn't need a murder to complicate things. He also knows I can't grab a shovel and hurry up dig a hole to steal the coins from under his nose. I'm no real threat to him. He doesn't know what I'm really after. That's my edge."

Lauren cast a concerned eye at him. "Be careful."

"I'm always careful." He leaned into the Jeep and gave her a kiss. "Love you."

"Love you too." She drove off.

Jack climbed into the passenger seat of Bobbie's Malibu. "On to Singapore."

Bobbie pulled out of the parking lot onto Griffith Street and headed north. They reached the Dugout Road turnoff on 66th Street in five minutes. She held her foot on the brake at the stop sign. "If you're right about this archeological dig being manipulated behind the scenes, our visit might not be a good idea."

Jack considered her a long while. "You told me you needed the coins to get out of trouble."

"I do."

"The only way to find them is to head down that road."

She hesitated. Lauren and Connor rolled up to Dugout Road in the oncoming lane of 66th and waited for the Malibu to move. Bobbie tapped her fingers on the steering wheel. "How sure are you that we'll find the clue on the bank rafters?"

"Ninety-nine percent."

"Why not a hundred percent?"

"I need wiggle room in case I'm wrong. Get moving."

She turned onto Dugout Road. Lauren followed in the Jeep. Half a mile down Lauren pulled into an off-road pocket concealed by a barb wire fence overgrown with wild berries. Bobbie kept driving. The road followed the contour of the river. Thick tree cover darkened the surroundings to the point the Malibu's headlights clicked on. Up ahead an old gray Chevy Tahoe appeared around a bend in the road. It was coming from the west, where Bobbie and Jack were headed. Loud music thumped from open windows. A mix of college-age guys and girls were crammed inside. They looked to be laughing and carrying on.

Jack watched them pass by. "Probably MSU students from the dig." He gave Bobbie a smile. "Remember those days?"

"Like it was yesterday." She eyed him. "This treasure hunt reminds me of some crazy thing we might have done back then."

"Yeah, it kind of does." Jack felt the Colt under his belt press against the small of his back. He recalled not feeling the need to carry such iron around with him in his college days. Life had certainly changed a lot between then and now.

The Malibu emerged from tree cover to open road. The fading sunlight at nine o'clock was still enough to switch the headlights off. They drove by a yacht building company on the right. The parking lot was empty. Jack figured their work day had ended hours ago. Apart from that large facility there wasn't much else to see on Dugout besides sporadic trees and, now that they were in the open, sand peppered with scrub grass.

The dig site appeared just north of the road ahead. Skeletal structures from Singapore's past and mounds of dislocated sand fashioned a unique landscape that in a strange sense resembled a place under construction rather than a place raised from the dead. A large beige canopy stood at the edge of the site and sheltered a spacious worktable built on legs made out of four-by-four posts. Water coolers, a rack of hand tools, and wooden crates stacked three high filled the space beneath the canvas. Someone was sitting at the worktable. It looked like Professor Dodd.

A Range Rover was parked just off the road adjacent to the canopy. No other cars were around. Bobbie pulled the Malibu in beside it and shut off the engine. "I don't see anyone walking around out there. That's a good sign, isn't it?"

"Might be." Jack hit the speed dial to call Lauren's phone. He let it ring once and then disconnected. "First heartbeat." He retrieved his camera bag from the floor and opened it. A glass flask and a digital camera were packed inside. He confirmed the camera battery was charged and that the disk was empty, and made sure the cap on the flask was tight. He definitely didn't want the gasoline inside spilling all over the place.

Bobbie eyed the flask. "Are you really going to burn the rafters after we get the clue?"

"Depends how well the engraving is preserved." Jack pulled a lighter from his shirt pocket and sparked a flame to make sure it worked. "If it's in real good shape someone is going to notice it sooner or later. They might even figure out what it means. I don't want to leave them that possibility."

"Dodd's not going to let you burn anything."

"I know. Let's hope we don't have to do it." He pocketed the lighter and closed the camera case. "Shall we meet with the good professor?" He climbed out of the car and shouldered the camera bag.

South of Dugout Road the Kalamazoo River flowed gently into Lake Michigan. A thirty-foot cabin cruiser decorated with an array of stowed fishing rods drove upriver. Jack checked the shore near the line of trees to the east but could not see Markus in the water. He must be waiting just out of sight.

Jack led Bobbie up a sandy slope toward the canopy. Dodd came out to meet them.

"Ms. Weller," he said, "it seems you found the site without issue. You're early." He regarded Jack. "All ready to get those breathtaking shots of Michigan's Pompeii?"

Jack patted the case. "You know it."

Dodd motioned them to follow. "Let me take you downtown."

Professor Dodd led them into the heart of the excavation. They walked on a wide path of trodden sand. Dilapidated structures in various stages of deterioration stood on either side. Grids of twine segmented various sections of earth. Skewed roof peaks, exposed trusses, and collapsed walls on the south side of the path outnumbered those to the north. Dodd gestured to the well-worn path. "We're walking on what was once Oak Street. The present elevation is about five or six feet above proper street level." He pointed to the ruined structures to the south. "Buildings are more densely clustered near the river. Merchants and other businesses lined up their shops to be closer to the commerce on the water."

Jack noticed a large section of ruins had been staked off and boxed inside a perimeter of red twine. He oriented himself with the Kalamazoo River, Oak Street, and the building remnants between and determined that the area cordoned off with red twine had to be the city block described in the clue from David's Bible. Any doubt remaining that the MSU archeological team's arrival in Singapore was coincidental to the treasure hunt evaporated. Jack gently pulled Bobbie close and whispered. "That's our city block. They're on to it."

Dodd turned around. "Merchant shops are great for finding business documents and discarded tools, but a residential home is the place to find personal effects that tell us so much about past culture."

"What's special about those buildings over there?" Bobbie said.

Dodd peeled off his sunglasses and studied the ruins in the red box. "That's our focus this month. We're hoping to unearth some nice pieces for the Blue Water Foundation's display."

Jack checked the time on his cell. He had to make his next call to Lauren in thirty seconds. "Can we get a closer look at those buildings? I think it would be a great picture to capture Bobbie standing in the ruins."

Dodd hemmed and hawed and scrutinized the excavation. "It's an active dig site. It'd be unfortunate if you stumbled in the wrong area and disrupted our work."

Jack hit the speed dial, allowed the phone to ring once and then ended the call. "We'll be extra careful. Trust me."

Dodd relented with a sigh. "Please be careful where you step."

Jack and Bobbie walked off the path and into the husk of a building. It smelled of mold and decomposing matter. They casually scanned a set of bare rafters overhead. No engraving was evident on the rotted wood. "Professor Dodd," Jack said. "Do you know what each of these buildings was used for back in the day?"

"Not all of them. Very few accurate maps of Singapore survived the years." Dodd looked in through a broken window frame. "This one was a general store, dry goods I believe."

Bobbie scooped a handful of sandy soil off the ground. "In my book I recount some interesting history concerning a local bank. Can you show me where that building stood?"

Dodd scratched at his beard. "A bank doesn't show up on the map we have. Did it exist very early on in the life of the village?"

"I think so. It must have dissolved before your map was drawn." Bobbie brushed the soil from her hands. "Just my luck."

Jack exited the husk through a collapsed section of wall. The neighboring structure didn't even have a roof. Fallen truss segments and broken roofing boards lay half buried inside three standing walls. A grid of white string mapped the area. Jack knelt to get a better look at the truss pieces. "You must be a patient man. Sifting through all this soil has got to be tedious work."

Dodd studied his wristwatch. "It's a rewarding profession." He smiled. "Sometimes very rewarding."

Jack stood. "Are we keeping you from an appointment?"

"No, I'm just fastidious with time. There's so little of it and I hate to waste any." Dodd glanced at Bobbie standing at the crumbled corner of the building. "Have you found what you're looking for, Ms. Weller?"

Bobbie's concentration on a collection of fallen boards broke. "Excuse me?"

"The perfect setting for your photograph. That is the reason you're out here, isn't it?"

She put on a defensive smile. "Of course. Why else would I be out here?"

Dodd didn't reply.

A little alarm sounded in Jack's head. The good professor seemed a bit on edge. Something had changed in his demeanor. Jack searched the skeletal ruins around them. They were still alone, but it didn't feel that way. A minute remained before he had to make the next call to Lauren. He wasn't so sure he should do it.

And then the cell phone vibrated in his hand.

Caller ID displayed Eugene Elliot's phone number. "Excuse me," Jack said, "I need to take this call." He flipped open the phone.

"Jack," Eugene said. "Sorry I didn't get back with you earlier. A power surge took out the power grid servicing my street. When it came back up my air conditioners blew out my breaker box. I've been melting all afternoon trying to get a serviceman to fix it."

"Sorry to hear that, Eugene. Did you understand my message?"

"Yes." He chuckled. "The buried town of Singapore lifts blackened bones on high."

"What?"

"It's from a poem by a man who called himself Friar Tuck. The wildcat's bones seemed to fit. Anyway, you want to know about the bank."

Jack glanced at Dodd. The professor was checking his watch again. Bobbie strained to see the face of a splintered rafter sticking out of the ground. Jack cradled the phone close to his ear. "What can you tell me about it?"

"You're looking in the wrong place," Eugene said. "You don't have to go to Singapore."

A beep sounded on the line and broke up Eugene's sentence. Someone was trying to ring in. Jack didn't hear the historian clearly. "What did you say?"

"You don't have to go to Singapore. When the mills closed the bank building was moved out of town. It ended up on Butler Street in Saugatuck. It's still standing there today as an art shop and bookstore."

Jack snapped his fingers to get Bobbie's attention. She turned around, but so did Dodd.

"What's the matter?" she said.

Jack waved her over. "Thanks, Eugene. I have to go. I'll call you later." He hung up and checked the incoming phone number. It was Lauren. He connected. "What's up?"

"That black 300C just drove by. It's coming your way."

Jack clapped the phone closed and glared at Dodd. "Bobbie, it's time to go."

The professor tensed and his face flushed red. "Now, see, we've got a problem."

Jack took Bobbie's hand and pulled her onto Oak Street.

"Who was that on the phone?" she asked.

"A friend. He told me we took a wrong turn."

Dodd followed them. "Where are you going? You didn't get that picture."

Jack picked up the pace and kept Bobbie in tow. "Trouble's coming."

Dodd called out in an irritated voice. "They need that second Bible, Jack, and they won't let you leave without it."

TWENTY-FIVE

Dodd knew something he shouldn't know. Not Good. Jack spun on his heel to confront him but Collin Dodd, Director of Field Projects, Department of Anthropology, was holding a .32 caliber pistol.

Bobbie drew an alarmed breath.

Jack clenched his fist. "You know about the coins."

"They made me an offer," Dodd said. "Ten percent of twenty million dollars sounded pretty reasonable."

"You sell out cheap."

Dodd scoffed. "It'll be a nice supplement to my pension plan."

Jack thought about the 300C driving up Dugout Road. He and Bobbie had to get out of Singapore. Dodd had to be dealt with quickly. Jack noticed the professor didn't seem comfortable holding the gun and took a step toward him. "What happens to your sweetheart deal when you don't find the coins in Singapore?"

"Once you give us the second Bible that won't be a problem."

"The coins aren't here. I deciphered the second clue and it points somewhere else."

Dodd shook his head. "You're lying. The coins are buried somewhere in that city block over there."

Bobbie stood a few steps behind Jack and focused on the outline of the Colt under his shirt. She moved closer to him.

Dodd keyed in on her. "Stay where you are, Ms. Weller."

The pistol barrel drifted and Jack made his move. He lunged, seizing Dodd's hand and pointing the gun at the ground. Surprise forced Dodd's eyes wide. Jack kicked his knee into the professor's wrist. The pistol fell. Dodd struggled to free himself but his slight frame was no match for his opponent. Jack threw a punch across Dodd's jaw. The professor went down. He didn't try to get back on his feet.

Jack lifted the pistol off the ground and handed it to Bobbie. "Hold this." A cell phone was clipped to Dodd's belt. Jack grabbed it and smashed it under his heel. "Let's move."

They ran up Oak Street, retracing the route they had followed into Singapore. The beige canopy sheltering the worktable loomed large at the top of the rise. Bobbie's Malibu was parked behind it. Jack reached back for the Colt under his belt and rounded the corner of the canopy. He skidded to a sudden halt. The camera case surged against the strap on his shoulder. He threw out his arm to stop Bobbie. She nearly ran him over and dropped Dodd's pistol. Escape plan A had just been foiled.

One of Ben's men was sitting on the hood of the Malibu toying with a handgun. The car's front passenger tire was flat. The man pointed the pistol at Jack. "Hello, Captain America. I didn't know you were interested in archeology."

Jack aimed the Colt at the man he recognized from the Ottawa Hills incident. "Put that Nerf gun down, Nate."

Nate Kisko smirked. "I've got nineteen shots in here. What've you got in that old Colt, seven?" He laughed. "I'd say you're outgunned."

"I'll only need one."

Kisko kept Jack in his sights and stood. "Someone cut the valve stem on your tire. You're going to need a ride home. Good thing my friends are on their way to pick me up. We can give you a lift."

Jack stepped in front of Bobbie and maneuvered closer to the Malibu.

Kisko took more careful aim. "You just hold it right there."

"You're not aiming at my kneecaps, Nate."

"Don't have to anymore. Rules have changed, and not in your favor."

"Haven't you heard? I have something you need. Shoot me and you'll never get it. On the other hand, if I shoot you I lose nothing."

"Bullshit."

Jack smiled. "Don't tell me Ben is withholding information. He must not trust you."

"Shut it, Sheridan. Ben will be here in a minute, and you two are going to have a little talk." Kisko glanced at Bobbie as if just noticing her there. "Good to see that nice ass again, Mrs. Weller. You should have helped us three months ago. Now look at the mess you're in."

Jack nodded at the ground in front of Kisko. "Hey, Nate, your shoe is untied."

"Asshole. How stupid do I look?"

Jack shrugged. "Let's try this one. What's that behind you?"

Kisko sneered but instincts forced him to glance sideways. He saw the weathered dock plank in his peripheral vision right before Markus struck him with it in the chest. Kisko cursed and folded. The pistol fired. A hole burst in a water cooler under the canopy. Jack shouted for Bobbie to get down. Markus followed through with the plank and swept Kisko's legs out from under him. Kisko tumbled and smacked the back of his head on the hood of the Malibu. He hit the ground and writhed in the sand half-conscious. Markus hovered over him. "El Pomposo strikes!"

Jack snatched up Kisko's handgun. "Nice work, Markus. Now get Bobbie out of here."

Markus nodded. "Got it."

Jack waved Bobbie forward. "Get to the water. They're going to be here any second."

"What about you?" she said.

"I'm right behind you. Go!"

Markus grabbed her arm. "This way." They ran across the road toward the river.

Jack crouched behind the Malibu. The roar of an engine echoed up from the tree covered stretch of Dugout Road. He needed more than a few seconds to get away clean. He needed to take Ben's eyes off the ball.

Kisko tried to get up but his floundering senses dropped him to his stomach. "You're screwed now, Sheridan."

Jack tore open the camera case. "Look who's talking." He pulled out the flask filled with gasoline and set it on the ground between his legs. His shirttail lay loose in his lap. He grabbed it and gnawed a tear in the seam, then ripped off a piece of material and rolled it into a large wick. The revving engine grew louder. He removed the cap from the flask and jammed the shirttail inside the neck. Gasoline soaked the material. He held the flask away from his body and fished the lighter from his pocket.

Dusk was settling in. A pair of headlights appeared on the road. Too far. Jack held still. Something shuffled on the ground behind him. Kisko had found an unsteady balance and stood poised to pounce. Hands full, Jack turned and kicked him between the legs. Kisko went down for the last time.

Jack sparked the lighter and lit the shirttail. It burst into flame. He hurled the flask for all he was worth, hoping to hit the mark, and hoping the mark was a black 300C with an ogre named Ben behind the wheel.

A sputtering trail of flame traced an arc through the air. Jack broke into a run across the road. The car's headlights landed on him. The flask came down. On target. It smashed on the road directly in front of the 300C. A mushroom of fire enveloped the front end and obscured the headlights. The driver swerved right. Flames peeled from the hood as the car careened off pavement and into a bank of sand.

Jack made it to the riverbank in time to see Markus whisking Bobbie away on a Jet Ski, a rooster tail of water kicking out behind them. Alyson glided in close on another Jet Ski. A couple hundred dollars for an after-hours rental was certainly paying off now.

"Good girl, Alyson." Jack stepped into the water. "No offense, but let me drive."

Alyson slid back on the seat. "Are you okay?"

Jack settled behind the handlebars. "I'm fine, they're not." He gunned the throttle.

On shore men spilled out of the 300C, cursing and kicking sand at the flames on the car. Alyson watched them scurrying about as Jack circled the Jet Ski around and started upriver. It wasn't long before they'd gotten out of sight of the scene. "Jack, you're crazy."

He took Kisko's pistol from his belt and tossed it into the river. "Crazy is as crazy does."

"Did you get the clue off the rafters?"

"It's not there."

"Are we back to square one?"

"No, I know where to find it for sure now."

Jack followed Markus around the bend in the river. The faint sound of a siren carried across the water from shore and rose just above the whine of the Jet Ski engine. Red flashers penetrated the trees flanking Dugout Road. The fire department was responding to a 911 call about a fire in Singapore.

Jack and Markus throttled down when they neared the docks of Saugatuck. They drifted into the slip at the ski rental and dismounted. The owner of the place met them on the dock and asked how their special twilight ride went. Jack smiled and tipped him a twenty. They all walked onto Water Street, Alyson and Bobbie chattering about the escape, Markus too wired to string together a coherent sentence. Jack noticed three missed calls from Lauren on his cell. He rang her up.

She answered immediately. "Are you all right?"

"Yes, we all are."

"What happened after we talked?"

"The professor wanted us to stick around and talk to Ben," Jack said. "We declined and rode out with Markus and Alyson."

"No shootouts or car crashes?"

"No shootouts."

"What happened to Bobbie's car?"

"Someone gave us a flat tire and we couldn't drive out. I think we need to report it stolen. By the way, thanks for the fire department support."

"Did you find the engraving?"

"Not yet. I'll fill you in on that when we're all together."

"Did you get away before Ben got there?"

Jack paused. "Sort of—hey, we're in town on Water Street. Come around and pick us up at the coffee house on Hoffman.."

"Hold on." Lauren muffled the phone and told Connor to find a map. They bickered a few seconds, and she came back to the line. "Okay, that's Uncommon Grounds. We'll be there in five minutes."

Jack led his troupe to the coffee shop. Once adrenalin from the Singapore incident receded, he contemplated Dodd's disturbing knowledge of Daniel's Bible. How did the professor learn about its existence and that Jack had already acquired it? Someone on that team was sharp. Jack doubted it was Dodd or Ben. Neither seemed the mastermind type. The specter of Rafferty rose again. That man was definitely capable of orchestrating everything he had seen. But Lauren's point that Rafferty was on the run argued against him getting involved in an elaborate treasure expedition. What about Lloyd? That weasel may not be the mastermind but he was a tool of Neptune's Reach, an industrial organization with plenty of resources. Then again it could be someone he hadn't thought of yet, or more likely didn't even know. Regardless of who was pulling the strings, Jack knew he had become a thorn in the competition's side, and unless he stayed a step ahead of them things would get even more dangerous for everyone.

He bought a round of caffeine for the group, and they waited for Lauren to arrive. Jack and Bobbie shared a small table outside on the sidewalk. Markus and Alyson did likewise.

"Here we are again," Bobbie said. She lifted her cup. "Discussing treasure over coffee."

Jack smiled. "We're going to keep doing it until we get it right."

"Finding the bank and the engraving isn't as easy as you thought it would be, is it?"

"No, it's going to be easier."

"Easier?" Bobbie laughed. "We ran out of Singapore empty handed. People were pointing guns at us."

"You get used to it after a while. Trust me; we're on the brink of great things."

"What did your friend say on the phone to boost your confidence?"

"He said I was stupid."

"And you found that inspiring?"

Jack leaned forward. "He didn't actually say I was stupid, but what he told me made me feel that way."

"What did he say?" Lauren's voice turned their heads. She stood beside the table near the curb with the Jeep keys in her hand. "You two look deep in conversation. Please continue."

Connor appeared and took the chair beside Alyson. Jack had them pull the two tables together so everyone could hear him. "Eugene told me we were looking for the bank in the wrong place," Jack said. "Before Singapore was buried, the bank building was moved."

"Moved to where?" Connor said.

"The Flats," Jack replied. "That's what it was called back then."

"What was called the Flats?" Bobbie asked.

Jack gestured to their surroundings. "Saugatuck. Eugene said the bank building was moved to Butler Street in Saugatuck. It's still standing."

Markus gave him an exaggerated double-take. "What?"

"It's some type of art shop and bookstore now." Jack frowned. "It's my fault we missed this little fact. I'm rushing us through, and I'm getting sloppy. I'll bet I walked by it three times."

"Let's get over there." Markus stood.

"Hold on, impulsive boy. The place is a business, and it's late. I doubt it's still open." Jack tapped his foot and added, "But I don't see any problem with doing a drive by."

They all headed for the Cherokee. Jack opened the door for Bobbie. Lauren noticed. She slapped the keys into his hand. "You drive."

"What's the matter?"

"Nothing."

Lauren, Bobbie, and Jack crammed into the front seat. Connor, Markus, and Alyson took the back. Jack pulled from the parallel parking space and headed east on Hoffman. Butler intersected the road at the end of the block. Jack turned south. All eyes searched for an old building housing an art shop and a bookstore. They didn't see such a place. Jack stopped at a visitor information booth at the end of the road and grabbed a merchants walking map of Saugatuck. He climbed back in the Jeep and noted Bobbie and Lauren were politely not talking.

They crowded around the unfolded map on the dashboard. Connor, Markus, and Alyson tried to see from the back seat. The map was a blown-up caricature of downtown, with numbers running up and down the street diagrams to represent shops and restaurants.

Lauren edged closer to the dash. "Did Eugene give you any idea where on Butler to look?"

"We've seen everything south of Hoffman," Bobbie said. "Where's the legend for these numbers?"

"Balls!" Jack jabbed his finger into the map. "Number seventy. East side. Singapore Bank Bookstore. Talk about being hit right between the eyes."

Connor laughed from the back seat. "Wow, Dad, you are getting sloppy."

"Let's go take a look." Jack turned the Jeep around and headed north. He slowed where the bank building should be located according to the map. "That has to be it." He swerved into an open parking space, and everyone got out of the Jeep.

They stood in front of a two-story building that looked more like a nineteenth-century home transformed into a shop than it did an old bank. A pair of striped awnings flanked the main entrance and hung over display windows where pieces of artwork were propped on easels. A sign over the door read SAUGATUCK GALLERY. A second door on the north end of the building beside one of the display windows had a narrow sign beside it. Vertical lettering on the sign read BOOK-STORE and a painted picture of a hand pointing up directed patrons to climb a set of stairs that were apparently behind the locked door. A trio of windows with decorative shutters spanned the upper level fascia.

Jack and the group stared up at the building. Passers-by on the sidewalk wondered what they were looking at.

"Okay," Connor said. "It doesn't look as obvious as it sounded."

Jack caressed his jaw. "This place definitely doesn't scream out 'I used to be a bank!'"

"I think we walked by it a few times ourselves," Alyson added.

"This is our secret," Jack said. "Can we all keep it until tomorrow morning?"

Everyone nodded and mumbled an acknowledgement.

Jack glanced at the upper-level windows but couldn't see in through the blackness. He lifted his gaze a bit to the peak above the windows. Behind the siding and wall board were the attic rafters, and on those rafters, hopefully, the engraving spoken of in the Bible clues.

Would it really be there? What would it say?

Standing there pondering, Jack realized he wasn't going to get much sleep that night.

TWENTY-SIX

Higgs pulled Kisko off the ground by his shirt collar and set him on the hood of the Malibu. Kisko slumped forward and took deep draws of breath. Several yards up the road, the front end of the 300C sat imbedded in sand with wisps of smoke curling up from the hood. Ehrlich was trying to suffocate the last remnants of burning gasoline on the ground with his foot. Barnett stood on the roadside smoking a cigarette. Fire engine sirens were getting closer. Higgs clenched his jaw and kicked the side of the Malibu so hard it rocked back and forth.

"What are you so mad at," Kisko said. "I'm the one with fractured ribs and nuts to match."

Higgs pointed an accusing finger at him. "You had Sheridan in your hand. What the hell happened?"

"Someone got the drop on me." Kisko tried to sit straight.

"This really pisses me off, Nate. I expect more from you."

Kisko sneered. "You're the one who said Sheridan was a badass. You said he took on a ship full of mercenaries. He's livin' up to your press. Why so pissed?"

Higgs grabbed him tight by the collar and glared. "Because a maritime garbage man made you look like a fool."

The move startled Kisko. "Sheridan got lucky, that's all. It's not going to happen again, I guarantee that."

Higgs released him. "You damn well better." He stepped off to cool down.

"Weller's wife was with him," Kisko said. "They're definitely working together."

"That's not earthshaking news; we knew she got him involved." Higgs kept his back turned and listened to the sirens rounding the last bend on Dugout Road. He dropped his chin. Another complication that needed to be diffused was rolling toward him. Picking up the pieces after tangling with Sheridan was becoming an irritating pattern.

Professor Dodd appeared around the corner of the canopy. He staggered through the sand like a car crash victim stumbling from the wreckage. Higgs exhaled a breath of disdain. "Freaking school teacher." He marched up the slope to meet Dodd. Near the top he picked up the professor's .32 from the ground and brushed grains of sand off the barrel. "All you had to do was keep him occupied until I got here. Was that too much for you?"

"Sheridan found out you were coming," Dodd said. "Someone called him."

"At which point you pull out your piece and tell him to stand still."

"I did."

"So how did it end up over here?"

Dodd bit back a response.

"Wait, don't tell me; you're a professor of archeology, not a soldier of fortune. Right?"

The fire truck arrived at the site, headlights blazing and flashers pulsing. Barnett waved to the driver as it approached. Ehrlich stopped smothering flames with his feet. Higgs glanced at the fire truck and then spit on the ground. "Professor, you're going to tell those firemen you had a little mishap with a gas can but it's under control now. Thank them for their concern and send them on their way."

Dodd watched the truck roll to a stop near the 300C. "Since when did our agreement include taking orders from you?"

"Since when did you think otherwise?" Higgs made the pistol safe and dropped it into his sports coat pocket. "Make it quick, we're not done talking."

Dodd started down the slope, but then paused. "Sheridan told me they're not here."

"What?"

"Sheridan told me the coins aren't in Singapore. Is that true?"

"Could be. I'll know for sure when I get a look at that second Bible." Higgs snapped his fingers. "Oh, that's right, my professor and my partner screwed me on that one."

"What happens to our deal if you find the coins someplace else?"

"No coins in Singapore, no cash in your pocket."

Dodd turned. "I worked this site for months. I deserve something."

"I thought you people enjoyed this crap. Digging up the past, preserving history, just finding an old piss bucket is payment enough, isn't it?"

"I was told ten percent for my participation. I upheld my end of the bargain."

Higgs squared with him. "There was never a guarantee. You took a chance like everyone else. Now get down there and handle the fire department."

Dodd stared at him a moment longer and then continued down slope.

Kisko hobbled up next to Higgs. "What's the problem with Singapore Jones?"

"Our agreement is starting to taste sour to him."

"Did Sheridan tell him something?"

"Maybe. Why do you ask, did Sheridan tell you something?"

"Yeah, he said he had something we need."

"He does." Higgs watched Dodd parlay with the firemen. "There's another Bible with another clue. The picture is not complete without both. I just found out myself."

"Then we need to get it from him."

"Why the hell do you think I'm so hot right now?"

"He's in town," Kisko said. "It's a small place. Let's find him and convince him to give us the second Bible. I'm sure he'll fold if Bobbie Weller has a knife to her throat."

"Or his son," Higgs said

Kisko cocked his head. "Huh?"

"One of the two guys tagging along with Sheridan is his son, and Sheridan is a concerned father."

Kisko chuckled. "Soft white underbelly."

A couple of the firemen unraveled a hose from the truck. Another inspected where the gasoline had splattered on the road. Dodd started back. Higgs scanned the fire truck. "Nate, find out if that engine has a winch to pull the car off the sand bank."

Kisko lifted his head. "Are we going to look for Sheridan?"

Higgs nodded.

Kisko smiled. "I feel better already. My nuts even stopped hurting." He headed for the truck.

Higgs walked beneath the canopy and stood over the worktable. He switched on a battery-powered lantern. A large chart of Singapore marked with notations concerning dig activities lay across the tabletop. A box drawn with a red marker encircled the block of buildings identified in the Coates Bible clue. Before Higgs had learned about the second Bible, he was certain the coins would be found in that red box. Now he wasn't so sure. After so long on the trail his frustration was becoming palpable, but he had to stay focused. He couldn't let his attitude slide like Kisko. It would all be worth it in the end. Hell, the money from the coins was just the tip of the iceberg.

"They're spraying off the road." Dodd approached the worktable. "Then they'll be on their way."

Higgs kept studying the chart. "Bobbie Weller contacted you, correct?"

"Yes."

"Give me her number from your cell phone memory."

Dodd reached for his belt clip. Empty. "Sheridan smashed my phone."

Higgs raised an eye. "Did he take anything else from you, Collin?"

"Quit trying to belittle me about it. You're not faring any better against him yourself."

Higgs wanted to reach over and throttle Dodd but the whinny archeologist happened to be right. Sheridan was bouncing around like a jack rabbit, popping his head up and springing away with a carrot before Higgs could draw a bead and take him down. That had to change. The motivational value of going up against a worthy adversary only went so far. At some point you have to stop him from scoring points, or he eventually wins the game.

"Sheridan made a mistake today," Higgs said. "He showed me a weak spot."

"What do you mean?"

Higgs shook his head. "You just keep the dig going. Proceed as if none of this has happened. For all I know those coins are right where I thought they were. Until I find out differently there's no need to change course."

Dodd stood there like he wanted to say something else. Higgs ignored him. Eventually Dodd sulked down to his Range Rover. Higgs called after him. "Be here in the morning at your normal time. Business as usual."

Dodd climbed into the Range Rover without responding.

The firemen finished washing down the road and coiled the hose. They were even good enough to pull the 300C off the sand with their winch. While they worked, Higgs formulated his strategy for the next day. He'd need to make a phone call or two to get some information, but in general his plan was pretty straightforward. By the time the fire truck had left the scene, the sun had completely disappeared from the sky. Night fell on Singapore. Kisko, Ehrlich, and Barnett gathered around the lantern on the worktable beneath the canopy. Sound of lake surf rolled in over the dune just west of the site.

"We didn't make any progress today," Higgs said to them. "The good news is we stopped Sheridan from making any progress either."

Barnett tossed a cigarette into his mouth. He hesitated before lighting up.

Higgs paid him no mind. "We did learn something, however. Sheridan is in possession of another important clue, and we need to get it from him."

"How are we going to do that?" Ehrlich said.

"We're going to flush the jack rabbit out of his hole and convince him to give it to us."

Barnett lit his cigarette. "It's gonna take a lot of convincing to make this guy give it up."

"Don't worry," Kisko said. "It'll happen."

Barnett and Ehrlich looked to Higgs for confirmation.

Higgs smirked. "It's a matter of leverage, gentlemen." He lifted the lantern off the worktable. "When you approach a problem from the right angle you can accomplish anything."

He switched off the light and sent them all into darkness.

- TWENTY-SEVEN -

The cottage at Beechwood Manor was full up. After the Singapore incident Jack thought it best for Bobbie and Alyson to stay the night with the group. The decision netted mixed reviews from the members of Jack's Treasure Expeditions, Inc. Connor and Markus whole heartedly agreed it would be safer for the women to stay at the cottage, although Jack was certain ulterior motives influenced their thinking. Lauren refrained from commenting on the subject. Her silence sounded pretty loud to Jack. She and Bobbie weren't exactly cozying up with chamomile together. He had hoped Lauren would strike a more congenial chord, but in retrospect he realized that was a lot to expect of a wife in regards to her husband's ex-lover.

He'd gotten the Jeep and the S-10 off the street for the night. A Saugatuck resident a few blocks away from the inn had a nice big two-car garage and didn't mind housing the vehicles without asking too many questions, for a fifty-dollar storage fee. Jack figured he needed to find the coins just to cover his mounting operating expenses.

As expected he didn't sleep much. He spent an hour trying to determine the best approach to get inside the bank and look at the attic rafters, and another wondering whether the engraved clue even existed. Of course, the whole issue of Dodd knowing about the second Bible still rattled him. There were sharp players on the other team, and they were very motivated to get to the coins first. He couldn't afford to be sloppy anymore.

Jack wasn't the only one losing sleep. He heard Connor, Markus, and Alyson talking in the kitchen late into the night. They were a good group of kids, even though they weren't kids anymore. Despite the fight in town the guys had proven themselves to be a valuable asset to have along for the ride. And Alyson fit right in like she'd always belonged. She was a strong girl, unassuming like Connor, capable of more than she let on. She mixed well with the guys, and they definitely didn't mind having her around.

And then there was Bobbie. Just spending time with her brought back a lot of memories he'd tucked away long ago. The chemistry between them hadn't become inert with the passage of time. Despite the years, or her marriage to Steven, or even his love for Lauren, a remnant of their bond remained. It didn't surprise him. They were close before the split, and but for a few missteps Bobbie would have been his wife. But that was a long time ago, and he had to make certain he didn't trip himself up with Lauren on the road to the treasure. Their marriage had rebounded from the brink, and he wasn't about to jeopardize it again.

Sometime after two o'clock he put his arm around Lauren and fell asleep.

* * *

Jack had his team arrayed in front of the shops on the west side of Butler Street beneath gray cloud cover. They stood across from the old bank building. The time on his cell read 9:57 a.m. The Singapore Bank Bookstore opened at ten. He singled out Connor and Markus. "Ben's got at least three men working with him, and you guys know what they look like. If they show up I don't want them getting inside the bank, and I definitely don't want to get cornered in an attic."

"They won't get in," Connor said.

"Right, if we see them we'll drop the hammer," Markus added.

Jack shook his head. "Wrong, El Pomposo, if they show up just keep an eye on them and Alyson will report a purse snatcher to the police. When the police arrive she'll tell them, 'I'm not certain, Officer, but I think those men right there stole a purse from a woman on Water Street.' That should be enough to get them questioned and out of action for a while."

"But what if they try to get into the bookstore while you're inside?" Connor said.

Markus raised his fist. "Then my knuckles persuade them to back off."

Alyson stifled a laugh.

Connor rolled his eyes.

"No," Jack said, "you call me immediately, and then you call the police and follow the purse snatching scenario. We want *them* detained, not you for instigating another street brawl."

"Look," Connor said. "They started this whole conflict thing."

"These guys are dangerous," Jack said. "So far we've managed to stay in one piece, and I intend to keep it that way."

Connor grumbled. "Pardon me. I didn't mean to be the trouble-maker."

Jack settled back on his heels. "That's not what I'm saying. Don't twist it." He let a few seconds of silence pass. "I need a volunteer to go in with me."

Lauren and Bobbie both made a move to come forward. They glanced at each other. Bobbie backed down, and Lauren took her place at her husband's side.

"Okay," Jack said. "We'll be back in twenty minutes with the key to twenty million dollars."

Bobbie raised a hand. "After you find the engraving, are you going to burn down the building?"

Jack frowned. "Different circumstance." He surveyed the group. "Any other wise comments from the gallery?" There weren't any. "Good. Spread out. Eyes open."

Jack adjusted the camera case strap on his shoulder, and he and Lauren started across the street. "I wasn't waiting for an invitation this time," she said to him.

He smiled. They crossed the yellow line and his cell phone rang. Caller ID came up with an unknown name and unknown number. He hated those. "Hello?"

"Jack Sheridan, how's the family?"

Jack stopped on Butler's east curb. "Who is this?"

"Think real hard and you'll figure it out."

"Let's see, cocky tone, linebacker baritone, it's got to be my buddy Ben."

Lauren whirled her head around.

"You're good," Higgs said. "I knew you'd make things interesting. Let me return the favor."

Jack scanned through the people on the sidewalk, wondering if Ben was close. "You're doing just fine. Don't do anything special on my account."

"Tell me, do you read those Bibles you're carrying around, or do you just strip away the clues and discard them?"

"I'll be honest; I'm lifting the clues and closing the book, just like you."

Higgs found a laugh in that. "Seriously, Sheridan, you should read II Samuel 18:33. Learn from scripture. Don't live the sad lessons it teaches."

Jack didn't know the reference but something in Ben's voice tightened his stomach. "What are you talking about?"

"The second Bible," Higgs said. "The second clue. You have it. I need it. Turn it over now and no harm done. You gave it a good go. If you keep holding on to it, then that no harm clause is going to change. Let me give you a hint. I won't be pulling out *your* fingernails. Capice?"

Veins pulsed in Jack's neck. "You go that route, there's only one way this is going to end between us and believe me, I've dealt with bastards like you before and you won't like the finish. Capice?"

Higgs paused. "I won't let this go, Jack. Those coins are mine. I won't let you rest until they're in my pocket."

"You going to stalk me the rest of my life, keep me looking over my shoulder? Get in line."

"Consider yourself warned. Whatever happens next is in your hands." Higgs disconnected.

Jack closed the phone in his fist. He met Lauren's concerned eyes. "Let's find this last clue and get the hell out of here."

"That was Ben," she said. "What did he say?"

"He said he wants the second Bible." Jack started up the stairs to the Singapore Bank Bookstore. "I'd like to know how he learned about it."

Lauren followed him. "You said he's been hunting this treasure a long time. He probably pieced it together with the information he has, just like we did."

"That doesn't explain how he knows I have it." Jack reached the top of the stairs and entered the small shop. Half a dozen tables piled with books filled the upper level of the old bank building. Bookshelves divided the room in half. Some new release displays were built right into the wall. An off-balance ceiling fan clicked overhead. A little countertop sat adjacent to the stairs. Leaflets, bookmarks, and books cluttered its surface. A woman in her middle years with long black hair and thin-framed glasses sat in front of an old cash register on the counter. Behind her a curtain closed off a doorway to a back room. She smiled at her patrons. "Can I help you find something this morning?"

Jack approached and noted her name tag. "Yes, Barb, I think you can." He stood at the counter and glanced around the little shop. "This might sound a little strange, but I'm a member of the American Historical Architecture Society, and I've got a fifty-dollar wager with a fellow member that this wonderful old building employs a king-post truss system. My delusional friend believes the builder used a queen-post truss system." Jack scoffed like the notion was ridiculous.

Lauren stood beside him and bit her lower lip.

"You're right," Barb said. "That does sound a little strange."

"If I'm right, I win his fifty bucks." He shook the strap of the camera bag. "All I have to do is get a couple of pictures inside your attic. Is that possible?"

She stared at him. "Are you serious?"

"You have no idea."

"Are you going to buy a book?"

Jack surveyed the tables. "Um..." He tapped Lauren on the shoulder. "Hey, sweetheart, I've got an idea. Let's see if there's a nice old edition of a Bible that Uncle Ben would enjoy."

Lauren's eyes fell deadpan. "Uncle Ben would just as soon burn a Bible."

"It never hurts to try."

Barb pointed to a table. "Check in the Spiritual section. I think we've got a few King James."

"I will," Lauren said, "but I'm dying to know if the king-post truss system is in the attic."

Jack turned back to Barb. "If I promise to buy a book, can I have a look upstairs?"

Barb called over her shoulder. "Carl, I'm taking some customers back. Button your shirt." She waved Jack and Lauren around the counter. "Come on."

They pushed the curtain aside and went into a back room where even more books were stacked. The floor creaked and the air smelled musty. A light without a fixture burned overhead. An attic access door in the ceiling aligned with the far wall. A middle-aged man who must have been Carl stood packing books into a box. He tucked his shirt in tight over his belly and adjusted his glasses. "Good morning, folks. A little adventure today, eh?"

Jack smiled. "Just a little one, if we're lucky."

Barb pulled a rope tied to a ring on the access door. The door folded open on a set of springs and a ladder slid down. "We upgraded the access when we started using the attic as a secondary storage space." She climbed the steps.

Jack felt his heart beating. The final answer was close. He followed Barb up the steps.

Poor lighting kept the reaches of the attic dark. At each end of the space a dim bulb dangled from a power cord. Wall board and 1x8 planks covered over the joists and provided a walking path, and islands on which to stack boxes. The air was warm and muggy. Sounds of conversation and the whir of cars from the street below flowed in through the vents at the roof peaks. Jack had to duck his head to avoid a nail in the scalp.

"In the wildcat's bones," he said under his breath.

"What was that?" Barb asked.

"Thanks for bringing me up here." Jack studied the nearest rafter. Its warped surface didn't contain any special markings. Engraved and sealed. Read north to south. He closed his eyes and pictured Singapore, the street layout, the bank's likely orientation to the river when still there. Which way was north? It had to be...

"That way." Lauren climbed up from the access door. "North would be that way." She pointed to the far side of the attic.

"No, that's east," Barb said.

Jack walked around her over the planks. "Not in 1842 it wasn't." He slowed his pace and searched the rafters to the right from top to bottom. Nothing. He searched left. Near the peak on a central common rafter he saw the first one. A faint marking blended into the aged surface of the wood. He moved closer. It seemed more like an etching than an engraving, but there it was, a crude scrawl in the shape of an H. There had to be more. He examined the next rafter to the south. In approximately the same location he spotted an F.

Lauren went over to him. "You look like you see something."

Barb peered into the shadowy depths of the attic. "Is it a king or a queen-post truss?"

Jack licked his lips. "Don't know yet." He nodded at the markings to show Lauren.

She grabbed his arm. "Read north to south."

"I'm heading north." He walked backwards with a hand on a truss for balance, making sure he stayed on the boards over the joists. It'd be a bad thing to fall through the ceiling at this point. He kept the engraved letters in sight. Now there were three. The letter T preceded the H on an adjacent rafter. He smiled. He understood the pattern.

Lauren opened the camera bag slung over his shoulder. "I can't believe it's really here."

Jack stood with his back flat against the north wall and leaned left. From one end of the attic to the other the rafters cascaded like a neatly spread deck of cards. The message that Harlan Coates left for his sons was revealed. S-O-U-T-H F-O-X.

"Well?" Barb said.

Jack caressed his chin. "King me."

"You won the bet?"

"I certainly did." He glanced at Lauren. "Honey, get a few shots of this."

Barb looked funny at the rafters. "Hey, I never noticed those letters before."

"It's an old builders' tradition," Jack said, "kind of a signature on their work."

Barb nodded. "Oh, I never knew that."

Jack shrugged. "My dad was a carpenter. He knew a lot of weird things like that."

Lauren grinned and lined up the camera to take a picture.

Jack walked down through the center of the attic, inspecting each letter of the message just to make sure he had read them correctly. At the end of the string of letters, he noticed a different marking on the next rafter. He pushed a stack of boxes aside to get a closer look.

A number had been engraved on this one: 217.

"Revelation awaits," he whispered. "Revelations 21:7."

To his left a symbol carved into the surface of the following rafter caught his eye. It was a circle with a shape like an obelisk in the center. A pair of lines projected from the tip of the obelisk. He studied the image. He had a hunch on what it might mean.

Lauren carefully stepped around the stack of boxes.

"Get a shot of the number on this one," Jack said, "and the symbol on the other."

She took the pictures. "I understand the number. Revelations, right?"

"Yup."

"What about the symbol?"

"I'm workin' on it."

"And what's the meaning of Southfox?"

Jack noted Barb approaching. "I'll tell you later." He smiled at the bookstore owner. "I can't thank you enough for letting me come up here. Boy, my buddy is going to be upset."

"Don't forget about your Uncle Ben," Barb said.

"I can't possibly forget him." Jack smiled at Lauren. "Let's go find that book for Uncle Ben."

Lauren handed the camera back to him. "Are we finished up here?"

"Nothing left to see. I have my answer. Let's let these folks alone."

Barb led them from the attic. In the little back room Carl stopped sorting through books long enough to give them a smile. "Adventure enough for ya?"

"All I can handle in one day," Jack said.

They went to the Spiritual table in the main bookstore and searched through the titles, but the engravings burned in the forefront of Jack's thoughts. South Fox. 217. The symbol. Mostly the symbol. He had to be sure of what it meant. Looking for an old Bible on an old bookshelf wasn't where he wanted to be. He wanted to get on the road, but he had to do this. Anything that might buy them some time was worth the effort.

Lauren pulled a tome off the shelf. Its black leather binding was worn and the edges of the cover split. Age had turned the pages a sepia tone. "It's a King James Version," she said.

Jack examined it, checked how old it was. "This is just about perfect."

"Perfect for what?"

"I'll tell you, right before I explain South Fox." He took the Bible up to the counter where Barb was waiting. She checked it out and told him a cost. He thought it relatively cheap and handed her his credit card. While waiting for approval on the card Barb put the Bible in a bag and handed it to Lauren.

Jack replayed Ben's phone call in thought. "Lauren, look something up in that Bible for me."

She pulled it out of the bag. "What do you need?"

"Second Samuel 18:33."

Barb handed him the receipt to sign. He did. Lauren flipped through thin pages. Jack thanked Barb again for the attic tour. "We need to get moving," he said to Lauren. They headed down the stairs to exit the bank building. She kept flipping pages.

They got halfway through the stairwell. "I found it."

Jack stopped a few steps ahead of her and turned.

"The king was shaken," Lauren read. "He went up to the room over the gateway and wept. As he went, he said: O my son Absalom! My son, my son Absalom! If only I had died instead of you—O Absalom, my son, my son!"

Jack stood rigid and anger flushed his face red.

"Why did you want me to look this up?"

"Ben told me to read it. He said I should learn from scripture and not live its sad lessons."

She skimmed through the verse again. "He's threatening Connor."

Jack continued down the steps. "Ben doesn't know where we are. He doesn't know where to go next. All he knows is that I have the answer he needs. This is a psychological tactic, an act of desperation. It's not going to work."

"Then why are you so angry?"

Jack didn't reply.

"You think he's going to try something, don't you."

Jack spun around. "I won't let anything happen to Connor."

She stayed quiet a moment. "That's a hard promise to keep."

"You said you believed I could get us to the coins and back again. Do you still believe that?"

"I believe you'll do everything in your power to make that happen. The problem is, not everything is within your power."

"I don't need everything in my power."

"Then what do you need?"

"I have it right here." Jack lifted the camera bag. "For the first time in this treasure hunt I'm in the lead. Ben has no idea just how far behind he is, and I mean to keep it that way."

TWENTY-EIGHT

They all gathered around Connor's laptop on the kitchen table at the Beechwood Manor cottage. The computer was hooked up to the digital camera and displayed the picture Lauren had taken of the message on the bank rafters. Jack stood back and gave everyone a moment to absorb the image. Bobbie stared deep into the screen. "Is that really where we're going to find the coins?"

"I think so," Jack said. "Behold the end of the rainbow."

Markus balanced a pencil on his fingertip. "What's Southfox?"

"It's an island in Lake Michigan," Alyson said.

"About seventeen miles northwest of the tip of the Leelanau peninsula," Connor added.

Alyson smiled at him and lifted her hand for a high-five. Connor obliged. Markus grumbled and let the pencil fall onto the table. "How do you know about this island, Sheridan?"

Connor laughed. "Are you forgetting who my dad is?"

Markus tilted his head toward Jack.

"I spent months on the Great Lakes working for Neptune's Reach," Jack said. "I know every island from Chicago to Sandusky. By the way, the name is two words: South Fox."

"How big of an island is South Fox?" Lauren said.

"About twice the size of North Fox."

She frowned. "That isn't helpful."

"South Fox is about five miles long and two miles across at its widest."

Bobbie turned in her chair to face the others. "That's a lot of ground to search."

"There's more to the engravings." Jack reached for the computer and advanced to the next picture. The 217 image appeared on screen. "Revelations 21:7. I think this is Harlan Coates' way of telling us we're not imagining this. We really found his clue." He brought up the picture of the symbol. "Bobbie, look at this engraving and tell me what comes to mind."

She examined the obelisk within a circle and the lines projecting from its tip. Something sparked in her eyes. "Alyson, do you see what I see?"

Alyson smiled. "It reminds me of that little picture dad kept on his desk."

"It looks like the seal," Bobbie said.

"The seal for what," Lauren asked.

"The official seal for the U.S. Lighthouse Service. Steven was big into the lights of the Great Lakes. I mean, he bought Granite Island so he could own one of his very own, and he sat on the board for the Lightkeepers Association. He had a copy of the seal framed on his desk. It was the image of a lighthouse on a rocky point inside a circle. This symbol looks to me like a crude version of that seal."

"In the early days the Lighthouse Service was known as the Board of Lights," Jack said, "and Harlan Coates served in it after he was discharged from the Union navy after the Civil War."

"Why did he put the seal on the rafter?" Connor said.

"He's telling us where to look," Lauren said. "He's sticking a thumb tack in the map."

Bobbie's eyes brightened. "There's a lighthouse on South Fox."

"That's what I'm thinking." Jack leaned back on the kitchen counter. "The South Fox light is pretty old. The era is right."

Connor pulled his chair up close to the table. "Did you know the Beechwood's got Wi-Fi?" He accessed the Internet and Googled South Fox. A Great Lakes lighthouse site hit near the top of the list. He found a page dedicated to South Fox and skimmed the text. "The island has over two thousand acres of unspoiled wilderness. Bring a machete." He read more. "No natural harbor so docking a boat isn't easy...The light tower is the classical schoolhouse type, constructed with whitewashed cream brick. Lantern height is thirty-nine feet above base, sixty-eight feet above lake level...First lit in 1867. What year did Coates go down on the *William Barclay*?"

"1868." Jack lifted his chin. "The Manitou Passage is just south of the island. Coates may have been returning from South Fox after hiding the coins when his ship went down. Talk about irony."

Lauren counted off on her fingers. "South Fox, the seal, Coates and the Board of Lights, an 1867 lighthouse; it's all adding up."

"It certainly is," Jack said. "Coates hid the coins in the South Fox lighthouse." He mulled it over a moment. It all made sense. "That's it. I really think that's it."

"What if we go to the lighthouse and find another clue?" Bobbie said.

"I don't think we will. Not this time. Daniel's Bible told us we'd find the answer to where the coins were hidden in the bank building, not the coins themselves. The answer we found is the lighthouse on South Fox."

"All right!" Markus yelled. Knuckle bumps all around. "Let's roll. We've got twenty million dollars in rare coins to get to auction."

Bobbie stood. "Jack, are you sure about this?"

"No doubt, that's the place." He smiled wide.

She went over and gave him a big hug.

Lauren narrowed her eyes and crossed her arms. Jack noticed and cut the hug short. He took his wife's hand. "We're almost there."

She didn't smile. "Save the celebration until we have the coins. Ben is still out there."

"Mom, don't be such a killjoy," Connor said.

Jack slapped the back of his head. "You mother's right. Ben's on a parallel course, and we've been clashing with him every step of the way. We need to deflect him in a different direction."

"How are we going to do that?" Bobbie said.

"I'm going to give him the second Bible clue." Jack lifted the bookstore bag from the counter and withdrew the Bible.

"Why?" Alyson said.

Markus scrutinized the old time. "Wait, that's not the second Coates Bible."

Jack appraised the book cover. "It's not?" He thumbed through some pages. "Let's have a look." He opened it to Revelations 21:7. "What do we have here? Something's written in the margins...Hmmm. A wildcat sleeps on the banks of the River, the wealth it once warded has slipped off shore, went across water, west beyond sight, four points north and into the light, the light that burns in death's door."

They all stared blank at him, all except Lauren.

Jack smiled. "Kind of a spooky clue, isn't it?"

"I like it," Lauren said.

Markus chuckled. "You're going to give him a red fish."

Alyson giggled. "A red herring."

Connor examined the phony clue. "This looks just like the writing in the Coates Bibles. How did you do it?"

"Your mother has been signing my name on checks for years. All that practice at forgery has finally paid off."

"Does this clue actually lead someplace," Connor said, "or is it gibberish?"

"It leads north of the Door Peninsula in Wisconsin. If Ben figures it out and follows it, the entire width of Lake Michigan will be between him and us."

Connor thought it over. "We originally thought the coins were buried in Singapore. Why not direct him there, just keep him digging where he's at?"

"Because I rather emphatically told Professor Dodd the coins weren't there."

Markus made a face. "Why'd you do that?"

"He had me at gunpoint and Ben was on the way. I guess I got caught up in the moment."

"Your clue is good," Alyson said. "It's clever."

Connor nodded. "It is pretty good once you hash it out."

Markus jerked a chair around and dropped in. "One of you geographical gurus want to explain it?"

"Sure," Jack said. "At the tip of the Door Peninsula, there's a hazardous passage of water that leads into Green Bay. It's choked with islands and shoals, and shifting winds stir up freakish currents. It's a mariner's nightmare to navigate, so much so that early French settlers named the passage Porte des Morts, or translated, Death's Door, hence the name Door Peninsula."

"And the light at death's door is the lighthouse built on Pilot Island at the entrance to the passage." Bobbie smiled. "It is clever, Jack. It's got an authentic feel, and if they follow it through they'll sail into dangerous water. Here's my problem with it. Why would they accept that you all of a sudden just give them the key to the coins?"

"Because Ben called me and asked for it." Jack paused. "To say he asked for it is putting it mild. Ben promised bad things would happen to me if I didn't turn over the second Bible."

A trace of concern crept into Bobbie's eyes. "Even so, the odds are they'll figure out your clue is a fake. As good as it looks and sounds, it doesn't fit in context with the first clue, and the Bible itself looks different. They're going to be suspicious of it from the get-go."

Markus scoffed. "They're stupid, they'll fall for it."

"We only need them to believe it long enough for us to get to South Fox Island and haul the treasure back. Then we disappear from the hunt." Jack closed the old Bible and brushed off the front cover. "Ben and his thugs will keep looking, hopefully forever. We'll need to sit on the coins for a while to convince them we've given up."

The group stayed quiet and digested the plan.

"Sounds good to me," Connor said.

Lauren shook her head. "I think we need to consider getting some outside help."

"Outside help from where?" Jack said.

She started to say something but held back. "I don't know. This Ben character makes me nervous."

"Ben I can deal with." Jack set the Bible on the counter. "The person pulling his strings is the one that makes me nervous. That's a wild card we haven't turned over yet."

Connor glanced around at the pensive faces. "It doesn't matter. We know where the coins are. We're hours away from getting them. How about a little more action and a little less conversation?"

"Tell 'em, Elvis," Markus said.

"Connor's right." Jack said. "We move fast enough, this all gets academic."

Bobbie agreed. "Then let's get going."

"I'm trying to get off the blocks here." Jack positioned himself as the coach in front of the players. "We need a boat to carry us all to South Fox. Markus, you have exactly what we need in that Boston Whaler of yours."

Markus stood. "*El Pomposo* is ready for action."

"At ease, Hornblower," Jack said. "Connor, get your S-10 out of storage and head back home with Markus to get his boat. I'll take Lauren and Bobbie with me to pick up equipment and supplies we'll need on the island. We reconnect tomorrow morning at the Leland Township Marina, seven o'clock. Mapquest it so you don't get lost." He tapped a finger on the old Bible. "I don't know how much time this ruse will buy us. It may not work at all. In either case we have to move fast. The less time the other guys have to think the better it is for us."

"What about me?" Alyson asked.

Jack regarded her. "Take your pick. Who do you want to ride with?"

She took a discrete step to the side and stood between Connor and Markus.

"Youth, intelligence, charm; it wasn't much of a contest, was it?" Connor said.

"Yeah," Markus added, "the old folks didn't stand a chance."

Jack scowled. "Guys, pack up and hit the bricks. It's almost noon, and you've got a lot of road to cover."

Markus howled and they dispersed in a flurry. Within fifteen minutes all three had their bags over their shoulders and were out the door. Jack watched them go.

"How are you going to get the fake Bible clue into Ben's hands?"

Bobbie said.

Jack grinned. "You'll see, but before we get there I want to write a note to send along with the Bible, give Ben a little icing to help swallow this fabricated cake we're feeding him."

Lauren handed him a piece of paper. "I've already written one."

Jack took the paper and read her note. It wasn't quite what he had in mind. He held his tongue and creased the paper. "Ben's not going to buy this."

Lauren tapped a pencil against her chin. "Why?"

He read the note. "Please accept this Bible as agreed upon in our bargain. I give it to you with the belief that you will honor your word and leave my family and friends alone. Their value to me outweighs any amount of gold I might find on this quest, and I gladly end all attempts to find the coins to secure their safety."

Bobbie shrugged. "What's wrong with that?"

Jack crumpled the paper. "He's never going to believe I wrote this. All it will do is make him suspicious."

Lauren glared. "Well then, what did you have in mind to get him to *buy in?*"

Jack snatched the pencil from her and went to the kitchen table. He thought a minute or two and then scribbled out a note of his own. He reviewed it, nodded his approval, signed and dated it, and handed it over to Lauren. "I think this will work better."

Lauren and Bobbie read it through. They shook their heads and turned to face him with a hint of incredulity in their posture.

"You think this is going to help us?" Lauren said.

"I know how men think, especially this guy. That message will spark the desired effect."

Lauren handed the note back to him. "I defer to your knowledge and experience in these matters."

Jack smiled. "Trust me; it takes one to know one."

The three of them packed their things and combed through the cottage, making sure not to leave any telltale signs of what they'd been doing or where they were going. Every scrap of paper they'd written on was either stowed in luggage or burned in the fireplace. Each piece of furniture was overturned and looked under. The cottage was cleaner when they left than when they'd arrived.

Jack went and got the Jeep from the garage. Beneath gathering rain clouds the three threw their bags in the back. Jack considered the load. Something would have to be lost to make room for the equipment. Later. Right now he just wanted to get moving.

They climbed in, Jack behind the wheel, Lauren in the passenger seat, and Bobbie in the back. They swung through Saugatuck to make arrangements to get the Bible to Ben. By 1:15 they were accelerating out of town. Exhilaration flowed clear through to Jack's fingertips. The rush had returned. He hated it and he loved it all at once. *Get a handle, Jack, too much is at stake.*

He took a deep breath and settled himself. After a few minutes of driving he calculated how long it would take them to reach Rezner's place, their first stop. It'd be good to see Rezner again. It'd been a long time, almost since Rafferty, but they wouldn't have much time to catch up on things. A stash of gold coins was waiting on South Fox Island, and Jack Sheridan was determined to be the first to get there.

A rakish smile dimpled his cheeks, and he put his foot down on the accelerator.

$* * *$

Lightening flickered above the ruins of Singapore. Professor Collin Dodd sat behind the worktable beneath the large canopy at the edge of the dig site. He stared at the map laid out before him, doodling around the edges with a pencil, trying to divine where he needed to concentrate his efforts to unearth the coins. The exercise might be pointless. If Sheridan had told him the truth, the gold wouldn't be found in the sands of Singapore.

Dodd threw the pencil down and stood. Off to the west the sky had turned dark. He figured rain had already started falling out over the lake. It wouldn't be long before it swept inland and ended dig activities for the day. He wouldn't mind that. He'd lost a measure of motivation to work. If the coins weren't in Singapore he'd leave the site empty handed, no million dollars, no early retirement.

A boxy brown UPS truck drove up Dugout Road and squealed to a stop behind Dodd's Range Rover. The driver hopped out with a small package in his hand. He jogged up the slope to the canopy, shielding his eyes from a mini sandstorm sweeping over the dune. The wind subsided and the driver straightened his cap. "Sir, I have a delivery for…" He checked the shipping label on the box. "Ben—c/o Professor Collin Dodd, MSU Dig Coordinator, 0001 Oak Street, Singapore, MI." He glanced around at the exhumed buildings. "Cool."

A fork of lightening danced in the sky. Dodd took the package and signed for it. The driver touched the pen to his cap and nodded. "Thank you, sir, have a good afternoon." He jogged back down the slope to the van.

Dodd inspected the package. It was intended for Higgs, so he figured he'd better not open it. It didn't feel that heavy. He wondered what it could be and read the shipping label. The sender's name surprised him.

Benjamin Higgs had just received a package from Jack Sheridan.

TWENTY-NINE

Lloyd Faulkner lifted a Styrofoam cup and took a large swig of a frozen mocha latte. He settled into the leather seat of his Cadillac CTS, one hand on the steering wheel and both eyes on the Jeep Cherokee barely visible on the road ahead of him. His speedometer hovered at seventy-five but cruise control wasn't locked in. He'd been adjusting his speed to keep a constant distance from the Jeep. Didn't want to get too close, no need to.

A GPS unit mounted on the center console displayed an arrow icon laid over a map background. It wasn't showing Lloyd his position on the road. It was showing him the exact location of the Jeep ahead of him, which happened to have a locator tag magnet-mounted to its inner frame. The GPS unit wasn't a standard commercial model. He had it on loan from the Neptune's Reach tech inventory. The company used the system to tag salvage sites and marker buoys at sea, but Lloyd found it quite adequate for tracking automobiles as well.

He activated his Bluetooth earpiece and hit a speed dial code on his phone.

"Yes, Mr. Faulkner?"

"Vince, contact the *Achilles*, tell Garcia to make preparations to get underway."

"Do you have a set of destination coordinates to relay to him?"

Lloyd watched the Jeep for a moment. "Not yet. Sheridan hasn't tipped his hand far enough to see where he's going. Just tell Garcia to make his heading dead north. I'll follow up with more detailed instructions as soon as I have them."

"Understood. Is there anything else you need, sir?"

"Vince, you're not in the navy anymore. You don't have to call me sir. Mr. Faulkner works."

"Yes, sir—Mr. Faulkner."

"Better. That's all for now. I'll be in touch." Lloyd disconnected and took another swig of frozen mocha. The Jeep disappeared over a hill a few miles ahead. He checked the GPS unit. The arrow icon stayed steady on screen, reporting that the Jeep was still there, heading north. "You're not screwing the company on this one, Jack." He set the coffee cup down and loosened his tie. "You're not screwing me."

Part III
REVELATIONS

Rain beat against the canopy overhead as Benjamin Higgs tore open the package. He dug into brown packing paper and extracted a book. A pair of rubber bands affixed a folded sheet of paper to the front cover. He appraised the tome with a skeptical eye.

Dodd stood with arms crossed. "Is that the second Bible you told me about?"

Higgs glanced at him but didn't answer. He pulled the sheet of paper from beneath the rubber bands and found a handwritten note inside.

> *Dear Ben,*
> *Per your request, Daniel's Bible complete with second Coates clue. I decided to give this to you based on two factors.*
> *1.   You're too stupid to figure it out anyway.*
> *2.   If you do somehow manage to do it, I'll be halfway to the Virgin Islands with the coins before you even get close to the empty hole in the ground.*
> *If you need any help just give me a call. You've got my number. We might be able to work something out - LOL.*
> *Best of luck. You're going to need it.*
> *Warm regards,*
> *Jack Sheridan*

Higgs crushed the paper in his fist. He thought about throwing it on the ground but decided to pocket it just in case he needed to review it after his blood pressure settled. He opened the Bible to Revelations 21:7. A clue was written in the margins just like the first Coates Bible. The handwriting looked the same. The age and condition of the Bible appeared similar. Higgs read through the clue but the thought of beating Sheridan to a pulp distracted his focus.

Dodd tried to peer into the book. "What does it say?"

Higgs scowled at him. "This doesn't concern you."

"If that clue reveals the coins are in Singapore then it certainly does."

"Don't overestimate your importance. It seems the coins have nothing to do with this dig anymore, and if that's the case, your role in this is over."

Dodd stood there with a cast of disbelief on his face. "The first clue led to Singapore. It doesn't make sense if the second ignores the first."

Higgs thought about that, considered Sheridan's end game. He tossed the Bible onto the worktable. "See for yourself. Those coins aren't here."

Dodd positioned his glasses and read the clue. He pondered it a long while. "Singapore is still part of the puzzle."

"It doesn't say a damn thing about Singapore."

"Not directly."

Higgs waited for an explanation.

"If I help decipher this clue I want some portion of the treasure, even if the gold doesn't get pulled from the ground at my dig site."

"Don't press your luck, professor."

"I want half of our original deal. That's just five percent of the total find. Not too much to ask if you ask me."

Higgs stared him down. "If what you tell me helps us find the coins I'll consider it."

Dodd read from the margins. "A wildcat sleeps on the banks of the River." He pushed the Bible off the map of Singapore that was spread out on the worktable and pointed to one of the roads. "River Street is the river, like in the last clue."

Higgs frowned. "That's it?"

"The wildcat is the other thing." Dodd motioned to the city block on the map boxed in red marker. "Remember, south of the Beach, north of the River, Cherry and Cedar flanking the find. This block of lots was defined by the first clue. The second clue tells us which building in the block to use as the starting point for the rest of the instructions."

"How does a wildcat relate to a building?"

"Mrs. Weller asked me about the location of a bank. It made me curious, so this morning I reread some historic Singapore records. The Singapore Bank was a wildcat bank, printing worthless notes and passing them along. I learned the old building is in Saugatuck now but it used to be in our city block right here. The second clue implies that the original site of the bank is the starting point for what comes next."

Dodd read from the clue. "The wealth it once warded has slipped off shore, west across water, west beyond sight, four points north and into the light, the light that burns in death's door."

Higgs surveyed the empty dig site soaking in the downpour. The rain had driven the college students into town. Wind shook the red twine defining the perimeter of the Coates city block. "West across water," he said, imagining a line extending from the ruins to a point out over Lake Michigan. "West beyond sight." He faced Dodd. "Four points. That's about forty degrees, right?"

"Yes," Dodd said, "and forty degrees north of a westerly heading is almost dead north, which leads to the next part of the clue, the light in death's door."

"I suppose you have some idea about that too."

"Death's Door Passage. It's a dangerous waterway into Green Bay. On maps it's called by its French name: Portes de Morts. And the light—"

"A lighthouse," Higgs said. "There's got to be a lighthouse located somewhere in that passage." He smiled. "Too stupid to figure it out? Sheridan, you prick." He swiped his cell phone off his belt and hit speed dial number one.

It rang once. "Have you found Sheridan?"

"Better," Higgs said. "It looks like Sheridan blinked. He sent me the second Bible. Dodd and I just went through the clue and I think I know where to find the coins."

"Why did he send you the Bible?"

"I applied some leverage to the situation. Guess he didn't have the stomach for hardball."

The phone line fell silent. A flash of lightening sent a hiss of static through the connection. "How did you apply this leverage, Mr. Higgs?"

"I told him his son would pay for his refusal to cooperate."

"That may have been the right chord to strike." Silence. "I want to see this Bible to authenticate it."

"No problem," Higgs said. "But if Sheridan is off and running with this new clue, we need to get on it as quick as possible. Let me read it to you over the phone. We can discuss it now and I can get rolling. I'll put the Bible at a drop point for you to pick up and study. That way we won't fall too far behind Sheridan."

"I admire your motivation. Read it to me."

Higgs recited the clue. They worked through it and came to agree with Dodd's interpretation. "What about the lighthouse?" Higgs asked.

"I'll do some checking at my end. Your assumption makes sense." Laughter. "The light at death's door. Coates has gotten more poetic."

"I'll collect Nate and the boys," Higgs said. "We'll need a boat and some things to help us search a lighthouse, provided that's where we end up."

"You have all my resources at your disposal. Just make sure you reach the coins ahead of Sheridan. You know the consequences if you don't."

"Understood. I'll put the Bible at the drop point within the hour."

The line disconnected.

Higgs regarded Dodd. "The man thinks you're right about the clue. You just might get your five percent after all." He watched rain fall over Singapore and the dunes. "Hell of a day for a boat ride. Hope Sheridan's keeping dry."

"Since when do you care about his well-being?"

Higgs gave Dodd a grave smile. "I want Sheridan safe, dry, and in one piece when I catch up to him. That way I'll get full satisfaction when I completely destroy him."

- THIRTY-ONE -

Carson City, MI

Jack tried to steer around pot holes in the narrow dirt road but there were just too many of them. The front end of the Jeep plunged, and a plume of muddy water splashed the windshield. The wipers were already on high to clear away the downpour, and they smeared the milky-brown mess until the rain washed it away. Great branches from aged pines reached out and brushed the sides of the Jeep. Jack grumbled, "Damn, Rez, what are you doing so far off the main road?"

The Jeep heaved again like it had hit a land mine.

Lauren used the dashboard to brace herself. "Hey, you missed one back there."

"It'd be better to go off-road and dodge tree trunks."

Bobbie hung on to the seatback in front of her. "Who is this guy we're going to see?"

"Joshua Rezner." Jack swerved around another pot hole. "We worked together at Neptune's Reach for ten years. We both called it quits after the Rafferty project. He decided to open a sort of army-navy surplus store."

"That's an odd career choice after Neptune," Bobbie said.

Jack chuckled. "You won't say that after you meet him." He bounced the Jeep into a small rustic parking lot fashioned from railroad ties and gravel. A single four-by-four pickup truck painted in camouflage was parked in the lot. A large log cabin surrounded by mature maples and pines sat just beyond the gravel. The timbers comprising the walls seemed to have suffered through several decades of Michigan weather. A plywood sign spanned the roofline. In black stencil it read JR SUPPLY and AMMO.

"Oh," Bobbie said, "I'm starting to get the picture."

Jack parked the Jeep near the front entrance and switched off the engine. "Rezner's not a militiaman. He's just like me, but amplified."

Jack led the women up to the cabin's front porch. A white sign with the word OPEN written in black Sharpie hung in the front window. He pushed through the door and entered. The place smelled of canvas, leather, and oil. Cami clothing and all-weather gear hung on racks at the center of the room. Camping and hiking equipment filled a four-tier shelving system off to the right. A wide selection of army boots and high-tech wilderness footwear ate up floor space on the periphery. Straight on in the back of the room a collection of hunting rifles and bows hung on a wall rack. An assortment of handguns, knives, and a survivalist's version of personal protection equipment were on display in a glass case below the rifle rack. A stocky man a few inches shy of six feet stood behind the case scrutinizing his customers. He wore camouflage pants and a brown army T-shirt that matched the color of his hair and short beard. A smile broke across his face. "Jack Sheridan?"

Jack walked up with Lauren at his side. "Rez, how've you been?" Bobbie stayed a step behind them.

Rezner came around the counter and thrust out a hand. Jack took it and they embraced. Rezner stepped back. "It's been a while, hasn't it?" He faced Lauren. "Good to see you too, Lauren. You look great." They hugged each other.

"Hey, Rez, you grew a beard," she said. "What's up with that?" Rezner ran fingers through his facial hair. "I'm going native."

"What's with the location?" Jack said. "Being a mile back over hard terrain has got to kill floor traffic."

"People looking for what I'm selling find me okay." Rezner shifted his weight from one leg to the other and drew down his smile. "Rafferty keeping in touch?"

Jack shook his head. "I haven't heard from him in about a year."

Rezner nodded to the Colt holstered under Jack's windbreaker. "Then why are you carrying?"

"I've managed to piss off someone else. Imagine that. How about you?"

"Nothing." Rezner patted a 9mm in a belt clip at his side. "But I'm ready if he decides to pay a visit."

Jack glanced at the rifles and handguns on display. "Looks that way."

Rezner noticed Bobbie standing behind them. "Who's this, Lauren, your sister?"

Lauren forced a smile.

"This is Bobbie," Jack said. "She's a friend helping us out on a little expedition, which is why we're here. We need to gear up."

"You've come to the right place." Rezner gave Bobbie a polite smile. "Sorry to hear you're mixed up with Jack Sheridan. That can only mean trouble for you." He laughed.

"If there's trouble, it's my doing," Bobbie said. "This is my expedition."

"Well then, you've got the right man on your team," Rezner said. "If it wasn't for Jack I'd be fish food in the Atlantic now. Wherever you're headed, he'll get you there and back."

Jack and Lauren exchanged a glance.

Rezner eyed them both and grinned. He climbed up on a stool beside the display case. "What's this expedition you're on and how can I help?"

"It's a treasure hunt," Jack said. "We're looking for a lost barrel of gold coins."

Rezner stared at him for a long while. He eventually chuckled himself into a full laugh. "For a minute there I thought you were serious."

"I am serious. My competition is serious, too. They almost shot me two days ago."

Rezner cut his laughter short. "Christ, Jack, why didn't you say so." He hopped off the stool and went to the front door. After checking through the window he threw the dead bolt and flipped the OPEN sign over to CLOSED. "If you need more hardware to defend yourself, I've got it." He went back behind the glass display case.

"Hold on, Rez," Jack said.

Rezner reached into a compartment behind the case and lifted a submachine gun out. "Heckler & Kotch MP5, fully automatic, weapon of choice for U.S. Special Forces and, if you'll remember, arms dealing mercenaries." He set the gun down on the surface of the case. "You got pretty familiar with the MP5, didn't you?"

"I didn't come here for guns."

Rezner retrieved another weapon from the compartment, this one a shotgun with a stubby barrel and a pistol grip. "Ithaca twelve-gauge Stakeout, thirteen-inch barrel, five-round magazine, perfect for concealment."

"Rez, I need equipment to help me search, retrieve, and transport the coins, not arms to wage a small war."

Rezner seemed stuck on the notion. "For real?"

"I need hand tools," Jack said, "a couple of shovels, a pick axe, and a sledge hammer. You have anything like that?"

"Yeah, guys building shelters and cabins come in all the time looking for that kind of stuff."

"How about a couple of metal detectors, the kind with precious metal discrimination?"

"I've got one. It's mine. I'll let you borrow it."

"A little Zodiac would be nice. I've got to land on an island without a good natural harbor. I need something that can carry three or four people and some supplies from my boat to shore. Got anything like that back in your warehouse?"

Rezner rested the short-barrel shotgun over his shoulder and let out a sigh. "Yeah, I have two ten-footers."

"And a GPS unit?"

"Of course."

"And plastic totes." Jack measured out a square of space with his hands. "About twenty by fifteen inches, a foot deep, with sturdy handles. I need about ten of them."

"Jack, you could have gotten this stuff at Gander Mountain and a home improvement store. Why come to me for it?"

"Because I can't get commercial grade explosives from Gander Mountain."

Rezner's eyebrow rose.

"I may come up against rock or a stone foundation," Jack said. "I won't have a lot of time to pick through it with the tools. I'll need to break it out fast. Blasting is pretty quick."

"Okay, you got my attention back." Rezner set the shotgun in the compartment. "Give me a minute to rummage through my inventory. I'll show you what I've got." He disappeared through a door behind the display case to a rear room.

Lauren and Bobbie stared at Jack.

"I told you," he said. "Me, but amplified."

Lauren spoke quietly. "And I thought you were paranoid. Poor Rez. Did he always like guns and explosives this much?"

"Not sure. Before the Rafferty project he was wound pretty tight. The experience seemed to liberate him in a strange way. He smiles more now." Jack shrugged. "Figure that one out."

Bobbie wandered over to the camping equipment. "You should ask him for a deal on a couple of these tents. We may be on South Fox longer than we expect."

"Can't afford to be." Jack joined her near a four-person dome tent on display. "We need to be in and out as quick as possible. We know the coins are in the lighthouse. It shouldn't take very long to find them."

Lauren sat on the stool. "Speaking of overnight stays, this detour to Carson City put us a few miles off course from the Leelanau Peninsula. By the time we get there it'll be late. We should try to find a hotel now and make reservations, especially with the holiday weekend."

"Good point." Jack thought about where they should pack it in for the night and then nudged Bobbie with his elbow. "Hey, do you remember Grand Traverse Bay?"

Bobbie laughed and put a hand on his arm. "Yes, and the little old man at the hotel registration desk who suggested we get a room with two beds."

"It scandalized him when we said one would be just fine." Jack chuckled.

The clatter of metal on glass turned his head. Lauren toyed with her car keys on the display case. "Rezner is coming back," she said glaring at Jack. "You want to talk explosives with him?"

Jack approached her. "Why the look?"

She shook her head ever so subtly. "Don't forget flashlights and battery-powered lanterns."

Rezner returned to the display case with a white cylindrical cartridge about a foot and a half long, some little silvery cylinders, and a coil of wire. He seemed rather animated. "Here we go." He held the white cartridge. "Tovex water gel explosive. Twenty-five millimeter package. It has a four thousand meter-per-second velocity of detonation at blast point." He lifted a silver cylinder and flicked a pair of wires protruding from the casing. "Standard #8 detonator." He gestured to the wire coil. "Detonation wire." He dug into a pocket and pulled out a module about the size of a fat Blackberry wrapped in red plastic with an angled lever along the side and two wire connectors at the top. Rezner squeezed the lever and let it spring back. "Boom." He pointed to the wire connectors. "Don't hook up your wires until you're ready to blow the Tovex."

Jack listened intently. "Good tip." They went over a few more details about handling explosives and setting charges until he felt comfortable. "Got it."

"Why do you stock blasting equipment?" Bobbie said.

Rezner grinned. "You'd be surprised how many miners and independent civil engineers operate in the area."

"Really?" Bobbie thought it over. "I hope those miners are law abiding, patriotic Americans."

"You've just described my entire customer base."

Jack appraised the blasting set up. "Can you pack this stuff so it doesn't blow up on my way to the site?"

"No problem." Rezner went about collecting the materials and making it safe for transport.

Jack glanced at the items beneath the glass of the display case. "Are those flashbangs?"

Rezner nodded. "Good eye. M84 Stun Grenade, a wise choice for the discriminating treasure hunter. Capable of delivering a six million Candela flash and an earsplitting one hundred and seventy-decibel blast, field tested to incapacitate affected personnel for up to one minute."

"Enough with the brochure, how much are they?"

"You're making my week here, Jack. For you, BOGO on the flashbangs."

"Pack 'em up, I'll take two."

Rezner obliged and began gathering the items from Jack's shopping list. Lauren and Bobbie helped collect the things and condense them into the smallest load possible. They still needed to lose half their luggage and stow the rolled up Zodiac on the roof of the Jeep. Rezner promised to keep the discarded travel bags safe until their return. "I've only got a ten-horse outboard motor for the Zodiac, so you'll be a little under powered."

"It'll work," Jack said.

Lauren and Bobbie carried a stack of plastic totes to the Jeep.

Rezner waited for them to get outside. "How likely is it you'll find these coins?"

"Confidence level is high," Jack said.

"How much of a threat is the competition you're facing?"

Jack considered the question. "If I let them get too close I'll be in trouble." He looked Rezner in the eye. "But I'm not going to let them get close."

Rezner scratched his beard. "I know how you can keep them away."

"Yeah?"

"Claymore."

Jack dropped his chin and chuckled.

"I'm serious."

"I know you are." Jack lifted his head. "The stuff you've supplied me already is enough."

"Are you sure you don't want to take some firepower?"

"Escalating is a bad idea. We're not on a ship at sea. Police don't like citizens walking around with illegal weapons, and they especially don't like them getting into public firefights with those weapons."

Rezner considered his friend. "If you need me to come along and give you a hand, all you've got to do is say the word. You know that, don't you?"

"I know, Rez, and I appreciate it. I've got the boys with me on this one. We'll be okay."

"Connor's a good kid," Rezner said. "Even that jackass Markus is all right. Don't tell him I said that."

Jack slid a credit card from his wallet. "How much do I owe you?"

Rezner didn't even look at the card. "Pay me after you find the coins."

"Come on, you're not a charity house. You've got bills to pay."

Lauren and Bobbie came back into the store and shook off the rain. Rezner walked away from Jack and toward the women. "Ladies, it's been a pleasure."

Lauren gave him a hug. "Thanks for helping out."

Bobbie offered her hand. "Mr. Rezner, you have a unique store." She added, "And I'm glad you do."

"Come on back if you need anything else, and good luck with your treasure hunt." He addressed Jack. "Let's get that outboard loaded and send you on your way."

They carried a ten-horse Evinrude from the stock room to the Jeep and strapped it to the roof beside the Zodiac. Rain soaked into their clothes. Jack gave Rezner a heartfelt thank you and a firm handshake. "I'll be back to pay up, with interest."

"See that you are," Rezner said, "and nail them before they nail you."

"I hope there won't be any nailing."

"But if there is…"

"It'll be them." Jack opened the driver's door and stepped up.

"Jack."

He stopped and turned around.

"We got through the Rafferty project all right. How hard could a treasure hunt be?"

Jack gave him a wary smile. "I'll let you know when I get back."

THIRTY-TWO

Milford, MI

"You're wrong, Sheridan, it wouldn't happen." Markus jabbed his finger into the S-10's dashboard to emphasize his point. "The Southfield Police would never catch him."

Connor raised his voice. "They're not going to let the guy who just leveled the Lawrence Tech campus get away. Don't be an idiot."

Alyson sat between them gazing at the roof of the cab.

"How are they going to stop him?" Markus said. "Once he rolls onto the Southfield Freeway he's gone, and it won't matter how many road blocks they set up. An Abrams tank will crush any police car that gets in the way."

"You know, the police have a riot tank with a battering ram," Connor said.

Markus jeered. "That sardine can on wheels? It's got like, aluminum foil for armor plating. No match for the M1A1."

"The armor doesn't matter. The Abrams gets something like six gallons to the mile. All they have to do is wait for the guy to run out of gas. Once he does, just force the hatch and it's all over."

Alyson glanced between the two of them. "How often do you guys argue over this kind of ridiculous stuff?"

"Depends what you mean by often," Connor said.

"Depends what you mean by ridiculous," Markus retorted.

"How did this subject ever come up?" she asked.

"Well," Connor said, "the origins of this debate go back to college days, during finals week if I remember correctly. Tensions were high, and we were discussing ways to relieve the pressure."

"Yeah," Markus said, "and I thought, what could be better than parking an Abrams tank in the center of campus and just leveling the place. It's a perfect set-up. School of Engineering: Gone. Ninety degrees right. School of Architecture: Gone. Ninety degrees right. School of Management: Gone…Well, there's a lot of concrete in the Buehl building. It might take a few rounds to do the job."

"Don't forget, another ninety right and we have the science building." Connor laughed. "There's a lot of glass on the science building. Lobbing two or three shells at it would be pretty spectacular."

"You guys need help."

Markus slapped the dash. "Exit here, Sheridan! Exit!"

"I know, I see it." Connor swerved the S-10 onto an off ramp and decelerated through the long curve. "Anybody back there?"

Alyson checked through the rear window of the cab. "No one behind us. No one changing lanes like a maniac to stay with us. Looks like we're in the clear."

Markus settled into the seat. "Seems Connor's poor driving skills have been an effective deterrent to tailing."

"Or there was never anyone following us," Connor said.

Alyson faced forward again. "I hope that's the case. I've seen enough of those men to last a lifetime."

"Ditto that." Connor stopped at the traffic light at the end of the ramp.

Markus rolled his window down enough to get some air, but not enough to let the rain in. "Me thrice. I'd rather those cork stackers not find out where I live."

The light turned green and Connor pulled out onto the road.

Alyson clapped her hands together. "I've got an idea. Let's discuss something that isn't ridiculous."

Connor laughed. "All right. What would happen if someone stole the old World War II submarine from that naval museum in Muskegon and went on a rampage in the Great Lakes?"

Markus glanced at him crosswise. "That's the stupidest idea I've ever heard."

"Let's think of a non-military subject," Alyson said.

The guys fell silent.

"Is this really that difficult?" she asked.

Markus repositioned himself in the seat. "I think *Iron Man* is the best big screen adaptation of a comic book character ever attempted. Connor, what do you think?"

"I agree. The deft screenplay and spot-on performance by Robert Downey Jr. as Tony Stark really sets the film apart from other super hero theatrical efforts. Ms. Weller?"

Alyson stared at the dashboard, wondering why she chose to ride with them. "Actually, the first Spider-Man delved much deeper into the psychological foundation of the protagonist and provided an effective counterbalance to the action elements of the plot."

Markus laughed sharp. "That's ridiculous."

"No kidding."

"You two are impossible!" She grabbed each guy's leg and dug in her nails.

Connor flinched. "Hey, I think you punctured my femoral artery."

Markus grinned. "I kind of like it."

She let go.

"You want to talk girlish talk?" Markus said. "I can play that game. Tell me about your mom and Mr. Sheridan."

"There's not much to tell. They dated once. They're friends now."

Connor glanced over. "There's more."

"I know there's more," Markus said. "Your parents have Bobbie discussions, and they're not talking about Bobby Kennedy or Bobby Brady or Bobby Knight. The topic of discussion is Bobbie Weller, so I ask: If there really is nothing to this dating thing, why does it cause such a fuss today?"

"I guess they were kind of serious," Alyson admitted.

Connor watched traffic ahead. "When I was younger my parents had a lot more Bobbie discussions. My dad always downplayed the affair, and my mom blew it up. When it comes to Bobbie, Mom gets whacked out. She shouldn't worry about it."

"How do you know she shouldn't worry?" Markus said. "I mean, Bobbie's kind of, well—she's hot."

Alyson turned. "That's my mom you're talking about."

Connor shot him a glare. "And what are you implying about my mom?"

"What? No, that's not what I meant. Connor, your mom is hot too—"

"Wait a minute. Markus, you can't think about my mom like that. It's disturbing."

"I can't win here."

Connor turned down a residential drive. "I wouldn't talk about your mom like that."

"Now what's that supposed to mean?"

Alyson slapped the seat. "Enough already."

"Back to my premise," Markus said. "What if Mr. Sheridan and Bobbie really do have something going on the side?" He glanced at Alyson. "Theoretically, of course."

"They don't. I asked my dad about it directly one time."

That surprised Alyson. "You did?"

"It was back when I graduated from Lawrence. My parents had a huge blowout, and Bobbie came up in the fight. I was getting ready to move out of state for my first job and didn't want to abandon my mom if my dad was cheating and divorce was on the horizon. I asked if he was having an affair with Bobbie. You might call me gullible, but he spoke to me with more sincerity than he ever had before, like he finally recognized that I'd crossed over from being a kid to an adult and he wanted to be straight with me. He said he'd loved Bobbie once, that he still cared a great deal for her, but Mom was the one he loved now and she's the one his life revolved around. He said it like he meant it, and I believed him."

Markus gnawed on that a bit. "Okay, I won't say you're gullible. I'll merely imply it."

"That sounded like a nice moment with your dad," Alyson said. "It seems like you have a close relationship with him."

"It wasn't always like that. When I was growing up he was hardly ever home. I barely knew him. I kind of resented him for it." Connor laughed. "It's weird to say but the Rafferty project was the big ice breaker for us. We spent more time together on that ship than we had the previous ten years, and the stress of the situation just stripped all the bullshit away. It got us back to basics. It got us back to realizing the importance of keeping our family together, because in the end family is the only thing worth hanging on to."

Markus sniffled. "I'm getting weepy, Sheridan, stop it."

"Connor, how close are your parents today?" Alyson said.

He shrugged. "Right now they're pretty tight. They were separated for a while before my dad left Neptune's Reach. That was the worst time for them. Mom's very principled and she wanted Dad to put the family first like he'd promised. She threw down the gauntlet. Turn it around or it's over."

"What happened?"

"Rafferty happened. That was the event that brought Dad back home. I guess that bastard Rafferty did my family a favor." Connor steered the S-10 through a subdivision of little tri-story and colonial homes that all seemed to have been built circa 1970.

Alyson mulled the conversation. "Would you say your parents have a passionate marriage?"

Markus rolled his eyes.

"Oh, you should hear when they argue. Now that's passion. But when they're in synch, I have to say, you see they really love each other."

Alyson sat quiet a bit. "I know my mom cared for my dad, but I didn't see passion between them. Their marriage seemed to be a quiet thing. There weren't any highs or lows. It just felt like they shared a comfortable companionship."

Connor gave her an assuring smile. "Maybe they just didn't wear their passion on their sleeves like my parents do."

"My parents had Jack discussions," she said. "They weren't big explosions. Like everything else with them, their arguments were quiet events. One time Dad said something about being a substitute. That really upset her. She sat crying on the porch all afternoon. I went out to talk to her, and she just hugged me for a real long time."

Connor coasted to a stop sign. "If there's one thing you can say about Jack Sheridan, it's that he has an inexplicable knack for leaving a trail of wrecked people behind him. He usually doesn't mean to do it. He just doesn't seem able to control it."

Markus fixed Connor and Alyson with an exasperated eye. "Would you two babies quit whining about your parents? At least you had dads to get pissed at. Mine took off when I was two and never looked back. Now that he's getting old, he's trying to buy his way back into my life." He let out a derisive laugh. "Let me tell you, it's going to cost him a lot."

Connor smirked. "There's that Sweetwood compassion I know so well."

"We're here," Markus said. "Pull up alongside the garage and make sure your little Tonka toy truck is out of the way."

Connor turned onto the cracked asphalt drive of a tri-level home wrapped in faded white aluminum siding. He slid the S-10 in beside a two-car garage and parked on the grass near the neighbor's property line. They all piled out and grabbed their bags. The rain had dwindled to a drizzle. Markus ran in through the front door. A moment later one of the garage door panels lifted open amid the hum and rattle of an electric opener. Markus' Explorer was parked inside. He started it up and pulled it out. They threw their bags inside. A second electric opener lifted the second door to reveal the bow of *El Pomposo*. Connor stood by the boat and guided Markus back to align the Explorer's ball hitch with the nose of the trailer.

Alyson checked out the old boat. "This has got to be a twenty-five-foot boat."

"Thirty," Connor said cranking the trailer down over the hitch.

"How did Markus fit it inside his garage?"

"He knocked a big hole in the back wall. The boat sticks out through it. He keeps a tarp over the stern. Some of the neighbors complain, but he's technically not breaking the neighborhood association rules."

Markus leaned out the driver's window. "You got it hooked up yet, Sheridan?"

"Not yet."

"Come on, we're burning daylight."

A dark gray cloud ceiling drifted overhead. "Daylight?" Alyson said.

Connor tightened the retaining tongue around the ball hitch and plugged in the cord for the taillights. "Ready to roll. All aboard." He and Alyson climbed inside the Explorer.

Markus howled and threw the gearshift into drive. He eased the boat trailer out of the garage and pressed the buttons on the garage door remotes. Both doors dropped into place as he accelerated away from the house.

"Hit a McDonalds or some other place with caffeine and Wi-Fi," Connor said to Markus. "We need to Mapquest Leland Township Marina."

"We need to hit a gas station, too," Markus said. "*El Pomposo* is thirsty." He checked the fuel gauge on the dash. "The Explorer isn't doing so well either."

The guys broke into a debate over whether FDR knew about the attack on Pearl Harbor before it happened or not. Alyson watched passing traffic through the window, thinking about her mom, and her dad, and Jack Sheridan, and how their complicated history had rippled through more than two decades. She wondered if those ripples would spread any farther.

- THIRTY-THREE -

Marion, MI

It'd been a long, quiet drive from Carson City. The alternating whir of the windshield wipers and the pattern of rain on the roof was all Jack had heard for over an hour. After leaving Rezner's place Lauren had clammed up. Jack tried to stir conversation a few times but she refused to participate. Bobbie kept her distance in the back seat, staying quiet as well, although Jack figured she was just attempting to keep the peace by holding her tongue. He didn't quite understand the shifting dynamic between them. Instead of kicking off a session of conflict resolution, he'd decided to let the situation simmer with the hope that it would fizzle out. So far no luck with that strategy.

A combination diner and rest area came up along the roadside. They'd been driving the rural route a long time, and a ten-minute stop to stretch legs and get something to drink might go a long way toward improving dispositions. He pulled into the gravel lot and parked beneath the bluish hue of an ancient street light atop a telephone pole. "Pit stop, ladies."

"Good timing," Bobbie said. "My bladder's screaming at me."

He switched off the engine. Bobbie jumped from the back seat, dodging rain and running for the diner's brick facade. Jack turned and started to speak to Lauren, but she unlatched the door and climbed out of the Jeep. He cursed under his breath. "Damn it."

She rounded the hood on her way to the diner. He popped from his seat to intercept her, splashing through a mud puddle and taking her hand before she got away. "What's the matter with you?"

"Me?" She stared hard at him. "Look in a mirror and ask that again."

"Hey, I'm not the one brooding in the corner."

"That's the problem, Jack. You don't see what you're doing."

"What am I doing? I'm searching for hidden treasure. We both are."

"And every step we've taken has gotten more and more dangerous. I went along with you at first because I thought you were making rational decisions, but you're not anymore."

"We've discussed every decision. Where is this coming from?"

"Our son has been singled out, threatened, and you just put on blinders and plow ahead."

"We agreed to keep going. We fed Ben the false clue to put him off track. Remember that 'we' part?"

"I remember you saying your family's safety was more important than ten million dollars in gold, but that was back when this was still Jack Sheridan's treasure hunt."

"Well, whose treasure hunt is it now?"

She kicked muddy water from a puddle at him. "It's Bobbie's, and everything you do and every decision you make is focused on her. You're not thinking about anything else."

"That's not true and you know it. Come on, Lauren, if we find these coins it does us a world of good, too. That's right, I said us. And as for Connor, he wouldn't stop looking for the coins now even if I told him. It's better that I stick with it to keep an eye on him."

She shot him a sarcastic smile. "For a year you've been playing it safe to a fault. Rafferty had you looking behind every door. The fear of him coming back made you carry that pistol around every day. It made you buy me a gun and teach me how to use it. It made you keep tabs on Connor's every move. All of a sudden Bobbie comes out of nowhere and you throw caution to the wind. You get into shootouts and car crashes. It doesn't faze you. You get Connor and Markus tangled up in street fights."

"They started that fight," Jack protested. "I told them to stay low."

"It wouldn't have happened at all if it wasn't for this treasure hunt, and this treasure hunt wouldn't be happening if Bobbie hadn't asked for your help."

He frowned. "Q.E.D., it's all Bobbie's fault."

"No, Jack, if you didn't feel for Bobbie the way you do you'd be handling this situation differently. Yes, she's the catalyst but she can't make you do things you don't already want to do. It's not her fault. It's yours."

Rain soaked him to the bone as he digested her words. "What do you think my feelings are for Bobbie?"

Lauren shook her head and turned away. Jack reached for her arm. She refused to look him in the eye. The streetlight buzzed atop the telephone pole.

"Whatever you're thinking right now," he said, "it's not what's happening."

She watched rain hit parked cars. "Just a few days with Bobbie and you're turned inside out. If seeing her again has knocked you this far off balance, what does that say about us?"

"You're reading between the lines and seeing something that isn't there."

"Then what is it I'm seeing, Jack? I see the way you look at her. I see the way you interact with her. I know it's something. What is it?"

He didn't reply.

She lifted his hand from her arm and squeezed it. "I need something warm to drink. It's pretty cold for July, isn't it?" She walked into the diner.

Jack watched her disappear inside. He whirled around and kicked the Jeep door closed. *What is it with women confronting me in the rain?* He stomped through slushy gravel and entered the shop section of the rest area. From the end cap of a magazine rack he could see through a corridor into the diner. Lauren sat in a booth near the front window. The restrooms were positioned off the corridor, and Bobbie stepped out. She spotted Jack. A bit of indecision set into her stance and she glanced the other way, straight into the diner at Lauren. She was stuck between them. Jack acknowledged her with a little nod and then picked up a newspaper and wandered into an aisle with snacks and medicine.

What is it I'm seeing, Jack? He didn't know how to explain it to her. He wasn't entirely sure he'd done an adequate job of explaining it to himself. Was it a vestige of guilt? A remnant of love? A glimpse down the road not traveled? He swiped a small bottle of Ibuprofen from a shelf. The songwriter got it right; love hurts, and at that moment it throbbed at the base of Jack's skull.

He paid for the paper and pills at the shop register and went into the restroom down the corridor. The mirror above the sink reflected an unkind image back at him. The rain had matted his hair to his head and flattened his mustache. Dark circles puffed under his eyes. His clothes were wet and disheveled. "What's the matter with you?"

He brushed his wet hair back and straightened the windbreaker to conceal the Colt better. The childproof cap on the pill bottle nearly foiled him, but he managed to circumvent the safety and dug out the wad of cotton to reach the tablets. He plopped two into his mouth and scooped some water from the antiquated sink faucet into his hand. He drank from his palm, closed his eyes, and splashed what remained onto his face.

He opened his eyes on the mirror. The image startled him.

Lloyd Faulkner's reflection watched him through the glass.

Jack spun around. Yes, Lloyd was really there, dressed in a wrinkled dark suit and a loosened silk tie. They stared at one another a suspended moment.

"What the hell are you chasing, Jack?"

Cogs clicked into place. Jack narrowed his eyes. "It's you."

"Yeah, it is me," Lloyd said. "Surprised?"

Jack sprang at him, pinning him against the wall with a forearm and yanking the silk tie tight around his neck. "I should string you up right here."

Lloyd coughed and worked his fingers under the tie to loosen it. "A little overreaction, don't you think?"

"Considering the men you sent after me, you're lucky I haven't shot you already."

Lloyd glared in a smug manner that seeped under Jack's skin. "Still haven't figured out who you're up against? Wish I could help out there, but at this point I'm a little more in the dark than you are. I have no idea who they are."

"You track me to a Marion rest area and expect me to believe you know nothing about those men or the coins? Don't play stupid."

"Coins?" Lloyd managed a smile despite his disadvantage. "I knew you'd find something bigger to go after than a job as a fishing charter captain."

"I go to Saugatuck and you anchor the *Achilles* just off the coast. Don't try and tell me that's a coincidence."

"Of course it's not. I've been keeping an eye on you ever since you turned down my offer to bring you back to Neptune's Reach. I knew you had something cooking when you refused. You need something to chase, it's in your blood."

Jack released him from the wall. "You don't know me like you think you do."

"I don't? Your visit to that historian in Portage, the urban violence you incited in Grand Rapids, the chaos you brought to that archeological dig—it's all classic Jack Sheridan finessing his way to the big prize." Lloyd shook his head. "We smoothed out a lot of your peripheral adventures at Neptune over the years but it was worth it. You always got the job done."

Jack turned a fraction and threatened to come at him again. "You're pissing me off, Lloyd. Tell me why you're here. Did Ben tell you I'm not playing fair?"

"Why do you insist those men are mine? We don't deal with their type at Neptune."

"You are their type."

Lloyd straightened his suit coat. "I think the pressure is getting to you. Old friends don't talk to each other like that."

"You said I'd regret turning down your offer. That sounded like a threat to me. Old friends don't talk like that either. Guess we're not old friends."

"You're having a lot of trouble you wouldn't be having if you had hooked up with Neptune's Reach on this quest of yours. I'd say that's grounds for regret."

"Hook up?" Jack said. "I don't want you or the company anywhere near this."

"We lost those contracts because you didn't come back." Lloyd tensed with agitation. "You can make up for that, Jack. These coins you're after, they must be worth an awful lot to pull you in this deep. Let's make a deal. I'll give you Neptune's Reach resources to find the coins and we split the take sixty-forty."

Jack drew the Colt and aimed it at Lloyd's chest.

Lloyd backed against the toilet stall. "A gun? You're pulling a gun on me?"

"What did you expect?" Jack snarled. "You stalk me across the state. Your gang of thugs kicks me around and takes shots at me. You threaten the life of my son. And now I'm supposed to forget all that and join forces with Neptune's Reach? Fat chance."

"You have it all wrong. I don't have anything to do with—"

"Quiet!" Jack kept the gun trained on him and opened his cell. He speed dialed Lauren. She let it ring four times before answering. "Honey," he said, "I've got a situation in the men's restroom that I need your help with."

"Don't try to be funny to break the ice, just apologize."

"No joke. Lloyd Faulkner's here, and I want him to stay here."

"Lloyd?"

"I need you to bring me a handful of those tie-wraps we got at Rezner's place."

"Tie-wraps? Okay, I'm on my way."

Jack closed the phone and planted his foot at the base of the restroom door to lock it in place. "Twenty years," he said. "After all that time you still can't resist screwing me over for your own interests."

Lloyd put a hand on his chest as if reciting the pledge of allegiance. "I'm not screwing you over. I'm offering you help. The fact that Neptune, and by extension I, will also benefit is just a bonus. Win-win."

"You like that expression, don't you?"

"I like it when everyone wins. It's good for business. But you're making a big mistake."

"Zip it." Jack and Lloyd stared each other down for a full minute. A knock rattled the restroom door. "Jack, it's me."

He stepped aside and opened the door. Lauren came in with Bobbie in tow. They each had a handful of large tie-wraps. Lauren glared at Lloyd. "You're really here. I can't say that surprises me. I knew you wanted Jack for something."

"Nice to see you too," Lloyd said.

Jack handed her the Colt. "Point this at him. Shoot if necessary."

"With pleasure." She took the pistol.

Jack went over to Lloyd with the tie-wraps. "Don't get too comfortable because Lauren's holding the gun. We just had an argument, she's really mad, and she hates your guts." He grabbed one of Lloyd's hands and cinched a tie-wrap around his wrist. He looped a second tie-wrap through the first and secured it to the corner post of the toilet stall. Bobbie repeated the process with the other hand on an adjacent post so that Lloyd was fixed in the stall doorway with his arms at his side. They did his feet next. Then Jack grabbed Lloyd's cell phone and threw his Bluetooth earpiece into the urinal.

Lloyd rattled the posts. "You're screwing yourself this time. I'm not your enemy."

Jack recovered the Colt from Lauren. "I know you're not my friend. And I know my best interests aren't at the top of your priorities list. Tying you up here is simply keeping you out of my way without having to shoot you dead. I guess you might call that a win-win." He holstered the pistol and looked around the restroom, and then went over to the paper towel dispenser and cranked out a length of towel. Wadding it up, he yanked Lloyd's jaw open and shoved it in his mouth. "Let's go, ladies."

They left Lloyd struggling against the tie-wraps and mumbling through paper towel.

A guy was making his way toward the restroom and Jack intercepted him. "Nasty mess. You don't want to go in there. I'm going to tell the shop manager about it now."

The guy stayed away.

"Who was that we just tied up in the restroom?" Bobbie said.

"My ex-boss," Jack answered. "He thinks I still work for him. He should be getting the idea that I don't by now."

In the parking lot Jack spotted Lloyd's Cadillac CTS. He opened his pocket knife and worked the tip of the blade into the sidewall of a front tire. Air hissed out. He sawed the cut larger and then folded the knife back up. Approaching the Jeep, he reached into his jacket pocket for the keys. They weren't there. He checked his pants pocket. Empty too. "I can't find the car keys."

"The Jeep was unlocked when we got the tie-wraps," Lauren said.

Jack remembered his quick exit from the vehicle to catch Lauren earlier. He hopped into the driver's seat and found the keys in the ignition. "Nice move, Jack," he said to himself.

The women took their seats and Jack started the engine. He twisted around to back out of the space. For a brief moment the three looked at each other, giving subtle recognition that something had changed between them. Jack pulled out of the parking lot and onto the main road.

No one spoke as they drove toward the Leelanau Peninsula.

- THIRTY-FOUR -

Frankfort, MI

Higgs and Kisko inspected the white MasterCraft 245-VRS tied up in a dock at the Gold Coast Marina. She stretched twenty-four feet from bow to stern and sported twin V-8 inboard-outboard motors. She could seat up to eighteen passengers, but on this trip she'd only be carrying four. The extra capacity would be eaten up with supplies and, if all went well, a load of gold coins. An impressive boat for sure. An expensive boat, too. No wonder she was laid up at an affluent condominium complex on the lake. It continued to amaze Higgs how well connected and how deep his employer's pockets seemed to be. Of course, the depth of one's pockets was a relative thing. Higgs knew he wouldn't even be out here bumping heads with Sheridan if the man pulling the purse strings thought his pockets were full enough, but then does anybody ever think that?

Kisko stepped into the boat's open bow. "I'm not a damned sailor. You going to get us across the lake in this thing?"

Higgs tossed him a book. "I know my way around a boat well enough."

Kisko read the title: The Great Lakes Lighthouse Companion. He opened it to a dog-eared page. "What's in here?"

Higgs looked down on him. "Do you even know how to read?"

"I read when I have to." Kisko skimmed over the text on the page.

"Let me save you about an hour," Higgs said. "Pilot Island is a little scrap of rock and dirt located at the inlet of Death's Door passage. There's an 1858 lighthouse standing on it. That's where we're heading."

Ehrlich and Barnett walked up the dock and threw a pair of duffle bags into the stern of the boat. Ehrlich hopped in and sat in a port section of wraparound seating. "Who's in the lead, Sheridan or us?"

Higgs shot him a glare. "If you have to ask that's not a good sign, is it?"

"How the hell did this happen?" Ehrlich said. "We went from pole position to hind tit."

"He was a step faster, we missed something. It doesn't matter now. If life gives you lemons, make lemonade. If life gives you Jack Sheridan, make him do all the work and then take the coins from him."

Kisko sneered. "Sheridan won't let it go if we take the coins from him."

"He can't come after us if he's dead," Higgs said coldly.

Barnett grinned and took a final puff on a cigarette.

Rays of sun broke over the trees behind the marina. Remnants of rain clouds drifted in thin sheets on an easterly breeze. Higgs noted the opening moments of a new day. "Rain finally stopped. It should be a smooth ride to Pilot Island."

Kisko tossed the book on a bow seat. "What if Sheridan has already found the coins and he's gone from the island?"

Higgs climbed down and took the captain's seat in the large cockpit. "He hasn't gotten there yet. He was still in Saugatuck yesterday morning. In the afternoon the storm kicked up the lake so bad he couldn't have gotten across. I'm betting he's shipping out right about now from some marina up the coast. If we leave within the hour we'll get there close to when he does. Then it's just a matter of time."

Barnett flicked his cigarette butt into the water. "What if we just can't find the coins?" He gave Ehrlich a wry grin. "You know, what if we come back empty handed? Sorry, boss, the coins weren't there. Know what I mean?"

Higgs set a hand on the throttle lever and studied the cockpit controls. "Barnett, you say something like that again and your body will never be found. Capice?"

"Hey, I'm only joking. No need to get serious."

"Joking about it means you've thought about it, and that shit isn't happening." Higgs turned to face him. "We find the coins, we bring them back, we all land in a bigger place. If I hear a whisper of anything different, this plan will carry forward with just three of us…or two."

Kisko laughed. "Barnett, you dumbass."

Higgs' cell phone rang with a call he'd been expecting. He gestured to Kisko. "Nate, help Ehrlich and Mr. Dumbass load the rest of the supplies and hardware into the boat." He answered the phone. "Yes, sir, what's the word?"

"It was a damn good try on Sheridan's part but not good enough," the caller said.

"You mean—"

"The Bible he gave us is a fraud. I had the clue analyzed and found it's not the same handwriting as in the first Bible. Furthermore, the ink is from a modern-era ball point pen."

Higgs mouthed a curse. "How'd you get it analyzed so quickly?"

"I know people. The important thing here is you are not to go to Pilot Island."

"Understood."

"The good news is I know where to send you."

Higgs sat straight. "Where?"

"South Fox. It's another island in Lake Michigan. The coins are in a lighthouse there. Get a chart, plot a course, and get moving."

"How did you figure that out?"

"I know people."

"Any special instructions?"

"Just get the coins. I want this behind us so I can move on to the next phase. Do you understand how important this is, Mr. Higgs?"

"Yes, sir."

"It's getting time critical. No more setbacks. I expect to hear from you with a positive report this evening." The call ended.

Higgs picked through one of the duffle bags and pulled out a chart of Lake Michigan. He laid it out on a bench seat. South Fox Island lie seventeen miles west-northwest off the Leelanau Peninsula. The route from Frankfort to the island stretched almost eighty nautical miles. The MasterCraft could get them there in four hours, given lake conditions remained calm and the weather favorable. Higgs found himself smiling. Once again the man's connections came through.

"Plotting a course to Pilot?" Ehrlich said hoisting a canvas bag off his shoulder.

"Not going to Pilot," Higgs said. "Plans have changed. We're heading to a different island."

Kisko and Barnett walked up with the last of the bags.

Higgs folded the chart and took his seat in the captain's chair. "Load up and get in." He fiddled with the GPS unit. "We've got an opportunity to put this hunt to an end today, and believe me, we're going to do it."

THIRTY-FIVE

Leland Township Marina

El Pomposo slid off the trailer and glided into the water. Jack and Connor guided her alongside the dock with the mooring lines. Markus drove the Explorer forward, pulling the trailer out of the lake. He poked his head out the window. "We clear?"

"All set," Jack said. "Take it away."

Markus drove off with the trailer bouncing over the split concrete of the boat launch.

Jack and Connor tied off the lines. Bobbie and Alyson walked onto the dock, chatting and sipping from water bottles. Jack watched them a moment. "How was the drive up last night?" he asked Connor.

"Good. Alyson is a fun girl to have around."

"You and Markus bumping heads like rams over her?"

Connor laughed. "Sometimes yes, other times...I don't know. I can't get a handle on it."

"You telling me Markus got the upper hand?"

"Please." Connor brushed sand from his palms. "What about you?"

"What do you mean?"

"How was your drive? Mom and Bobbie weren't gelling that well in Saugatuck."

"Things haven't improved. Your mother apparently has a problem with Bobbie and I working together."

"Should she?"

"Don't start."

Bobbie and Alyson approached. Jack said, "Boat leaves in fifteen minutes, ladies."

Bobbie saluted him. "Aye, Captain." They continued walking the dock. Alyson wiped condensation from her water bottle and flicked it at Connor. It hit him in the eye and he blinked. "Nice."

Jack smiled at him. "I'm going to find your mother. Make sure the load in the boat is evenly distributed and secure." He started for the marina parking lot.

Markus came toward him clapping his hands. "All right, let's go.

The sun's been up an hour already. Hey, Mr. Sheridan, you're going the wrong way."

"How much coffee have you had this morning?" Jack said.

"Not a drop. It's all me."

"Well, get all of you to the boat and help Connor secure the load for shipping out."

"Wait a minute, I'm the captain. I should be the one giving orders."

"You may be captain, but I'm the admiral. Snap to."

Markus kept walking. "How'd I get stuck in this Mickey Mouse navy?"

"Hey, Markus, I've been meaning to ask you. That Boston Whaler is a sixty thousand dollar boat. How did you get your hands on it?"

"My dad," Markus said. "He's got a guilty conscience and a big bank account. He used the boat down in Florida for fishing a couple of years and then gave it to me as a bribe to be his buddy."

"Did it work?"

Markus kicked some gravel and seemed uncharacteristically unsure what to say. "Let's put it this way. Right now you're more like my dad than him."

"Give it time. At least he's trying."

Jack walked into the parking lot and found Lauren buttoning up the Jeep. She buckled a hiking pack around her slender waist and closed the rear hatch. He watched her adjust the pack and then lock the Jeep with the remote. She became aware of him and swept a wisp of hair from her eye. Sun lit her face in a way that took him back twenty-five years to a South Haven beach. He offered her a smile. "You still do mornings better than anyone I know."

She considered the comment but didn't respond. It seemed she had something else on her mind. "We ready to go?"

"Yeah, everyone is at the dock." He motioned to the pack on her waist. "Did you transfer everything from your purse into that?"

She nodded, not a hint of cheer in her expression.

"Chin up, sweetheart. South Fox marks the end of this marathon coin trick. Starting tomorrow we go back to normal."

"After this week, what is normal for us?"

"The same thing it was last week."

"I'm not so sure about that. Something tells me all of this doesn't end with the coins."

Jack pondered that thought a long while. It hung with him as they shoved off the dock. Markus took the helm and nudged the twin

Evinrude engines from idle to low rumble. He swung *El Pomposo* around and steered her toward the mouth of the harbor. Jack fired up the GPS unit and entered destination coordinates 45° 22' 41", 85° 50' 18", which would land them right at the doorstep of the lighthouse on South Fox.

The sky cleared to deep blue and the sun warmed the air. Lauren slid a pair of sunglasses on and sat in the stern beside Connor. Jack couldn't tell if she was avoiding him or if she really wanted to spend some quality time with her son. A little of both he decided. In the cabin Markus drove the boat. Alyson stood beside him, threatening to hit switches and throw levers just to annoy him. He had his hands full keeping an eye on the GPS display and warding her off the controls. Jack chuckled and made his way forward to the bow pulpit. He plopped down. The green hills and bright sand of North and South Manitou Island drifted far to the west. He lost himself in thoughts of time past, gold coins, and a dangerous man named Ben.

Bobbie watched him a long while from the shade of the cabin. She came and sat beside him and drank in the view of sky and water. Wind blew her dark hair from her face. "Ten million for your thoughts," she said.

"Just trying to piece together a search plan for us once we reach the lighthouse," he said.

She contemplated the horizon. "I didn't want to become a wedge between you and Lauren. I'm sorry for the trouble I've caused."

Jack shrugged. "I've been informed that it's not your fault, it's mine."

Bobbie smiled, but only for a moment. "I'm going to tell you something that isn't going to make it any better with her."

Jack looked at her funny. "What do you mean?"

Bobbie started to speak but stopped and turned away. A glassy shimmer appeared in her eyes. Jack sat forward. "What's the matter?"

"You need to know something."

Jack suddenly felt apprehensive.

"Do you know why we stopped talking after you moved to Virginia?" she said.

"We drifted. Remember the young and stupid discussion on the paddleboat?"

She gazed at him. "No, I stopped calling and writing letters because I knew I could get you to come back home, and if I did that every plan and dream you had for your career wouldn't get the chance it deserved."

He gave her an empathetic smile. "In case you haven't noticed, I'm pretty stubborn. You couldn't have changed my mind about Virginia."

"I could have done it," she insisted. "I know you, Jack. I knew you back then. You always do the right thing. You're stubborn and determined but you're also responsible, and I wouldn't use that against you."

"How could you use that against me?"

She wiped a tear from her cheek. "If you knew you had a baby to take care of at home, you would have come back."

He stared at her, dead silent.

"She's yours," Bobbie said quietly. "Alyson is your daughter."

Jack sat speechless.

"I wanted you to come home but I didn't want you to resent me for crushing your dreams. I couldn't live with that, so I told you the baby was Steven's." She averted her eyes. "I'm terrified you're going to resent me for this."

"Resent you?" Jack stammered. "You—you kept this from me for twenty-four years. How should I feel, grateful you did a good job raising her?" He looked through the cabin window at Alyson. "My God, Bobbie, you should have told me."

"I was afraid you'd think that I got pregnant just to snare you. What life would we have had together if every time you looked at me you saw the person who ruined your greatest career opportunity?"

"So instead of facing that unlikely possibility you kept me in the dark."

"I didn't want to win the battle and lose the war."

"I would have come back," he said, "and I wouldn't have resented you for it."

"You say that now but back then your heart and soul were anchored in Virginia. I knew you—"

"Stop!" He moved across from her in the pulpit. "You know me. Lloyd knows me. Lauren knows me. Everyone on this planet claims to know me better than I know myself. I've got news for all you people; the planet's got a crappy track record at predicting Jack Sheridan's next move."

"I didn't keep Alyson a secret to harm you for leaving, if that's what you're thinking."

He frowned. "I don't think you did it to be malicious, but that was a big mistake."

"And you've never made a mistake, Jack?"

"Not this big."

"You better give that a little more thought. Your history isn't snowy white."

"This would have changed everything for us," he said. "You shouldn't have kept it from me."

She didn't reply.

He glanced over his shoulder at her. "Did Steven know?"

"He suspected but never asked. He loved Alyson as his own, and that's what mattered."

"And what about Alyson?"

Bobbie shook her head.

"We need to tell her."

"We do, but would now be the best time?"

Jack watched Alyson through the cabin window. She caught him looking and gave him a wave. He nodded and smiled. *That's my daughter. Good Lord, that's my daughter.* Bobbie kept staring at him. He faced forward. Far ahead of the boat, a small green land mass appeared in the haze between water and sky. South Fox Island lie dead ahead. A handful of miles farther and they'd be ashore, and then the job of finding the coins would begin. Would now be the best time to tell Alyson that the father she'd known all her life wasn't really her father?

"No." Jack stood and strained to see the island. "But this conversation is going to happen as soon as we get back from South Fox." He turned. "Lauren and Connor need to know, too. Everybody finds out at once."

Bobbie stood beside him. "I agree."

Jack watched the island grow larger as they approached. The surreal impact of Bobbie's confession had his head swimming in emotional soup. How different would the last twenty-five years have played out if he had known the truth about Alyson? He'd have started down a completely different path with Bobbie, and his memories of Lauren and Connor wouldn't even exist. What would that reality look like from the present vantage point?

He closed his eyes and forced the thoughts from his head. He had to focus. The coins were within reach, no time to get feebleminded. Everyone on that boat had joined the treasure hunt because they believed he could make it a success. He promised them, but he couldn't guarantee that promise if he allowed this revelation to possess his thoughts.

"I'm sorry I didn't tell you," Bobbie said quietly.

He lowered his head. "Me too."

THIRTY-SIX

The Zodiac slid onto the beach strewn with rock rubble and zebra mussel shells. Jack stepped over the bow and pulled the craft ashore. Lauren disembarked next. Connor secured the outboard motor and began handing bags and equipment to them. Up the beach a short distance the remains of an old jetty littered a stretch of sand from the water to a dilapidated boathouse. The roof of the boathouse sagged and the exterior walls were brutally weathered, but it stood pretty straight and the boards that remained on the roof provided ample shade inside the structure. Jack figured that made it a good place to store the Tovex cartridge for the time being. He carefully set the black hard shell case that Rezner had packed the explosive in just inside the entryway.

Connor and Lauren set the last of the bags on the beach.

Jack returned from the boathouse. "Connor, you and Markus bring the rest of the stuff ashore and then shuttle Bobbie and Alyson over. We're heading up to the lighthouse to start looking around."

"Got it," Connor said. "Give me a push off."

Jack and Lauren reached down and launched the Zodiac back into the lake. Connor waited to drift into deeper water and then lowered the outboard motor and fired it up. He drove the little inflatable toward *El Pomposo*, which was anchored a quarter mile east of the landing site.

"Let's go," Jack said.

They started inland from the beach, weaving through a thin tree line toward the heavier forested island interior. A lightly worn trail guided their footsteps. Jack noted the signs that others had beaten this path recently. Ahead and a bit north, a faded white tower capped by a rusted lantern room with broken windows rose above surrounding trees. Wind whistled through the exposed cast-iron frame.

The trail turned north and a narrow corridor opened up through the trees. Amid thicker vegetation the signs of a maintained trail appeared more evident. Clipped tree branches, trimmed shrubs, and cleared ground cover revealed a hard-packed walkway leading up the rise in the terrain and straight to the base of the lighthouse. "Somebody's been visiting the island and caring for the light station," Jack said. "There's probably a renovation project getting underway."

Lauren walked a few more steps. "What were you and Bobbie talking about on the boat?"

He gave her an irritated eye and made a poor attempt at imitating her voice. "Yes, Jack, it does look like someone has been here maintaining the grounds."

She exhaled an annoyed breath. "Yes, Jack, it does look like someone has been here maintaining the grounds. By the way, what were you and Bobbie talking about on the boat?"

"The coins, the hunt, the aftermath."

"It must not have gone well. You two seem mad at each other." She smirked.

"Nice."

They walked past a decrepit brick shanty on the east edge of the path. Rust infected the metal roof and the entry door was missing from the frame. "Oil house," Jack said. They continued on in silence. West of the lighthouse another building appeared through the trees, a two-story brick house with a set of dormers extending from a pitched roof. Every window across the front elevation had been broken out.

"Assistant keeper's quarters," Jack said. "Considering the years it's not too bad off."

Lauren appraised the keeper's quarters and the lighthouse. "This might take longer than we thought if we have to search both buildings."

"We don't. The assistant's house was built in 1910. That's forty years after Coates hid the coins here. We stick to the light."

They reached the white brick tower. A padlocked black iron gate barred entrance through the front door. A pair of windows was stacked vertically above the gate on the face of the tower.

"Let's check the perimeter," Jack said. They moved around the side of the schoolhouse-style building. Bushes and tree branches had been cleared there as well. Bars blocked the windows. Along the back wall of the building, the roof of an attached shed sat partially collapsed on rotting rafters. Lauren peered inside through an empty door frame. "This place is falling apart. There's a rear door but it's banded and bolted shut." They walked between the keeper's quarters and the lighthouse. A cellar entrance at the foundation on the west side of the lighthouse had been sealed with a rusty chain strung through the door handles, and dozens of nails pounded into the doors. "What do you think?" she said. "Did Coates bury the coins outside or hide them inside?"

Jack scrutinized the faded cream brick comprising the wall. "I don't know. Coates supervised construction of this lighthouse, so he had access to dump them anywhere he wanted. My gut says he hid them inside."

"Think Ben is following your red herring?"

"Hope springs eternal, but if he's not following the clue he won't know where to turn."

"What are the odds he'll find the engraving in the old bank building?"

"Slim to none. What concerns me is Lloyd. He's been following me around a while now. If he's got Neptune digging into this they just might come up with all the right answers."

"Then we better find these coins and get off this island as fast as we can."

Jack regarded her. "I'm glad we're talking again."

"We never stopped talking," she said. "You just didn't like what I was saying."

"Let's go meet the others at the landing point."

"Sure. What did you and Bobbie have a disagreement about?"

"The past, the present, and the future. We need to find the coins. Come on."

She heckled him all the way to the beach. He refused to crack open the Alyson issue with her. Too many complications would come with it. Instead of escalating to an argument, he inspected the staging area on shore and found that more equipment had been dropped off. Out on the lake, the Zodiac drove inbound through light waves, carrying the rest of the group to the island. When the inflatable bottomed out near shore he walked into the water and helped them to the beach. They disembarked and arrayed around him.

Jack stood with his back to the island interior and jabbed a thumb over his shoulder. "That's our lighthouse behind me. It's locked up pretty tight. We need the equipment up there right away. There's no telling how much time we have to mess around."

"You don't think Ben took the bait?" Markus said.

"I'm not counting on anything," Jack replied. "I won't relax until we're back on the mainland with totes full of coins. Everybody grab something and move out."

Jack's treasure expeditionary force mobilized. They shouldered bags, boxes, and tools and marched up the path toward the lighthouse like a platoon of soldiers advancing through enemy territory. Jack took point, leading the advance. At the base of the tower he directed the troops where to disperse their loads. "Connor, break out a hammer and chisel. Pop those hinges on that gate across the front door. Markus, give him a hand."

"Why don't we cut that big lock?" Connor asked.

"I didn't think to bring bolt cutters," Jack said. "Besides, if we cut the lock we'd be breaking and entering. At least this way we're just entering."

"That's splitting hairs," Bobbie said.

"I'll split 'em where I can." Jack singled out Alyson. His stomach fluttered. "Ms. Marine Biologist. Are you good with tech tools?"

"Depends what kind of tools you're talking about."

"There's a metal detector in that hard case behind you. I'm told it's a nice one capable of discriminating gold from junk metal. I want you to get familiar with it and sweep the perimeter of the lighthouse. Find out how accurate it is reading through wood and plaster, too. The coins might have been built into this place."

Alyson opened the case and went about assembling the detector.

The pound and clang of metal echoed from the gate. With four hits the guys had the first hinge out. Jack retrieved a printout of a hand-drawn floor plan of the lighthouse from his equipment bag. "Ladies, your attention, please."

"Where did you get that?" Lauren asked.

"The same place I learned about the dates of these buildings. Our son isn't the only one who knows how to use the Internet. I researched last night at the hotel while you were sleeping."

"And?"

"Coates left no reference to the hiding place on the architectural record. There's nothing peculiar in this floor plan, so we need to search every square inch of this building."

Connor and Markus started hammering out the second hinge.

"What should we look for?" Bobbie asked.

"Anything and everything. Search with all your senses. Your instincts will red flag things your eyes miss. A wall where there's no reason for a wall. A shallow closet. An offbeat pattern of crown molding. A room that feels smaller than it should be. Look for the number or the symbol from the bank engravings, too. The coins are here somewhere, and there has to be a marker to find them."

"Got it!" Markus dropped the hammer and grabbed the iron gate. He and Connor swung it open about the padlock and rested it against the wall. Jack reached for the rusted front door knob. It wasn't locked.

He took a deep breath and pushed. The warped door resisted, screeched in the jamb. He put his shoulder into it. The door surrendered and swung open amid popping hinges.

Jack stumbled into a tight square room and caught his footing just before crashing into a set of iron stairs. The steps wound around a center post, spiraling up through the throat of the tower overhead. With nowhere to go but up Jack climbed. Five feet above entry level the tower opened to a short hallway scarred by peeling paint and cracked plaster. He walked into the hall a few steps. The air tasted stale. He studied the floor plan to get his bearings.

Connor and Markus rushed up the stairs behind him, their voices reverberating in the brick tower like a megaphone. Jack spun around. "Guys, settle down, this search is going to be organized."

They both posed indignant. "What?"

He repeated the guidelines he'd just told the women. "And I'm assigning search areas for everyone."

"Wow, Mr. Sheridan, you're going to take all the fun out of this," Markus said.

"We'll break into teams of two."

Connor raised a hand. "Alyson's on my team."

Jack balked. "Uh, no…Connor, you and Bobbie are a team. I'm with your mother, and Markus will stick with Alyson."

"All right." Markus smiled and punched Connor in the arm.

"Are you kidding, Dad, you're acting like my Little League coach."

"I benched you in little league," Jack said. "At least I'm letting you play now."

The women crowded into the tower behind them. "What's happening in here?" Lauren said.

"We're forming search teams." Jack checked the floor plan. "Bobbie and Connor, head up the tower. You have a room and a bunch of crawl space storage to search through on the second story. Markus, help Alyson with the perimeter sweep and then move inside. We'll likely be on the main floor by then, and there're lots of nooks and crannies to consider. Lauren and I are starting at foundation level in the cellar. Everybody watch their step. This house has been deteriorating for a hundred and fifty years; no telling what's rotting under our feet."

They scattered as directed: Markus outside with Alyson, Bobbie and Connor up the steel spiral. Jack grabbed a flashlight and a battery-powered lantern from the equipment outside. Lauren took the lantern. They followed the floor plan down the little hallway and branched right into a kitchen with warped floorboards. The ceiling, cabinets, and doors were white and the walls a dark shade of beige, but the years had taken their toll and the colors flaked on every surface. The thud and shuffle of Connor and Bobbie's footsteps upstairs bled through the peeling ceiling. All in all, though, it looked in decent condition. An open green door on the south wall near an empty pantry led to a narrow stairwell. Jack flicked on the flashlight and started down.

The stairs creaked and the air smelled a mixture of mold and dust. The cellar floor was an uneven slab of cracked concrete. The walls were built of stacked and mortared concrete block with a rough stucco face. A block wall from ground to ceiling divided the space evenly down the middle, with a doorway near the center to allow access between the halves. Scant daylight filtered in through the frosted glass of a foundation window to the south.

Jack ducked under a ceiling joist. He guided the flashlight beam through a slow arc, inspecting the space on this side of the cellar. Apart from scattered concrete fragments and a few pieces of aged lumber the place was pretty well cleaned out, which seemed more evidence of a renovation project underway.

Lauren came up beside him. "Any shiny coins down here?" She peered through the doorway to the other side of the cellar and frowned. "No treasure chest. Now what?"

Her voice bounced off the floor and block walls. Jack scuffed the surface of the concrete with his boot. "We look for a concealed compartment in the floor." He swung the flashlight beam back and forth across an exterior wall. "And we search each block for some sign of a hidden crawlspace."

"Okay," she said. "I'll start with the wall."

"I'll probe the floor." Jack rushed up the steps. His legs cast distorted shadows on the foundation window when he grabbed a sledgehammer from the equipment stash. He returned in under two minutes and began tapping the hammer head against the floor at various locations, listening for a hollow thud. Lauren continued inspecting each block. Half an hour into their efforts a sharp knock on glass startled them. Jack swung around and faced the foundation window with hammer in hand. A big shadow blocked the light and Markus' muffled voice came through the opaque glass. "Any luck down there?"

"No," Jack said. "Get back to work."

"We're done out here. The detector didn't pick up anything."

"Then start searching the main floor."

"Right." Markus' shadow disappeared.

Jack continued probing. After he finished thumping the floor, he leaned the sledgehammer against the wall and helped Lauren inspect the blocks. Neither found the number 217 or the symbol, or any other peculiar thing on any of the blocks. A little over an hour after they'd begun he kicked the sledgehammer over. "Damn it, Coates, where did you hide them?"

He rallied everyone to a meeting outside the lighthouse. No one had anything of substance to report. Jack paced back and forth in front of the tower. "Those coins are here, we just missed them on the first pass."

Nobody rebutted him.

"We go back and hit it again. Take your time, probe deeper, get creative."

The group flooded into the lighthouse. Before joining them, Jack collected three more lanterns and another flashlight. He marched into the cellar with an armful of illumination. Lauren took two of the lanterns from him. "No matter how bright you make it down here, we're not going to be able to see through these blocks to the other side."

He smirked. "It's good to know you can still be a smart ass with me." He cranked the dimmers on the lanterns up to full intensity and set them in a row a few feet from the west wall under the cellar doors. Loose concrete pieces served well to tilt the lantern bases and aim the light at the wall. The flashlights had focal adjusting lenses, and he widened their beams and set them up on the floor as well. With four lanterns and two flashlights illuminating the rough face of the blocks, he stepped back to observe. "Maybe we weren't seeing the forest for the trees," he said. "Coates might have been thinking on a larger scale."

He and Lauren gazed at the wall for ten minutes. Nothing popped out at them through the mortar and block. Jack clenched his fist. "Son of a—"

"Don't kick anything," Lauren said. "This is a good idea. Let's set it up on the opposite wall."

They recreated the lighting arrangement on the east side of the cellar and stepped back. Jack knelt down, closed his eyes, opened them again and tried to look at the wall as a whole. He let his focus go blurry. An image slowly lifted off the rough surface of old blocks. His heart skipped.

"I think I see the forest," Lauren said.

"Yeah, I see it! I see it!"

Faded colors and a layer of dust had concealed Coates' marker, but Jack's lighting penetrated the camouflage. From ceiling to ground and spanning ten feet, a large number 217 became visible within the wall. A group of blocks with dark gray surface shading were mortared in a deliberate pattern amongst blocks of lighter color to form the numbers.

Jack started wiping dust from the crags and pocked surface of the dark gray blocks. Lauren did likewise. In a few minutes they had cleaned them all and the 217 stood out like a beacon. He stared at the number a full minute and then shouted up the stairs. "Guys, get down here. We found something!"

Markus came bounding down the cellar steps. "What?"

"Go get the other sledgehammer, quick."

Markus didn't ask questions. Jack's urgency was enough to put him in motion. Alyson came into the cellar. Jack pointed to the number in the wall. She smiled wide. "My dad was right."

Jack paused. "Yes, he was."

Markus returned with the sledgehammer. "All right, what are we destroying?"

"Stand here," Jack said. "Look at that wall and tell me what you see."

"Cinder blocks."

"Concentrate on the dark gray ones."

His eyes widened. "Hey, 2-1-7. That's the number. What do you want me to do?"

Jack took a step back and pointed at the wall. "Hit it!"

Markus howled and drew back his sledgehammer. He swung hard, smashing the twelve-pound steel head into the wall at the center of the number.

* * *

Connor looked out at the southern tip of South Fox Island through a broken window in the lighthouse lantern room. After searching the upstairs room with Bobbie and finding nothing, he moved to the crown of the lighthouse and found the same. Taking in blue sky, sparkling water, and the lush green of the island from this perch worked to take the edge off his frustration. A ship steaming through the lake below the horizon held his interest as well. He'd been watching it a while now. It appeared to be a large vessel. Something about it struck a nerve. Something about it...

A heavy crash suddenly carried up the tower to the lantern room. Connor turned from the picturesque view. He dropped his legs through the hatchway in the floor and sat on the rusted steel. Another crash rolled up to him.

"Bobbie, did you hear that?"

She stepped out of the second story room and lifted her gaze to him. "Yes, and before that I swear I heard Jack's voice…I'm going to check it out."

"Let me know what's going on."

She descended the tower steps.

Connor lifted himself from the hatch. That ship on the horizon seized his attention again. It had covered a lot of distance since he first spotted it. The vessel was taking a more discernable shape now. The sweep of the bow, the configuration of the deck, he could almost make it out. A blue splash of color appeared on the starboard bow quarter. Connor leaned through the window frame as if it would help him to see clearer. Somehow it did.

"Oh no!"

He wormed through the hatch and scrambled down the spiral stair, leaping over the last five steps. He rushed through the central hallway as a pair of crashes echoed up from the cellar. At the fork he spun around, uncertain which way to go. Another crash of concrete and steel drew him into the kitchen, then down the stairwell to the cellar. "Dad, Dad!"

Jack and Markus stood amid a cloud of mortar dust, sledgehammers in hand and squaring off with a gapping hole in the block wall. Lauren, Bobbie, and Alyson watched them from the far corner. Dust muted the lantern light and everybody had a towel or some kind of garment covering their mouth to filter the particles in the air. Jack looked like a gang member in the Great Train Robbery. He turned away from the hole. "What is it?"

Connor's eyes danced around the distracting scene and he stumbled over his words. "South of the island. A ship is out there. It's heading this way."

Jack pulled the kerchief from his mouth. "You sure about that?"

Connor nodded and coughed on dust. "Real sure. And Dad, I think it's the *Achilles*."

THIRTY-SEVEN

Jack stood on the walkway outside the lantern room and peered through a set of binoculars. It took a few seconds to locate the ship in all that water. He steadied his hands and adjusted the focus. The lines of the vessel sharpened, and the fuzzy blue marking on the bow morphed into the Neptune's Reach trident.

"Damn it, Connor, you're right. It's the *Achilles*." Jack watched the ship a few more seconds. "How the hell did Lloyd find us out here?"

"I don't know but he's coming this way," Connor said.

"It won't take him long to get here." Jack dropped the binoculars and let the strap around his neck catch them. "We've got to be gone with the coins by the time they make shore."

"Do you think Lloyd will try to take them from us?"

"I'm not giving him that chance." Jack moved into the lantern room, crawled through the hatch, and hurried down the tower steps.

Connor stayed with him. "We haven't even found the coins yet."

"We might have." Jack rushed through the kitchen and down the stairwell into the cellar. Dust still clouded the air. Everyone except Markus stood gathered around the hole they'd pounded through the wall. A pair of shovels lay at their feet. Light flickered from inside the cavity.

Lauren came over. She'd taken off her waist pack and her hands were dirty like she'd been clearing debris from the sledgehammer work. "There's a passage that goes back about ten feet and ends at a sheet of granite. Markus crawled in there to see if he could break through."

Jack handed her the binoculars. "Lloyd's coming. We have to figure this out fast."

"We left Lloyd tied up in Marion. How did he get out here?"

"The more zeros you tack on to a dollar amount the more resourceful he gets." Jack walked over to the hole in the wall. Bobbie and Alyson stepped aside to let him have a look. Connor joined him and they knelt at the entrance. "Markus," Jack said. "What have we got back there?"

Markus came crouching out of the passage. "Big freaking slab of granite. Nice inscription on it. He that overcometh shall inherit all things. I think we found the right place."

"Let me in there." Jack switched spots with Markus. He took a flashlight and worked his way into the passage, noting a series of timber support beams overhead keeping the earth from collapsing in on him. After a hundred and fifty years, he figured the beams were due to give way any second. He reached the slab of granite and read the inscription. Definitely the right place. He studied the slab. There didn't appear to be a hinge or pivot mechanism anywhere around the edges. He dug his fingers between the dirt and rock, clawing back, looking for an edge. High clay content in the soil prevented him from digging very far, and all he managed to expose was more granite. He called back through the passage. "Get me a sledge."

Connor crawled in and handed him the hammer. "Any luck?"

"Not yet. Get back now."

"I tried that already," Markus said.

Jack grumbled. He took the sledgehammer in both hands and drove the head into the granite like a ram. The slab didn't budge. He did it again and again, each time with more force. Particles of dirt fell onto his head, timber supports creaked, but the slab stood immutable. "Son of a bitch!" He crawled out of the passage.

Connor, Markus and the others gathered around.

"What are you thinking?" Lauren said.

"I'm thinking of blasting."

"If you blast that whole passage is going to collapse," Bobbie said.

"Most likely, but if we're lucky the granite will direct the velocity of the blast out the passage. It might minimize the collapse enough so that we can dig through the debris and reach the coins."

"Sounds like wishful thinking," Lauren said.

"It is but it's all we've got. I'm not leaving the coins or this passage for Lloyd." Jack brushed lumps of dirt from his hair. "I'm going to get the Tovex. We've got five minutes to figure out a non-explosive way to get through the granite." He ascended out of the cellar.

Bobbie followed him up. "We're breaking things now, Jack."

"Huh?"

"Now we've broken and entered."

Jack kept walking. "We actually entered and then broke. I'm not even sure there's a law against that." He gave her a smile. "Four minutes. Figure out that granite." He hurried out of the lighthouse and down the path to fetch the case with the Tovex from the boathouse on the shore. All the way it gnawed at him. How did Lloyd Faulkner find them at South Fox? Probably the same way he found them at the

Marion rest area. Jack lifted the case from the boathouse floor and started back. A recollection stopped him cold. He'd left the Jeep unlocked at the rest area. All the equipment they brought to the island had been in the back of the Jeep. That had to be it.

He ran the path to the lighthouse and tore into the cache of equipment. Lauren and Connor came out and met him. "What are you doing?" Lauren asked.

Jack ripped open a canvas bag. "Lloyd didn't stop by the rest area just to talk. He planted a tracking device somewhere in our equipment. Help me find it."

Lauren and Connor began rifling through bags and containers alongside him. They dumped a box of work gloves and spread open a canvas roll stuffed with hand tools on the ground. Connor overturned a box of water bottles. "What will this thing look like?"

Jack ripped out a small black module that had been duct tapped to the inside of a plastic tote. "Like this. Neptune's Reach standard GPS locator tag." The device appeared to be a rectangular bar made of plastic composite about the size of a stapler with a blinking red LED on its face and a stubby antenna protruding from its end. Jack pried open an access plate on one of its sides with his pocket knife and revealed a set of dip switches. He set the tip of the blade in a black switch and clicked it to the opposite position. The LED went dark. "This is an active tag so it can be powered down. It's off now. Too little, too late but at least Lloyd will have to search the island a little harder for us."

Bobbie appeared in the tower doorway. "Alyson found something."

Jack threw the GPS tag into the tote and carried the Tovex case into the lighthouse. Bobbie turned. "Please leave that up here. We might not need it, and it makes me nervous having it so close."

He set the case near the door in the tower and followed her down to the cellar. Connor and Lauren stayed close. They all crowded around Alyson at the breach in the cellar wall.

Jack acknowledged the metal detector in her hands. "Show me."

She switched it on. "I didn't think Coates would expect his sons to dynamite the slab. I figured there had to be a mechanism to open it buried in the dirt somewhere around the periphery of the passage. I dialed down the detector's discrimination circuit so it will pick up iron and steel. Guess what?" She waved the head of the metal detector near the ceiling of the passage between the first two support beams. A low octave tone pulsed loud. "There's some kind of metal shaft concealed in the dirt that runs from the top of the slab to just above the first support beam in the passage here." She slapped the timber cross member nearest the hole.

"Good job, Alyson."

Markus crouched down and brushed the face of the beam. "When we smashed through the wall some debris lodged into the wood here. I cleared it away, and look what I found."

Jack moved closer. A hole the size of his pinky was bored into the center of the beam at an angle directed toward the ceiling of the passage. Words carved into the wood above the hole grabbed his attention. "Conquer by this." Jack glanced back at the others. "That sounds familiar."

"It does." Lauren smiled. "I know what we need to do."

Jack stood. "Please share, sweetheart."

"We need the Coates cross."

"Why?"

"It's the key that will open the slab. 'Conquer by this' is a reference to Roman Emperor Constantine's vision."

Jack thought back. "I remember the story. Before a crucial battle Constantine saw the image of a cross of light in the sky with the words 'conquer by this' inscribed above it. He took it as a sign from God that he'd win the battle if he converted to Christianity. He did, and had his men decorate their shields with the symbol of the cross. They won big."

"Yes," Lauren said. "Coates is telling us to use his cross to fit into that hole and release the latch that locks the slab. Conquer by this."

"The bad guys have the Coates cross," Connor said.

"I don't think we need the cross," Jack replied.

"Everyone needs the cross," Lauren said.

"I'm speaking literally." Jack inspected the size and shape of the hole in the beam. "I spent a lot of time studying the picture we have of the Coates cross. No part of it is machined in any way to function as a unique key. The intersecting members are simple four-sided silver rods. An Allen wrench of similar diameter should work." He ran a finger over the hole. "I'd say a three-eighth inch will do."

"I'm on it." Connor fetched a set of Allen wrenches from the equipment and returned in under a minute.

"Good boy," Markus said.

Jack selected an extended length variation of a three-eighth wrench and inserted it into the hole in the beam. It slid through the bore until an obstruction stopped it. He rotated it about. It didn't seem to mesh or interface with anything inside. He tried to finesse it but it wouldn't go farther.

"You need the cross," Lauren said.

"No, I don't." He lifted a sledgehammer and tapped the end of the wrench, driving it a fraction of an inch deeper into the hole. Somewhere a metallic linkage clinked. The rumble of shifting stone spilled from the passage and then stopped. Markus jumped and swung his flashlight into the dark space. The slab of granite still blocked the passage but something had changed. A sliver of dark space had opened up at the top edge.

"It moved!" Connor yelled.

Jack twitched his eyebrows at Lauren.

She scowled. "You're lucky."

Jack tried to spin the Allen wrench, but it had engaged a mechanism up there that locked it tight. He struck again with the sledgehammer. Something clicked and sucked the wrench into the hole. The beam split and a cascading clatter of chain through a tackle swelled with the rumble of stone grinding against stone. The granite slab dropped straight down, crashing into a cavity below. It stopped sharp with a heavy thud that shook the ground. A plume of dust rolled from the passage and into the flashlight beam.

"We're in!" Markus shouted.

"Jack, you did it!" Bobbie said.

"We all did it," Jack replied. "Now let's see what we did." He took the flashlight from Markus and crawled into the passage. Light chased darkness from the compartment that a moment before had been sealed behind the granite slab. Three wooden crates sat beneath a sprinkle of loose soil and a layer of cobweb. He reached for the closest one and tried to pull it from the compartment. It scraped heavy against the earth. Connor crowded into the passage and grabbed the other side of the crate. They drug it out to the cellar floor. All eyes locked on. Jack felt around the lid. It didn't seem to be nailed down. He took hold of a rope handle and yanked off the lid.

A mix of gold and silver coins packed in a bed of multi-colored paper filled the crate to the brim. Nobody spoke. Dust particles floated in the lantern light like tiny pieces of confetti. Jack took a gold coin from the pile. The inscription identified it as a Betchler five-dollar piece. Eugene Elliot was right. But there were silver coins too, Seated Liberty dollars, also very valuable according to Mr. Elliot.

Alyson ran her fingers through the coins. "I can't believe it."

Jack noticed numbers printed on the colorful pieces of packing paper. He pulled one out and grinned. It was a two-dollar bank note from the Singapore Bank. Coates had packed the coins in notes of every denomination that the bank had printed. "People, we're rich."

Markus whooped and danced around. Connor high-fived him so hard their hands should have bled. Bobbie stood staring into the crate, tears streaming down her cheeks. Alyson hugged her tight. Lauren met Jack's gaze and surrendered a subtle smile. "You got us to the coins," her eyes were saying, "now get us back home."

"Listen up," Jack said with raised voice. "This is all very nice, but there are people on the way to this island who want to take these coins from us. We need to get out of here, and we need to get out now. Ladies, start bringing down the plastic totes. Guys, help me get the other two crates out. We fill the totes as fast as we can and get them down to the Zodiac without stopping. I'll shuttle them to the boat, and then we leave South Fox in our wake. Everyone understand?"

The celebration ended. Jack's treasure expediters took to their assigned tasks. By the time the men had the second crate sitting on the cellar floor, the first load of totes arrived. Alyson and Bobbie began filling them with coins. Jack and Connor wrestled the last crate out of the passage.

Jack found the binoculars on the cellar floor. "Guys, the first tote's full. Take it to the beach. The bucket brigade starts now."

"Where are you going?" Markus said.

"Recon." Jack climbed out of the cellar. He met Lauren in the hallway. She had an armful of plastic containers. "That should do it for the totes," he said to her. "Those crates should empty into about ten containers. Bobbie and Alyson have started transferring the coins."

"How close is Lloyd?"

"I'm going to check." They split apart, he climbing the tower, she descending to the cellar. Outside the lantern room Jack scanned the waters south of the island with the binoculars. The *Achilles* had made good time. She'd almost reached the tip of South Fox. She'd be looking for anchorage soon. At least her deep draft would keep her farther from shore than *El Pomposo*. It would take them a little longer to reach the beach. It wasn't much but every second counted. Jack expected to see her launches in the water within thirty minutes. He had to get his group and the coins onto the boat in a damn hurry. Timing would be tight.

On ground level at the base of the tower, Connor and Markus squeezed out the front door carrying a tote filled with coins between them. They double-timed it over the trail to the landing site. Jack took one last look at the ship and then came down from the lantern room. He helped fill totes in the cellar until the guys came back. Markus was wired. "Come on, let's go. Give me another one!"

Alyson shoved him on the shoulder. "Hey, I'll help you carry this one."

"All right." Markus lifted his end of the tote. "Connor, take a break. The girl is doing your work for you." They carried the coins up the steps.

"Penis," Connor said under his breath.

Jack pulled him aside. "The *Achilles* is dropping anchor. We're going to have company real quick."

"How much trouble do you expect?"

"There's a pistol in your mother's hiking pack lying on the floor over there. Get it."

"That much, huh?"

"I don't want you going to the beach without protection. After all we've seen on this expedition and knowing Lloyd like I do, I'm not taking any chances. Plan for the worst, hope for the best, remember? But don't let your mother see you take the gun. No need to worry her about something born from my paranoia."

Connor met his gaze. "Your paranoia has saved us more than once."

Jack gave him an appreciative smile. "I'll occupy her while you grab the pistol. Check on the *Achilles* from the lantern room before you make your next trip to the beach. I'll be heading down to shuttle coins on the Zodiac in a few minutes."

Connor nodded.

"You okay with this?"

"No problem. We've been through worse before, right?"

"Yeah, we have." Jack put a hand on his shoulder. "Watch yourself, and keep an eye on Alyson."

Connor acknowledged and moved toward Lauren's pack on the floor.

Lauren and Bobbie scooped handfuls of gold and silver coins into totes. They sat together in awkward silence. Jack knelt between them and set a container near a crate. "Wonder what price Wallace Garity would put on that sailboat of his if I told him I wanted to buy it." He reached into the crate and grabbed a bunch of coins. "I'll bet this would make a good down payment."

* * *

Markus and Alyson dropped the second tote on the beach next to the first in front of the Zodiac. It thudded over sand and zebra mussel shells with a chink. Markus shook off the ache in his arm from carrying the heavy load two consecutive trips.

"Too much for you?" Alyson said.

"Of course not." Markus checked on *El Pomposo* anchored beyond the shallow water. "But next trip I'm a lefty." He regarded her. "So, are you still going to get a job as a marine biologist, or are you just going to be a rich chick with a little red sports car?"

"I'll probably be a marine biologist with a little red sports car. What about you?"

Markus shrugged. "I'm not sure how the shares will shake out. I might not be able to retire just yet, but I'll tell you what, I'm definitely taking a year off to pick a direction to follow." He thought a bit. "Do marine biologists have assistants?"

She laughed. "Sometimes, but they have to know what they're doing."

"Oh, I know biology, especially the female kind. Just give me a shot and I'll show you." He paused and looked beyond the ruins of the jetty to the water surrounding *El Pomposo* again. "Ever get the feeling you're being watched?"

"Connor said a Neptune's Reach boat is close by. Maybe that's got you on edge." She tugged on his shirt sleeve. "Let's get back to the lighthouse."

Markus turned. "About Connor. Do you two have something going on?"

Alyson smiled and started to speak but the words caught in her throat and she froze.

"What's the matter?" Markus followed her stare over his shoulder.

A dark, imposing man was standing on the beach beside the boathouse: Ben Higgs.

Higgs appraised them with contempt and spat on the ground. Nate Kisko stepped from the shadows of the decaying boathouse toting a pump-action shotgun. He chambered a round and took aim with the weapon.

Markus pushed Alyson toward the path. "Aly, run!"

Kisko sneered. "You suckered me with that plank, numb nuts. It's payback time."

Markus spun, tried to find cover.

A blast of fire and shot belched from the shotgun barrel.

- THIRTY-EIGHT -

"Rejoice with me; I have found my lost coin."
— Gospel of Luke 15:9

Connor spiraled into panic. From the lantern room he could barely make out the old boathouse through waving tree branches, but he'd seen enough. Two men were on the beach. One of them fired a weapon. The only targets to shoot at down there were his friends.

He scrambled down the tower stairs and into the hallway.

Jack ran into him. "What did I just hear?"

"People are shooting at Markus and Alyson on the beach."

"Who are they?"

"I couldn't tell. We have to get down there." Connor backtracked to the tower.

Jack followed him. "Are they from the *Achilles*?"

"I don't know. I didn't see any boats. I didn't see anything but those guys shooting."

They ran down iron steps and out the front door. Connor pulled the Kel-Tec pistol from his belt and headed for the landing site. Jack seized his arm. "Hold up! If we just rush the beach we might get shot ourselves. Now calm down and tell me how many people you saw."

Connor breathed heavy, tried to see through the woods to the landing site. "Two. I saw two. There might be more. Trees blocked my view."

Jack rummaged through the equipment scattered on the ground. "What kind of guns do they have?"

"Uh, one guy had a rifle or a shotgun. That's the only one I saw."

"Sounded like a shotgun." Jack found the box containing the stun grenades. "They haven't fired again. It might have been a warning shot. Markus and Alyson are probably okay." He attached a Velcro pouch to his belt and slid the grenades inside. "There's a little oil house about forty yards down this path, brick exterior. We'll take cover there and try to get eyes on the beach. Understand?"

Connor nodded.

Jack drew the Colt from his shoulder holster and disengaged the safety. "Follow me. Keep that pistol pointed at the ground until you have a real target."

They moved along the path leading to the boathouse, scanning ahead and into the trees beside them for any signs of movement, any indications someone might be advancing from the beach. Jack pressed his back tight against the brick wall of the oil house and peered around the corner. Connor came up alongside him.

Over eighty yards of distance and a long stand of elms still obstructed their view of the landing site. Jack leaned close to Connor. "Stay put. I'm going to get a better look." He broke from the cover of the oil house and maneuvered along the tree line. He stopped behind the last sizeable oak just beyond the bend in the path. The move landed him less than sixty yards from the beach. Better visibility, but bushes, shrubs, and some trees near the boathouse were still a problem. Two totes sat in front of the Zodiac, and Ben Higgs stood over one of the totes. Alyson walked from behind a tall bush, prodded forward by the guy named Nate. That weasel had a shotgun pointed at her. A fire ignited in Jack's gut.

He rolled behind the thick trunk and took a deep breath. Connor stared at him from the oil house. Jack made his way back. "It's Ben and one of his men," Jack said. "I saw Alyson. She seems all right, but they've got her at gunpoint."

"What about Markus?"

"I didn't see him, but that doesn't mean he's not okay."

Connor set his jaw. "Let's go."

"We need a plan before we march down there." Jack glanced over his shoulder. "The terrain leading to the beach is pretty sparse. Not enough cover to get us there undetected. We can try to circle around from the north but it's not much better. We might have to come at them with a ruse to—"

"A ruse to what?" Connor said.

"Hold on. Bobbie's coming. This is going to complicate things."

Bobbie approached from the lighthouse. Jack waved her forward, signaled her to hurry. She ran to him and they all huddled inside the small oil house. "What's going on?" she said. "Why do you have your gun drawn?"

Jack hesitated. He and Connor exchanged a glance. "Ben and Nate are on the beach," Jack said. "They've got Alyson."

Bobbie shook her head. "No. We sent them the false clue. They should be across the lake right now."

"Neptune's Reach tracked us to the island. Ben must be working with them."

"What are we going to do?"

"We're going to get her back."

She read his demeanor. "Where's that Jack Sheridan confidence? Why don't you tell me this will be easy?"

"I won't lie to you. Ben's desperate and dangerous. Anything we do will be risky."

Bobbie touched his arm. "She's my daughter."

They held each other's gaze a long moment. Without using the words Bobbie had really said, "She's *our* daughter." Jack put his hand over hers. "Alyson will be okay."

She looked at the Colt in Jack's hand. "They want the gold…we should give it to them."

"It's not that simple anymore," Jack said. "I know these guys. I've seen them do some bad things. We slugged it out over this treasure, and they won't just let it go if we surrender the coins now. They're not the type to leave loose ends to come back and bite them."

Connor caught his eye. "Then we make them think we're giving them the coins, just long enough to get Alyson and Markus back, then we get out of Dodge."

Jack stared at him. "You have details to go with that plan?"

"Not yet."

"Try this. We've got some empty totes left. We fill them with stones and rig a flashbang inside one. We carry them down to the beach like we're paying a ransom. When Ben opens the tote to inspect the coins, the stun grenade incapacitates him and we take Nate down."

The three contemplated the idea in silence. Bobbie spoke first. "Let's do it."

"I second," Connor said.

"Motion carried. I'll get the totes." Jack stepped from the oil house. He immediately sensed movement in front of the keeper's quarters up the rise. Two men with pistols raced from the old brick home on a bee line for the lighthouse tower. Jack recognized them from Saugatuck: Ehrlich and Barnett. He crouched and aimed the Colt at the lead man, Ehrlich, but lost his bead when they dashed behind the bushes between buildings. They emerged from the other side in a blur and got through the tower doorway before he could reestablish his aim. "Damn it!" He rolled back into the oil house. "Connor, the men you and Markus fought in Saugatuck just got inside the lighthouse."

"Mom's in there alone," Connor said.

Jack kicked the door frame. "I know she's in there alone!" He rested the cool barrel of the .45 against his forehead. He had to go after those men to protect Lauren, but that meant abandoning Alyson and Markus. He couldn't be everywhere at once. He couldn't protect everybody. Lauren turned out to be right. His façade of invincibility melted away and left him sitting on the dirty oil house floor feeling painfully mortal.

"Dad, what do we do?"

"Jack, they're going to hurt Aly."

Their urgency burned through the fog in his head. He had to come back. "Connor, listen close." He lifted himself off the concrete. "I'm going to the lighthouse. You get down to the bend in the path and keep watch over the situation on the beach. Don't make a move unless you absolutely have to. When I get back, we go in together. We'll knock this wall down one brick at a time."

"What if you don't come back?" Connor said, a trace of fear underlying his voice.

Jack ignored the question and pulled a stun grenade from his pouch. "Take this. It works best in confined areas, but use it however you can. Pull the pin and throw; when you do, look away and cover your ears. Got it?"

Connor nodded.

Jack turned to Bobbie. "I'm sorry, but we have to do it this way. Alyson is all right for the moment. If those men get Lauren and the coins in the cellar, it's all over. The only thing left for Ben to do then will be to shoot us dead one by one and bury the bodies. I'm not going to let that happen, but I have to hit the lighthouse first."

Bobbie shook her head. "I'm the one who's sorry. I got us into this."

He raised a finger to silence her. "Don't even go there." He looked to Connor. "One brick at a time, son."

Connor offered him a weak smile.

Jack poked his head from the oil house. The grounds around the lighthouse and keeper's quarters appeared clear. He lifted the Colt in both hands and started up the rise. At first he took cautious steps. As he advanced he moved his legs faster. He followed the pistol, keeping an eye on the tower doorway and the windows across the front of the building. His heartbeat matched his footfalls. It seemed to take an eternity to cover the forty-yard distance. His boot hit the first iron step in the lighthouse, and he pointed the Colt up the throat of the tower. Nothing but the black spiral staircase above him. He stopped dead and listened.

A man's voice shouted from inside the house. He couldn't tell where but guessed the cellar. The crash of something knocked over in a scuffle bounced off the peeling walls. And then Lauren's voice rose, "Jack! Jack!" Another crash.

He wanted to run blindly to the cellar but held himself back. Tactics. He had to think tactics. Two men went inside the lighthouse. How were they dispersed? He started climbing the steps to reach the first story.

Jack decided that if he were in charge of those men he'd send one off to search the house for the coins and the other to stand watch to protect their back. The lantern room would be too open a perch to post a sentry. He'd have the guy stay inside, watch from a second story window, far enough back so as not to be seen by an advancing enemy.

Jack had seen no one on his advance to the lighthouse.

Five steps up and his eyes came level with the first story hallway. Another clamor echoed from the cellar. Lauren called out to him again. He nearly broke into a run to reach her but tapped every bit of strength to hold his position. *Keep your head, Jack, or you'll get it blown off.*

Tactics, damn it!

The sentry would hold his fire if a single man approached the lighthouse, waiting instead for him to come inside and walk into a trap.

Jack stepped up to the first floor and moved cautiously into the hallway, slowly sweeping the Colt in synch with his shifting gaze.

The sentry would set up a kill zone on which he could throw down fire from a position above and to the rear of his prey.

Like from the spiral stairs into the hallway.

Jack spun around. Glowing daylight through a tower window captured the form of a man in silhouette crouched on the steps just below the second story. Jack jumped to the side, slamming into the wall as the man on the steps opened fire. Sharp, cracking 9mm reports exploded in the hallway. Floorboards cracked and craters burst through wall plaster all around Jack. He responded with the Colt, blasting three rounds into the tower. One slug pounded the center post of the spiral stair and deflected out through the window behind the shooter. The man jumped like he'd taken fire from all directions and scurried up to the second level, discharging a haphazard pair of shots in his flight.

Jack knew where both men were now. He turned and raced into the kitchen. Lauren shouted to him from the cellar. Her voice cut short like she'd been struck. Jack bounded down the stairwell in four strides.

Across the cellar against the far wall, Barnett struggled to get his left arm around Lauren's neck while a pistol flailed in his right hand.

She fought against him, trying to get free. Her bra was exposed through a long tear in her shirt. Blood flowed from a slice on her lip. Her face twisted in a panicked frown.

Jack aimed quick and fired the Colt, shattering Barnett's collar bone and spattering the cellar wall with his blood. Lauren broke free and ran. The pistol clattered on the concrete floor. Barnett howled in pain and threw a fierce glare at Jack like he might charge. Jack aimed straight at his forehead and didn't say a word. He wanted to pull the trigger. They stood frozen like that for five full seconds. And then Jack slid his aim to Barnett's leg and blew a hole in his thigh. Barnett went down writhing in pain. Jack picked up his pistol.

Footsteps thudded across the ceiling. The man from the hallway firefight was coming. Jack went to Lauren and threw his arm around her. "Are you all right?"

She clung to him and nodded.

Jack guided her back away from the stairwell. The man started coming down the steps. His legs appeared. Jack fired once into the stairwell and pulverized a chunk of wall plaster. The legs stopped and an answering volley of gunfire shot into the cellar. Jack held Lauren close and cradled her head, trying to protect her from possible ricochet. He studied the studs and boards of the external stairwell wall and estimated where behind it the guy might be standing. He aimed the Colt at his best guess and blasted a hole through the board. The guy shouted a curse and scampered to the top of the steps.

"There's no way out, Sheridan," the man hollered from the kitchen. "You're trapped."

Barnett squirmed on the floor. "Ehrlich, Higgs is coming. Wait for him to rush the cellar."

Jack drew Barnett's 9mm from his belt. "Lauren, are you okay to take this gun and point it at that guy to shut him up?"

She snatched the pistol from him. "Absolutely." She aimed across the cellar at Barnett and placed a finger across her lips. "Shhhhh."

Jack sprang the empty clip from the Colt and reloaded with a full magazine from his holster. "You're here for the coins, aren't you, Ehrlich? I've got eight totes full of them down here. Come and get 'em, you candy ass."

"We'll get them soon enough. Just sit down there and sweat it out a few more minutes."

Jack holstered the Colt and grabbed the stun grenade from his pouch. He took hold of the ring connected to the pin and moved closer to the stairwell.

Barnett saw him maneuver. "Ehrlich!"

"Hey!" Lauren waved the 9mm, reminding Barnett to stay quiet. He eyed her with distain but held his tongue.

Jack signaled Lauren to get ready. "Ehrlich," he said, "how bad do you want the gold?"

"You'll find out." Ehrlich's voice placed him in the kitchen doorway leading to the cellar.

Jack pulled the pin, counted down the delay, and tossed the stun grenade up the stairs. He covered his ears. The grenade clunked on the top step an instant before it detonated. A burst of white lightening and hundred-and-seventy-decibel thunder rocked the stairwell. Blast concussion surged into the cellar. Lauren shuddered, brought a hand to her ear. Jack drew the Colt and aimed up the steps.

Ehrlich stood with mouth agape, eyes wide, jerking his head back and forth like he was trying to restart the freeze frame burned into his retinas. "Barnett!" He dropped the pistol and cupped his deaf ears.

Jack swiped a shovel off the cellar floor and raced up the steps. Ehrlich didn't respond in any way to his charge. At the last instant he seemed to see something coming at him. Jack shoved him into the kitchen. Ehrlich lost his footing, falling sprawled on the dirty floor. He spat a string of profanity as he tried to right himself amid washed-out sight and deafness. Jack swung the shovel and rang the spade against Ehrlich's head to put him under.

Jack dropped the shovel and hurried down to the cellar with the Colt in one hand and Ehrlich's 9mm in the other. Lauren still held Barnett at the point of his own pistol. Jack walked over and pinned him against the wall with a boot in the chest, and then aimed the Colt at his head. "You're living on borrowed time after what you did to my wife. Tell me how you communicate with Ben."

Barnett grimaced under the pain of his gunshot wounds. "Cells," he rasped. "But they don't...work here."

Jack grabbed Barnett's cell phone off his belt clip. Its display window indicated 'No Service.' Jack checked his own cell. Same problem. He shoved Barnett against the wall with his boot again and stepped away. Lauren watched him in silence. She wiped some blood from her chin and tried to pull her shirt closed over her bra. Jack fixated on her a moment and then spun around with the 9mm and pointed it at Barnett's uninjured leg. "Kneecaps only, remember that?" He jabbed the barrel into Barnett's knee. "Pretty damn funny back then, wasn't it?"

"Eat me."

Jack kicked the gunshot wound in his leg, sending Barnett into a screaming fit.

"Stop!"

Jack glanced over his shoulder. Lauren's frightened expression gave him pause.

"Enough," she said. "You stopped him. He can't hurt us now. That's enough."

Jack stepped away. "You're lucky she's here."

Barnett slumped forward.

Lauren regarded him a short while and then turned to Jack. "Where is everyone else?"

"Connor and Bobbie are down at the oil house waiting for me. We still have problems. Ben is holding Alyson and Markus on the beach."

She tried to pull her shirt closed again. "How did all this happen?"

"These guys got to the island a lot quicker than I thought they would. They came at us from two fronts. Tide's turning, though."

Lauren knelt beside Barnett and started removing his shirt. He looked at her odd but didn't resist or respond.

Jack watched with slack jaw. "What are you doing?"

"I'm going to put a tourniquet on his leg and dress his shoulder wound. I need something to bandage with."

"He almost killed you. It looks like he tried to rape you. Let him bleed out."

"He might," she said. "But it won't be because I let it happen."

"How far do you turn the other cheek?"

She tried to rip Barnett's blood-stained shirt in half. "At the moment he's not a threat, he's helpless. Believe me, different circumstances would net different results."

Jack took the shirt from her and tore it down the middle. "He's really lucky you're here."

She ignored the comment and grabbed one of the shirt halves to tie around Barnett's leg. "What's our next move?"

"Hook up with Connor and devise a plan to confront Ben."

"Is this what it was like on that ship with Rafferty?"

"It's getting close."

She cinched the tourniquet above Barnett's wound. "I'm starting to understand you better."

* * *

Connor and Bobbie carried a tote half-filled with rocks between them. They held their free hand in the air as they neared the beach. Nate Kisko trained the shotgun on them. Higgs stood near the Zodiac with Alyson at gunpoint, and considered their approach with a wary eye.

Still several yards from the beach, Connor spoke low so only Bobbie could hear. "When we get there let's try to stay ten feet apart. Scattered targets are harder to manage."

Bobbie stared at her daughter. "What if Ben doesn't open the tote?"

"Then I'll pick an opportune time to move. Follow my lead."

"You sound like your father."

"That's the idea, isn't it? WWJD."

"What would Jesus do?"

"No, Jesus wouldn't get into this situation. What would Jack do?" Connor eyed his adversaries on the beach ahead. "Still don't see Markus. That worries me. Can you tell I have a pistol on my back under my shirt?"

Bobbie casually glanced over. "No, it's covered up pretty good." She walked a few more steps. "There's a hole in my pocket. I feel the sand falling against my leg."

"Don't let them see it."

They closed within ten yards of Nate Kisko. "Hey, it's Jack Jr.," he said. "Hold up, piss-ant."

Higgs looked them over. "Thanks for bringing me my gold. Put it down next to the others."

Connor and Bobbie walked the tote near the first two and gently set it down. Bobbie rushed to Alyson and hugged her. Connor scanned the area. Up the beach Markus lay propped against a piece of driftwood, sand soaked red beneath him and his left shoulder and chest tore up by buckshot. Connor fought back a surge of panic. "I want to see if Markus is okay."

Higgs considered the request. "You've got two minutes, and then you're going back to get more of my gold." He gestured his pistol toward Bobbie and Alyson. "But these two will stay here."

Alyson stood on the verge of tears and watched Connor's every move.

Connor tried to calm her with a reassuring smile. He walked to Markus and knelt beside him, praying the Kel-Tec under his belt wasn't visible through his shirt.

Markus' eyes fluttered open. "Sheridan, if you let them get you I'm going to be pissed."

Connor inspected the gunshot wound under Markus' shirt. "Holy shit," he said. "How bad does this feel?"

"Not as bad as it looks, I hope." Markus checked on Kisko standing guard ten feet away. "I've been playing it up, but to tell the truth it hurts like hell and I'm getting lightheaded."

"We've got a plan," Connor whispered. "Get ready."

"Don't klutz it up."

"He's not dead," Higgs called over. "Now get your ass moving back to the lighthouse." He stepped up to the tote that Connor and Bobbie had delivered.

Connor pivoted about to get him in sight.

Bobbie's eyes locked onto the tote.

Higgs lifted his foot to flip the lid off. A group of crackling reports sounded in the distance. They came from the lighthouse. Higgs lowered his foot. "Sounds like Ehrlich is saying hello to your dad." He laughed.

Kisko joined in, glancing over his shoulder at his partner.

Connor felt nauseous. His dad might have just been shot. Higgs might not open the tote, and even if he did, the stun grenade wouldn't go off. Connor had not figured out how to rig it to the lid. The best he could hope is for the sight of the grenade to panic Higgs long enough for he and Bobbie to take action.

But then why go two-against-two when he could go three-against-two and swing the odds into his favor? He subtly tapped Markus' foot and whispered from the corner of his mouth. "Pistol under my shirt...take it."

Their eyes connected. Markus understood.

Another group of gunshots crackled from the lighthouse.

Higgs quelled his chuckle. "I have to give your husband credit, Mrs. Weller. He knew what he was talking about."

Bobbie faced him. "How did you find out about Steven's research?"

"It wasn't very hard," Higgs said. "He came to us."

"Us?"

Kisko kept the shotgun pointing at the guys and turned. "Yeah, he went to the—"

Higgs silenced him with a glare.

Markus reached under Connor's shirt and slid the pistol out.

"Your husband wasn't a very honorable man," Higgs went on. "After asking for help with the coin search, he decided he wanted all the gold for himself and tried to cut everyone else out. He shouldn't have done that."

Grim realization seemed to settle over Bobbie. "What are you saying?"

"I'm saying your husband had it coming, just like you will if I don't get the rest of the coins."

"You killed my dad?" Alyson said through a bitter frown.

Kisko sneered. "Settle down, little girl, before you get yourself into trouble."

Markus concealed the pistol under his leg.

Higgs put his attention back on the tote with the stones and the flashbang, but kept the women in check under the barrel of the pistol. "Weller chose his own fate."

Connor stood and walked toward him. "No, Ben, you chose his fate."

Kisko tensed. "Keep your distance, Junior."

Connor held fast just ten feet from that shotgun. "Now you want me to deliver that hard earned blood money."

Higgs rested his foot on the tote. "Yeah, that's about right. Your loudmouth friend is down for the count and the totes are too heavy for the women to carry. That leaves you. Get moving."

Connor didn't budge. He stared Higgs down. Neither one blinked.

And then a deep boom rumbled from the lighthouse.

Higgs' eyes narrowed on the tower among the trees.

Connor's hope resurrected amid the fading echo of the detonation. "That was a grenade," he said. "My dad just said goodbye to Ehrlich."

A hint of uncertainty compromised Higgs' confidence.

Kisko turned, letting the shotgun drift away from his targets. "What's going on?"

Connor made eye contact with Bobbie and then fixed Kisko in his peripheral sight. He drew a breath. "Markus, take Nate down."

Kisko's eyes popped and he whirled around.

Markus steadied himself against the chunk of driftwood and fired three shots from the Kel-Tec. A bullet passed through Kisko's bicep and another grazed his temple. Connor lunged for the shotgun.

Bobbie slung a handful of sand from her pocket into Higgs' face. He recoiled, raised his arm to protect his eyes. She grabbed Alyson's hand and made a break. Higgs spat a slug of sand from his mouth. The women tried to skirt around him to get to the trees beyond the beach. Higgs kicked Alyson's legs out from under her as she passed, sending her tumbling and tearing her hand from Bobbie's. He reached for her on the ground. Bobbie came at him with claws bared. Higgs made a quarter turn and punched her hard in the jaw. She crumbled like a sack of rocks.

Connor seized the shotgun and forced the barrel into the air. He kicked Kisko square in the abdomen, stealing his wind and staggering him backward. Kisko's finger dragged on the trigger and discharged the weapon. The blast rang Connor's ears. A spread of shot splintered the corner of the boathouse roof. Connor wrested control of the shotgun and gained some distance from Kisko.

Reeling and gasping, Kisko righted himself to go after Connor again.

Markus rose to his feet and stood in the gap, stopping Kisko's advance with the threat of a bullet in the brain. He stood a shambling triage; blood-stained shirt sticking to his body, shredded arm hanging at his side, sweat dripping from his face.

Connor pumped a shell into the chamber and swung the shotgun around. His gut tightened. Higgs held Alyson like a shield, a fistful of her blonde hair in one hand and pressing a 9mm against her head with the other. "I wanted to get my hands on you," Higgs said, "but she'll do in a pinch."

Bobbie slowly picked herself up from the beach.

Higgs kept Alyson close and maneuvered near the water. "You're definitely your father's son, Sheridan, I'll give you that."

Connor tracked him with the shotgun. "Let her go."

"Fire that scattergun and you'll tear up her pretty face. Don't want that on your conscience, do you?"

"You're after the gold," Connor said. "You want coins, not a hostage. Take these totes right here and I'll let you walk away."

Higgs chuckled. "Don't insult me. I didn't come all this way for pocket change. I want the whole pot." He kept moving up the beach toward the boathouse.

Kisko pressed his hand over the hole in his arm. "You don't look so good, Marko."

Markus struggled to keep the pistol on target and straightened himself as best he could. "Don't worry, if I feel myself fading out I'll empty this clip into your head."

Connor moved with Higgs, shadowing his every step. "How are we going to resolve this?"

Higgs scoffed. "You talk like this is a negotiation." He jerked Alyson's head back to get her moving quicker. "Here's how it's going to go. I'm taking your sweetheart with me. If Jack is still alive, you two will collect all the coins and deliver them to me at a point of my choosing. I get the coins, and when I'm satisfied, you'll get the girl back." He glanced at Kisko. "Come on, Nate."

Kisko stepped away grinning. Markus aimed at his leg and squeezed the trigger but sand had worked inside the slide and jammed the Kel-Tec. Kisko laughed at the misfire.

Connor stayed focused on Higgs. "I can't let you take her."

Higgs didn't stop his withdraw. "Let's not waste any more time with this, Sheridan. You made your move and it didn't work out."

Bobbie came forward. "Alyson, it's going to be okay."

Alyson reached out. "Mom!"

Connor tried to find some angle to take a shot at Higgs and not hit Alyson, but the spray of the shotgun factored too unpredictable. "Damn it, Ben, don't force me to do it!"

Higgs smiled. "Don't fool yourself. You want her alive more than you want me dead." He and Kisko scurried over the ruined jetty and headed for the trees north of the boathouse.

Connor felt the moment slipping away. He couldn't shoot. He couldn't take the chance of killing Alyson. He slowed his steps.

Higgs and Kisko melded into tree cover with Alyson between them.

Connor lowered the shotgun, shoulders slumped in defeat. Bobbie quietly wept. Markus dropped to his knees. Oppressing silence settled over them.

THIRTY-NINE

"Connor!" Jack jogged around the bend in the path on his way to the beach. He'd heard gunfire there, small caliber pops and a shotgun blast. He spotted his son holding the twelve-gauge between the boathouse and the Zodiac. "Are you all right?" Jack said to him.

Connor's eyes brightened. "We heard shooting in the lighthouse. We thought you might have—"

"We're okay." Jack scanned the beach. Bobbie was tending to Markus' wound and clearing away tears. No sign of Alyson. "What happened here?"

"Bobbie and I decided to go to the beach after you went into the lighthouse."

"I told you not to come down here until I got back."

"We weren't sure you'd make it." Connor rested the shotgun barrel over his arm. "If those guys you went after made it out and joined the ones on the beach we'd be screwed."

"One brick at a time," Jack said. "What happened to that?"

"They tried to divide and conquer us. That calculation works both ways. They were half strength down here."

Jack searched the beach again, more impatient this time. "Where's Alyson?"

Connor dropped his chin. "They have her."

"Where did they go?"

"I offered them the coins in these totes but Ben wouldn't take it. He wants everything."

"Connor! Where did they go?"

"Into the trees north of the boathouse. They're going to set up an exchange."

Jack took the shotgun from Connor and handed him Ehrlich's 9mm. "How long ago did they leave?"

"Two, maybe three minutes."

"This isn't over." Jack heard Lauren coming down the path. She arrived with a first aid kit from the equipment stash. He gave her the twelve-gauge.

"Why do you keep handing me guns?"

"Force of habit." He nodded to Markus lying on the beach. "He needs to be bandaged up pretty bad. Give Bobbie a hand with that. Connor and I are going after Alyson."

Connor lifted his head. "We are?"

"We have the advantage on the island. If they leave and pick an exchange location, they're in command again. Can't let that happen. Here they're outnumbered, outgunned, and on our turf."

"Our turf?" Connor said. "They're using Alyson as a human shield. They've got the trees to cover their escape. We don't know where they're going. How is any of that to our advantage?"

Jack started north up the beach. "Ben didn't come ashore at the southern tip of the island. We would have seen him approach from the lantern room. He must have landed farther north. That's where his boat is, and that's where he's heading right now."

Connor jogged to catch up. "How is that better for us?"

"There are low-lying dunes just beyond these trees that stretch the width of the island. The expanse runs about two hundred yards before the forest picks up again. When Ben crosses those dunes he'll be completely exposed." Jack drew the Colt. "And when we catch up I'll be shooting at him with something more accurate than a shotgun."

"Okay," Connor said, "maybe I didn't completely screw this up."

Jack caught Bobbie's attention in passing. "We're going after Alyson. Stay put."

Bobbie stood. "You can't expect me to do that."

"I don't expect it, I just want you to do it."

She fell in line with them as they entered the trees, leaving Lauren to tend to Markus. They pushed through vines, hopped over fallen timber, and ducked under low branches. They'd soon be through the short band of forest and onto the dunes. Jack and Bobbie caught themselves looking at one another and then at Connor. Jack figured they were thinking the same thing. Connor needed to know that Alyson was his sister. Now just wasn't the right time.

Bright dunes materialized through the trunks and branches ahead. Jack clicked off the Colt's safety. "Connor, get behind that big maple over there and search for Ben on the sand."

Connor nodded and did as instructed.

Jack took post behind an old ash tree. Rolling dunes scrolled out before him, dividing the southern tip of South Fox from the denser wooded wilderness to the north. The hot belt of sand spanned half a mile and connected the east and west coasts. The western dunes rose nearly thirty feet into the air, tapered off to quarter that height at the mid-point of the island, and then settled to a shallow amplitude on the east side. The relative flatness of the east passage is where Jack figured he would find Ben, treading the path of least resistance.

And he did.

Higgs, Kisko, and Alyson had covered half the distance across the eastern portion of the dunes. Three trails in the sand led right to them. Ben had a hold of Alyson's arm and pulled her along, physically insisting she move faster. Kisko trod on the other side of her. She wasn't quite a human shield but she was close, and the hundred-yard distance put them out of the range of pistols.

"They got farther ahead than I'd hoped," Jack said to Connor. "We've got to move now. Spread out and stay low. Use the depressions in the terrain to conceal your approach as best you can. I'll make the first move. Understand?"

Connor acknowledged.

"Bobbie, stay behind us. Let's go." Jack broke from the trees. His feet sank into the sand. The ground absorbed the power of his stride. He kicked his legs higher to compensate. Thirty yards to his right, Connor ran parallel. Bobbie trailed a few paces behind.

Far ahead of them Higgs marched forward, struggling to keep his grip on Alyson. He turned to secure his hold and Jack signaled everyone to drop. They fell flat and disappeared in the valley between the low dunes. Twenty seconds felt like an hour. Sand burned against Jack's face. He lifted his head. Higgs had continued his march. Jack signaled his troops to move again. They rose in unison and scurried forward.

Sweat mixed with the sand on Jack's face. He judged their progress. They were almost close enough to pose a threat to Higgs and Kisko, but not quite yet. He checked on Connor, exchanged an "okay" hand gesture.

And then things weren't okay anymore. Higgs suddenly picked up his pace, practically dragging Alyson behind him. Kisko turned around and opened fire with a pistol. Slugs peppered the dune and sent little geysers of sand bursting up at Jack and Connor's feet. They dived behind the low crest of the nearest rise. Kisko let off the trigger. Jack counted down on his fingers to Connor: three, two, one. They popped above the crest and returned fire. Kisko turned tail amid a hail of .45 and 9mm rain.

Jack stopped squeezing the trigger after pumping three rounds down range. "Let's go!"

He and Connor charged over the dune.

Higgs and Kisko escalated to full flight. Fifty yards of sand separated them from the edge of the northern wilderness. Jack felt himself gaining ground on them. Kisko spun again with the pistol, this time firing just to hear the noise. Jack ducked his head and kept running, fighting the sand sucking in his feet, breathing hot, dry air deep into his lungs. Connor fired two rounds at Kisko. They closed the distance.

Higgs had nearly reached the tree line. Alyson skidded and flailed behind him like a kite on a string. Jack cursed and worked his legs harder. If Higgs got into the trees he might lose them. Time to throw the Hail Mary. He planted his feet and drew a bead on the broad space between Higgs' shoulders. Alyson skirted through his line of fire. "Come on, girl, move!"

Higgs entered the shade of the forest.

Jack fired the Colt. Its kick shook his arms. The bullet flickered along its trajectory. Higgs and Alyson tumbled forward into the woods. Jack lost sight of them amid shadow and undergrowth.

Bobbie shrieked.

Connor kept running. Jack hustled to catch up. Thirty yards out, a barrage of 9mm gunfire came at them from inside the tree line. Kisko had found a spot under the branches to hold them back.

Connor kept charging. He shouted something obscene about Kisko's mother and opened fire into the foliage. At the edge of the forest he jumped on top of a large fallen tree trunk and sprayed the area with bullets until the action on the 9mm locked open. Jack raced up and pulled him to the ground by his shirt collar.

"Getting yourself killed isn't going to help her!"

Connor gasped for air and held up the pistol. "I'm empty."

"You're staying empty, and you're staying down." Jack pressed tight against the tree trunk and checked behind them.

Bobbie scurried up, crouching low and keeping her head down. "Did you get him?"

"I don't know."

Connor scooted to a sitting position "We have to keep going."

"Is Alyson okay?"

"Everybody quiet!" Jack listened. No more gunfire was coming at them. A rustling noise rose from the forest floor several yards inside the tree line. The crackle of snapping twigs even farther away. "They're moving," Jack said. "Come on." He scrambled over the tree trunk and bounded into the woods. Connor and Bobbie followed.

Jack pushed through bushes, catching shadows of movement far ahead. An exposed root tripped him up. He stayed on his feet and kept going, and then realized he didn't have a bearing to follow anymore. He stopped dead, listened hard, scanned the thick forest around him. Nothing. Senses were coming up empty. He switched to instincts.

Higgs had to be making for a beach to reach his boat. Jack stood still, felt a slight breeze filter though the trees, reconciled it with the wind direction he recalled from earlier near the boathouse. "This way." He changed his course and ran through a large path of ground cover and down a slope. The trees opened up to a narrow band of beach on the east side of the island. Jack halted on the wet sand. Far north three forms waded through the water, heading for a white boat anchored just off shore. It was Higgs, Kisko, and Alyson.

Jack kicked into a run up the ribbon of sand. Water lapped at his feet. The distance was too far to cover in time. Higgs reached the boat while Jack and the others were still dozens of yards away. Kisko stood in the stern and fired a handful of bullets at them for good measure. The slugs fell short and kicked up plumes of water. Inboard engines rumbled to life. The boat's propellers bit into the water, and the craft snaked northeast away from South Fox Island. As it did, someone threw a yellow box into the lake.

Jack stood in water up to his knees, watching that son of a bitch Ben speed away with his daughter.

Connor ran up and realized the boat had gotten away. He bent forward with hands on knees to catch his breath. "I messed this up bad. I should've waited for you."

Jack holstered the Colt. "This isn't your mess. It's mine." He splashed through the water to Bobbie and hugged her tight. "I'm going to get her back," he said with as much confidence as he could muster. She sobbed in his arms.

The yellow box bobbed its way toward shore. Jack waded deeper into the lake to check it out. It was a tackle box with bold writing in black Sharpie across the top. It read, <u>ALL</u> THE COINS. VFH CHANNEL 78. 2:00.

Jack lifted the box from the water.

Bobbie met him near the shore. "What is it?"

He looked somber at her. "Our first set of instructions."

FORTY

Jack drove the Zodiac away from South Fox Island for the last time. Connor sat in the bow. The final two totes filled with gold and silver coins rested on the floor in the center of the craft. No conversation passed between father and son. They sat quiet and listened to the purr of the outboard motor. There wasn't much to say. Alyson's life hung in the balance, and the price Ben had placed on it was twenty million dollars. At two o'clock they would learn when and where that price would be paid.

They approached *El Pomposo*. Jack noticed the water line had risen on her hull quite a bit higher from when they'd first arrived at the island. With eight totes packed with precious metal, three people, and miscellaneous equipment aboard she weighed heavy in the water. She was about to get a little heavier.

"How much time do we have?" Connor said.

"It's twenty minutes before two o'clock, if that's what you mean," Jack answered.

"What else could I have meant?"

"I checked on the *Achilles* from the lantern room right before we shoved off. She has three boats in the water coming this way. They'll be here in about five minutes."

"Aren't Ben and the *Achilles* boats the same bad news?"

"An hour ago that's how I figured it but I'm changing my mind. Ben got to the island before the *Achilles* dropped anchor. There's a good chance they're not working together. That's interesting but it doesn't much matter at this point. It just means that the inbound boats are different bad news than Ben. Right now Ben is enough bad news to deal with. We're not going to stay here to contend with Lloyd's flunkies too."

Connor turned to face Jack. "When the *Achilles* crew finds the empty passage in the lighthouse they won't stick around on the island long. They'll probably come after us."

"Negative," Jack said. "While you were tying up Ehrlich and Barnett in the keeper's quarters, I rigged the Tovex to blow the support beams in the passage. The tunnel will collapse when the front door upstairs is opened. Those guys will spend a bunch of time trying to figure out what happened and determining if anything worthwhile can be salvaged from the mess."

"I hope you're right."

Jack guided the Zodiac alongside *El Pomposo*. Lauren and Bobbie helped them off-load the totes and they climbed aboard. Connor tied a tow line to a stern cleat so they wouldn't waste time deflating the Zodiac, they'd just pull it behind them. Jack fired up the old Boston Whaler's engines.

Markus rested on a seat in the shade of the cabin. Lauren had done a good job patching up his gunshot wound, but he looked ready to drift off into a week-long nap. He gave Jack a perturbed look. "Go easy on her until she warms up, Mr. Sheridan. I want my boat back in working order when I'm up and around again."

Jack made sure the anchor was secured and inched the throttle levers forward. "No problem, Hornblower." He leaned close to Markus. "You know that competition you've got going with Connor regarding Alyson? Guess what. You won."

Markus lifted weary eyelids. "Huh?"

"I'll fill you in later. Just keep it to yourself for now."

Markus laid his head back and closed his eyes. "Is she going to be okay?"

"I don't know." Jack steered *El Pomposo* northeast toward North Fox Island. "But I'll do whatever it takes to get her back safe. Count on that."

They'd traveled a good distance from South Fox when the three boats from the *Achilles* came around the point of the island and nosed into shore near the boathouse. The men in the boats didn't notice, or didn't care to notice the Boston Whaler driving toward the little sister island to the north. At two minutes before the hour Jack dialed *El Pomposo's* VHF radio to channel 78. Bobbie, Lauren, and Connor crowded into the cabin a silent brood. Jack glanced at their pensive faces, and then at the radio. He took the mic from its cradle. His hand was shaking. Weakness. It made him angry. He willed the tremor to stop. Two o'clock.

"Jack Rabbit, Jack Rabbit." The voice from the radio startled everyone.

Jack frowned. It had to be Ben calling. He keyed the mic. "This is Jack Rabbit. Identify."

"Quarterback is hailing. Confirm receipt of transmission."

Ben wasn't taking any chances. He knew anyone could be monitoring the public channel. Nothing would be said concerning a hostage, gold coins, or a ransom. Communication would all be in code, hopefully a code Jack could understand. "Quarterback—Jack Rabbit. Transmission confirmed. I want to talk to her."

"Patience, Jack Rabbit. I call the play first, and then you talk. Capice?"

"Are you an Italian Quarterback?"

Silence. "Jack Rabbit, confirm your understanding or the game is off."

Jack's expression hardened. He squeezed the mic and keyed the switch. "I understand."

"Run a pattern to 44° 57', 86° 27'. Execute in three hours. Hand off the ball. Cheerleader to follow. Confirm."

"Say again, Quarterback." Jack wrote down the coordinates as Higgs restated the instructions. "Play confirmed, now let me talk to her."

A stretch of silence followed. Alyson's shaky voice emerged from the radio. "Jack, I'm okay." Static. "They say you only have three hours. If you…don't complete…the pattern…they'll call a more difficult play."

"We're coming, honey, sit tight. Be strong."

Higgs' voice returned. "If you want to see her again in one piece, you best follow the playbook. Confirm your understanding."

Jack and Bobbie stared at one another.

"Jack Rabbit, confirm."

"I understand."

"Come alone to the field. Keep this an amateur game. If you involve professionals, throw the playbook out the window and kiss the cheerleader good-bye. Quarterback out."

Static on the radio.

Jack studied the mic a moment and then clipped it on the cradle. "That's it then. We take the coins to the coordinates and we get Alyson back. It's that easy."

Connor sank to the deck and sat. "Nothing's easy."

Jack entered the coordinates into the boat's GPS unit and called up an overview map. The numbers identified a point in Lake Michigan roughly fifty miles southwest of *El Pomposo's* current position and twelve miles off shore. It would be a waterborne exchange in the middle of the vast lake without anything or anybody around for miles. That didn't sit well with Jack, but then if roles were reversed it's exactly how he would have set it up. He steered *El Pomposo* to a heading that would lead them to the exchange point and throttled up the engines, mindful to stay well clear of the *Achilles*.

For an hour he navigated the boat, imagining possible exchange scenarios and playing them out in his head. They all ended the same; every member of Jack's treasure expedition, his family and friends, dead at the bottom of Lake Michigan and Ben sailing into the sunset with a cache of gold coins. Jack needed an impregnable negotiating position to avoid that end. After an hour of thinking he only came up with one way to get it.

He pulled the throttle levers down to idle and walked to the stern. Lauren watched him, as did Connor. Bobbie continued staring out over the water. Jack rifled through a canvas bag he'd packed on the island and pulled out the Neptune's Reach locator tag.

Connor sat forward. "What are you doing?"

Jack pried the side plate off the tag with his knife and adjusted a set of dip switches. The LED on the face of the tag began to blink.

"Dad, you just activated it."

"I know what I did." He heaved a full tote of coins from the deck and set it on the stern bench seat, and then dug into the canvas bag again. "I configured that tag to emit a coded distress signal per Neptune's Reach standard operational protocols. When the *Achilles* gets word this tag has been activated in distress mode it will set course to investigate immediately."

"You're calling Lloyd to come here?" Lauren said.

Jack produced a roll of duct tape and began taping the locator tag to the side of the tote. "That's exactly what I'm doing. More specifically, I'm calling the captain of the *Achilles*. Last I heard Garcia was her skipper. He's a good man. Rafferty Project alumnus. I think we can trust him."

"How can you trust anyone at Neptune's Reach?" Connor said.

"Lloyd and Ben aren't working together. That became clear on South Fox. Neptune crews came looking for the coins after Ben had already left. Whoever it is pulling Ben's strings, it isn't Lloyd."

"How can you be sure?" Lauren said. "Lloyd's slimy, you know that."

"Yes, he's slimy, greedy, and self centered, but after working with him for eighteen years I think I've gotten to know him pretty well. The crap Ben's been pulling is over the line even for Lloyd."

"Regardless," Connor said. "Lloyd still wants the coins. Why call him here? We need the coins for the ransom."

Jack lifted the tote with the tag tapped around it to the edge of the boat. "No, we don't." He pushed the tote overboard, sending it splashing into the lake and sinking to the bottom.

Bobbie whirled around in her seat. "Jack! What are you doing?"

He lifted another tote to the edge of the boat. "Think about it. If we show up at the exchange with these coins, Ben has no incentive to keep us alive. If we show up with just the location of the coins, he has to negotiate to get what he's after, and we'll actually have a shot at getting Alyson back." He shoved the second tote into the water.

Connor helped him lift the next one. "This is a good plan. I'm all for staying alive."

"I thought you might be."

Bobbie seemed uneasy with the idea. "Ben said not to involve anyone else in the exchange. What do you think he'll do if he sees the *Achilles* show up?"

"The *Achilles* won't be showing up at the exchange."

"Then why set the distress code to get them here so fast?" Connor asked.

"Because I want Garcia to pick up the people I leave behind here in the Zodiac." Jack pushed the third tote into the lake. "We're not all going on from here."

"You're not doing this alone," Lauren said.

Jack said nothing and lifted another tote.

Connor helped him toss it overboard and then regarded his father a long moment. "Who do you think you're leaving behind?"

"Markus needs medical attention. The *Achilles* has a licensed EMT aboard. I'm leaving him here to be picked up, but I won't leave him alone. Someone needs to look after him." Jack stared into his son's eyes. "You're staying."

"No way. I'm helping you get Alyson."

Jack stepped forward and jabbed a finger at him. "This isn't open for debate. You'll be a liability to me at the exchange. I don't want you there. What you need to do is make sure Markus survives this."

Connor looked back at his friend sleeping in the cabin. Blood from Markus' gunshot wound saturated the gauze that Lauren had bandaged him with. Jack was right. Markus needed better care than they could give him on their own, and he needed it quick. "All right," Connor said. "But as soon as I get Markus into good hands I'm going to find some way to help with Alyson."

"By that time we'll be celebrating her release in a Traverse City bar," Jack said.

Bobbie found a little smile in the thought. "Lord, I hope so."

"Lauren, I want you to stay behind with Connor."

"No." She shook her head. "I'm going to be there when you rescue Alyson—your daughter."

Jack stood silent, thinking he didn't hear her right. Bobbie flushed with surprised.

Connor whirled around. "Your what?"

"How could I miss it?" Lauren said. "Her eyes, her face, her hair, her height; I see you in there, Jack. Her laugh is like Connor's. I see them together and it's obvious."

Connor shook his head. "It wasn't obvious to me!"

Markus let loose a little rumble of laughter from the cabin.

"I just told him this morning," Bobbie said. "He didn't know, Lauren, I swear."

"When I saw Alyson at Steven's funeral I suspected." Lauren searched Jack's eyes. "Didn't you ever wonder if she was your daughter?"

Jack didn't reply. He slapped Connor's arm to snap him out of shock and they heaved another tote overboard. "We need to get her away from Ben, that's what's important now." He faced Lauren. "And I still want you to stay behind with Connor."

Lauren frowned. "You can't do everything alone. When will you learn? Sometimes you need help. One day you might actually need my help."

Jack reflected on that moment in the oil house, sitting on the concrete, becoming mortal. He jerked another tote off the deck by himself and tossed it into the lake. "Did you consider the possibility that I know I'm not all powerful, that I can't guarantee your safety, that I love you and don't want you to get hurt?"

"That's exactly why I want to come, Jack. We'll be stronger together."

He wanted to argue that there were situations in which her viewpoint wouldn't be true but he kept quiet. He looked to Bobbie. "I won't even ask. It'd be pointless to try and get you to stay behind, wouldn't it?"

Bobbie nodded.

They heaved the rest of the totes overboard and then carefully transferred Markus to the Zodiac. They loaded water bottles, protein bars, wheat crackers, fresh gauze bandages, a bottle of Ibuprofen, and a blanket into the inflatable. No telling how long it would take the *Achilles* to find them. They also packed one of the 9mm pistols, just to be on the safe side. Lauren gave Connor a long embrace before he swung his leg over the side of the boat to climb down to the Zodiac. Jack took hold of his hand to steady his descent. Connor dropped his feet into the craft.

Jack didn't let go. "Take care of Markus, and take care of yourself."

Connor gave him a nervous smile. "Go get my sister. I've got a lifetime of harassment to catch up on."

Jack smiled back. He released his son's hand. Connor sat in the stern of the inflatable and leaned over Markus. "Okay, genius, explain again why FDR sacrificed the Pacific Fleet when he knew the Japanese were attacking on December 7th."

Jack untied the tow line and tossed it into the Zodiac. He went to the GPS unit in *El Pomposo's* cabin and wrote down their present coordinates. He gave Connor one last wave and then pushed the throttle levers forward. The bow rose and the boat gathered speed. Jack steered her back on course. Lauren and Bobbie watched from the stern as the Zodiac shrunk smaller and smaller in the distance.

Jack took the paper with the written coordinates and tucked it into his boot. He drove north through the vast lake, trying to steel himself for the coming encounter. Lauren and Bobbie joined him in the cabin but sat out the journey in silence. He considered his trio. They were all aware of what lie ahead. They were on their way to barter for Alyson's life, and in the process risk their own lives. A tall task, hard to grasp its gravity, hard to quantify the odds of success or failure, but it had to be done.

Jack began throwing out his thoughts on how to approach Ben, what tone to take, possible reactions. Treating the ransom negotiation like a project to be accomplished seemed to defray the women's nerves. Noting tasks and roles got their minds working and muted the impact of emotion. That's exactly what Jack needed, everyone thinking, functional.

They came within a few miles of the coordinates Ben had given them and a boat appeared on the horizon. Jack checked the GPS unit to verify they were on track. It showed him they were. *El Pomposo* closed the distance to a mile. The ship seemed to be a fairly sizeable sail vessel, not the boat Ben had used to escape South Fox. Closer still. She spanned nearly eighty feet from stem to stern with tall aluminum fore and mizzen masts. The little hairs on Jack's neck pricked. Something felt wrong. Very wrong. That ship looked too damned familiar. He double checked the GPS unit.

"No, no, this can't be right."

Lauren noticed his face had turned to ice. "What is it?"

Jack's mouth went dry and he stared at the sailboat. It was a transom gulet of Turkish origin. Her keel was laid in '97. She had once been owned by an Exxon executive but was sold to a Michigan Supreme Court judge.

Jack tried to speak but his voice faltered. He found it on the second try.

"That's Wallace Garity's ship."

FORTY-ONE

Jack spun the wheel and pulled *El Pomposo* hard to port. He didn't want to get too close too fast. He needed time to think. He wouldn't get it. A white MasterCraft slid out from behind the sailboat and fishtailed to an intercept course. Jack recognized that boat too—the one Ben had taken Alyson away in.

Lauren fought to stay on her feet with the deck pitching beneath her. "That can't be Garity's ship. He can't be here."

Jack maxed out the throttles, pushing *El Pomposo* to her limit. "That's his ship. It's no coincidence he's sitting out here at these coordinates. Garity's the man at the top. Ben's working for him. Damn, I can't believe it!"

Lauren retreated to a corner of the cabin and covered her mouth with her hand. "My God, Jack, this is my fault. All this is my fault."

Jack white-knuckled the wheel, tried to angle away from the MasterCraft. "What are you talking about?" He glanced over. She seemed on the verge of breaking down.

"It's Ben and Nate," Bobbie said with eyes on the approaching speedboat. "They're closing."

Jack acknowledged, adjusted course again. "Lauren, what do you mean this is your fault?"

She looked horrified. "I thought he could help us. With his connections to the police I thought he might be able to keep Ben away."

"Oh no, Lauren, honey, don't tell me…"

"I've been calling Garity," she cried. "I told him about the second Bible, about South Fox."

Jack pounded his fist against the console.

"They've got a shotgun," Bobbie called from the stern. "And they're getting close."

Jack cursed. "Ben thinks we've got the coins aboard. He's got us where he wants us, and he's decided to screw the negotiations. Stupid jackass."

A boom sounded over the noise of the engines. A chunk of molded fiberglass shattered on the starboard side of the cabin. Lauren flinched and squeezed tighter into the corner. Jack ducked his head. "Bobbie, get up here and take the wheel."

She stumbled over to the captain's chair.

"Stay on this heading, straight and true." Jack reached into the equipment cache and snatched the shotgun that Connor had taken from Nate. He aimed as best he could with the boat slapping the waves, tried to target the MasterCraft's pilot area. He fired. Pumped the shotgun. Fired again. Pumped the shotgun. Fired a third time. The speedboat's windshield cobwebbed. A section of chrome railing along the bow burst apart. Higgs and Kisko crouched for cover. The MasterCraft came within twenty yards of *El Pomposo* and veered off. Kisko twisted about and fired two blasts as they sped away. A spread of shot splashed in the water. The second spread tore off the cover plate of the starboard motor.

Jack set the shotgun down and retook the wheel from Bobbie. "Those dip-shits are going to mess up our plan."

"How do we get them to stop?" Bobbie said.

A burst of squelch came out of the VHF radio, and then a voice. "Jack Rabbit, power down and hand off the ball. Now!"

"Answers that question," Jack said. He scooped up the mic and keyed the switch. "Back off, Ben, the coins aren't aboard. If you kill us you'll never lay eyes on them. That'll really frost Garity."

Dead silence in reply.

"Garity." Bobbie spat the name like bitter rind off her tongue. "I wish I could say his involvement surprises me."

Lauren began to emerge from shock. "I didn't see his hand in any of this."

"How could you?" Jack guided *El Pomposo* into a wide circle around the sailboat. The script lettering across her stern was barely readable at this distance: *Distinguished Gentleman*.

"Jack Rabbit—Quarterback," Ben said through the VHF. "Heave to fifty yards off the sail's starboard side. Kill your engines and stand in the stern with hands on your head. Oh, and mention a name on this channel again and she loses a finger. Quarterback out."

"Understood." Jack cradled the mic and slowed to half speed. "Okay, let's get this situation under control."

"Control?" Bobbie sounded doubtful. "Our old college friend Wallace Garity has been trying to kill us and is holding our daughter hostage. I don't see us gaining control here."

"The fact that Garity is at the top doesn't change how we have to deal with this situation. It might even give us an advantage. We have history with him. We know him."

"We know him and he knows us," Bobbie said. "That makes it worse, doesn't it? He'll want to make sure we don't turn him in for revenge after the ransom is paid, more so than if he was dealing with complete strangers."

Jack didn't reply.

"I'm so sorry," Lauren said. "He has Alyson because of me."

Jack nosed *El Pomposo* into a heading toward the *Distinguished Gentleman*'s starboard side. "We're all so busy apologizing to each other for getting into this mess the son of a bitch really responsible is getting a free pass. I say we quit laying the blame on ourselves and throw it at Garity." He met Lauren's eyes. "Hell, I spoke with Wallace face to face and he duped me."

She gave him the slightest hint of a grateful smile.

"Bobbie," he said. "Take the wheel again." She did and he picked up the shotgun. "Now stand back from the console." He chambered a round and blasted the GPS unit to smithereens.

"What was that for?" Bobbie asked.

"That GPS electronically stored a record of our trip from Leland Harbor to South Fox to here. We don't need Ben figuring out where the coins are by where we stopped along the way." He stood behind the wheel again to drive *El Pomposo* into position.

The *Distinguished Gentleman* rested still in the calm lake to their port side, sprawling two and a half times the length of the Boston Whaler. Jack scanned her deck for Garity but didn't see him. To their starboard the MasterCraft glided in close with Higgs at the helm and Kisko wielding the shotgun. Jack shut down *El Pomposo's* engines and put his hands on his head. "Ladies, it's time to negotiate. Let me do the talking."

They walked from the cabin to the open stern as instructed.

The MasterCraft drifted two yards to starboard, her engines rumbling at idle. Kisko stood in her open bow, feet spread to steady his stance and training the shotgun on them. He craned his neck to inspect the Boston Whaler's deck. "Don't see them," he said to Higgs.

Higgs rose from the pilot's seat with visible irritation. "What the hell did you do with the coins, Sheridan?"

"The coins?" Jack raised his eyebrows in mock surprise. "You think I'm stupid enough to bring them to a meeting with you in the middle of nowhere? You might try something crazy like kill me and take them instead of releasing Alyson."

"Where's your son?"

"Same answer."

Higgs slid a 9mm pistol from a belt holster. "Before we go any further, you're going to carefully remove that Colt and toss it into the lake."

Jack didn't want to comply. The old Colt had gotten him out of a lot of tight situations, but he had no choice in the matter. He gingerly removed it from the shoulder holster by pinching the handgrip with his thumb and fingers.

"Hold up," Higgs said. "On second thought I want that as a souvenir. A remembrance of the day I bested Jack Sheridan. Set the safety, reach over, and set it on my bow."

Jack did as instructed.

"Now do the same with that pouch on your belt, real careful now."

Jack exhaled in frustration and removed the pouch in which he had put the second stun grenade.

"Now tell me where the coins are or the girl starts losing pieces. Capice?"

Jack did not put his hands back on his head. "I'm through dealing with low man on the totem pole. No offense, Ben, but unless I meet with Wallace Garity I'm finished negotiating."

Higgs stood rigid, smoldering. "You're what?"

Kisko sneered and fidgeted with the shotgun.

Jack thought he saw flames lapping out of Higgs' ears. "I'm dead serious. I speak direct to Garity or twenty million dollars stays lost forever."

Higgs lifted a mic from the MasterCraft's console, never taking his eyes off Jack. "Sheridan doesn't have the coins aboard. He says he wants to meet with you or he's not negotiating."

"Of course," Garity's voice said through the radio. Aggravation was evident. "Invite Jack and his companions over to my boat. Be persuasive, as we discussed earlier."

Higgs smiled. "The honorable Judge Garity requests your presence aboard the *Distinguished Gentleman*."

Jack shook his head. "Have him come to us."

"Nate," Higgs barked. "Persuade Sheridan to board the sailboat."

Kisko tipped the shotgun barrel toward *El Pomposo's* water line and fired a spray of shot into the hull. He racked in another shell and fired a second time. Lauren and Bobbie recoiled from the blast. Fiberglass shattered amid brittle screams. Kisko blew another hole amidships. Jack pulled the women back from errant shot and bursting hull fragments. Kisko put a fourth hole in the stern and then cackled with delight. Water rushed into the ruptures. The Boston Whaler began listing.

Higgs watched with an amused grin. "Hop into my boat if you don't want to get wet. Otherwise you're swimming to the sailboat."

Jack half-heartedly encouraged the women to jump to the Master-Craft. His mind raced. He hadn't anticipated this move. Their ride home had just been blown out from under them. That left Ben's boat and the *Distinguished Gentleman* as the only vehicles for escape. Things had just gotten a bit more complicated.

Bobbie leapt across first. Lauren followed. *El Pomposo* took on water fast. She listed at thirty degrees already. Water sloshed up to Jack's ankles on the angled deck. He crouched low and jumped, barely landing his foot on the MasterCraft's bow lip and tumbling onto the wrap-around seating.

Higgs held them under the barrel of his 9mm. "Sit tight now." He gunned the engines and the MasterCraft lurched forward. Kisko sat next to him feeding shells into the shotgun. Jack righted himself and checked on Lauren and Bobbie. They both looked rattled. He shared their concern. The lake continued to consume *El Pomposo* in the wake of the MasterCraft. She completed her ninety-degree roll and lay full on her side, sinking. Jack interpreted the message: Garity did not intend on letting them leave.

They covered the distance to the sailboat in no time, coming alongside near an aluminum ladder. Kisko climbed the rungs with the shotgun slung on a strap over his shoulder. The hole in his bicep slowed him down. He tied off the MasterCraft's bow and stern lines on stainless steel cleats. Higgs insisted his guests climb aboard. Jack led the women up the ladder and stood on the deck of the boat he had admired in Grand Haven five days before. And there was Wallace Garity, standing beside the low profile deckhouse dressed in khaki shorts, a white polo shirt, and dark sunglasses like five days before. Inappropriate for the situation, he gave his guests a wide smile, flashing teeth as white as the hair on his head. "Jack, I said I wanted you and Lauren to join me on my Fourth of July cruise and here you are. Funny how things work out, isn't it?"

Jack wanted to run over there and punch him in the nose. "Where's Alyson?"

"You're still wrapped up in business. You need to learn how to relax." Garity considered Lauren and Bobbie. "Ladies, I have to say that seeing you two standing together gives me a perverse sense of amusement. I almost feel sorry for Jack."

Lauren seared him with a glare. "Go to hell."

"Don't get angry at me for your error in judgment. And don't be hard on yourself. We all make mistakes."

Kisko walked beyond the deckhouse and stood post behind Garity. Higgs stayed to the rear of Jack and the women to hem them in. Jack noted their positions. "Get Alyson up here, now."

Garity's demeanor shifted from jovial to irritated. "Do you really think you're in any position to demand anything?"

Jack glanced into the water off starboard. A scant six inches of *El Pomposo's* port side remained above the lake's surface. Make that five inches. And there was no land visible clear to the horizon. "Why are you doing this? You don't need the money."

"Don't presume to know what I need. That's always been your problem, Jack. You try to equate us. You never saw the difference."

"I'm seeing a big difference now."

"Whether people choose to believe it or not, American society is divided into a caste system. There's the working class and the governing class. You're the bare-fisted, beer-drinking worker, down in the trenches. That's where you're happy and you know it. My family has always been in the ruling sect; my father the senator, his father the governor. That is our station."

"How do you fit into that scheme, Wallace? Is judge as close as you're going to get to ruler?"

Garity smiled, not so much out of amusement. "What did you do with the coins?"

"They're in a safe place."

"And so is the girl."

"Show me."

Garity leaned against the deckhouse and looked skyward. "We seem to be at an impasse."

"Nothing we can't overcome. Just bring Alyson up here, hand me the keys to the MasterCraft, and as we shove off toward shore I'll tell you where the coins are hidden."

Garity studied him through dark lenses. "Reverse the order of those events and we might have a deal."

"We working-class folk aren't stupid. Your hired knuckle-draggers have been trying to burn me all week. If I tell you where to find the coins without some guarantee of safety I'm finished."

Garity removed his sunglasses. "Are you saying you can't trust an old friend?"

"You can't be serious."

"You have to admit your late arrival to this treasure hunt has obstructed my longstanding efforts to find the coins. My actions to this point have merely been an attempt to protect my business interests. It's nothing personal."

"Nothing personal?" Bobbie said. "Was it an impersonal business decision to have Steven killed?"

Garity advanced toward her, his face flushing red. "Steven came to me when he couldn't find the coins on his own. He came to me after he failed. And when he'd expended my resources and we'd gotten close to the prize, what did he do? He tried to walk away from our agreement, just walk away so he could claim the coins for himself."

"I knew Steven pretty well," Jack said. "He was my friend. He wasn't the type to weasel out of a deal. He must have figured out you planned to take all the gold from him."

"Your friend." Garity laughed. "Is he the same friend who never told you that Alyson was your daughter?"

Jack tensed.

Garity smirked. "Well, he told me. He had to confide in someone. He poured out his soul and agonized over the fact that his dear wife still pined for her lost love."

Bobbie's face flared with anger. "Shut up, Wallace!"

Garity fixed his gaze on Jack. "Bobbie just couldn't seem to get over you. Poor Steven. He tried desperately to make up for the fact that he wasn't Jack Sheridan. He lived in your shadow, and he decided that if he couldn't win Bobbie's heart he'd try to buy it with a trove of gold coins."

Jack cocked his arm to strike Garity but Higgs kidney-punched him and knocked him to his knee. Garity shook his head. "What a dysfunctional group of friends we are. Keeping secrets from one another, hiding our agendas, putting ambition above loyalty—we really have no business calling each other friend, do we? Perhaps we should stop."

Jack winced at the pain in his side and gasped for air. "No argument here."

Garity knelt down to meet him eye to eye. "You really want to see Alyson, don't you?"

Jack stared hard at him.

Garity rose back up. "If it means that much to you, I won't let it happen. You have to learn your place, Jack. You don't control me." He nodded to Kisko. "Take the women below to see the girl. Give them quality time together in the cabin. Sheridan stays on deck with me."

Kisko acknowledged and then gestured to Lauren and Bobbie with the shotgun. "This way, ladies."

Lauren hesitated at Jack's side.

He stood, straightening his back and recovering his bearing. "It's okay," he said. "Wallace and I will do some catching up." He gave her a little nod. "It's okay."

The women started for the hatch in the deckhouse under Kisko's eye.

"For the record," Garity said to Bobbie in passing. "I did not order Steven's death. It was Mr. Higgs who took the initiative." He paused. "But don't mistake my honesty for compassion. I would have given that order if Steven didn't change his mind about breaking our agreement. And I'll give a similar order to discover where Jack hid the coins now if I have to."

Bobbie kept silent and moved toward the hatch, closer to her daughter.

Garity allowed her to pass and shifted his attention to the next in line. "Thanks for all your help, Lauren. I couldn't have done it without you."

Lauren's fuse burned to the quick in a heartbeat. She lashed out and slapped his face so hard it staggered him backward. Kisko swung the butt of the shotgun around and struck her in the stomach. She doubled over. Jack jumped into the fray on instinct, stinging Kisko in the jaw with a quick right. He made a quarter turn to square off with Garity when something very hard struck him in the back of the head. His consciousness blinked and he dropped to his knees. The deck of the sailboat spun in his vision. Lauren shouted his name. Garity ordered Kisko to get the women below. Jack felt the coolness of a shadow fall over him, a shadow from behind. He closed his hand into a fist and twisted about. Higgs towered above him, massive fist drawn back and a bar of metal gleaming across his knuckles. Jack had half a second to contemplate what was about to happen. He tried to throw his punch, but before his arm even twitched the bear paw banded in steel struck him hard just below the eye. The world went real dark real fast.

FORTY-TWO

Kisko shoved Bobbie and Lauren into a cabin below deck and slammed the door closed, throwing a deadbolt before leaving the corridor. Bobbie regained her balance from the push and scanned the surroundings. It was a fairly large space considering the overall size of the boat, probably designed to accommodate two. Mahogany adorned the cabin walls and floor. A wooden chair upholstered in burgundy fabric stood behind a round hardwood table affixed to the tongue-and-groove decking. A private bath done in white marble tile with a toilet and shower sat off to the right. A king-sized bed sat against the outer hull beneath a pair of small port holes. Alyson knelt in the center of the bed trying to see out through one of them. She turned when her visitors were thrown in. A large bruise marked her cheek and a cut ran along her neck.

Bobbie rushed over and hugged her tight. "What did they do to you?"

"They convinced me to settle down on the boat."

Bobbie showed the bruise Higgs gave her on the beach. "A matching set."

Lauren gave Alyson a short embrace. "Are you okay?"

"I'm fine, considering…what about you two? I heard a lot of commotion topside."

Bobbie's eyes lifted to the mahogany deck overhead. "Jack is up there with Garity and Ben. We're in some trouble."

"Garity wanted the coins for your release," Lauren said. "We didn't trust him to make the trade so we hid them and tried to negotiate with him instead."

"It didn't sound like negotiations went so well," Alyson said.

Lauren crossed her arms. "Not yet. The only thing keeping us alive is Jack's knowledge of where the coins are hid. He's holding on to that, trying to swing a deal."

"Is Markus okay?"

"I hope so. Connor is with him. They're trying to get aboard the Neptune's Reach ship for medical care. I'm glad they didn't come with us."

Bobbie tried to open the cabin door. "Locked tight. Deadbolt." She glanced around the room. "Aly, have you looked for another way out of here?"

"There is no way out," she answered. "The door is the only exit, the port holes are too small, and there are two guys playing cards in the cabin across the way standing guard. I think they're Garity's deck hands."

A clink and rumble carried through the boat, and then the hum of an electric motor.

"They're weighing anchor," Lauren said. "We're going to move."

"Do you think Jack told Garity where the coins are?" Alyson said.

Lauren and Bobbie stared at each other. It was the longest time they'd held eye contact since being together on the treasure hunt. Lauren said, "There's no way Jack gave up that information, not so quick and not without getting something in return."

"I agree," Bobbie said. "Garity's up to something."

"We have to get out of here." Lauren launched into a search of the cabin, checking for a concealed maintenance panel to reach another compartment, or a weak backing in a cabinet that might let them crawl to the next cabin, or something that could be used as a tool to remove the door from the frame. Bobbie and Alyson joined her. Halfway through their effort the *Distinguished Gentleman's* diesel engines started and the boat got under way. The view from the port holes indicated they were heading east, toward the Michigan shore.

Their search turned up nothing. A sense of foreboding crept into the cabin. Bobbie sat with Alyson on the bed. Lauren sat in the burgundy chair. They all seemed to be thinking about the things they were afraid to talk about. What would happen next? How soon until Garity decided to turn up the heat to get the location of the coins out of Jack? They thought but didn't speak.

Fatigue and exhaustion eventually took its toll on Alyson and she drifted off to sleep on the bed at her mother's side.

Lauren pulled a knee up to her chin and hugged her leg. She stared blank at the wooden deck, contemplating. The hum of the engines coaxed buried thoughts to the surface. She felt eyes on her but didn't look up. "I'm afraid of you, Bobbie."

Bobbie tilted her head. "You're what?"

"I've spent a lot of years learning how to be brave. Being married to Jack it's something I had to do."

"Anyone marrying Jack would have to be brave, but why—"

"He almost died working with Neptune's Reach on four different occasions."

"I only knew about the Rafferty incident."

Lauren put on a weary smile. "Everyone knows about Rafferty. A few years earlier a group of Columbian privateers nearly killed him. And then there was the hurricane in the Caribbean, and the diving accident in the South Pacific. Each time I got a phone call telling me he might not make it home. Each time I had to consider the possibility of carrying on life without him, raising Connor alone. Each time I prepared to bury a part of myself right along beside him."

Bobbie slid to the corner of the bed, careful not to wake Alyson. "Jack told me how difficult the early years with Neptune were for you."

"His career became the enemy," Lauren said. "He was always gone and a lot of the time in dangerous situations. At first I tried to live with it, and then I tried to fight it. It almost destroyed our marriage. When Jack left Neptune after the Rafferty project I thought it had finally ended. I wouldn't get that phone call again. But he loved the work he did. I knew it would draw him back. Lloyd knew it too, and he kept trying to lure him into the fold. I couldn't let that happen. Our marriage wouldn't survive. I tried to keep the monster at bay. I did everything I could to keep Neptune's Reach away from Jack. That's where I went wrong."

"You didn't fail," Bobbie said. "Jack doesn't want to go back there."

"That's not what I mean." Lauren regarded her a long while. "I prepared myself to confront Jack's desire to return to Neptune's Reach. I didn't prepare myself to confront his desire for you."

Bobbie closed her eyes. "That's not what's happening, Lauren. Please believe me."

"I believe you two have an unresolved history, and I believe that Jack is trying to resolve it with this treasure hunt."

"I asked Jack to help because I had nowhere else to turn. If I had it to do over again I'd do it differently."

"I wouldn't want you to," Lauren said. "I'd rather the last chapter of your open-ended story gets written now regardless of how it ends."

"I'm not trying to get him back."

"Garity said some things about you and Steven up there. Was it true?"

"At one time, yes, it was true. But I grew apart from the person I was back then. I carried on without Jack like you imagined you might have to do. I've lived half my life with Steven and Alyson and don't regret the way it's turned out. Going back and trying to relive the old days with Jack isn't why I called him. Our being together is a memory, not a pursuit."

"It doesn't matter if you're pursuing him. You're a question he's never been able to answer. You've been lingering in the back of his mind for years. That's why you frighten me. You don't need to do anything to get into his head and heart, you're already there."

"He loves you, Lauren. You took the risk I was afraid to take. That means more to him than any memory of us he has in his mind. He's not trying to reverse the course of his life with this treasure hunt. He's trying to put the past in order so he can move forward with you and Connor. Even if I wanted to I couldn't pull him away."

Lauren searched Bobbie's eyes, sensing a benevolence she never thought possible from the women she'd considered an adversary for two decades. "When this treasure hunt is over, things are going to be different for all of us."

Bobbie panned the cabin. "I'm thinking this hunt is pretty much finished."

"Don't call it quits yet," Lauren said. "Jack knows how to pull a rabbit out of his hat. He's done it four times now."

"I hope he's got another one in there."

* * *

Jack stirred awake. For an instant he thought he'd had an odd dream that his old college buddy Garity had captured him and was threatening his life to get possession of the coins. Reality crashed in on this notion when he realized he was lying with his hands bound behind him on the *Distinguished Gentleman's* bow solarium. This was no dream.

He felt metal cuffs clamped around his wrists. His arms ached and his head throbbed. Ben really rattled him with those brass knuckles. Except they weren't brass, they had appeared more like chrome plated steel. That bastard really had it coming.

Jack rolled to get a look at the sky. The last few minutes of dusk shaded the sailboat. He'd been out a long time. It had to be close to ten o'clock. He twisted his hands inside the cuffs. They were snug but not tight to the point of pain. If he had to guess he'd say Garity had clamped them on. Ben would have wrenched them so tight the blood would have been cut off from his fingers. Jack tested how difficult it might be to pull a hand through a manacle, careful not to inadvertently tighten it.

"Welcome back, Jack."

Garity's voice. Crap.

Jack strained to see over his shoulder. Garity stood near the forward hatch in the deckhouse with one hand in the pocket of his Bermuda shorts and the other holding the pouch containing the stun grenade. Higgs stood beside him with an infuriating grin on his face. Garity gave his minion a nod. Higgs walked to the solarium and took hold of Jack by the arms, applying just enough upward pressure to send a surge of pain into his shoulders and force him to his feet.

Jack steadied himself on wobbly legs. Breeze blew from the west as if generated by the movement of the rapidly setting sun. A few miles to the east, the Michigan shoreline stretched across the horizon. They'd moved closer inland while he was unconscious.

Garity held up the stun grenade. "What were you planning on doing with this?"

Jack shrugged. "I wasn't sure. Right now I'd like to shove it up your ass and pull the pin."

Garity chuckled despite the tension. "Always with the juvenile remarks. You may like to know that I've sent plenty of men capable of spitting out snappy retorts to prison for life sentences. Their attitudes never got them anywhere, besides deeper into trouble."

"I'll make a note of that, your honor."

Garity tossed the grenade into the corner of the solarium and looked at the deck as if thinking over the situation. "We still need to hammer out some agreement before we can enjoy the night's festivities."

"I told you my terms," Jack said. "They're not open to further negotiation."

"I've been giving that some thought and have come to the conclusion that you really mean it." Garity pointed toward shore. "There's a fireworks barge anchored off the coast that an affluent lakefront community has commissioned to celebrate Independence Day. They put on a fantastic show. I try to catch it from the lake here every year. Wouldn't you like to celebrate your own freedom tonight? Just tell me where the coins are and it can happen."

"You know what I want; the women, the MasterCraft, and a five-minute head start. Nothing's changed. No theatrics are going to alter those terms."

Higgs forced Jack over to the deckhouse and shoved him against the wall. He leaned in close and whispered, "I told you to pull the trigger in Saugatuck. Regretting it yet?"

Garity brushed him back and planted himself in front of Jack with an authoritative stance. "Perhaps clarifying my situation will help things along."

Jack eyed him with a measure of defiance. "It couldn't hurt."

"You asked where I fit into my family's social stratum. I'll answer that now. I intend to win back my father's senate seat."

A laugh somehow found its way out of Jack. "Murder, kidnapping, assault, and larceny doesn't fit well into a winning campaign strategy."

"Internal statewide polling gives me a thirty-point advantage over every opponent in the field this November. Our esteemed incumbent representative has become so unpopular the people are clamoring for the good old days when my father held the position. Name recognition carries a lot of weight for me, and my father's supporters have mobilized a grassroots movement that will bolster my late entry into the race. I'll be seen as the savior coming onto the scene who understands Michigan's needs and can get things done with the power of my family's position on the Hill. I only have one small problem."

Jack quelled his laugh at the black comedy. "You've got more than a small problem."

"Those damned Indian casinos were bad enough," Garity said embroiled in his confession. "But when MGM and Motor City opened in Detroit, I got in over my head with people a respected public official shouldn't be affiliated with. I need to wipe the slates clean with them before I reveal my official candidacy. Sure, I might have to offer them special consideration on certain political issues once I reach the Hill, but it will be a small price to pay to take that first step."

"First step?" Jack began working with the handcuffs behind him. "What's the second step?"

Garity brimmed with self-confidence. "The country is starving for real leadership in the White House. After nearly two decades of wars, economic downturns, and indiscrete scandals, they've finally had it with the miserable leaders they've elected. They want a solid hand at the helm, like when this country faced down the Soviets over Cuba, or tore down the Iron Curtain and won the Cold War. My family name has been there for this country at each critical juncture, and it will be again."

"You're overplaying your hand, Wallace. I assume you understand that expression given your current problems."

"On the contrary, my chances are excellent. There is precedence for a one-term senator to capture the White House. Oddsmakers would put good money on me to make it."

"I wouldn't put a dime on you, not if I have anything to say about it."

Garity stepped back. "The good thing for me is you don't have anything to say about it." He leaned into the forward hatch on the deckhouse and called to someone inside.

Higgs stood close beside Jack on the narrow walkway between the portside and the deckhouse and drew a 9mm pistol from a belt holster. Jack noted the movement from the corner of his eye. Something was coming. He felt he didn't have much time to act. He tried to force the cuff on his left wrist down over his hand as nonchalantly as he could. It wasn't going to be easy. He would likely have to break some bones in his hand to get it free. Doing that without showing the pain or effort would be tricky.

Near the darkening horizon to the east a trail of fire lifted into the sky. The first rocket had launched from the barge. It shot straight up and ended its flight high above the water with a single brilliant flash. Higgs turned his head to the light, waited for the sound. Jack pulled hard to force the cuff over the base of his thumb and over the spread of his hand below the knuckles. It felt like a vice compressing his bones. Pain made his eyes squint.

It took two seconds for the firework boom to reach the boat. Higgs returned his attention to his captive. Jack stopped working the cuff and leveled his expression, fighting every instinct to react to the pain radiating from his hand.

Garity stepped aside to let someone out of the hatch. "I thought the ladies would like to see the fireworks display as well. We could all enjoy the show together if you would just cooperate."

Jack said nothing. A pair of rockets took off from the barge. Lauren and Bobbie emerged from below deck. Kisko prodded them forward with the barrel of the shotgun. Garity instructed them to stand side by side at the edge of the bow solarium as the rockets burst into great spheres of blue and green sparks. Their brilliant light illuminated the deck and faded away.

Garity spoke into Kisko's ear and then faced Jack. "Allow me to demonstrate my effective and efficient leadership qualities. You've emphatically stated your terms are non-negotiable. I know you'll stand firm on that. I won't waste time pressuring you by breaking bones and distressing you in other nasty ways. That won't work with national hero Jack Sheridan, so I'm cutting to the chase."

Jack knew what was coming. He fought the panic surging into his chest.

Lauren and Bobbie stood twenty feet away, also seeming to sense an imminent threat. Kisko had set down the shotgun and positioned himself directly in front of them with a pistol in hand.

Higgs still hovered close by, brandishing his 9mm and watching the grim scene unfold.

Jack glared at Garity. "How could you possibly think you'll come out of this clean?" He clamped his right thumb and forefinger over the left cuff and pushed it farther down over his hand. Skin split beneath the steel. Bones shifted. Something popped but a string of explosions from the fireworks display covered the noise. Jack kept his eyes fixed on his old friend. Sweat glistened on his face.

Higgs smiled in the wash of a strobe light effect from a series of rocket bursts. "You look nervous, Sheridan."

Garity lifted a hand to his chin in the classic thoughtful pose and waited for the crackle and bangs from the rocket barrage to fade. "The loves of your life stand before you, Jack. You either tell me where those damned coins are or one of them dies right here, right now. Five seconds."

Kisko readied himself, setting his stance with the pistol and keeping both women in his sight. Lauren stared fearfully ahead, her composure holding by a thread. Bobbie's eyes darted nervously about. Higgs chuckled. Jack counted down in his head. Three seconds.

A lull in the fireworks show dipped the ship into darkness. Jack squeezed his hand and pushed the cuffs. It felt like a knife twisting between his bones. The eastern sky suddenly lit up with dozens of white fire trails corkscrewing through the air.

Garity smiled. "Which woman do you want to spend the rest of your life with?"

Jack didn't reply. Garity shook his head and nodded to Kisko. "Do it."

Kisko pointed the pistol at Lauren. Jack shouted and wrenched the handcuffs as hard as he could. Bobbie jumped forward and tried to get her hands on the gun. Kisko fired. The muzzle flash flickered against Bobbie's shirt and a dark hole burst open on her chest.

Jack's broken hand came free. He shouldered into Higgs and reached for the 9mm, latching onto the fist holding the gun with a death grip. Higgs was caught flat footed and staggered. Jack forced the 9mm to target Kisko and wedged his finger inside the trigger guard. He managed to fire the pistol four times. Kisko caught each round in the body, convulsing with each hit and crumbling down.

Higgs reared back and head butted Jack hard. The impact jarred Jack's whole body, shaking loose his grip on the 9mm. He felt himself falling, and swung wild with his right arm. The flailing end of the handcuffs connected and split a long gash across Higgs' chin. Jack landed awkward on his back against the deckhouse. He scurried back on his elbows to gain some breathing room.

Higgs loomed over him with a stream of blood flowing from his chin. He lifted the 9mm. "Good game, Sheridan. You came real close."

A fiery red blossom burst open in the sky. Its glow lit Higgs' face in a hideous way, exaggerating his features into a mask befitting an angel of death. Jack drew back his heel to smash him in the knee. The boom from the red blossom rumbled over the boat. Higgs flinched and turned his head sideways. The lower half of his ear was missing. Two more reports crackled, but they weren't from fireworks. They sounded a lot closer and seemed to emanate from a smaller pack of powder. Higgs jolted as two bullets blew through his body, back to chest. He tumbled face down toward the deck.

Jack rolled out of the way and pinned his bleeding, broken hand against the outer hull. The agony rushed from his hand to his head and out his throat. He struggled to his feet and realized he was screaming. He stifled his cry through clenched teeth and whirled about to where the gunshots had come from.

Lauren stood with Kisko's pistol in hand, locked in a perfect firing stance that Jack had taught her. She seemed frozen in the moment and slowly lowered the weapon. "I told you you'd need my help."

Jack rushed to her. "You were right, sweetheart. I stand corrected." He scanned the deck. "Where's Garity?"

Lauren shook her gaze from Higgs' body. "He went below when the shooting started."

Jack noted where she had been staring. "Don't even think about bandaging that guy up." He dropped to his knee at Bobbie's side. The bullet had missed her heart but hit a prime location to puncture her lung. She breathed in quick draws. Blood soaked through her shirt. Jack tore open the buttons to check the wound.

She somehow smirked. "Hey…your wife is watching."

Lauren knelt on the other side to assist.

"What were you thinking, jumping in front of that gun?" Jack said.

"That you couldn't…stand…to lose her."

Jack compressed his right hand against the wound, being mindful of the cuffs still secured to his wrist. "I want to keep you both around."

Bobbie suddenly took hold of his hand. "Aly's down…in the cabin."

Jack bolted upright. "Lauren, take over here." He searched the deck. The shotgun was missing. He went to Higgs' body to look for the 9mm. Instead he found his Colt tucked under the big Italian's belt. Jack reclaimed his pistol and brought it to Lauren. "Honey, I need you to work the action for me."

She grabbed the Colt and pulled back the slide, snapping it forward to cock the weapon. Jack took it into his right hand, gingerly holding his left at his side. "Stay with Bobbie. If you see Garity pop up somewhere…"

"I know what to do."

Fireworks still flashed in the sky. Their bright light and loud booms reminded Jack of the stun grenade that Garity had tossed aside. He dashed across the open deckhouse hatch and retrieved the pouch containing the flashbang from the solarium. He set the Colt down, extracted the stun grenade from the pouch, jammed it into his back pocket, and took up the pistol again.

Wall lamps inside the deckhouse were lit, illuminating the space enough to show that Garity wasn't there. Jack descended the steps into the mahogany galley, holding the Colt out in front of him and sweeping the area. The handcuffs dangled from his wrist. He recalled sharing a drink and discussing the coins with Garity in this very compartment. He still couldn't believe it.

A red sheet metal box with a white cross on the cover hung on the portside wall above a small dining table. A first aid kit. Jack set the safety and tucked the pistol in his belt, and then tore the box off the wall. He tossed it up through the hatch at Lauren's feet. He drew the Colt again and approached a door in the bow bulkhead beside the wet bar that led below to the cabins. It was open a crack. Jack licked his lips, clicked off the safety, and reached forward with his foot to pull it open farther.

The clap of wood smashing against wood rose from the lower deck. "Clear this door, girl!"

Garity's voice. Jack kicked open the door and leapt through the hatch, over the steps into the lower space. He landed crouched at the base of the steps in a narrow corridor stretching up to the bow. Two doors were spaced evenly along the portside wall, two doors along the starboard. Garity had his shoulder pressed against a starboard door fifteen feet away with a grimace on his face and the shotgun in hand. Jack's crash landing startled him. Garity pivoted but fired before setting his stance. The spread of shot splintered the wood framework around the hatch above Jack's head.

Jack sprang left against the portside wall and blasted two rounds from the Colt. Close quarters, his shattered hand, the dangling handcuffs, and his frantic motion threw his aim off the mark. The slugs flew high and wide, imbedding in a mahogany panel near Garity's face. They hit close enough to fluster the judge. Garity withdrew farther down the corridor to the second starboard door, pumping the twelve gauge as he went. Jack rose to pursue but Garity leveled the shotgun at him. He burst through a portside cabin door as Garity fired another blast. Steel pellets pulverized the door's center hinge.

Jack steadied himself, taking deep breaths and gripping the Colt tight. He glanced across the corridor to the cabin Garity had been trying to enter. Its door was ajar but barred by something on the other side. "Alyson, are you okay?"

Her voice called from inside the cabin. "Jack? Thank God. Yeah, I'm okay. I wedged the bed frame against the door. I couldn't get out so I figured I wouldn't let anyone in."

Jack smiled. "That's my girl."

He peered down the corridor. The door to the cabin Garity had run into was half open. "You're trapped, Wallace, and your boys are out of action. Give it up."

No reply.

Jack trained the Colt on Garity's cabin and stepped into the corridor. He whispered, "Aly, I need your help. Open up."

She slid the bed frame away and opened the door. Jack set the safety with his thumb and handed her the Colt. She took the pistol but seemed awkward handling it. Jack lifted the stun grenade from his pocket and held it up to show her. "Grab that ring and hold it tight," he whispered. "I can't use my left hand."

She seized the ring.

Jack yanked the grenade downward and dashed across the corridor into the port cabin. Alyson stood staring at the pin in her hand. Jack counted off half the delay and tossed the flashbang into Garity's retreat.

A brilliant flash burst from the cabin and lit the dim corridor like mid-day sun. A great boom detonated in concert with the light. Jack rushed to a stunned Alyson and took the Colt from her. He ran into Garity's cabin. The judge stood with flash-frozen retinas and hands clamped over his ears. The shotgun lay at his feet. Two stacks of wooden crates ate up half the floor space. There were six of them in all. The grenade had exploded on top of one and had set it ablaze. Words stenciled on the side of the crates made Jack's heart jump:

Cascade Fireworks Co.

He shoved deaf and blind Garity into the corridor. The judge collided with the wall and collapsed to the deck. Jack stepped into the cabin's restroom and stuck the Colt with safety engaged under his belt. He stuffed a white towel from a rack into the sink and soaked it under the faucet. He lobbed the sopping wet towel onto the flaming crate, spreading it out to douse the fire.

Jack marched over to Garity. The judge lay still on the deck. His vision would be returning soon, and Jack didn't need him trying anything funny. He stuck the Colt into the back of Garity's head. "Handcuff key. Now."

Garity didn't move.

Jack rolled him over with his boot. Garity was out cold. Right. Jack nodded to Alyson. "Aly, search his pockets for the handcuff key."

She did. The left pocket was empty but she found a little key in the right. Jack had her unlock the cuffs and then instructed her to bind Garity's hands behind his back with them. "Now let's get topside," he said to her. "Your mother's hurt."

She rushed ahead and up the steps that Jack had jumped over.

Jack stowed the pistol and picked up the shotgun from the cabin floor, and then followed Alyson up. He remembered the judge's invite to a Fourth of July cruise five days ago, and the mention of a private fireworks show. If Garity knew Jack was after the coins back then, why did he extend an invite to the cruise, and why bring the crates of fireworks aboard? His charade nearly killed them all. Taking refuge in that cabin during a gun battle was a dangerous move.

Jack climbed the stairs into the galley and then went topside. Lauren had Bobbie patched up as best she could with the materials from the first aid kit and had her lying on the bow solarium. Alyson was holding her mother's hand and was trying to comfort her. Jack set the shotgun down on the deck.

"We need to get Bobbie to a hospital," Lauren said.

"And we need to get Garity into custody. Sorting all this out with the authorities is going to take some time." Jack studied the sailboat's deck and masts. "You think we can bring her into port?"

"Between you, me, and Alyson we can probably figure it out." Lauren's eyebrows lifted. "Wait, Alyson said there are a couple of deck hands aboard. We might be able to get their cooperation."

"I didn't see anyone else below deck. You sure they're aboard?"

"They should be, unless Garity sent them ashore. He might have wanted fewer witnesses to what he was doing."

Jack looked beyond the bow of the sailboat. "I don't see the MasterCraft."

"Let's find it."

Jack and Lauren crossed the deck to the starboard side and worked their way along the *Distinguished Gentleman's* length, searching the water around the sailboat for the MasterCraft. No sign of it. They checked the water beyond the stern. Nothing. The only other water craft available was an eight-foot dingy hanging from davits at the rear of the boat.

"They're gone," Lauren said.

"It's just us. We'll have to take her in ourselves."

They started back to the bow via the portside deck. They made it amidships when Jack heard a click of metal and the sound of a footfall on the wood deck behind them. He drew the Colt. "Somebody's astern," he said to Lauren. "Get forward and check on Bobbie and Alyson."

She nodded and kept moving.

Jack pulled his blackened, bloodied left hand close to his body and doubled back. He rounded the rear of the deckhouse, keeping the Colt in front of him.

The rear hatch was open, and Garity was at the dingy, messing with the davits to release it. He must have been feigning unconsciousness and had a second key Alyson missed, or had one stashed below deck. Damn tricky politician.

Jack stepped toward him. "Wallace, stop right there!"

Garity froze. He turned slowly about with hands half-raised. In the dim light of low voltage deck lamps, he extended a hand toward Jack like he was warding off Dracula with a crucifix. Except he wasn't holding a crucifix; it was a device about the size of a keyless remote for a car with a green light flashing on its face.

Jack aimed the Colt at his chest. "What the hell do you think you're doing? There's no place to run to. It's all over."

Garity actually smiled. "You're so wrong. I spent a lot of time planning this out, setting up contingency upon contingency."

"Did one of your contingencies include losing all your henchmen and staring down the barrel of my .45?"

"Believe it or not I did consider a worst-case scenario similar to this. I'm no fool. I knew who I was up against. The great Jack Sheridan."

"The great Jack Sheridan is telling you to sit your ass down so I can cuff you again."

"You don't control me. I've told you that already. I'm the authority, I call the shots."

Jack regarded the remote in his hand. "I don't suppose that's for your Mercedes."

"If you're as smart as I think you are, you know what this is."

Jack had a pretty good idea. It all started to make sense; the firework crates, Garity taking refuge in that cabin, the invite to the Fourth of July cruise. "You've rigged this ship to blow up, and your finger is on the detonation button."

"Bravo. Right now Bobbie is sitting on top of six crates of explosives. You see, when I said I needed to wipe the slates clean before my campaign, I meant all of them."

"All of them, huh? I guess our twenty-five year friendship never meant all that much to you."

"There you go again, equating us, equating our values. You just don't understand me. Never did. I know where I belong, where my family belongs. I will get there regardless of the means. I have clarity in my direction, and nothing will stand in my way. That's a hell of a lot more than you can say. You can't even decide which woman to love."

"There *you* go again, showing your ignorance. The simplest things just confuse the hell out of you, don't they? Friendship and love and integrity just don't make sense."

Garity ignored the lecture. "Like I was saying, I couldn't leave any skeletons in the closet for the press to dig up, so I had to find some way to explain the death of my dear friends." He seemed to be relishing his brilliant plan. "A tragic Fourth of July accident on my boat seemed the optimum solution. Bodies of evidence strewn about the floor of Lake Michigan would not be recovered." He chuckled. "If I spin the incident right, I might even be able to cast myself the sympathetic hero."

"Two problems," Jack said. "First off, if you blow the ship now, you die too. You may be an ambitious gambler but you're not a suicidal fanatic. Second, you don't have the coins. You may eliminate witnesses but you're still in financial straits. Between your debtors and your gambling vice, your campaign will be destroyed by September."

Garity reached into the dingy and threaded his arm through a life jacket. "Winning my senate seat is very important to me. I've gone to extreme measures to make it happen. Don't think I'll stop short of my goal now. If I detonate those fireworks when I'm in the water, I'm confident I'll survive."

"There's still the issue of no coins. Oh, and the fact that I'll shoot you dead before you jump overboard."

"I've been judging characters for fifteen years, and I've known you for twenty-five. You won't shoot me in cold blood, even if it means you might die as a result. If you were capable you would have done it already."

"You think you know me that well? That's a sucker bet. I see why the casinos stuck it to you."

Garity switched the remote detonator from one hand to the other to pull the life jacket over his shoulders. "As far as the coins go, I'll bet Connor knows where they are. Good old Uncle Wallace is going to take real good care of him in his time of grieving for his parents. We'll finish Dad's quest together, in his memory."

Lauren appeared at the stern from the starboard side and absorbed the scene. "Jack, what's going on?"

"He's got explosives wired in a forward cabin. You need to get Bobbie and Alyson off the ship now."

"It's over three miles to shore. Bobbie will never make it."

"None of us will make it if we stay here. Move!"

Lauren ran off, shouting a warning to the other women.

Garity backed toward the safety chain across the stern. "It's too late for them."

Jack bit his tongue. He had to shoot Garity, kill him right there. The great unknown was the remote detonator. Did Garity have it set up with a dead man's switch? Would the ship go up in flames as soon as his lifeless hand released the button?

Jack had to take his own gamble. He tightened his aim on Garity's chest over the left side of the life jacket and blasted a round from the Colt. A hole blew through the jacket and shoved Garity back to the chain. The detonator popped from his hand and clattered on the deck. Jack cringed, waiting for a concussive firestorm to consume him. It didn't happen.

Garity plopped to a seated position with a stunned expression frozen on his face. "You shot me, you son of a bitch."

"You're not very good at this gambling thing, Wallace." Jack set the safety on the Colt and shoved it in his belt. He walked two steps to the detonator and knelt down to pick it up. The green light was still flashing. He studied it a moment, careful not to touch the button in the center. He glanced over his shoulder and shouted up to the bow. "Lauren, I got him."

And then Garity's heel smacked him in the side of the head. Jack reeled with the force of impact. Instincts threw his right hand out to break his fall and kept his shattered left in close and protected. The detonator skidded across the deck.

Jack's off-balance tumble left his side exposed. Garity zeroed in on his weak spot and kicked him square in the broken hand. A surge of agony shot up his arm. Jack screamed and rolled and struggled to right himself. The Colt fell from his belt.

Garity took a second to revel in triumph. He stuck a finger in the hole in the life jacket. "Type IIIA Kevlar backing. It hurts like hell but there's no blood. I hedge all my bets now."

Jack stabilized his footing and read the situation. The Colt lay on deck between them. The detonator had come to rest five feet away. If he went for the gun, Garity might be able to grab the detonator, hop over the side, and blow the ship before Jack could take him down. If he went for the detonator, Garity could grab the gun and shoot him dead. Whichever way Garity went, Jack would have to go as well.

Garity lunged for the detonator.

Jack launched himself at Garity. They collided and grappled and crashed down six inches from the remote with the flashing green light. Garity reached for it. Jack slammed his right hand over the judge's arm and yanked it back. Garity reached with his other arm. His outstretched fingers flicked the little remote another six inches away. The thought of batting the thing overboard flashed into Jack's mind but he didn't know for sure if the water would kill it or short it out in such a way as to trigger the detonation. He decided he needed to get it in his hand.

Garity heaved his whole body forward, grunting and clawing to reach the remote. His fingers touched it again. Jack couldn't keep grappling like this, not with his broken hand. He seized Garity's life jacket between the shoulders, rose to one knee, and yanked the judge back so hard he thought he'd pop the veins in his neck. Garity slid across the deck with arms and legs flailing like a turtle and then scrambled to all fours on the way to his feet.

Jack didn't let him get that far. He rose on his left leg and round-house kicked the judge solid across the jaw with his right foot. Garity groaned and flopped on his side. Jack whirled around and dove for the remote. He slid to the edge of the boat, swiping the little device into his hand. Splashing noises drew his eyes to the water.

Flashes from the fireworks show illuminated people swimming away from the sailboat. Two were helping a third in the middle stay afloat. Lauren had gotten everyone off the ship.

And then a klaxon went off in Jack's head. Garity. The Colt.

Jack spun around.

Garity frantically searched the deck in the low light. He spotted the pistol and snatched it up. Jack clutched the remote in his fist and heaved himself over the side of the sailboat, splashing into Lake Michigan. Darkness enveloped him, cold water shocked his senses, but he stayed submerged and waited for the detonator to short out and set off the fireworks.

The water stayed calm and dark. No explosion. Garity was still up there. Jack considered hitting the button but he was too damn close to the boat, and he didn't know if the women had gotten to a safe distance yet either. He needed time and distance.

The boots on his feet retarded his swimming, but with his left hand broken and the detonator in his right he couldn't untie the laces. He gave up on the idea and kicked his legs instead, heading in a direction he calculated was away from the *Distinguished Gentleman*. Cold numbed his hand, adrenalin kept his limbs moving. He struggled on until the oxygen in his lungs depleted. He said a short prayer and came to the surface.

Treading water fully clothed and in boots was nearly impossible, but he kept his head above the waves and checked his surroundings. He'd only made it about twenty-five yards from the sailboat. To his left the women hadn't gotten too much farther.

Garity stalked his prey from the sailboat's stern quarter, scanning the water and sweeping the pistol over the lake. He locked in on Jack's head bobbing in the waves amid flashing lights from the fireworks show's grand finale.

Garity seemed to have the Colt dead on target but there was no muzzle flash, no bullet. Jack knew what the problem was, and the judge figured it out the very next second. Garity had not disengaged the safety.

Jack prepared to go under again but stopped himself. Popping up and down like a target in a carnival fair only played into Garity's favor. There were five more rounds in the Colt and who knows how many boxes of 9mm ammunition available on board. Garity would win this turkey shoot if Jack let it go on. It had to end now. Jack had to detonate the explosives and sink the boat. He could only hope the women had gotten far enough away and that Bobbie would survive the long swim ashore.

Garity rectified his error with the safety and aimed again at Jack's head. This time he fired a round. The bullet sizzled through the air and drilled into the water two feet from the mark. Time had expired. Jack yelled across the waves. "Lauren, get underwater. The ship's going to blow!"

Garity shouted and fired again and again. "You—will—not—stop—me!"

Slugs from the .45 kicked up the lake in a chaotic pattern. Jack pressed his thumb hard into the button on the detonator and sank below the surface. Six crates of packed gunpowder ignited in the starboard cabin. The bow heaved and broke apart atop a ball of fire, shattering into countless fragments of mahogany and stainless steel. Garity pushed off the edge of the stern, leaping into the air and out of the boat as a wedge of flame peeled back the roof of the deckhouse and shattered its windows. The fore mast screeched and tumbled to port, and the mizzen mast shuddered as blast concussion severed the *Distinguished Gengleman's* stern from her body. Rockets took flight out of the firestorm in all directions; whistling, booming, hissing into the water.

Jack hovered six feet below the surface and covered his ears. Debris splashed into the lake above him and drifted down in sizzling chunks. Flashes from the explosion illuminated the water a ghastly orange, revealing to him glimpses of Lauren, Bobbie, and Alyson's forms floating nearby. The intensity of the blast wavered, then subsided, then darkened until only the fire consuming the hull of the sinking sailboat remained.

Jack surfaced and gasped for air. The hulk of the once beautiful sailboat crackled in fire and hissed as she sank below the waves. The *Distinguished Gentleman* had been blasted to flinders. Among the floating debris, a body in a life jacket bobbed in the lake with a two-foot shard of mahogany plank skewered through the neck.

Three heads popped to the surface to Jack's left, wheezing and coughing and sucking in oxygen.

"Lauren, is everyone okay?"

One of the heads turned left and right. "Jack, where are you?"

"Over here." He dropped the detonator, pulled the laces loose on his boots and then kicked the boots off and swam over to his wife. "Are you okay?"

Lauren nodded and brushed a strip of hair from her eye. "Yeah, all in one piece."

"How's Bobbie?"

"Still here," Bobbie said with a hand over Alyson's shoulder to stay afloat.

"Can you make it to shore?" Jack said.

"I don't know." She coughed. "I can't breathe very well."

"We're all going to help you. We're all going to make it."

"Come on," Lauren said. "Put one hand on my shoulder and the other on Alyson's. We'll get you to the beach."

Jack hoped they wouldn't have to go that far. The explosion made for quite a distress signal, and with so much activity on the lake for the fireworks show there should be no shortage of rescue craft homing in on them. He found a shank of wood burning on a floating piece of debris and held it above his head as they started in.

Inside of twenty minutes the first boats arrived, crawling through the area with spotlights sweeping the lake surface. Voices called for survivors to answer. Jack and the women shouted and guided them in. A sixty-foot Brunswick Meridian yacht fished them out of the water and made for shore at maximum speed to get Bobbie to a hospital.

A guy who called himself Captain Bob distributed blankets and fell all over himself trying to accommodate his rescuees. Jack answered the question of what happened with a simple fireworks accident explanation. That's all that needed to be said until the full story could be rolled out to the police. He could already picture the morning newspaper headlines.

Jack sat next to Lauren and across from Alyson in the warmth of the Meridian's cabin. He watched his daughter a long time until she noticed his stare. Jack smiled at her and tapped the boat's skipper on the arm. "Captain Bob, do you have a VHF radio aboard?"

"Yeah, sure, Jack." Bob lifted a mic from the cockpit console and stretched the cable to its limit to hand it to him.

Jack had Bob switch to a standard channel that he knew the *Achilles* would be monitoring and looked again at Alyson. "*Achilles, Achilles,* this is Jack Sheridan."

A voice responded to his hail in less than five seconds. "Jack! This is Garcia. Man, I'm glad to hear from you. Listen, we picked Connor up and he told us what was happening. You all right?"

"Yeah, yeah, I'm all right. I think we'll all pull through. Hey, is Connor around?"

"Sure, he's standing ten feet away from me."

Jack made eye contact with Alyson. "Tell him we got his sister back and she's okay."

- EPILOGUE -

Bobbie underwent several hours of surgery at Grand Traverse City Hospital. The doctors gave her a good prognosis when they wheeled her into recovery the next morning. Alyson stayed at the hospital the whole time, worrying about her mother and pondering the news that Jack was her father. At dawn, Connor and Markus put into a slip at the Grand Traverse Bay Marina aboard the *Achilles'* runabout. They rushed over to the hospital to check on Bobbie, and to have a doctor inspect the work the ship's EMT performed on Markus.

Jack and Lauren spent all night giving their statements to the police. They had a lot to explain; after all, a respected Michigan Supreme Court judge had just perished in a spectacular blaze on the Fourth of July, and their account of his criminal actions leading up to the incident bordered on the fantastic. Despite the best efforts of the state police to keep the story under wraps, a loose-lipped sergeant managed to leak salacious tidbits from their statements to the media.

Word of the *Distinguished Gentleman's* demise and Garity's alleged criminal activity spread quickly. Local news stations and newspapers latched on to the story and were saturating the region with coverage by morning. Jack Sheridan returned to the headlines, embroiled in a pieced together story about high-level corruption, political ambition, and a cache of gold coins lost, found…and lost again.

Of course, Jack didn't talk to the media. He wanted the furor to settle down and fade away as soon as possible. Work still needed to be done, and the sooner he got to it the better.

He had told the police everything concerning his clashes with Garity's henchmen during the treasure hunt and about those last hours on the sailboat, but he left out one small detail. Jack failed to mention the fact that he knew the exact coordinates of where he had dumped the coins in Lake Michigan. His official statement read that in all the excitement he couldn't remember where he was when he threw the totes overboard, leaving the issue nice and ambiguous. He rationalized that it really didn't matter to the police where the coins were, as far as their investigation was concerned, so he thought it prudent to protect his hard-earned find by not disclosing the numbers. He didn't need every treasure hunter within five hundred miles of the Great Lakes converging on the scene.

Jack hammered out a deal with Lloyd after leaving the police station. In exchange for the use of Neptune's Reach resources and mutual confidentiality, he would give the company twenty percent of the take. Four weeks later he led a salvage team aboard the *Achilles* to recover the coins from the lakebed. It turned out Eugene Elliot's estimated value of the trove was accurate if not conservative. The combination of Bechtler coins, Seated Liberty silver dollars, and the historically significant Singapore Bank notes netted just over twenty million dollars in private auction.

A week after the sale of the coins, Eugene Elliot took delivery of a new central air conditioning system. The Granite Island mortgage was paid off a few days later. Jack hand-delivered a check to Rezner to cover the cost of the equipment JR SUPPLY and AMMO provided, with a substantial bonus for the mileage he got out of the flashbangs. Jack also unhitched a new thirty-foot Boston Whaler in front of Markus Sweetwood's little tri-story house to replace the ill-fated *El Pomposo*. Markus was still nursing his shotgun wound, but chomped at the bit to get his new toy into the water. Jack didn't purchase his own sailboat right away. Since the *Distinguished Gentleman* was no longer available, he wanted to take his time to look around and make just the right choice.

By Labor Day weekend Markus had healed enough to take the skipper's chair and invited everyone over to christen *Grande Pomposo*. Jack's treasure expediters gathered at South Haven Marina for the event. Even Bobbie was well enough to venture out and join the group. They shoved off into Lake Michigan under the warm sun of late summer. Alyson had a good time toying with a whole new set of controls and levers to pester Markus as he navigated along the coast. Jack plopped down in the stern bench seat between Connor and Lauren. "Son, I promise I don't have any other daughters out there."

"You better not have any other sons out there either," Lauren said.

Bobbie covered her mouth. "Don't make me laugh. I'm not all healed up inside yet."

Jack lifted an ice cold beer bottle from a cooler near his feet. "Who wants to hear the final numbers?"

Every hand went up.

"Right." Jack twisted off the bottle top and leaned back. "Markus, shut her down and get back here." He waited for the inboard engines to fall silent and for Markus and Alyson to join them in the stern.

"Okay," he said. "Total take from the auction was twenty million and some change. Deduct the Neptune's Reach percentage, the share we agreed to give to the surviving Coates family, and our total operating expenses, and we're left with eleven million, give or take a few thousand. Since Steven discovered the existence of the coins, and his research led us to them, Bobbie and Alyson get fifty percent of net. That leaves five and a half million to split between you two guys and Lauren and me."

Markus quickly calculated in his head. "That's almost 1.4 four million a piece."

"That's all?" Connor said.

"Sheridan, at your current salary, including all that overtime you put in at the plants, you'd have to work twenty years to make that much."

"Don't forget Uncle Sam's cut," Jack said.

Markus shook his head. "I don't think so. Uncle Sam wasn't out there with us searching for the coins; why should he get a cut?"

Jack frowned. "Play it straight with the government. You can't hide this from them. Once you start buying expensive toys and opening huge bank accounts they'll find out, and if they decide you're evading taxes you've got real trouble. Don't forget, that's how they got Al Capone."

"How much of a hit are we going to take?" Connor said.

Jack shrugged. "Forty, maybe fifty percent."

"Fifty percent!" Connor made a flustered calculation. "I can't retire on six or seven hundred thousand dollars."

"If you're smart, it'll take you a long way," Jack said.

Markus just about stamped his foot. "This just isn't fair."

Alyson wrapped her arms around him and kissed his cheek. "I'll give you a loan from my share if you need one. I've got a little more to work with."

Markus eyed Jack. "I mean, half a million might be fine for a guy at the end of his career who can pool his cut with his wife's share."

Jack grinned at him. "Wise ass."

"Seriously, Mr. Sheridan, this money means you're done working. Permanent vacation time."

Jack didn't reply.

Connor studied his expression. "He's got an iron in the fire. I know that look."

"What kind of iron?" Markus said. "Tell us. We might want in."

Jack looked crosswise at Lauren.

"Jack's not the retiring type," she said. "I've come to grips with that just in time."

"In time for what?" Connor said.

"Nothing is agreed on yet." Jack leaned forward and dangled the beer bottle by its long neck. "Remember my friend Abner Wilson?"

"The admiral guy with the navy?" Markus asked.

"The rear admiral guy, and yes, that's the one. Admiral Wilson has been appointed to head up a special operations unit for the navy, and he wants to contract Neptune's Reach to execute some projects for him. He wants me on those projects."

"What, like search and destroy, covert mission type stuff?" Connor said.

Jack smiled. "No, research and salvage type stuff, but it will all deal in some regard to national interest, security, or historical significance. Lloyd and I are in negotiations to determine just what my role would be in all this."

"Think you might need our help?" Markus said.

"Not at this point." Jack tipped the bottle at him. "But stay tuned."

Markus retook *Grande Pomposo's* helm and they cruised a while longer up the coast, reveling in their victory, dreaming about what might come next for them. The vibration from Jack's cell phone clip surprised him. He didn't think they were close enough to a tower to be connected. He checked caller ID: unknown name, unknown number. He hated those but took it anyway. "Hello?"

"Jack, hope you're well. I just wanted to call and congratulate you on your recent success."

The voice sent a chill through him he hadn't felt in over a year. He stood and turned in a slow circle, scanning the horizon of water, searching for something out of place. "Who is this?"

Laughter. "I'm hurt. I thought our experience together made more of an impression on you. Let me give you a hint. I got you the cover of *Newsweek*."

Jack didn't need the hint. "Rafferty."

Lauren, Connor, and Markus turned with dropped jaws when he said the name.

Jack's hand instinctively reached for the Colt but it wasn't there. "What do you want?"

"Not too terribly much," Rafferty said. "I've been busy getting back on my feet lately and was concerned you'd forgotten about me."

Jack gripped the phone and looked to the shore. "Don't worry, I haven't forgotten."

"Excellent. Then let's call this a friendly reminder that we have unfinished business between us."

"Better yet," Jack said, "let's pretend this call never happened. It'll save you a lot of trouble down the line."

Rafferty laughed. "I've missed your bravado. Let's get together soon to discuss old times. I'll be in touch." The line disconnected.

Jack slapped the phone closed. "Markus, take us in."

"Was that really him?" Lauren said.

Jack nodded. "Positive."

"It's a scare tactic," she said. "He wouldn't dare come back. Too many people are looking for him."

"Maybe." Jack clipped the phone and met Lauren's eyes. "But if he does come back, you can be damn sure I'm going to be ready for him."

For more information on *Inherit All Things*, the state of Michigan, and other works by J. Ryan Fenzel visit the author's website at www.jryanfenzel.com.